COURT OF LIES

Dawn Kunda

ROMANCE
BookStrand
www.BookStrand.com

A SIREN-BOOKSTRAND TITLE
IMPRINT: Romance

COURT OF LIES

ISBN-10: 1-60601-936-8
ISBN-13: 978-1-60601-936-8

First Printing: November 2010

Cover design by Jinger Heaston

Printed in the U.S.A.

PUBLISHER
www.BookStrand.com

DEDICATION

To my husband who is a one hundred percent supporter and to my family members who are watching from above.

ACKNOWLEDGEMENTS

I have many interests and hobbies in life, if only there were time for everything. One autumn afternoon when I told my wonderful husband, "I think I'm ready to write now." He told me to do whatever it takes and since has been my biggest supporter. I love you for that and many other things. Thank you, Mom, for listening to my constant chatter about where I'm at in my writing career. You're the best. Other family members constantly listen to my writer's talk and keep asking when they can read my work. I appreciate your genuine interest and now's your chance.

Thank you to my dear group of friends who have supported me through constant urging along with necessary technical knowledge. Brenda Kunkel, Stephanie Ninnemann, and Jennifer Paswaters are my computer savvy saviors. Anne Ullius took time from her hectic schedule to educate me on her fantastic art of stained glass. I wish I had the time to make it a hobby of my own. To all the sexy landscapers out there who give my hero in *Court of Lies* sex appeal before a reader even meets him.

Professional friends have contributed their expertise to help me write realistic fiction. Thank you, Lee Bliss, for your medical knowledge shared over many cups of coffee. Many thanks to Connie See, Victim Witness Specialist, and Attorney Andrew Myer who both filled me in on realistic variations to actual laws in the state of Wisconsin. If I have misinterpreted or incorrectly used any of their knowledge, I am solely responsible for this infraction.

I definitely need to thank the writing groups that have guided me on the intricacies of publishable writing. Romance Writers of America, your support, information, networking capabilities, and friendships are incredible. To my critique group, the Kettle Moraine Writers' Guild, your knowledge and support are invaluable. Special thanks go out to Terri Dulong, Lisa Lickel, and Donna Baker for their honesty about my scripts, their intelligence, and of course, their friendship.

My editor, Jennifer Colgan, and publishing manager, Alison C., deserve a huge thank you for their insight and expertise in helping me make *Court of Lies* come alive for all the dedicated romance readers across the world. I'm very fortunate to have you on my side.

COURT OF LIES

DAWN KUNDA

Laws vary from state to state according to the needs of its citizens. There is a lot of gray area in law, but beware of the black scenes.

Chapter 1

Brooke focused on the half-naked trees overhead as the sun attempted to penetrate a handful of plump clouds in the southeastern Wisconsin sky. Mature maples, oaks, and scented evergreens signified the Kettle Moraine Forest. Their branches creaked as a sharp breeze undressed the rustling leaves and caused the needles to dart to the forest floor. From a distance, a metallic clicking filtered through the late autumn agenda.

"Hurry, Scott. I have something to tell you, and I will say it this time." She glanced at her watch. Goose bumps scattered over her arm.

* * * *

The dull barrel felt heavier as the crosshairs steadied on their target.

Now is the time.

Now is the time. 5:12 p.m.

* * * *

Brooke looked down the walking trail. She wanted to see Scott's long stride aimed for her and his neatly trimmed beard below a smile created when they were together.

The goose bumps multiplied. In lieu of a jacket, Brooke folded her arms across her chest.

* * * *

5:12:46 p.m.

Previously damp, now dry, the forefinger tightened on the trigger.

The head is a death shot.

The heart will hurt more.

Decide.

The distant clicking continued.

A quarter inch movement of the trigger shattered the tranquil woods. Brooke toppled to the ground while the thunderous boom echoed between the overhead branches.

* * * *

The sound deafened her to everything except her quick gasp for air. An avalanche of pain streamed through her muscles and spewed red at the finish line. Blood-soaked strands of hair stuck to her shoulder and turned her pink shirt a dirty maroon.

Brooke's eyes fluttered as her head turned in imaginary circles. A mess of dirt and blood mixed with her freshly bathed scent. The stench of death, sure to appear if she closed her eyes too long, would be worse.

The creaking branches held their tongues. Her ears beat the rhythm of the blast she last heard. The sound became less audible as her head rested on the walking trail.

Brooke didn't know whether she whispered it or simply said it to herself, "This is proof that I shouldn't consider more than a business relationship with you. Someone agrees with me."

Aware that the rhythmic clicking ceased, she closed her eyes.

Chapter 2

At the entrance to the state forest, Scott Marshall parked his truck next to Brooke's car. He glanced at his watch and cursed himself for being his typical ten to fifteen minutes late.

With a deep breath, he readied himself. Able to admit his true feelings, he repeated them to convince himself they were possible and real. Brooke didn't mind his bohemian lifestyle, the odd hours he worked for his company, Marshall's Superior Landcraft. She expected nothing and asked for nothing, yet she must need something. He hoped she needed him. Maybe the shell she encased her feelings in had dissolved.

In the few months he had known Brooke, she wouldn't take anything for free. Scott carried a surprise for her, not in the physical form, but rather he was able to offer her another job with his business. Her stained glass art mixed with the hardscape of his current landscaping project attracted attention. He wasn't giving her money, just an opportunity to acquire it. He could give her so much more, if she let him.

Scott's hurried stride led him to the blue-marked walking trail as his thoughts energized him.

The iridescent hands on his watch clued him in on the unusual darkness crowding the woods as he stepped between the towering hickory and pines. Breathing in a sweet, earthen smell, he picked up the pace. He wouldn't miss Brooke. More likely, he would run into her. Further in, he couldn't help but notice the exchange of air fragrance as he crunched the leaves on the well-worn path. Sweet became sour.

Rounding a bend in the trail, Scott breathed stale air. At the same time, his eyes focused on a body, posed at an awkward angle. Two more steps and he would trespass on this motionless body that claimed the path for its resting place.

Scott gasped for more air as he attempted to understand and discern what lay in a sticky mess of darkened and wet dirt. He couldn't do anything. He couldn't think. He stared for an interminable length of time. With his feet planted to the ground, each constriction of his heart caused his chest to tighten. He wanted to get closer, but his body remained petrified.

"Scott. Scott, do something." Stepping on his nerves to get a reaction, Scott stooped down to Brooke's still form. Before he touched her, he pulled his cell phone from its belt holder. His fingers trembled as the beeps of the numbers 911 echoed against the trees.

The chaos in Scott's startled mind began to clear as he recalled the first-aid training he religiously maintained for his landscaping crews. While he spoke to the emergency dispatcher, he firmly held Brooke's wrist without hesitation for the results.

His arm trembled as he felt small pearls of perspiration trickle down the back of his neck. Scott's hair dampened and clung to the collar of his shirt.

He knew what to do before the dispatcher instructed him. Keep Brooke warm. Keep her air passage clear of debris. Check her breathing and circulation.

Brooke gave no intimation of coldness, but he needed to do something. Scott wrapped his denim shirt around her. Warmth would encourage the faint pulse.

He searched his mind for a miraculous plan to make his Brooke complete again. Frustration sank into the synapses of his taut nerves. His skin reddened with heat, which he wished he could transfer to her limp form.

"What happened here? Who did this?" Scott asked to the no one listening.

It wasn't quite an answer, but he heard a faint screech of sirens which steadily grew closer.

"Brooke, I won't let you go this way. The ambulance will be here soon. Stay with me, baby," Scott whispered over her shoulder as he watched the color of life seep from her in a steady rhythm. He leaned as near as he dared, careful not to add his weight to her labored breath.

Leaves crunched in the distance. Scott turned to see a troop of medics with their emergency apparatus along with police officers in the lead with less baggage. The officers gripped weapons of .40 calibers as they scattered in trained surveillance.

"Sir, you need to move back." A skinny young medic, half Scott's age and size, rounded to Brooke's far side.

Scott touched her cheek lightly and moved back.

He rose to his height of two inches above six feet and backed into an officer matching his brawn.

"Sir, I need your name as a civilian on-site. Did you see what happened or know anything?" The officer wasted no time.

"I'm Scott Marshall." There wasn't the usual acknowledgement of Marshall's Superior Landcraft firm but rather suspicious eyes and raised brows. "I came here to meet Brooke. Brooke Bellin is her name, and I found her like this."

"We'll need to talk to you again. Write your name, address, and phone number here." The officer thrust a half-used notepad into Scott's hand.

Surprised at the lack of in-depth questions common in TV practice, Scott scribbled the information. The officer took the notebook, nodded a quick thanks for the cooperation, and turned to take pictures of the scene as the medics got ready to remove the victim.

Scott's emotions stewed. He feared for Brooke's recovery, mixed with anger at the shooter, and was also laden with guilt for his tardiness. He stood with his hands clenched, ready for a call to help, which didn't happen.

Goose bumps formed under his t-shirt. Scott remained alert while Brooke's privacy evaporated into the officer's lens as it captured angles of her despair. The officer proceeded routinely to photograph scenes not intended for Brooke's scrapbook but rather the files and stacked desks of the legal officers notified of their next client.

Interrupting the photo shoot, the paramedics maneuvered Brooke's extremities to fit the gurney, followed by the sound of endless leaves crunching back down the path.

"What hospital are you going to?" Scott faced the back of the skinny medic as he caught up to the rescue team.

Without a glance to see who asked, the medic automatically answered, "Mercy Medical."

Scott knew the complex's location but remained focused on Brooke's unreserved limo as he hastened to his truck to follow. He shuttled himself into the driver's seat and wondered, "Will Brooke make it to the hospital...alive?"

Chapter 3

Scott followed the ambulance as it sped a course amidst slow going sightseers of the Kettle Moraine Forest. He briefly noted the sun's retirement behind the western line of colorful maples. Passing the same vehicles as the emergency carrier, he strained his eyes against the blaze of red lights accompanied by a scream of sirens.

With a swerve into the emergency lot, he found an empty spot. Scott parked and straightened his arms as he gripped the steering wheel and pushed his back against the rigid seat. Every muscle flexed before he let go and swung the truck's door wide and jumped out. His legs pumped a quick rhythm to the hospital entrance.

Halting at the information desk, he urged, "Can you tell me anything about Brooke Bellin?"

"Is she a patient here?"

Scott met the clerk's blank stare. "Uh, she just arrived by ambulance. She's been shot." Hurtful words. Painful words.

"Oh! Uh, if you're family, a doctor will inform you of her prognosis when they have the situation under control. A waiting room is near the emergency department." A plump finger pointed left. Scott noted the calm tone behind the directions, probably protocol for visitors of the emergency department.

It wasn't the right answer, though. He wanted more. It was obviously too early to know anything and the wrong time to see Brooke. He wasn't family. They should be family. He had been stubborn not to admit he had fallen in love with Brooke. He wanted another chance to let her know because he wouldn't hold back this time.

Scott found himself a worn seat in the waiting room. He sat with his legs splayed, elbows dug into his thighs, and his damp hands clasped in the middle. His head hung down letting his shoulder length hair surround his face to disguise his misery. Scott returned to the scene he'd walked into this afternoon. The scene hadn't changed. The more he scanned his mind's pictures, the more unreal they became.

Brooke wasn't the sweet, beautiful, and sexy woman Scott worked with. Instead, red pain stained the memory. "Where was I? I should've been there before this happened."

He raised his head to check if any waiting room attendants noticed his odd behavior. An older man and probably his daughter sat together, one with tears, one with angry red cheeks. Behind him, Scott heard the flip of pages from a magazine. A burly man with a sleeve of tattoos sat rigid, without expression.

No one watched him. No one noticed.

Scott lifted his head another notch and stared past the entry of the waiting room. He hoped to see a doctor walk his way with a smile to assure Brooke's good fate. Not a chance. No one would inform him. No one knew how much he cared.

Scott viewed other visitors as they checked the signs and room numbers. The click of their shoes faded in seconds. An occasional aide or nurse calmly walked by to make their rounds.

An hour later Scott noticed two men in gray business attire, each with a grim expression. He dismissed them as family visitors due to their official appearance. Scott doubted they were attorneys because of the weekend and they usually didn't travel in pairs in the small village of Creek Willow.

The next couple hurried by in a huddle. As they left his view, Scott realized their identity. His eyebrows shot up, followed by a frown. Brooke's ex-husband and his female companion made a surprise visit.

Chapter 4

"Let me see those photos again." Officer Shears wriggled his fingers toward Officer Kaehne.

"They turned out good considering the medics were in a hurry to get her out of here." Officer Kaehne unhooked the digital camera from his shoulder harness. "Look at this one." Kaehne clicked through a dozen quick shots. He stopped at one picture and then continued until he reached the operative photo.

"Look at the way she fell to the ground." Kaehne tapped the camera screen. "It looks like she was shot from a slight angle. A straight shot would've pushed her directly back, but with the wound in the shoulder, she fell to the side. I'm sure it was at an angle."

"Get the rest of the team together to designate search regions." Officer Shears shoved his hands in his pockets. His elbows pointed to opposite sides as he viewed the section of the woods they needed to search. He looked straight ahead, from where the victim most likely faced, and didn't see any obvious clues to reveal the shooter's name and whereabouts without all the investigation of an attempted homicide.

As other officers circled around him, Shears spoke. "There's not much light left, so let's get the evidence while it's fresh. I want you to line up in front of where we located the victim and angle off from there. Make sure you include a good portion of the meadow to the south and cut high into that grove of oaks to the north." He paused here as he restudied the picture.

Shears looked at a picture of an apple. It lay in front of Brooke, covered in blood-soaked mud. He shook his head. "Guys, on your way back make sure you recheck your paths from the same angle. See if you find any apples out there."

"Apples? What are you getting hungry or something?" An officer smirked.

"Seriously, it looks like the victim carried apples. Maybe she was supposed to meet someone on the trail. Maybe they brought her an everlasting surprise, too, in the form of a bullet she won't forget." Officer Shears kept his eye on the picture.

Officer Kaehne added, "There aren't any tracks to indicate a struggle near the scene. She either knew the sniper or wasn't aware someone had her in their sights."

"Either she knew the perp or she didn't. That's a good place to start." Shears rolled his eyes as he looked up.

"Who hit you on the head with a branch on your way out here?" Kaehne returned the stare.

"Shit, it'd be nice if we could prevent the crimes as many times as we solve them." Officer Shears changed the subject. "Detectives from Milwaukee were radioed and should arrive soon to get whatever information we have to pass on. Keep the guys moving, and let me know what they've found as soon as they get back."

"I'll finish with the scene before they return. There are a few things that look interesting that I haven't been able to get to, yet."

"Carry on, Kaehne. I'm going back to the van to see if there's any contact with the hospital." Shears retraced the marked trail.

As the other officers continued to spread away from the scene, Kaehne kneeled next to where Brooke Bellin had been. He studied her features from the photos. Strands of dark hair formed clumps in the muddied blood. A scan of her body, revealed sun-touched legs and an unnatural twist of her waist. The lay of her shoulder foretold where the bullet entered.

Kaehne changed his focus to the swished and swirled dirt around her body. He studied the turns of dust and mud soaked with Brooke's blood. The blood had solidified like the skin of chocolate pudding. Time enhanced some details.

The dirt and blood mixed in one area. From previous pictures, Brooke hadn't tossed or put up a fight against the sniper. Now there were many footprints, but fortunately, he took pictures timely before the medics departed and added excessive prints. He scanned a photo of the ground and noticed a partial print left from a size twelve or possibly thirteen shoe. It was a whole print and as fresh as Brooke's step of seven when he had aimed the camera lens on it.

Officer Kaehne didn't acknowledge the distant years spent together in high school when he requested Scott Marshall to jot his information on the notepad. To this day, Marshall was unaware of the one-sided rivalry. Kaehne would have to check if it was Marshall's print. He also knew the shot was not at close range. Marshall could have been any distance from Bellin at any time. In Kaehne's mind, anyone could be a suspect.

Officer Shears returned with two detectives in his shadow. The first detective followed too closely and wore an intent expression. Stone gray eyes looked straight ahead. His hand hugged a pistol at his belt.

Shortly behind Officer Shears and the first detective followed another detective who had the "in training" look.

"Gentlemen, this is Officer Kaehne, our photo genius. He got a few snapshots of the victim. We can always count on him for that." Shears started his explanation to the detectives as they arrived at the newly roped area. "Officer Kaehne, these are Detectives Gaynor and Rell from the Milwaukee PD. They were twenty miles from the scene and were called in to assist our department."

Officer Kaehne felt Detective Gaynor's eyes settle on him as he remained with a knee planted in the dirt and leaves close to the crime scene. "Give me a list of the basics and then tell me what else you have," Gaynor requested without a formal greeting.

Officer Kaehne raised his brows as he obliged. "The victim, about thirty-seven, five foot four, and Caucasian without any record was shot with a rifle, known due to the lack of scattered shot. Other than the victim's shoeprint, there was another fresh print of male attitude, size twelve or thirteen. Both prints came from the same direction, time of both arrivals unknown. Victim carried a bag of apples possibly for the secondary person. Not determined yet whether the secondary person arrived before or after the shooting. Secondary person alleges he appeared after the shooting and was the one to call 911."

"You spoke to the secondary person?"

"Yes, briefly. He stated he arrived to meet the victim to talk."

"To talk?"

"He wasn't specific."

"Keep going." Gaynor sniffed with a follow-up cough.

Officer Shears stood to the side and watched the woods while Kaehne continued. "The shot appears to come from due west with a nominal southerly angle." Kaehne left out details of his reasoning as more questions accumulated with each piece of evidence. He glanced from Gaynor's cold, gray stare to Detective Rell's friendlier expression and then continued, "The victim was shot in the shoulder." Why wasn't the shot in the heart or head? Was the gun faulty? Was the aim inaccurate? Was the victim misidentified? He didn't offer his theories. "It doesn't appear the sniper is an expert. I'm sure the officers will find where the shot came from. Amateurs leave a lot of clues."

"That's police work 101," Gaynor interrupted. Kaehne wasn't sure if the detective insulted him for his description or just responded to his last statement. Gaynor added, "That's a good start. We still have a lot of roads to cover, which shouldn't be a problem with the force at hand and I was informed that the hospital admitted a living victim."

With validation, Kaehne sighed with relief, not used to scrutiny from an outsider. He'd investigated murder scenes before, but not in a small community where the procedures played out differently. People knew more in lesser-populated areas. The police just had to find them and obtain statements.

"Anything else?" Detective Rell circled the crime scene.

"There's one other odd detail. The bag of apples in Kaehne's pictures left the scene. I'm not sure who took them or why. I have a gut feeling they may have some significance." Officer Shears shifted his weight from one foot to the other.

"They shouldn't have been removed. Who left from the scene since the shooting?" Detective Gaynor continued his stern stare.

"The only persons we're aware of are the medics and Scott Marshall. The one who claims to have made the 911 call." Kaehne stood and wiped the dirt from his knees.

"We have his address and number." Officer Shears attempted to cover for his partner.

"Give us the information, and then we'll head to the hospital to joust the victim and catch any first visitors." Detective Gaynor reached inside a jacket pocket.

Detective Rell flipped through forms while Gaynor pulled his pen out and walked over to the blood soaked apple that remained off to the side. As he leaned over it, he poked it with the pen. “This apple is as fresh as they get. There’s still the untainted scent apples wouldn’t have if they were picked awhile ago or were left lying more than a couple days.” Detective Gaynor paused, then continued, “Maybe we’re just not used to seeing people carrying fresh orchard apples in the woods. Personally, I would’ve left the bag in the car until I left the park.”

“We’ll let you know what the search team comes up with when we put the stats together.” Officer Shears handed over Marshall’s information.

“We’ll be in touch.” The detectives jotted a few notes, nodded to the officers, and walked back to the parking area.

After the detectives were out of earshot, Kaehne said, “I heard those guys are quite the team. It’s been said they can tell which clump of dirt came from which tire on a vehicle. Then tell you the vehicle needs an alignment and oil change.”

Shears shook his head. “With our team and the evidence already uncovered, this case looks too obvious. Yet, the chief called in detectives from Milwaukee. That worries me.”

Chapter 5

"Ty Bellin."

At the sound of his name, Ty Bellin and Marla Vrahn stopped short of Brooke's hospital room. They missed the doctor's report after she came out of the emergency room.

Ty and Marla turned to face the authoritative voice. Two men in suits stood with legs parted and hands held together at waist level. They waited for acknowledgement. Ty gave a quick sideway glance toward Marla, as if she would give him some last-minute advice.

"Yes, that's me." Ty wasn't sure he wanted these unknown men to have any information on him until he saw Brooke. He had received a call from the police, telling him she remained in stable condition after a gunshot wound. His visit at the information desk of the hospital lasted long enough for him to acquire the room number. He needed to see her for himself.

Detective Gaynor announced their identity while he flashed a silver badge. "We need to have a few words with you about the attempt on your wife's life." Detective Gaynor's voice held no emotion. "Who's this with you?" He nodded toward Marla as she leaned away from Ty.

Before Ty could swallow away the sudden dryness in his throat, Marla spoke up, "I'm Marla. Marla Vrahn. I'm Ty's therapy nurse. And a good friend of the family's." She emphasized the claim of friendship as she made eye contact with each of the detectives.

Detective Rell wrote the names down as Gaynor held Marla's gaze. She broke the trance first.

This gave Ty enough time to croak out a response. "Detective, Brooke's my ex-wife. I'd like to see her first, if you don't have any objections to that."

"We'll give you ten minutes. Separately." Detective Gaynor scoped the hall for a clock and then pulled his shirtsleeve from his wristwatch.

"I'll let Ty go first," Marla murmured as she cocked her head. "I can visit with Brooke when you talk to him."

"Miss Vrahn, we'll need to speak with you, too. Separately." Rell mimicked Gaynor's rules.

Creamed with friendliness, Marla said, "I'm not sure what I can tell you gentlemen, but I will tell you Brooke and I have become quite good friends in the last two years. I would never guess she has any enemies."

"Miss Vrahn, we'll take this conversation in private. I'll give you the ten minutes with Ms. Bellin, or we can go now."

"Go now? I don't have to go to the police station, do I?"

"No, not right now. We'd rather have the conversation in private, though. There are meeting rooms close by." Detective Rell glanced at the doors leading down the corridor. "We don't want to bother the other patients."

"Yes, I suppose that must be considered." Marla rose on her toes and fell back onto flat feet. "I think I'd like to see Brooke before I talk with you. I'm so worried about her. I'm sure she'll be tired and won't want visitors to stay long." Ty watched Marla smile softly as she lowered her eyes and focused on the polished badge attached to the detective's belt.

"We'll wait down the hall. Just remember, you have to go in separately. Just our procedure in these situations."

As detectives Gaynor and Rell walked toward the common metal chairs with vinyl cushioning placed halfway down the hall, Ty caught Marla's attention. They both had questions in their eyes, but neither one dared say them aloud.

"I'll wait here for my turn," was all Marla dared.

"I'm sure I'll be quick."

* * * *

With her eyes still closed, Brooke heard the sweep of the solid wood door a few feet from her bed. The low, steady beep of the machine to her right continued along with the rubber-soled step of a visitor.

A slight touch to her arm caused Brooke to flutter her eyelids until they remained half-open. "I'm glad you're here for me." Surprised at her own sincerity, she watched a single line of moisture curve along his cheek.

"Of course, I hurried as soon as I was notified."

Brooke whispered, "I don't know much of what happened. The doctor told me I was shot." Admitting the crime caused a stream of tears to readily outnumber the already dried tear on Ty's roughly shaven face. She continued to speak between sniffles. "Ty, I don't know what happened. I don't even remember most of what the doctors probably told me. I think they said I'd be all right. That my injury won't be a permanent problem."

Brooke didn't understand what she saw. Was Ty genuinely concerned? Why else would his eyes be glassy other than from tears? Those eyes only stared at her injured shoulder.

"Ty, what did the doctors tell you when I came out of the emergency room?" An inner alarm alerted her senses. "Is it bad? Is it worse than what I thought they said? Why do you look so…so…? I don't know what your look is telling me. Don't keep anything from me, Ty." Brooke stared at him with her eyes as wide open as the morphine allowed while it surged through her body.

Ty lifted his shoulders and let them fall back into place. "No, Brooke. The doctors didn't tell me you're in any type of trouble. You should heal fine," he answered as if he'd spoken to the doctors personally.

Brooke settled back into the hospital's excuse for a pillow. "I'm going to be okay? I'm going to be okay. You had a miraculous recovery from your stroke. You…you can talk normally again, your walking is quite good now, and your arm is functional again. If you heal this well, my arm should be a snap to get back to normal." Brooke spoke her thoughts out loud, more for her own benefit. "Ty, why did you look at me like that then? Do I look bad? I haven't really seen what my shoulder looks like." With a faint laugh she added, "What am I thinking? I'm sure I'm not ready to have a picture taken."

Ty didn't comment as he watched Brooke attempt to raise herself in the bed.

Her face grew serious once again. "Ty, do you know exactly what happened? Who did this to me? Was anyone caught by the police? Was anyone at the trail with me?" Now the questions began to flow. Brooke knew she'd be okay. Chloe, a dear friend with an uncanny sixth sense, always told Brooke that she'd make it through anything thrown her way. She'd have to call Chloe as soon as she had the energy.

Ty leaned against the bed rail. “I don’t have any information yet, but the police are investigating. I’m sure they’ll catch him soon.” Ty paused as his lips formed a line of steel. “If they don’t, I will.”

An unexpected sigh of partial relief escaped Brooke’s dry throat. She welcomed Ty’s assurance, but she also recalled his betrayal, which caused their divorce two years ago. His necessary therapy after a stroke, which had occurred shortly before their divorce, was the only reason she allowed contact. With a false feeling of obligation, she occasionally helped the visiting nurse, Marla Vrahn, conduct his exercises. The therapy had been at the house Ty lived in. He was legally bound to sell the house after the divorce, but hadn’t made an effort.

Interrupting Brooke’s reminiscing, a knock on the door echoed against the steel and emptiness of the hospital room.

“Uh, Brooke, I’m only allowed ten minutes. You need to rest, so I should get going. Marla’s here to see you, too.” Tapping his hand on the bed railing, he walked back a few steps, gave a weak smile and turned to leave.

“Ty.” Brooke didn’t understand the distasteful feeling he left with her. As he turned back to her, Brooke saw a cold stare and didn’t finish the good night she’d planned.

“I’ll send Marla in now.” No “good-night.” No “take care.” Ty quietly opened the door and stepped back into the hall.

The look Ty gave Marla when their eyes met had more concern than he felt when he had seen Brooke. Ty and Marla did not exchange words, only a stare which told each other to be careful of what they said.

Chapter 6

Scott looked at his watch again. The silver hand had barely moved fifteen minutes since Ty and Marla surprised him with their tardy appearance he witnessed from the waiting room. No surprise it took them so long to get here.

Scott could wait forever for Brooke, but not today. Not right now. He needed to see and touch her. He needed her to know he would do anything to help her through this. His energy level peaked, even with the long day of anticipation and wondering. Realizing this, he stood and walked the length of his row of chairs. This wasn't nearly enough, as he rounded the end of the row within five seconds. A whole round of chairs would only take ten seconds. Eleven seconds if he slowed for the turns and maybe a whole twelve seconds if he knocked his knee on the corner metal chair arm again.

Mentally tabulating his walking time wasn't what he had planned to do this morning. He stopped his rounds at this thought and turned toward the entry of the waiting room.

"There's nothing wrong with being a visitor," Scott said aloud to convince himself.

Approaching the information desk once again, Scott asked, "Has there been any development with Brooke Bellin's injury?" It may have sounded awkward, but Scott didn't want to use the more accurate description of attempted murder.

Looking pleased that someone needed her help as the evening set in, the reception girl responded with a smile, "Could you spell Brooke's last name? I can look up her status."

Excited with this small amount of progress, Scott readily spelled Bellin for the receptionist.

While lightly clicking her keyboard, she hummed a tune of her own until she stopped typing. She peered closer as her eyes traveled the chosen screen. Scott saw a small frown form at the corners of the girl's mouth. As he considered getting nervous all over again, her mouth relaxed after a couple more taps of her fingertips.

Scott leaned in as close as he could to the computer screen, which he still couldn't read because of the angle. The girl turned her eyes back to him with a report. "Sorry that took so long. Apparently Ms. Bellin has been removed from the emergency ward." The receptionist paused before relaying the rest of the report as she absently dug office dirt from her manicured nails. She finally continued, "Looks like she was moved to room 225. She's only allowed one visitor at a time tonight until nine o'clock. Do you know…?"

Before the girl finished her question, Scott turned around and headed for the stairs. He knew how to find the second floor. The signs could direct him the rest of the way.

With one foot poised on the top step, he paused at the end of the stairs to scan the wall for signs always present in groomed hospitals. Scott was right about this. There were at least two feet of numbers, titles, and arrows. He reviewed them too quickly the first time and forced himself to slow down. This made it easy to locate the arrow for rooms 210-225.

Scott turned to his left as the sign directed and stared down the hall. As he guided his trembling heart to the next left turn, he needed to slow down again. He had to check for Brooke's ex-husband. She had mentioned that he had a jealous streak, and Scott wasn't in the mood to deal with it. Any other time would be fine.

With a glimpse down the next hall, Scott saw the same two suited men waiting for something at the far end. He wasn't too interested in them, but they did have an official appearance. As he recognized this, the door to room 225 opened.

Scott had only seen Ty Bellin a couple of times, but there was no doubt the man who emerged with a slight limp was Brooke's ex-husband. Scott was also surprised that he hadn't noticed the woman who stepped out of an alcove furnished with more waiting chairs. He didn't recall ever meeting her, but she had to be Marla. Who else would grab Ty's hand with a strangely serious expression? This was a strange incident and a serious one on top of that, but her look said more.

Scott retreated to the last hall he had come from. He glanced at his watch. It was already 8:50 p.m. Afraid of this, he knew there would be no way to see Brooke tonight. Scott had tried to kid himself into thinking he would find a way to see his beautiful Brooke before the doors of the hospital closed to visitors. Now he'd failed at this. Fortunately, the day was nearly over. There wasn't much time left for anything else to go wrong.

He glanced around the hall corner one more time and saw Brooke's door close as Marla entered. He wasn't surprised. What did surprise him was to see the previously viewed suited men stand up and aim their gazes at Ty. It was as if they expected him, or was it the other way around?

Scott watched one of the suited men lead Ty down the hall. He wouldn't be too concerned about any involvement of Brooke's ex-husband, except she had warned him about Ty. The warning didn't scare him, but he also realized that this wasn't the time to test Ty's volatility. He didn't know who the men were, or whose side they represented.

If Ty or the unknown men saw him, it could get ugly.

Chapter 7

"Mr. Bellin, please come with me." Detective Gaynor wasted no time in vacating the hall chair.

Ty practiced keeping his mouth shut and followed without a word. He would only say what was necessary, although curiosity made him peek at Detective Rell who stayed behind. Ty hoped this meant it wasn't too serious of an interview.

Gaynor answered his mute question. "Detective Rell will speak with Ms. Vrahn when she's done with her visit to Ms. Bellin."

Ty stupidly asked, "Will they join us?"

Detective Gaynor stopped and looked straight into Ty's startled eyes. "We interview everyone alone." The stare held for an acknowledgement.

"Yeah, sure. That makes sense," Ty mumbled.

Detective Gaynor continued at Ty's slower pace. He could walk quite well, but he wasn't ready for any races.

Gaynor paused at the chosen door and pushed it open, waiting for Ty to enter first. He pulled his shoulders back, took a deep breath and entered the small conference room. It was a closed room with only one window to show the viewers a parking lot that became increasingly barren as the five-to-niners departed. Lights from the lot left ghostly patterns on the poor excuse of a cheery paint job splashed on the walls.

Gaynor flipped the lights on as he entered. The furnishings consisted of a medium sized oval table with six padded chairs skewed around it. A crooked print of a vase of nearly wilted daisies adorned one wall with its sister of irises on another. The carpeted floor was a dizzy pattern of southwestern colors.

"Take a seat."

Ty obliged and picked the chair facing the door.

With a low note of sympathy, Gaynor began, "I'm sorry for what brings us here together. I wish Ms. Bellin the best of luck in her recovery, and we'll do our best to apprehend the shooter."

"Thank you. I trust you can do that for her."

"You have the right to counsel while I question you. The questions are pretty basic, so I'm sure you won't have any problem with them."

Ty wasn't convinced. He shook his head in a motion for Gaynor to continue freely.

"We'll start with the easy part. Where were you around five p.m. on this day of October the twelfth?"

Ty's shoulders relaxed for a moment as he cast his eyes to the right after this calculated question. "I was at the shooting range."

"Do you have any witnesses to your whereabouts?"

"Yes. Marla and another friend, Roger, were with me."

"Please state Marla and Roger's last names." Gaynor poised a pen that matched the ink smeared on his knuckles.

"It's Marla Vrahn and Roger Detris."

"Did anyone else see you?"

"I talked to some other guys sighting their guns. I don't know all their names, though." Ty paused slightly to think harder and added before Detective Gaynor came up with another question, "We also signed in at the registry. Everyone is required to when they use the shooting range."

With a quick note to his battered notepad, Gaynor piled on more specific questions. "What kind of gun did you use?"

"I brought my 12.0 gauge." Ty slowed his response as he thought of the 30.06 he'd taken out of his car before the visit to the hospital. He had intended to wipe it down with gun oil but only got half through with the ritual before an interruption caused him to hurry it back to its resting place in the gun cabinet. He had left the 12.0 gauge in the backseat for his ride to the hospital.

As if he already knew more than what Ty revealed, Detective Gaynor asked, "Is that the only weapon you carried?"

"Oh yeah, I forgot. I also had my 30.06. My friends wanted to see it because it was custom made. I only fired that one once." Ty circled one thumb with the other with his hand clasped in a fist on top of the conference table.

"What guns did Ms. Vrahn and Mr. Detris use?"

"They both had 12.0 gauges." He tried to distract the attention away from his own guns and added, "Some of the other guys had 12.0 gauges, 30.06's, and 16.0 gauges."

"So there were all types of guns being used?" Ty appreciated the useless, follow-up question, which gave him time to regroup.

"Yes. There were probably others, but I didn't keep track of them."

"Were there any 300 Win-Mags or 9 millimeters?" Detective Gaynor's expression didn't change.

"Is that what shot Brooke?" Ty asked with hope of an agreement.

Gaynor evaded Ty's question and changed course. "What were you doing before you went to the shooting range?"

Ty squeezed his eyes shut. "Ah, I was at home. I had walked down to Brooke's studio to talk to her, but she had mentioned she was going for a walk at the State Park, so she must've left already."

"Do you frequently see Ms. Bellin, even though you're divorced?"

"Occasionally she stops over to check on me. I still require therapy due to a stroke a couple years ago. Ah, we still have a friendly relationship."

"I'm sure you do." Detective Gaynor kept his steel gray eyes on Ty while he continued with the timeline. "What time did Brooke leave for her walk?"

"She left about twenty minutes before Marla picked me up. I'm not sure exactly what time, but it must've been around four o'clock."

"Could it have been later?"

Ty continued to circle his thumbs, slower when he listened and faster as he answered. "It may have been a little later. Like I said, I don't know exactly when she left."

Detective Gaynor underlined a phrase in his half-full notepad. Ty knew the time was important, but he figured it would be better if he hadn't been totally aware of every minute. Normally he wouldn't be.

"You were the last one to talk to her before she left for her walk?"

"Yes, as far as I know," Ty answered with a touch of defiance.

Gaynor flipped his pen and tapped the covered end on his pad. "These are standard questions. We have to cover all possibilities. Was she walking by herself or meeting a friend?"

Ty forced his fingers to slow their circles. "I assumed she would be by herself."

"Does she frequently see other people she does or doesn't know when she walks?"

"I'm sure she's not the only one out there. The trails are public property."

Switching tactics, Gaynor continued, "Why do you think she was only fifty to seventy-five feet into the trail, if she had been there for, say, at least half an hour already?"

Not sure how to answer this question, Ty put up his guard. "I was wondering that myself." Thinking this addition would help, he continued, "Maybe she had to stop for something on the way to the trail."

Detective Gaynor switched routes again. "Does Ms. Bellin have any enemies?"

Ty had waited for this question. "I'm not aware of any." He squinted his eyes and glanced to the sea-green ceiling, which matched the walls, and feigned an afterthought with good timing. "She had a few calls lately. The caller hung up when she answered."

"Really? Does she have caller ID?"

"I don't know."

Gaynor made another note. Firing from another angle, he asked, "How good is your aim, Mr. Bellin?"

A thin line of moisture appeared above Ty's upper lip. "My aim? I'm not sure what you mean."

"Your aim. With a rifle. Do you usually hit your target?"

Ty wondered if the detective wanted to hear that he always hit his target or that it was a rare occurrence. "I can usually hit what I'm aiming for."

"What about moving targets?"

"It's been a while, but I've gotten my share of pheasants." A nervous laugh edged his response.

Detective Gaynor leaned forward as if he had the final clue and wanted to reveal it. "Anything else you want to tell me?"

Relieved that the questioning was over, Ty found it easy to wear the concerned ex-husband appearance again as he answered, "No. I wish I did know more. You'll find who did this, won't you?"

"That's my mission." Gaynor rose from his seat and led the way out of the room. At the door, he turned abruptly, causing Ty to stop in mid-step, and added, "Do you like apples?"

"What? Apples? I guess so. I wasn't really thinking about food right now."

"That's what I thought." Gaynor left a distasteful afterthought to coat Ty's mental palate. "If you think of anything, keep in touch." He produced a rigidly new black and white business card.

"Definitely." Ty gave one last effort to appear grateful to the detective.

Back in the sterile corridor, Ty let out an exhausted breath. He hoped the detectives would grill their other suspects better than what Gaynor had done to him. Most of the questions were simple and expected. To make the interrogated stumble over an imaginary hurdle, the detectives would have to make them nervous. It didn't work with him.

Ty looked toward Brooke's room and didn't see Marla anywhere. He knew her ten-minute visit was over a while ago. He noticed other dark conference rooms with their doors ajar until he came upon a closed door with a blind covering an illuminated window. He glanced casually toward the light and attempted to look between the dustless slats. He saw the shapes of two people conferring. It had to be Marla with the other detective. He wondered how long they'd been in there and what had been said.

Ty chose a signature chair in the hall to wait. Detective Gaynor disappeared.

* * * *

"How long have you been using firearms?" The question came with an accusation. Detective Rell wasn't as soft spoken as he appeared.

"Firearms? I never thought of a shotgun in that way. You make it sound so serious." Marla attempted a shot at humor. When he didn't respond, she corrected her answer. "I've been using guns my whole life. My brothers and I used to shoot tin cans. Actually, we shot BB guns at each other with an occasional hit. Once in a while I hunted with them, but I'm not big on hitting live targets." Marla thought her last comment was fitting, considering the recent shooting.

Detective Rell reverted to current activity. "We're aware you were at the firing range with Ty Bellin, the ex-husband of the victim. How did you get there and at what time?"

The hospital wasn't overly warm, but Marla proceeded to re-cross her legs as she felt heated moisture sticking them together. "Ah, I drove there after I picked up Ty at his home. I think I signed us in before five o'clock."

"Who is 'us'? Doesn't everyone sign themselves in?"

"I signed Ty, his friend, Roger, and myself in. It was just easier that way."

"There were three of you together, and Mr. Bellin and his friend do not actually know what time they were signed in at the firing range?" Detective Rell remained cool, his back pushed against the chair and his legs spread to the corners of the seat.

"What does that matter? If they looked at their watches, they knew. Besides, it's written down," Marla slowly added with regret at getting upset during the questioning as she watched Detective Rell jot down a quick note.

"Explain exactly what your relationship with Brooke and Ty Bellin is."

Marla told him what he needed to hear. "Over two years ago I became Ty's visiting nurse to help him with therapy after he had a stroke. His wife, or ex-wife now, used to be involved in the sessions. The three of us have become friends."

"Anything more than that?" Rell demanded.

"More? No, I haven't moved in with either one." Again, Marla attempted to lighten the air without success. "Well, Ty lives in the same house by himself now. Since the divorce, you know."

"Did you have anything to do with the divorce?" Detective Rell was all business.

"Excuse me? I still am Ty's therapy nurse, and I do talk to his wife at times. I certainly didn't have anything to do with their divorce, if that's what you're accusing me of."

Changing topics, he asked, "Miss Vrahn, do you like apples?"

"Why, are you offering me one?" Marla's lips twisted slightly as she couldn't stop herself from this question. The late hour evaporated any humor Detective Rell might have had, so Marla resubmitted her answer, "Autumn is a good time for apples. Yes, I like them. Does this have anything to do with the shooting?"

"We may need to talk to you again. If you leave town, please notify me in case we need your help with any information." The interview must be over and the question remained unanswered. A typical practice for those with the upper hand.

"Definitely. Anything I can do to help." She'd play his game.

"We're done for now. Here's my card," Detective Rell offered as he stood up while he moved his chair out of the way with the side of his leg.

"Thank you." Marla reached for the card as she also stood.

Detective Rell glanced at Marla's hand as her fingers touched his business card. A swatch of dried mud clung to the surface. Instead of releasing the card to her, Rell pulled it back and urged, "Miss Vrahn, please follow me."

Chapter 8

Scott was up before the birds, the sun, and his alarm clock the next morning. He looked around his room at the colorless walls and the basket of dirty clothes, which kept the north corner of the floor from collecting dust. A new, but cheaply made oak dresser stood next to the mounded basket. Lining the west wall, but not an interruption of the window, stood a set of golf clubs, fishing poles, and a nylon pair of snowshoes. The first two items remained barely used. They were poor choices for hobbies since Scott worked hard at his landscaping during the three seasons they were useful. The snowshoes were a whim from last year. He'd used them twice, but without a partner, he didn't experience the expected thrill. Not too long ago when he focused on them, Scott wondered if Brooke would join him. He'd buy her a pair, if she'd try it.

With a broken night of sleep and dreams, Scott still felt entirely energized with the thought of seeing Brooke. He could also kick himself for letting his feelings get out of hand. He wasn't supposed to fall in love. Typically, the women he chose couldn't understand the hours his business required, or they always waited for a gift. Love was supposed to be sweet, comforting, and warm, but he didn't experience any of those emotions when he thought of Brooke surrounded by painted cement, cold medicine, and strangers.

Scott cut his typical morning routine in half. This meant he was in the house for a mere ten minutes after he awoke. As he put his truck into reverse, he remembered what he had wanted to bring for Brooke. He jammed the truck back into park and raced back to the house to retrieve the information for the next job, which he felt would cheer Brooke up. He also grabbed what was left of the bag of apples along with a muddied note he hadn't read.

Scott's eyes scanned the parking lot as he turned into the nearest entry. He didn't see any squad cars parked for him. On the way to the hospital, Scott had received a call. The detectives wanted to talk with him. He wasn't going to wait for them, and he knew they would catch up with him if they were in earnest about an interview. Actually, Scott looked forward to finding out if there were any leads. Above all, he just wanted to see Brooke.

Anyone who saw Scott cross the parking lot would know he walked unnaturally fast. Near the mirrored entry doors, Scott noticed the same two suited men from yesterday. He shifted the bag he carried, and the men caught and held his gaze. As if invited, they met up with Scott.

"Are you Scott Marshall?" The nearest man reached out a hand. He seemed to be in charge because he started the conversation.

"Yes. You must be Detective Gaynor," Scott remembered the phone call.

Once again, Detective Gaynor introduced himself and his partner. "Why don't we sit over here and have a little talk?" He motioned to a nearby outdoor table and chair set.

Scott noticed a not too friendly tone with Gaynor's suggestion, but he didn't let it bother him as he sat.

"You're the one who called 911, I understand. Tell us your itinerary from yesterday. Let's start with noon and on," Gaynor requested, wasting no time.

Not knowing why, Scott began with a touch of nervous adrenalin, "Noon? Yeah, noon. Let's see. So much happened since noon." He kept repeating the time to get a focus on what he needed to say. Slowly he pulled the answer from underneath the other memories of the day. "At noon I was doing paperwork at my office. My office is at Fourth and Madison in Creek Willow. I made a few phone calls to customers, but mostly paperwork."

Detective Rell broke in here. "What's your work?"

"I own Marshall's Superior Landcraft," Scott answered with a touch of pride.

Without an acknowledgment, Gaynor said, "Please continue."

More in control of his recount of the hours and minutes of the previous day, Scott continued, "I talked to Brooke around four o'clock. We talked about meeting at the blue trail at the State Park for a walk together. I was supposed to be there around five, but I was tardy. I didn't get there until five twenty." At this admission, Scott lowered his head in regret. He tried to explain his first mistake, "I have a habit of being late. I wanted to stop and check the job Brooke and I are working on together. Well, she's doing stained glass art for me to enhance the hardscape at Maple Haven, the bed and breakfast which is undergoing and extensive remodeling. I got to the B&B at four forty."

"Are there any witnesses to collaborate your time there?" Gaynor squinted as a streak of sunlight grabbed a hole in the clouds.

With relief Scott said, "Sure. I talked to my foreman, Jeff Carbell. A couple of my other guys were there, too, Justin Bedecker and Andy McGrath. Some workers from other crews were also in the area, but I'd have to check with the project manager for their names. They probably saw me, but I'm not sure."

"We'll check into it." Detective Rell wrote the names on lined paper. "Be specific with the rest of the afternoon's timing."

"Okay. At Maple Haven, I showed some of Brooke's work to Jeff Carbell, which took longer than I wanted. When I noticed it was already ten after five, I decided to get out of there. I left the site and traveled west on highway 28 until I came to the exit for the park. I arrived at five twenty-two. I remember because I kept watching the clock to see how late I was. I went right to the trail where Brooke said she'd meet me. It took me four or five minutes until I found her." Scott stopped, took a deep breath and looked up at the blue and gray sky. His nerves became active with goose bumps under his jacket. He didn't know if he'd ever forget what he'd seen.

Scott dropped his gaze to each of the detectives. With a touch of humanity, Detective Gaynor paused before his next request. "Tell us exactly what you saw and did from there."

As if more air was necessary to continue with the gruesome story, Scott took an extended breath and resumed. "As I walked about fifty feet into the trail, I saw a form lying on the ground. It took me only a split second to realize it was a person and not much longer to know it was Brooke." Because Scott knew Brooke was alive and out of critical care, he could proceed with the story. "I went over to her and bent down to see what happened. When I saw the blood on her shirt and in the dirt around her I immediately called 911 from my cell phone." Scott continued to tell the detectives how he did his best to help her until the paramedics and police arrived.

After Scott recounted everything, he waited for their reaction.

He watched them pause and flip through their notes. Detective Gaynor looked up first. Without a comment on the last twenty minutes of explanation, Gaynor began another line of questions with, "What kind of relationship do you have with Ms. Bellin?"

Surprised at the direct line of attack, Scott answered, "I hired Brooke to do her stained glass art for my landscaping project."

"What else?" Detective Gaynor rubbed the back of his neck, as if he waited for a long explanation.

"I suppose you could say that we've become friends."

Detective Rell added his thoughts. "This wasn't a work meeting? At the park."

"It basically was a meeting about work. She likes to go for walks, so I asked if I could join her. I told her I had some work information to pass on." Scott rubbed the palms of his hands together.

With a slight touch of sarcasm, Gaynor took his turn. "Do you think Mr. Bellin was having a hard time accepting his ex-wife taking walks with her business partner?"

"I don't think he knew," Scott claimed. "You don't understand Brooke's relationship with her ex-husband."

Rell came in with the researched history. "We understand Ms. Brooke Bellin divorced a Mr. Ty Bellin approximately two years ago. Are you saying Mr. Bellin is still interested in his ex-wife after this long?"

"Well, from the little she, uh Brooke, has said about it, I think he tries to control her. She still sometimes helps with his therapy because of a stroke he had right before they got divorced. I don't think it's good for her, but I can't tell her what to do."

Detective Rell continued flipping pages of notes. "Maybe Ms. Bellin still has feelings for him?"

"No. We had talked about that one time, briefly. She inferred that she keeps away from him unless he absolutely needs her help." The look the detectives passed indicated they wanted more. "Brooke's ex-husband had remodeled a studio for her stained glass art when they were first married. It's on the property adjacent to where they used to live. I sensed she felt as if she owed him something, or couldn't ignore him when she worked so close to his house."

Detective Gaynor looked to his partner, and then offered his theory. "So, it would be easier if he, Mr. Bellin, were out of the picture? If Brooke thought Mr. Bellin hurt her, say by shooting her, then she'd turn to you and completely negate him from her life."

"No. I mean… What are you saying? That I shot her? I found her after she'd been shot." Scott's voice rose an octave. The accusation surprised him, so he repeated his part at the scene. "I'm the one who called 911. I'd never hurt her. I...I wouldn't hurt her."

"We're just covering all bases, Mr. Marshall." Getting back to the questions, Detective Gaynor asked, "Were you anywhere else other than the first fifty feet of the trail and at the scene of the crime?"

"No. I may have walked around Brooke, but I didn't go any further down the trail."

The detectives seemed to be taking turns as Rell prompted the next concern. "Are you familiar with the use of a shotgun or rifle?"

"Yes, I've used guns before."

"What kind would that be?"

"I've used both. Shotguns and rifles. I've done target shooting and some hunting. It's been a while, though. I haven't had much time for it," Scott answered.

"Would you consider yourself a good shot?"

"I used to be. A still target isn't that hard to hit. Trapshooting is more difficult, but I got my share of clay pigeons."

With a mask of innocence, Rell asked, "Did you use the rifle for the clay targets?"

Scott smiled at this question. "It's unusual to use a rifle for a moving target such as a bird or clay target. I used a 12.0 gauge for those." As soon as he completed his answer, the smile faded. His shoulders became tight as he assumed they knew the answer to a question about gun usage.

Detective Gaynor changed the maze of questions again. "How close are Ty Bellin and Marla Vrahn?"

Scott lifted his eyebrows in thought. "As far as I know, they're a nurse and a patient. Possibly, they've become friends along the way. You'd have to ask Brooke. I don't see them often and never thought about what they do."

Gaynor tapped the end of his pen on the table. "Is it possible they have more than a nurse and patient relationship?"

"Like I said, I don't know much about what they do together," Scott repeated. "Brooke hasn't said anything about them to me."

"Maybe Ms. Bellin knows something disturbing about her ex-husband and his nurse that caused the divorce. Maybe she wants to 'see' you out of revenge?"

The accusation bothered Scott. Scott kept his tone calm as he responded, "I don't believe that. Brooke doesn't have that type of personality."

Detective Gaynor broadened his question. "You speak as if you know Brooke well. If you do, wouldn't she tell you her thoughts about her ex-husband and their relationship?"

"Brooke and I don't make a habit of talking about her previous marriage. We had our initial discussion and that's it."

"You don't seem to want Mr. Bellin to know how much time you spend with Ms. Bellin. Would he have animosity toward you? Or would it be the other way around?" Gaynor drilled.

"From the little Brooke has said, I don't think her ex would want her with any other man. I have no reason not to like him, except for the fact that he didn't respect her. In exactly what ways, I don't know."

"So, you were going to the woods to plan your getaway?"

"We weren't trying to get away from anyone. The trail was one of Brooke's favorite spots. I probably do like her more than she likes me, but I never had the chance to find out."

"So you want a future with her?" Gaynor kept his eyes locked on Scott.

Scott realized he said as much as he wanted about his and Brooke's relationship. He felt his blood begin to boil. Before the steam revealed itself, Scott said, "I've told you what Brooke and my relationship consists of. We have nothing to hide."

Apparently satisfied with this conclusion, Detective Rell took another tangent. "Have you talked with the men at your jobsite since the shooting?"

"I haven't had a chance. Last night I waited to see Brooke, but wasn't able to." He remembered a call to his foreman this morning to dismiss himself from the jobsite. "I did talk to my foreman, Jeff Carbell, this morning. It was brief. I only told him I wouldn't be at the site this morning and that I'd call later. I didn't specify a time because I didn't know how long I'd be able to see Brooke."

"Did you say anything about the shooting?"

"No. I didn't mention it. Jeff didn't say anything, so I don't know if he knows about it."

Both detectives fell silent for a moment. Detective Rell looked at Gaynor with an insignificant nod. Detective Gaynor looked back at Scott, and then asked, "Mr. Marshall, did you take anything from the scene?"

"No, I can't think of..." Scott felt the pressure of the bag of apples against his leg. "No, I didn't take anything."

"I guess we're done then. We don't have any more questions right now. If you have anything else to tell us, please call." Detective Gaynor handed over his customary business card.

"Will do. I'll help as much as I can." Scott picked up the bag of apples in an offhanded manner while the detectives briefly eyed his handful.

Chapter 9

Three light taps on the door caused Brooke to wake from a light sleep. She glanced around the stark room, with its medical machinery that lighted up with a slew of numbers. Her vacant stare followed the many wires and tubes attached to the equipment, many of which ended somewhere on the body.

Another tap on the door and a soft swoosh as it opened alerted her to what initially woke her.

Scott peered around the edge of the door and proceeded to Brooke's side. "Hey, did I wake you?"

He looked good. With a temporary lapse of manners, Brooke studied his features. She noted the light brown hair touching the top of his shirt collar, the hazel eyes catching the morning sun from the window, and the strength in his legs that filled out the worn Levi's.

"Did you sleep well?" Scott approached the edge of her bed, setting the bag of apples on the nearby chair.

Brooke quickly returned her stare to his face. "I slept on and off. I expected to sleep better after everything yesterday." She briefly smiled, and with a false laugh said, "You didn't have to come. Our meeting was supposed to be yesterday."

"I was worried."

"I'm in good hands. I'm still alive, aren't I?" She paused to take a sip of water from her bedside. "How'd you find out I was here?"

Resting his hand on the edge of the bed, Scott bent over her. "I was there, Brooke. I found you."

Not searching for more details, she nodded her head.

"I brought our unfinished business. I thought it might cheer you up."

Looking to the chair as Scott reached for the dirty bag packed with apples, Brooke snickered. “How did you get those? Is the note still attached?”

“I borrowed them after the medics left, thinking they might be important to you.”

“Well they were…are important because I brought them for you.” Brooke noticed the note was still intact and motioned for Scott to look at it.

“I wanted to wait ‘til I was with you to look at it.” Scott brushed crusted dirt away from the seal of the miniature envelope before he opened it and pulled out a note. He read it silently, then looked up at Brooke as she watched. “It says ‘I picked the sweetest apples for the sweetest man, Brooke.’ Does this mean you accept me for more than just an employer?”

Not answering immediately, Brooke commented, “They’re Jonathan apples. Very sweet. We can be friends.”

“And…”

“We’ll see.” Brooke became serious, looking out the window at the morning sun. “I just began to trust again, and now I don’t know if I’ll be able to.” She shifted her look back to Scott and locked his stare with hers.

With a shocked expression, Scott froze for a minute.

“I was shot. Who did it? Even if I want to trust someone, should I?”

Scott pulled the chair closer to her side and sat at the edge. “I don’t know who’d even think of hurting you, but I’ll find out if I have to do it myself. That’s a promise.” Brooke remembered the familiar statement. Ty had said almost the same thing.

For whatever reason, she let her guard down. She was probably too exhausted to hold on to it any longer. “Scott, I’m sorry. I’m acting as if you did something wrong.” Holding her uninjured arm to him, he took the offer and gently held her hand. “Just give me some time, and I’m sure I’ll want to get to know you as more than my boss. That’s all I can offer right now.”

Scott caressed her hand. “I’m not asking for anything else.” With a comforting squeeze, he released his hold and rose from the chair. “I’ll leave you alone to rest.” As he turned to the door, with the bag of apples and note in is grip, he added, “If you need anything, just call.”

She nodded and watched him exit.

* * * *

After a few hours of doctors, detectives, and a call to her friend, Chloe, Brooke convinced herself to talk to Scott again. The doctors told her she could leave. The detectives told her where not to go and why. Chloe helped her decide where to go, or at least who should pick her up.

Brooke figured she'd make a better habit of listening to Chloe. If she had listened to Chloe the first time, she wouldn't be in the hospital. If she had taken the reading seriously, she would've altered her plans and not gotten shot.

With shaky hands, she dialed the familiar numbers.

"Hello."

"Scott, it's me." She didn't know where to start with the unexpected information piled on her since his early morning visit. "I'll be released this afternoon, but I can't go home." Brooke held her breath.

"I can take you home. It's not a problem." She could hear the excitement in his voice.

"No. No, I can't go home. They told me I can't go home." Brooke began to choke on sobs.

"Slow down, Brooke. Who said you can't go home?"

"The police or the detectives who talked to me today. Scott, I can't go home. They want to investigate my apartment. They'll investigate Ty's house, too. I can't believe this is happening."

"Brooke, I'll be at the hospital in a few minutes. I'm on my way right now, and I'll bring you to my house. Don't try to tell me anything. Take a deep breath, and try to relax. You can let me know what's going on when I get there."

"Okay. Okay, I'll try. I'm so confused by everything. It's all like a horrible dream and I can't wake up. How can I wake up from this? Maybe I'm going crazy." Brooke's voice faltered as she absently kneaded the edges of her hospital gown.

"You're far from crazy. This is a stressful situation for you, and I'll help you through it," Scott confirmed and then changed subjects. "I'll make you whatever you want for dinner. If it's something I can't make, I'll get us a carryout."

With a laugh mixed amongst her fading tears, Brooke responded, "You really will take care of me, won't you?" She didn't wait for an answer. "It's a nice feeling after taking care of someone myself for so long. Not that I minded helping Ty, but…" She recalled the reports from the officers.

"Brooke. Brooke, are you still with me?"

"Yeah, Scott, I'm here. Just keep talking to me." She rested her head on the stiff pillow behind her.

Scott did as requested. "There's a slight chill out of the west, so I could build you a fire, and we could eat by it. Maybe you'd like a glass of wine or maybe something a bit stronger?" Scott paused, "That probably wasn't as funny as I intended it to be."

"It's okay. I know you're trying to cheer me up." Without effort, Brooke smiled as much as her dry and cracked lips allowed. "Actually, I probably will want a drink, but I'll have to find out if it's okay with the pain medicine. How long until you're here?"

"I can be up to your room in a quick two minutes. I just pulled into the hospital parking lot. I'll have to hang up before I enter, but I'll be there before you have time to forget about me."

"Mm…. I don't think I can forget you." Brooke turned her head to the door.

As if he had run to the entry, Scott said, "Well, I'm at the entrance, so I have to go now. I'll be right there."

Within a few minutes Brooke looked up as Scott ignored the greeting from a nurse who mistook him for Ty while he entered her room for the second time. Brooke gingerly tested her ability to pull a sleeve onto the arm with the injured shoulder as she dressed herself. She watched him respectfully cast his eyes to the floor.

Brooke's pasty lips formed a small curve upward. "Hi, Scott."

Her greeting was as good as an invitation. Scott moved close to her and righted her sleeve. Brooke knew Ty had purposefully brought this blouse for her the night before, as she habitually left her apartment door unlocked. He had presented the top as a Valentine's gift a few years back.

She fingered one of the delicate buttons as she gazed blankly at the wall for a brief minute. Shaking her head, she formed another small smile. "Scott, I don't remember if I've thanked you, yet, so thank you." With her next thought, the smile vanished. "I have to tell you what I was told since I saw you this morning."

"Wouldn't you like to leave here first?" Scott's leg rubbed against Brooke's thigh as she sat at the edge of the bed.

"I would, except we have to discuss, uh, where I'm going to." She looked at Scott with a question in her eyes.

Scott spoke with an edge of alarm. "Have you changed your mind?"

"I didn't change my mind. The detectives did."

Scott's voice wavered as he questioned, "What'd they tell you? I only told them the truth when I talked with them this morning."

Brooke continued as if they were talking about the same thing. "You couldn't have known this morning. They made their decision after they talked to you."

"Why would they think I'm not good for you? Brooke, I did the best I could. I'll hunt down the shooter and kill him for you, if that's what you want. Please, make the decision for yourself. Don't let them tell you what to think or do." Scott spread his hands to the side.

Brooke looked him in the eye. "I am making my own decisions."

Scott rolled his neck while he rubbed his palm across his chin. "Brooke, can I take you to my house and we'll talk?"

"Maybe it'd be better away from here."

Chapter 10

They snapped powdered latex gloves over their hands and reached for the doorbell. The bell rang twice with a knock to follow each. No one answered. Officer Shears twisted the doorknob. "The door's open. Apparently people don't lock their doors around here."

The stained glass center of the door glittered and changed colors with the movement as it swung into the entry. Officer Shears studied the tiled floor before he entered. "There isn't a scrap of dirt or dust on the floor. Either the house is cleaned every day or this entry isn't used much." Shears explained his assumption of the Bellin housekeeping. "It's unusual not to have tracks from shoes at this time of the year with the rain, mud, and all the leaves blowing around."

"Maybe that's just your house," Officer Kaehne chided. Serious again, he continued, "Most people come in through an attached garage door or the kitchen. Let's take a look at that."

Officer Shears listened while his gaze learnedly traveled the perimeter of the entry room. "Take a look to your left." Nodding his chin, he continued, "When we get back to this area we'll have to check out the goldmine in that corner."

Officer Kaehne swiveled his stance toward the indicated corner. "Could it be any easier? That's quite the stocked gun case. Yeah, let's save the best for last." He pulled out his camera and photographed the slightly ajar door of the gun cabinet. Kaehne snapped a few more shots of the floor and an overall view of the entry.

Moving with care, they entered the adjoining kitchen. Again, it looked like a magazine picture. Everything was in place. There weren't any dishes in the sink and not a crumb to be found on the counter. In the center of the table was a production of apples with cinnamon sticks nestled amongst the shiny redness. "That's worth a picture." Again the camera flashed. "What's with all the apples in this case? Bag one of them to see if they're the same kind as at the scene." He stood and stretched his back. "I talked with Gaynor and Rell while you were sending orders out for the other guys. They told me Marshall had a bag of apples at his feet during the interview. The bag had a slight rip and dirt smeared on the side. I asked the detectives why they didn't take it from Marshall."

Peering into the basket, Officer Shears commented, "Those detectives are pretty sharp, so they must've had a reason."

"They're taking a softer approach with Marshall. I'm not sure if it's because they suspect Marshall and don't want him to be clued in on it or they don't have much interest in him. He already confirmed his presence at the scene, so a lot of evidence against him can be explained away." Kaehne walked around the table, tapping the edge. "Taking evidence from the scene is a strike in my book. If the detectives won't watch Marshall, I certainly will. A criminal always makes a mistake. We just have to find it."

While Officer Kaehne announced his intentions, Shears thumbed through an orderly stack of paperwork stored on a small desk beneath a corner cupboard. "You think Marshall has something to do with this?" It was a serious question. Something Shears hadn't spent much time contemplating.

"Possibly. Isn't it convenient that Marshall was at the scene, called 911, but yet he took probable evidence from the scene? He could be playing the game 'If I can't have her, no one can.' Marshall probably knows the ex-husband is an automatic suspect and relies on that. Maybe Ms. Bellin was going to break it off with Marshall, and that was why they met."

"You don't have a personal affiliation with any of the involved, do you?" Officer Shears stopped his paper search and raised his brows.

"Of course not. I wouldn't be on the case, if I did."

Officer Shears gave his partner a sideway glance. He couldn't help but add with a smirk, "Or are you an expert on dating divorced women?"

"Give it up, Shears. I get my share, but I stay away from those who are harder to convince to stay the night," Kaehne replied.

With one last male jab, Officer Shears cajoled, "Bellin would be out of your reach, anyway." Officer Kaehne shot him a hot look that lasted only a second as he covered it with forced laughter.

Shears shuffled the paperwork and set it back on the desk. “Let’s check out the garage. That’s always a good place to hide evidence or leave it and forget about it. There’s a door, which will probably lead us to it.”

Shears examined the door handle due to habit as he placed a gloved hand over it and turned. Eave lights surrounded three sides of the garage and exposed it to a lot of light. He took a moment to peruse the surroundings and then motioned Officer Kaehne to follow him to a workbench littered with gun cleaning cloths and oils.

“Take a look at this.” Officer Shears zeroed in on the cleaning equipment. “It’s all set out, but none of it’s used. I would think if Mr. Bellin cleaned his guns and threw out the used cloths, he would’ve put the rest away.”

“Either he didn’t get to it or he was interrupted. This appears too obvious. Maybe someone else left these for us to find. We didn’t have to look hard, that’s for sure.” Kaehne walked over and eyed the apparatus.

“Bag the stuff up. Toss in the oilcans and the rod cleaners, too. We’ll check on who’s been using them.”

Officer Kaehne pulled more zip lock bags from his evidence satchel. He carefully set the clean cotton cloths at the bottom of the bag followed by the new can of cleaning oil. He meticulously stored the unassembled pieces of the rod used to push the cloths down the throat of a gun and wipe away firing residue.

During Kaehne’s procedure, Officer Shears pivoted to view the rest of the garage. Tools used to maintain the yard hung neatly lined against one wall. Each rake, shovel, and gardening hoe seemed to be nestled in its own designated spot. Each hanger was a precise distance from the next. Nearby, a length of yellow nylon rope, daisy-chained, hung over a larger hook. A six-foot length of shelving held bottles of oils, car maintenance liquids, tightly sealed and half empty cans of paint with all drips wiped away, neatly stacked leftover tiles, and other carefully reserved extras from projects.

“Quite the obsessively neat home, wouldn’t you say?” Shears commented.

As he finished zipping the bags, Kaehne walked to his partner’s side. “That means anything out of place must have a reason or be a sign.” As if he already knew the layout, he turned to the opposing wall and headed for an unusually high bottom shelf. Under it were two olive green, rubber garbage cans. Pulling one out, he flipped the lid. Two tightly knotted, white plastic kitchen bags were pushed down to leave breathing room for the next.

Kaehne glanced over his shoulder as Officer Shears's cell phone rang a nondescript bell tone. Shears answered his phone while he watched his partner look at the top white bag. Methodically he pulled it from its container and set it on the cement floor.

Shears peered over the edge of the can as he listened to his call. Even the garbage seemed clean. There wasn't any obnoxious odor or indescribable elements. Naturally, there were apple cores. Kaehne reached in and pulled out a relatively fresh core. Stuck to the stem was a used gun cleaning cloth. "Bingo," Kaehne yelled out. "Looks like Mr. Bellin took the time to clean at least one gun." He dug deeper into the house leftovers.

Officer Shears ended his call. "There aren't any more cleaning supplies?"

"No, I'm not finding anything else in this bag. I'll take the whole bag with us, but I still need to look through the last one. I doubt there'd be anything in it because it was probably from before the shooting."

"Evidence doesn't only appear after the crime. You seem to have found one thing already, and there could be more planning paraphernalia in the older bag. Why don't we take a look at the other one at headquarters, too? Let's get back to the gun cabinet."

Officer Kaehne nodded in agreement, as he quickly pulled the remaining bag from its resting place. "I'm going to run these out to the squad. I'll meet you in the entry."

When Kaehne reentered the front of the house, Shears said with a defensive tone, "Oh, the call I got while we were in the garage was from Detective Gaynor."

"What's the problem?"

"Apparently Gaynor and his partner were here early this morning. They didn't collect the evidence because they took pictures and were going to come back to see if anything was added or deleted or changed in any manner today."

"Shit, why didn't they let us know? It'd be nice if they would keep us informed. What are we supposed to do with the evidence we already collected?" Officer Kaehne came up with more questions about his own welfare. "I suppose we're going to get written up for this? Why were we given a search warrant, if the detectives didn't want anything removed, yet?"

"Hold on. I smoothed it over; otherwise, we would've dropped everything when he called." Shears proceeded with his reasoning. "I told Gaynor we took pictures of everything before moving the evidence. That held pretty well with him. Gaynor thought Ty Bellin might come home and leave a trail of some sort, if he hadn't already."

"You talk as if they know who the shooter was."

"Oh, did I forget that part?" Shears stopped sweeping the fingerprint powder across the handle and glass on the gun cabinet as his mouth slowly curved up on one side. "The District Attorney sent a couple other officers to arrest Ty Bellin and his mistress, Marla Vrahn."

Kaehne stopped with an exasperated look, "They came up with tangible proof this quickly? What about Marshall?"

Shears's expression quickly changed as he said, "Do you have something up your sleeve about Marshall?"

Ignoring the silent accusation, Officer Kaehne asked, "How could they investigate all tangents in such a short time? From what we found, the evidence does point toward Bellin, but what if he's being set up? Were they at Vrahn's house already, too?"

"Whoa, I can understand you having a lot of unanswered questions still. I do, too, but Gaynor wants to meet with us tonight and fill us in on what they've found. They must've turned in more evidence than we discovered because I wouldn't have made an arrest with what we've found so far." Officer Shears turned back toward the gun cabinet to finish the procedure.

"How can you remain so calm?" Referring to the detectives, Kaehne continued, "They couldn't have found what we have here. Even if they did, they didn't take any of the evidence to have it analyzed. They better hope for more than just their reputation to cover for them."

"Unfortunately, their authority overrules ours. They want us to finish the house investigation, get any possible fingerprints on this cabinet, and bring the 30.06 with us."

"They've pinpointed the gun used?" Kaehne asked incredulously.

"I didn't get any details. Like I said, they'll fill us in tonight." Officer Shears peered at the prints that appeared as he dusted the gun cabinet. "Let's finish this up and get out of here. Maybe we can catch a bite before we meet with the detectives. I'm sure it'll be a long night."

With a resigned sigh, Kaehne admitted, "It'll be interesting to hear what they came up with."

Shears didn't answer as he finished wiping down the glass door. Next, he turned his attention to a finely crafted 30.06 honoring the center holding grooves of the gun cabinet. He whistled softly through his teeth as he admired the custom fittings and markings on the stock. "They want us to bring the gun to the lab to be dusted. Gaynor must be expecting something great from this. Who knows? Maybe, this is an open and shut case."

"It would be nice to have one like that. Being so obvious worries me, though."

"Yeah, me too."

Chapter 11

"Let me help you," Scott commanded in a gentle voice as he reached for Brooke's waist to hoist her into his truck. She acknowledged him and waited for his help before taking hold of the handgrip between the door and front windshield. All of a sudden, her voice didn't exist. Her eyes looked nowhere.

Brooke felt an eerie change come over her. Was it because she'd finally digested what had happened yesterday? Or because she couldn't fathom the reality that someone, an unknown someone, wanted to hurt her or even kill her? Brooke felt herself tighten in reaction to the sweep of a cold, late fall chill tumbling over the faded asphalt of the parking lot. The surrounding trees held no warmth as their nearly bare arms reached to the sky for the hidden sun. A few leaves left to dangle precariously from their perches were withered and dry.

Brooke felt the same way the leaves did. Life drained from her soul. This was not her normal self. The person she knew could see peace and beauty in nearly everything. Brooke didn't like or want this change. She took a deep breath. She had to pull herself out of the foreign land into which she was slipping.

Brooke purposefully turned her aching neck to face the man who released so many warm emotions from deep inside her. Feelings she'd kept hidden. At the same time, she felt Scott's hands firmly encircle her waist. She dug deep into her mind to find the pleasure she vaguely remembered from the innocent touch of his hands when they had worked together.

She looked from Scott's concerned face to the massive hands on her waist. She remembered them as powerful and gentle. Brooke couldn't feel the unusual softness of his skin through her thin jacket, but she recalled the pleasant memory. She concentrated hard on this memory. She wanted to get back into her sweet world more than ever. "Bring me back to this world."

"What, Brooke?" Scott bent in close to her. "Am I hurting you?"

Brooke flashed her eyes back to Scott's soft brown stare, which attempted to bring her back to this moment. "Scott. Scott, just bring me back," was all she could muster.

"I'll take you anywhere you want to go. Just tell me. If you'd rather go to your home, we'll go there."

His voice helped her dismiss the depression she had felt climb through her soul. With a preemptory half smile, she corrected him. "No, I want to go with you. I want to be with you at your home. I'll feel safe there."

"I'll keep you safe. I promise." Scott tightened his grip and lifted Brooke onto the front seat. She shimmied in further as he set her small overnight bag in the backseat before he closed the door.

Brooke convinced herself she shouldn't wander off into the silent world she'd just escaped. It was a strange and fearful experience. As soon as Scott positioned himself in the driver's seat, she shifted her thigh against his. She needed to feel his warmth.

Brooke watched a quiet smile touch his lips, slightly covered by a thin mustache. She glanced over Scott's unshaven jaw and guessed he hadn't the time for a shower.

Scott darted his eyes back and forth from the road to Brooke as she stared ahead. He took the corners and turns with care while she stiffly sat at his side.

Brooke sensed that he was on the verge of asking her what the police had told her. This was not the time. She didn't know how she'd react after she revealed the authorities' decision. He'd have to wait. She simply wanted to make it to his home safely.

With an escaped sigh from Scott, Brooke turned her head to him and readjusted her focus before it slipped again. With a look at Scott, she saw what she wanted most, a beautiful man whose only concern was to please and take care of her. She knew it was his intention, but the clouds in her mind continued to be an infraction on her judgment. Brooke felt like everything she knew, trusted, and counted on for as long as she could remember, changed with the reverberating of a bullet against her weak flesh.

She had no reason to question the feelings and intentions of the man who insisted on protecting her. He repeatedly revealed his feelings in actions. Why hadn't she told him her thoughts? Was it because she couldn't find her voice at the right time? She imagined them naked together in every way, with their minds and bodies melted together. Why did she hold back?

There probably wasn't an answer to this worldly question. Brooke gently laid her head on Scott's shoulder and accepted the silence of the ride. As tired as she felt, her mind was on high alert. She noticed the rhythmic clipping of the tires over the cracks in the road, the hum of the truck's engine as it shifted gears at the stop signs, and the incessant buzz of the radio, which Scott turned low so she couldn't make out what the buzz stood for.

She turned her face into his shoulder and caught his masculine scent. A safe place, warm and perfectly scented. With this thought, her adrenalin shifted, allowing her eyes to close.

Scott glanced down at Brooke as he detected an even breathing pattern. Gladly he noted she was comfortable enough to rest in his presence. He didn't notice the road sounds around them or the near silence in the cab of the truck. His main thought was what Brooke had on her mind. He considered a multitude of avenues the promised conversation might cover.

The way she warmed up to him gave no evidence of her not wanting a relationship, but this could be because of her exhaustion. At the hospital, she was adamant about something he needed to know. Maybe it was selfish to think about himself. It could easily be about her injury. Maybe it was more serious than he knew. Scott didn't think he left the investigators with any negative connotations about his involvement with Brooke and the shooting, but she certainly needed to tell him something after he spoke to the detectives.

Relieved, Scott pulled into his driveway. "Brooke, we're here. At my house."

Apparently awakened from a challenging dream, Brooke jerked her head up, followed by a cry of alarm as she guarded her injury. She pushed away from Scott with her uninjured arm and gasped, "What happened? What'd I do to you?"

Startled by Brooke's sudden change from a quiet sleep to eyes intensified with fear, Scott carefully grabbed her forearm and said, "Brooke. Brooke, it's just me. You wanted to come to my home." He noticed the fear continue in her stare, so he tried again. "Brooke, I'm here to help you. You didn't do anything."

Brooke shifted her gaze from Scott to her new surroundings. They parked in front of a small, but older and well-kept cape cod. The siding had a grayish tint with a darker charcoal trim around the windows, and the entry door led to a small patio of cobblestones. A scant few pieces of furniture encouraged an evening of watching the sun set over the scattered maple and oak trees. A frequently used fire pit to the right of the patio had a well-stocked pile of wood for the next chilly night spent outside.

Brooke's eyes softened as she turned back to Scott. "I'm sorry. I don't know what I was thinking. We can go in now. I'm okay. Just a little on edge, I guess."

Scott leaned back and released her arm. "Stay right here, and I'll get on the other side and help you out." Scott jumped out and hurried to her side of the truck. She leaned back in the seat to let him take over.

With everything so fragile at this point, Scott transferred the gentleness of his movements to open the passenger door. "What'll work best for you in getting out?" He tried to figure out where to place his strength.

"I can't hold onto the door with my left arm, so if you let me put my weight on you while I step down, I should be okay," Brooke told him as she met his gaze with tenderness.

Scott did exactly as instructed. He didn't want to smother her and knew she could walk to the door. Yet, he did insist on carrying her bag.

Brooke paused before she ventured to the entrance. "I never thought about it, but I hadn't imagined where you lived before. I'm not sure a Cape Cod is what I would've thought."

"I'm comfortable here. Actually, I lease this place. I'm not here much, anyway. Work keeps me too busy to really care about a home of my own right now." He avoided an explanation that if he had a home, he wanted to share it with someone. He found it easier to talk than listen to silence, so he continued, "This is centrally located for my work and a lot less of a hassle concerning maintenance, Although, I did offer to exchange some landscaping and lawn maintenance for rent. Guess I can't overlook an ignored yard, can I?" Scott gave a small chuckle as he revealed his passion for his landscaping career.

"I'm sure you have great ideas. You'll have to tell me about them because the only work of yours I'm familiar with is Maple Haven's huge land remodel." With a sigh, Brooke added, "We'll have to talk about my stained glass for that project, too, and how I can get it done for you."

"I'm not worried about it right now. We'll figure something out. I can probably get an extension on the time in the contract, considering what my stained glass artist has just gone through," Scott responded with an encouraging smile.

"You're right. We have a lot to discuss. I think I need to start with what's going on right now. I'm also a bit chilled, so I better get moving to see the inside of your home." The wind had increased with the end of the afternoon.

He didn't need more excuses to get inside and led the way to the door. Sidling in front of Brooke, he opened the door and pushed it wide enough for her to step inside.

He stopped with Brooke in the entry as she looked around.

When he had rented the small house, he had furnished it comfortably with an oval, wool rug to partially cover a dark and slightly scuffed hardwood floor. The rug sported cranberry and muted browns, which blended with a slightly beaten, soft brown love seat. In front of this, a newer and purposefully scarred coffee table held multiple stacks of paperwork and project photos. At night he often did office work at this table. On the other side of it perched the only additional seating of an over-stuffed matching, brown chair.

The chair canted toward the fireplace, which stood at the far end of the table. Behind the chair and against the partial wall towered a stereo system with multiple sets of wires scattered between speakers.

Scott remained patient as he watched Brooke take in the surroundings. With a contented sigh, she signaled she finished examining the room, so he took the opportunity to make her feel comfortable. "Brooke, remember I promised you dinner? Why don't we go into the kitchen."

She followed him as he led the way. "I have so much to tell you."

"Do you want to talk about it now?"

"No. No, let's have a nice dinner first."

* * * *

They had taken their meals into the living room to eat by the now roaring fire. With the clatter of silverware against his empty plate, Scott decided to refill it. Maybe Brooke needed another moment alone while he went to the kitchen to contemplate what she had to say. He let his mind wander in an unfavorable direction. One minute he was ready to kiss her and the next minute she became distant. *Just concentrate on the dinner. She'll let me know soon.* .

"I'm ready to talk," Brooke announced as Scott returned to the living room. He paused before the table, then collected his nerves as he set his plate down. Looking toward the adjusting fire, he commented, "Let me stoke the fire and add another log or two. Then you'll have my full attention."

Without a disagreement, she smiled and waited until he sat down.

Neither one took another bite, as Scott's wondering eyes focused on Brooke. With a deep breath, she began, "I don't know where to start with this, and I'm not even sure what it makes me feel."

Scott held his breath and waited.

"Late this morning, the police visited me. They arrested Ty and Marla," Brooke blurted out as she looked down, while tears rolled down her cheeks.

Scott jumped up from his seat. It hadn't occurred to him an arrest had happened already, least of all that it'd be Brooke's ex-husband and his nurse. He had a flash of guilt for his thoughts about his own feelings for Brooke instead of the shooting at hand.

Scott rounded the table and sat next to her. He wrapped his arms around her with a gentle touch. Without adequate words, he just held her as her shoulders began to shake beneath his hands.

Brooke succinctly told Scott the news, but then the control was gone and she began to spill out her thoughts and feelings and details in-between chokes and sobs. "I don't even know how they came up with the idea that Ty…that Ty was the one."

Scott was at a loss for an explanation. "Brooke, they must know more than we do. When they talked to me, I wasn't aware of anything that pointed to your ex-husband."

Brooke raised her head from his chest, where it had felt so comfortable. "Why didn't I even suspect them? Why would he do this to me? I've tried to remain his friend since the divorce. And with Marla, too. Maybe he was upset that I actually have a life without him.

"Do you think he knew about us? Not that there's much to know, but I was apprehensive about how he would react. He had no right to make me feel that way. God, our divorce was two years ago, and I've lived up to my side of the deal. He hasn't. He was supposed to sell the house we lived in. I should've made him follow through."

Brooke's voice began to rise in frustration and fear. "I didn't do a thing when he 'worked overtime,' and I knew what he was really doing. I still stood by his side. I didn't accept or want to see what he was doing because everything at home still ran smoothly. I didn't want to be the one to change things, so I let his actions go. I always felt obligated to keep him happy no matter what. It was my job." Scott wiped the moisture on her cheek and remained intent on her story. He didn't allow himself to take offense as she reverted her discussion to her former marriage.

"But what about me? I haven't felt like I've had the company of a man in years. And not just since Ty's stroke and the divorce." With a pause she connected her gaze with Scott's and softened her tone. "And now I've accidentally found you."

Scott gave her a slight squeeze as she said this. "Brooke, first, I'll be here for you as much as you want me to be. I don't have all the answers you need right now, but I'll help you find them." Scott also wanted to ask her what she knew about the investigation because the officers must have given her some reasons for their arrest. He wasn't going to push it. Brooke had been through a lot already and was sure to go through more.

As if she knew what Scott wondered, Brooke added, "The investigators wouldn't tell me what they found or why Ty and Marla were arrested so quickly. They just told me not to go home tonight."

After a moment of silence, Scott suggested, "Let's give this a rest. You're getting tired. I can see it in your eyes." She slowly nodded.

He disappeared to gather blankets and on impulse, grabbed a sleeping bag for himself.

He wanted to be close to Brooke and able to protect her. For whatever reason, Scott didn't expect the night to stay quiet.

Chapter 12

If it weren't so large and imposing, it would be a replica of a dentist's office. The bland and colorless brick, broken up indiscriminately by narrow windows, rose tall and powerful over a lawn washed out by the late fall freezes. Five smooth cement steps led to a landing followed by five more steps, another landing and then the double, smoked-glass doors. Over the sterile atmosphere the building's label, Wisla County Police Department, greeted a weary Officer Shears and his partner.

Shears grabbed the handle of one door and held it open for Officer Kaehne to enter before him. "What room are we supposed to meet them in?"

"Room 2c, I was told." Officer Kaehne stepped into the building. They didn't talk the rest of the way to the designated room. It had been a long two days of investigations with more to come. Their shoes echoed in the hall and a random discussion between officers in rooms they passed were the only sounds in the early evening on a weekday at this municipal building.

* * * *

Detectives Gaynor and Rell had their notes in order when a draft from the door brought the officers in. Without a greeting, Gaynor began, "We've got a mess to sort through, gentlemen. It seems the District Attorney felt he was ready for action." He shook his head as he told this to the officers. "Unless you guys have a lot more than we do, I don't know where Attorney Sabin got his information from."

Officer Shears straightened his shoulders. "What did Sabin do?"

"Your District Attorney had Ty Bellin and Marla Vrahn arrested." Gaynor focused on the officers as if they had something to do with this rash decision.

"Are you sure? That's crazy," Officer Kaehne said.

"We've turned in rough reports on possible physical evidence, but haven't talked to Sabin personally." Officer Shears began to open his bag of notes.

"He doesn't have much more than that. We haven't turned anything over, yet," Detective Rell added.

Gaynor decided to take over and get the meeting started. "Under the circumstances, I think we'll start with what the officers have discovered, collected, and theorized so far."

Officer Shears took a seat at the conference table. "I'll take this one. Kaehne, jump in, if I miss something." He paused here to unload the thickening folders, in which he stored the last two days' information. Shears laid the forms and scribbled notes in chronological order.

"I'll start at the beginning." Officer Shears summarized the search of Ty Bellin's home.

Detective Gaynor interrupted here, "We had a chance to scope the other officers' reports. I'll fill you in when you're done."

Shears nodded. "We have a list of visitors from the hospital and just received a list of calls Ms. Bellin made. The only visitors were her ex-husband who was with Marla Vrahn, his nurse or girlfriend, or whatever you want to call her. The only calls Ms. Bellin made were to Chloe Heathlan and Scott Marshall."

"We'll be talking to her tonight." Detective Rell made a note to get Chloe's address.

"Getting kind of late, isn't it?" Officer Kaehne suggested.

"The sooner we talk to everyone, the more likely their input hasn't been tainted and their memory hasn't changed," Rell answered with conviction. Officer Kaehne looked back at his notes.

"Those are the main points we've come up with." Officer Shears tapped the blunt end of a pen on the last page of his reports. "Officer Kaehne, did I leave anything out other than a possible detail or two, which will be in the reports?"

"I think that's about it," Kaehne answered. Both officers turned their attention to the detectives for comments.

Detective Gaynor directed his question to Officer Kaehne. "What's the hang-up with the apples?"

Fidgeting in his seat, Kaehne kept his head up as he answered. "I find it odd that Ms. Bellin was nearly lying on top of a bag of apples in the initial pictures I took, but then they disappeared. The only person at the crime scene not in uniform was Scott Marshall. This leads me to believe he was the one who removed possible evidence, and the only reason someone removes evidence is to hide something. Why would Marshall want apples covered in dirt and probably blood?"

With his thumb and forefinger angled across his chin, Detective Gaynor held a lengthy pause before he responded. Using the spring in the chair, he purposefully leaned into the table. "I don't know why Marshall wanted those apples, but he had them with him when we questioned him at the hospital." The officers did a sideways glance at each other. "Marshall came to visit Ms. Bellin and brought the bag of apples with him. He also didn't say a thing about taking them from the scene. Maybe, she had brought the apples as a gift for Marshall."

"Or maybe Marshall thought she didn't want anything to do with him other than work, so he shot her and then went back to the scene to act as the hero. The apples were just a gift to himself as a perverted reminder of her," Kaehne added.

Shears looked to his partner with disapproval.

Gaynor jumped on the new idea. "Do you feel confident with pointing the finger at Marshall?" He didn't wait for an answer. "Marshall cooperated when he talked with us. Although, he could be over-confident thinking we wouldn't suspect someone who called in an emergency."

"If we're putting him on the suspect list, we're going to have to get her out of his house," Detective Rell mentioned.

"Even if Marshall is only being considered, she needs to be gone from his home. Shears, get an officer out there yesterday. I don't want an arrest or any reason given to Marshall," Gaynor commanded.

Shears took out his radio and called the nearest patrol unit. Gaynor waited until he finished. "We still have a lot to cover this evening, so we'll have the same information. As far as the interviews we've conducted, I'll give you copies of the paperwork, and you can read them. They're self-explanatory or just ask, if there are questions.

"Quickly, about the missing gun from the gun cabinet. It's probably the 12.0 gauge, which Mr. Bellin left in the backseat of his car. He rode to the shooting range with Vrahn, so he must've moved it. We aren't concerned with that gun, though," Gaynor stated as he prepared to continue with information that was more pertinent.

"What's your reason for ruling out the 12.0 gauge?" Officer Shears questioned.

Gaynor raised his eyes while his head stayed at the same angle toward the notes. He thought it was obvious to leave out the 12.0 gauge. As if the question wasn't asked, Gaynor outlined the rest of his discussion.

"We bypassed Miss Vrahn for consent to investigate her home. Her landlord gladly let us have full reign of the place, which makes the search legal in the state of Wisconsin because the landlord owns the property. The landlord, an older woman who'd probably trust anyone, made certain to repeatedly inform us that Miss Vrahn was a friendly and considerate tenant.

"We'd like to think otherwise after finding a few interesting articles. Miss Vrahn had a swatch of dirt on her hand and we found similar dirt in her apartment. The soil has been sent to the forensic lab along with a handful of bullet casings found in jean pockets from her laundry basket." Gaynor glanced up to see the expected skeptical looks from the listeners. "Dirt and bullet casings after being at a firing range. Sounds relatively normal. Put enough facts together and a different story might come out.

"Also, there may be a discrepancy about the sign-in time at the range. Of those interviewed, many thought Bellin and Vrahn, along with a third, Roger Detris, arrived twenty to thirty minutes later than documented."

Detective Gaynor flipped to his last page. "Seventy-five feet from the scene we found apple cores and indentations from a possible tripod." This raised an eyebrow from Officer Kaehne.

"The third item is the biggest. The bullet found in a red pine tree served as a direct line from the previous mentioned evidence. Partially damaged, of course, but with a semi-rotten tree, there was enough shape left to the bullet to determine what gauge of gun it came from.

"As soon as we get the results from the forensics lab on the evidence, we'll have a more solid list of suspects," Gaynor finished with.

"What are the most likely suspects you're considering at this point?" Officer Kaehne asked.

"We hate to make a list right now, but since the district attorney has already arrested two people, we can say there are at least three people we're now watching, maybe four."

"Obviously they would be Bellin, Vrahn, Detris, and…."

"Yeah, you made your point about Marshall," Gaynor agreed.

Chapter 13

"What the hell are we doing here?" Ty demanded with a slight slur.

"Calm down. I have a reason for getting you in here this quickly. It'll work to your advantage," District Attorney Sabin said.

"You need to get me out of here, now. I have patients to see in the morning. Their needs don't go on hold for emergencies," Marla's rattled voice added.

Remaining low key, District Attorney Sabin responded, "You both know you're on the list of suspects?" He turned his attention to Marla, didn't wait for an answer, and continued with a severe look. "You may have to give up a couple days of work, but this will be better than a whole lot of years."

After a minute's delay, Marla wiped the worried look from her face and said with defiance, "Many years? You sound as if you already have it figured out that we're responsible for this horrible shooting. Maybe I shouldn't be here period."

Ty followed her lead. "I don't want to be here long, either. Considering what we've been through, Attorney Sabin," he stated snidely, "What makes you think you have the right to bring me in here without payback?"

"Trust me. I know this seems backward, but it's in your best interest." District Attorney Sabin stood and put his papers back into a brown and tattered brief case. He shoved the steel chair underneath a rickety, matching table provided in the bleak conference room of the county jail.

Frustration replaced the smugness on Ty and Marla's faces as the guards surrounded them to lead them back to their separate cells.

Sabin approached Ty's escort. "Leave him behind. I need a few minutes with him yet."

The guards left the room with Marla in tow. As their footsteps faded, Ty shot out of his seat and turned on District Attorney Sabin. "I want that piece-of-shit Marshall away from Brooke."

"Hey, I'm working on keeping you from being committed for attempted murder. I don't think I owe you anything else."

"I don't care what you think. I have your job and your life in my hands right now. There's no limit to what you owe me for not turning your ass in."

District Attorney Sabin scowled and shook his head. "Okay, you tell me how I'm going to keep Marshall away from Ms. Bellin. You've got me there."

Ty spoke slowly, enunciating his demand. "I don't care how you do it. Charge *him* for trying to kill Brooke. Then you can arrest him. If you can't do that fast enough, put a restraining order or something on him."

"That's impossible. I can't charge him right now and she has to petition for a temporary restraining order."

Ty glared and slammed his fist on the desk. "Then fake it."

"Can't do that." Sabin paused and looked over Ty's head, thinking. "I'm not the only one dealing with the evidence for the shooting, and the only way we can get a TRO on Marshall without her consent, would be if she had a guardian and that person petitioned. Marshall doesn't have to be charged or arrested to be served a restraining order. We just need the right person to file for it."

"Get her a guardian then."

"Not that easy. It would take months and a mental or physical reason to have one."

Ty calmed before he asked, "How does a person get a guardian?"

"The purpose that would best fit Ms. Bellin is to have a court order based on a referral by a psychiatrist claiming she's incompetent. The court would appoint a guardian. The guardian can petition that she's an individual at risk against a certain person, Marshall for instance." Attorney Sabin shook his head. "I don't see it happening."

A sly smile escaped Ty's lessening anger. "I can do that."

"What do you mean?"

"Well, what do you think I did for the last two years when I was recovering from a stroke? I played games. Games on the computer, and not the kind that you buy at the store to download." Ty rubbed his jaw. "Get me a pass to the computer lab, and I'll be back in a couple hours with a form making me Brooke's guardian."

"Not gonna work."

"Sure it will. I'll get the form, scribble a psych's name on it, and then you call in a quick favor from your buddy the judge. How long will it take to get Marshall the news?"

"If it works, which I doubt, the TRO has to be executed within one day." Sabin's mind began to whirl as he realized Ty was serious. If the document appeared authentic, he considered how long it would be until someone figured out the game. Wiping his hand across his forehead, he prayed that it would last long enough to convince Ty to keep his mouth shut.

"Perfect." Ty locked stares with the district attorney. "Get Marshall away from my wife."

Sabin adjusted his briefcase under his arm. "She's not your wife."

"She will always be my wife."

Chapter 14

The last thing Brooke noticed before she fell asleep was the fire dying down to embers. Bright sparks of orange, coral and crimson tumbled off the logs and fell between the slats of the grate. Small flames sporadically leaped as they fed on the scattered remains of charred wood.

Barely an hour and a half of peaceful sleep passed in Scott's scantily decorated home when an obnoxious pounding on the front door changed the atmosphere. With a quick jolt, Scott sprung from his unusual sleeping arrangement.

Brooke grimaced as she awoke and jerked her shoulder.

"Brooke, just stay there. I haven't any idea who'd be visiting tonight, but I'll take care of this." Scott threw a quick glance toward Brooke as she watched his every move.

The barrage of bangs on the door continued along with, "Open up, this is the Sheriff."

Hastily pulling on his pants, Scott rose to his powerful height of six-foot-two and trotted to the door. He swung the door open and came face to face with two uniforms lacking in his height, but with a power established by other visual means.

Scott spoke first. "Did you find something out?"

"We're serving you with a temporary restraining order and to retain Brooke Bellin or have arrangements made that she leave the premises with us." The Sheriff relayed the message minus any details.

"What? The detectives know she's here. They approved of her coming home with me. What's going on?" Scott wiped the palm of his hand up his forehead.

"I never filed a restraining order." Brooke immediately jumped into the debate as she wrapped the blanket around her, ready to get up. "This is crazy."

The Sheriff avoided Scott's question and didn't offer an explanation. "May we come in?"

With a cooperative movement, Scott stepped back as he opened the door wider. A gust of cold air slipped past the Sheriff and a deputy, causing the dwindling fire to reenergize. "Come in."

As another bluster of frozen air whistled into the living room, Scott shut the door before he repeated his concern. "What's going on?"

The Sheriff and deputy remained standing at ease as the deputy answered. "We don't know the details of your case. We were ordered to remove Ms. Bellin from your care. A petition for the TRO has been issued by the judge."

Scott's voice tightened a notch. "You can't come in here and take her away without a reason." Disagreement crossed the Sheriff and deputy's faces. Scott changed his course. "Brooke was finally resting. You can't expect her to get up and move right now. She needs her rest. Besides, her ex-husband and his nurse have already been arrested."

The Sheriff reentered the debate. "That may be so, but you're now aware of the order and will be arrested, if you don't comply."

Scott clenched his fists and glanced at Brooke, wide-awake now. "Who gave you these orders, and on what basis?"

"You can call the Sheriff's department and verify the order." The Sheriff averted his attention from Scott to Brooke who jumped up from the couch, ready to argue. "Ms. Bellin, do you have somewhere else we can relocate you to?"

"This isn't right." Brooke looked to Scott for help.

"Can't you tell you're upsetting her? How's she going to find somewhere else to go this late in the evening?"

"I asked *her* if she knew of somewhere else. If not, we can take her to the station until arrangements are made," the Sheriff said as if it was an everyday occurrence for a person to find a new home in a matter of minutes.

Scott eyed both officials and barked, "What, so they think I have something to do with the shooting?"

Silence. Silence again, but it wasn't peaceful.

The Sheriff remained in charge, looked straight into Scott's blazing eyes, and said, "Like I said, we don't know the details."

Brooke's lips began to tremble as she jumped in. "That's impossible. Scott got help for me."

The deputy turned to Brooke. "Ma'am, we aren't suggesting anything. You'll have to talk to those assigned to your investigation." He continued with the main subject. "Do you have someone you can call? A relative or friend in the area?"

It looked as if a boxer threw a couple punches below the belt and had knocked the wind out of Scott. He moved to the freed up space on the loveseat and sank onto the cushion. She noticed the forced control as Scott muttered, "I'm allowed to do this, aren't I?"

The Sheriff ignored the sarcasm. "Until we leave."

Brooke had fantasized about their first night together many times. Never did she consider such circumstances as tonight, but rather being inseparable with nothing in-between their naked skin. She hadn't considered where this would take place, just that it would. It certainly wouldn't turn out this way at his home tonight.

Scott turned his gaze to Brooke as tears began to fill the corners of her eyes. "Brooke, don't worry. I'll get this straightened out. I don't want you staying at the station tonight. Just do what they say for now. What about your friend, Chloe?"

Brooke's energy drained, and she knew she couldn't fight the law. "It's getting late, but Chloe offered her home when I talked to her earlier today. Under the circumstances, I'm sure she'll let me come over."

"I suggest you call her. We'll give you some time to make whatever calls you need. We can't leave without separating the two of you," the Sheriff interrupted.

More awake after the initial shock, Brooke contemplated what she knew. Scott was at the scene. She only knew him through work. She thought they were becoming friends, maybe more. That was pretty much it. Whether she had to or not, she needed to follow the Sheriff's advice.

Brooke nodded toward Scott.

Minus a friendly expression, Scott politely said, "I'll get the phone." He took his time returning with the receiver before he set it on the table.

She regretfully picked up the phone and dialed the familiar number. As she listened to it ring, the thought hit her that she didn't have anyone else to call. She was uncomfortable with a call to any of her other friends who were slightly more than acquaintances. One more ring and the answering machine picked up.

Brooke didn't need to listen to the invitation to leave a message, but rather pushed the off button and looked up with stinging eyes as moisture collected in the corners. "What am I going to do?"

"I could call some of my friends," Scott offered.

"Probably not a good idea," the deputy stated before Scott had a chance to follow through. "It's not against the law, but not a good idea, either."

Scott understood. "Can I stay with her at the station until she can speak with her friend?"

"No, that would be breaking the order," the Sheriff answered as the phone rang.

Scott automatically reached for it. "Hello." After a pause as he listened to the caller, he smiled and handed the phone to Brooke. "It's Chloe."

Brooke took the receiver. "Hi, Chloe."

From the other end of the line, Chloe said, "I had Scott's number on my caller ID, so I figured it was important."

Brooke didn't waste any time and hurried her explanation. "I'm sorry to bother you this late, but something has come up. I need a new place to stay, and I was hoping your offer was still open."

"Of course. You can come over whenever you need to." Chloe didn't hesitate.

"Actually, I would need to come over right now."

"The door's open. I'll have some hot tea ready."

"Chloe…"

"Honey, you don't have to give me the details right now. We'll have plenty of time to talk when you get here."

"Thank you, Chloe. I'll be over soon." Brooke didn't have the energy to explain the whole situation. She knew Chloe would be patient and let her speak when she was ready.

Back to business, the Sheriff told her, "We'll need to know your friend's full name, address, and phone number, so we have record of where you are."

Scott sat on the edge of the love seat with his elbows supported by his spread knees. His frame of mind was obvious as he bowed his head while Brooke recited the information to the Sheriff.

She looked at him with saddened eyes. "Scott, I'm sorry." She glanced toward the Sheriff and his deputy with a silent request for a semblance of privacy, if only for a minute.

The Sheriff coughed into his hand as he turned toward his partner. "Make the call to the station to see if we can take Ms. Bellin to her friend's house," he ordered as he moved closer to the entrance to the kitchen, but still stayed within viewing range of the couple.

With appreciation Brooke looked back to Scott, "I'm sorry. I'm sorry for getting you into this."

"Brooke..."

"No, let me finish." She continued her supplication. "Originally, I was excited about having my stained glass art displayed so prominently at a four-star bed and breakfast. If I knew such a harassing situation was going to come my way, I wouldn't have gotten involved with you."

Scott interrupted, "Brooke, you didn't drag me into this, and I think you're forgetting an arrest has already been made." Brooke sensed his nerves tighten as her eyes clouded.

Not able to meet his look, Brooke murmured, "But he, Ty, couldn't have done this to me. Maybe, someone else was jealous because you were spending time with me." It was a feeble effort to find another explanation.

"I won't let myself, or you for that matter, start to think that way." Scott reached his hand to tilt her chin and gain her full attention. "I'm not going to accuse anyone right now, but don't think it'll change my feelings for you."

Before Brooke could acknowledge what Scott said, the Sheriff and his deputy returned to the living room, ready to go.

The Sheriff stated, "Ms. Bellin, your friend is approved. It's time to go." He turned and referred to Scott, "You must stay at least one hundred feet apart, no phone calls, no meetings, and no contact until a hearing, which will be scheduled to be within fourteen days."

Sadness, frustration, and everything else that can twist the nervous system like a kaleidoscope, careened through Brooke's blood, and she was sure Scott felt the same. With no choice, he offered, "I'll get Brooke's bag. Brooke, stay here until I get back."

By the time Scott returned with her tote of personals and the few articles of clothing, the Sheriff had Brooke headed for the door.

Brooke became silent as she struggled with separating the facts from fiction. She would have to call the District Attorney's office to find out what was going on. Why were Ty and Marla in jail, and yet a restraining order was served on Scott? It didn't make sense.

Chapter 15

"Brooke, sit down. Let me get you some tea." Brooke didn't have the energy to disagree with anything she was told to do. Following the request, Brooke pulled out a kitchen chair. The only thing that kept her from plunking down hard into the chair was she knew the vibration would continue up her shoulder. She already felt a mild throbbing begin with the activity since she'd left the hospital this afternoon.

A comfortable silence settled in the kitchen as Brooke vacantly stared at Chloe's back while she stood at the counter assembling the pot of green tea. As Brooke watched Chloe squirt a golden stream of honey into each cup, Brooke wondered how so much had changed in the handful of hours since Scott had picked her up at the hospital. Worse yet, since she woke up this morning she had been educated on her nonfatal injury, her ex-husband and his nurse were in jail, Scott was banned from her life for who knew how long or why, and now she was in her third residence to attempt a much needed rest.

Without saying anything more, Chloe turned from the counter and swayed her colorful skirt toward the table, always keeping the tea steady until it was set in front of their respective spots.

"You look awful, honey." Because of the special bond of friendship the women shared, Brooke didn't take offense to this remark. Instead, it drew a half-hearted smile.

"I can only imagine. I haven't had a chance or the energy to worry about how terrible I look." Brooke added, "Scott was probably glad to have me kicked out of his house with all the problems I've caused along with having a wreck of a human being take up room in his small home."

"You still have a sense of humor, which is a noble thing after what you've been through." With a perceptive look, Chloe affirmed, "I know Scott would never think that way about you."

Brooke didn't have the strength for an in-depth discussion, but she had to comment. "If I had only listened to you, this wouldn't have happened."

Chloe cocked her head and smiled.

"You knew what was going to happen," Brooke stated. "I should probably want you to 'read my mind' again and tell me what's next, but I don't want to go there." She sipped the steaming tea. "Not that I don't trust or believe your abilities, Chloe. It just scares me because you virtually told me what was going to happen, and I didn't realize it or understand. Maybe, I didn't want to believe anything bad could happen, so I didn't listen."

With modesty, Chloe took a turn. "Brooke, I can't see everything. Usually big or important issues come to me without my looking for them. If I concentrate, I could probably surmise what the eventual outcome of everything will be, but I won't think about it unless you truly want me to." Brooke didn't feel pressured with Chloe's offer of her intuitiveness. "One thing which might be helpful, though, is to take things at face value without mixing your kind intentions and thoughts with the answers."

"You might have to repeat that to me tomorrow. My brain is tired and overloaded right now."

"And I think it's time for you to go to bed. You can tell me whatever you're comfortable with tomorrow." Chloe stood up from the table and removed the drained teacups. "I'd offer you another cup, but I'm taking charge of your welfare tonight, and you need sleep more than anything."

Brooke placed her hand on the table and pushed herself out of the warmed up seat as an answer. "I was considering taking a Vicodin before bed, but nothing will keep me from sleeping now."

"I'm glad you feel that way because you certainly deserve a restful night." Chloe led Brooke down the hall to the spare room. As Brooke settled on the bed and began to undress herself, Chloe helped her with the sweater. It was a simple cardigan draped over Brooke's injured shoulder. Chloe laid her clothes on a nearby chair leftover from the kitchen set and turned before exiting the door. "If you need anything at all, don't be afraid to wake me up." Brooke accepted the offer with a smile as she laid her head on the pillow.

Storm clouds rolled overhead. Spatters of rain pecked at her cheeks. Disrupted, the dust on the trail formed swirls of gritty dirt around her tennis shoes. Branches from the dead trees waved overhead and extended their shadows over her body like an apparition tangling her into its darkness. Threatening fingers rolled around her forearms and lengthened to reach for her torso and grab at her breasts.

Faces appeared, laughing. Vacant eyes glinted with madness as lips twisted upward. The disguised identities rushed in and out of her vision, taunting her intrusion into their bleak forest. Hair of dried and curled leaves crumbled and shed its foul stench over her tired shoulders.

Brooke thrashed her arm overhead to shove away the malicious gloom that closed in around her, to no avail. Her arm went straight through those who groped her body and infringed on her privacy.

They ripped at her clothes. The endless arms reached for her exposed skin. What began as a tickle turned into a scrape of dead skin. Blood oozed and dripped in streams from her abdomen, lower back, and left breast.

The faces laughed maliciously.

You deserved it.

You earned it.

You will lose him.

The unknown faces grew more hideous as the same blood began to drip from the empty eye sockets and drop over Brooke's neck as she stretched up to gasp air.

The air was thick and poisonous. Small flecks of a scaly substance rushed into her nose and down her throat, leaving Brooke with no relief. Dried leaves. Dried skin. Dead blood.

She tried to scream, but her voice didn't cooperate. She briefly recognized the faces. Again, they laughed at their detection. They wanted Brooke to see them. They wanted her to know who would torment her until she humbled her soul.

"Brooke," Chloe commanded as she shook Brooke's trembling shoulder. "Brooke, wake up!"

Brooke turned her head to the voice as she forced her eyes open. She attempted to recall where she was. "Chloe?" Brooke's mind hadn't quite returned to reality. "What's going on? Who were those faces?"

"You must've had a bad dream. I don't know what faces you're talking about."

Quickly Brooke remembered her injured shoulder as she supported herself with the other to focus on the room around her and Chloe. Brooke blinked her heavy eyelids to clear the picture. "Yeah, I must've been dreaming."

"It's already ten this morning, so I can get a pot of tea going, if you'd like." Chloe didn't ask questions about the dream. She acted as if it were any other day. "I was just opening my store for the day. It's awfully cold and windy out there again. It feels like winter's coming a tad early this year."

"Oh, I haven't even looked outside, yet."

"Do you need any help, Brooke, with your sweater or getting cleaned up?"

"Good question. I don't know, but I'll call for you if I get stuck in the bathroom," Brooke answered as she realized this would be her first morning away from the hospital and technically on her own.

As Chloe glanced back with a warm smile, she exited Brooke's borrowed room. When she disappeared down the hall, Brooke looked around. It was a cheery room with light colors and warm scents wafting from the baskets and bowls of potpourri. Brooke's eyes focused on the window that viewed the northern slant of the house and the back edge of the business located up front. The cold and nearly colorless trees whipped around and brought a chill through Brooke that pulsed in her left shoulder. The dream came back in fragments. Who were those faces, and what were they trying to tell her? That she deserved being shot? Whom was she going to lose?

She squeezed her eyes shut and shook her knotted hair. Brooke slowly got up from the warm bed and made her way to the bathroom at the other end of the hall. She brushed her teeth and combed her hair with her right hand, which was normal, yet she realized how much her left hand used to assist her in these simple tasks. After a fifteen-minute interval in the bathroom, Brooke finally emerged feeling refreshed and partially cleansed of the disturbing nightmare.

Brooke entered Chloe's kitchen where a warm melon colored paint covered the walls. Dried herbs hung between the half a dozen different sized windows, which hosted various stained glass samples.

"Good morning, honey," Chloe greeted affectionately. "Don't look outside and we'll have a warm and peaceful morning. I doubt that I'll have any customers for a while. They usually don't venture out early when the weather takes such a sudden change for the worse. The bell on my door will tell me if anyone enters. So, have a seat."

Chloe continued a light chatter as Brooke attempted to gather her thoughts and add to the conversation. She started by saying, "I appreciate you letting me stay here. If you need me to do anything, just say so."

"It's a treat for me, too. I rarely have someone to take care of, which brings me to a couple of questions. First, do we need to get you to the doctor at some point? I'm sure you must have at least a couple follow-up appointments."

"Actually, I'm supposed to go to the doctor this afternoon. I can get myself there, though. I don't want to disrupt your work or be a problem for you."

"You're definitely no problem, and how do you plan to get yourself there? Your car is at home, and can you drive with your arm in a sling?"

"Well, I think I'd be able to drive. The drugs from yesterday wore off. I suppose not having a car is a bit of a problem."

"Normally I'd let you take my car, but I can take you myself because, like I said, I doubt the store will be busy today. I can hang a 'gone for lunch' sign, so I can escort you, if you like."

"I think I'd like that. I guess I'm probably slightly unsteady, yet," Brooke admitted without revealing the distress she felt from the chilling visit her dream left her.

"Great, that's what we'll do, but first we can start with this coffee cake," Chloe told her as she pulled a steaming pan from the oven. A scent of nutmeg and cherries wafted across the table to where Brooke sat. Chloe studied an open cupboard, filled with various patterns of mismatched china until she pulled two small plates down.

She dug for teacups and came up with another set of mismatches. "Close enough," Chloe commented as she laughed at her unorganized cupboard. She proceeded to deliver a large cut of cake onto each plate followed by a rimmed cup of tea.

"Thank you. Again," Brooke added. "I seem to be saying that a lot." Brooke looked down into her cup for a long moment. As a ripple of anger ran through her nerves, she caught her friend's attention. "Chloe, what's going on? I made it through the first problem, the shooting, and now someone put a restraining order on Scott. It wasn't me, and I don't know how else it can be done."

Pushing her fork into another piece, she hesitated and looked up. "I'm not going to ask what'll happen next, but you must have known this was going to happen."

"Possibly. I can't predict everything and sometimes what I see isn't completely clear." Chloe paused. "I knew a lot. I can't say I knew exactly how and when you'd be injured, but I also knew you would be okay at the end. That was the important part.

"Even though you didn't remember to take another trail at the park, it was destined. Who knows, at some other time or place the outcome may have been worse, so don't beat yourself for not following my suggestion."

Since the subject had been ripped open, Brooke proceeded to indulge Chloe with what happened in the last couple of days with no mention of this morning's dream. It disturbed her, but it was only a dream. *Forget it.*

"Do you think the shooter had wanted to kill me?" As soon as she asked, Brooke lowered her head. She didn't want the answer. She surprised herself with this question.

Chloe slipped her hand over Brooke's. "I don't know. You'll figure it out in time."

As they got ready to leave for Brooke's appointment, Chloe made a decision while starting her car. "Brooke, I'll close for the rest of the afternoon. It's been a slow day, and I don't expect anyone in particular to come in."

"Chloe, you don't need…"

"I know I don't have to, but I want to. Besides, do you want to stop at your apartment and pick up a few things?"

"Actually, that's a good idea. The police are done looking it over, so I'm allowed to go in. No one'll be there."

"What about your stained glass work with Scott?"

"Chloe, I didn't even get a chance to talk to him about it. I know he has deadlines, and I don't want to mess up this job for him." A tone of frustration seeped into her voice. "I'm not supposed to see him or talk to him until further notice. Whatever that means.

"Well, I do know that I have to make some calls and find out about the restraining order. If I decide not to spend time with Scott outside of work, then I want it on my terms."

"I think that's a good idea. As far as the work, why don't you bring the supplies to my house. We'll see what we can do together."

"You know what I want to say again, so I won't. I like that idea. I'm sure I can still do the work since it's my left shoulder with a bandage." Partially convinced, Brooke added, "Yeah, I'm sure I can still do the work, maybe a bit slower, though."

Arriving at the hospital, Chloe turned into the parking lot. "We'll have fun doing the glass. I think we can even get ahead of schedule with the two of us working on it."

"I worried about it, but I think you may be right. That's the first good news I've heard lately." Brooke got out of Chloe's car and took a deep breath before she headed for the entrance. "Wish me luck for my check-up."

"I don't think you need any, but good luck." Chloe followed Brooke to the second floor of the hospital.

After the checkup, Brooke returned to the waiting room.

"All is well?" Chloe asked.

"Yes, there's no infection and it's healing well. My shoulder has a long way to go, but so far, so good. I didn't even realize it, but the doctor told me it went all the way through and exited," Brooke explained, purposely leaving out the word "bullet." "I was probably told before, but under the circumstances I don't think I heard or remembered everything."

"Good, I'm glad you're on your way to recovery." As they walked back to the car, Chloe asked again, "Do you want to stop at your home or was this enough for you today?"

"I think getting out today is really good for my mood or mind or whatever it's good for, so one more stop will probably be fine," Brooke suggested with a new lilt to her voice. "Actually, I'd like to skip my house and simply stop at Ty's. I never did get all of my things from that house when we got divorced. I can also get the stained glass supplies from my studio next door."

"I'm surprised you still have so many of your things at his house." Brooke caught the disbelief in Chloe's eyes.

"I left things I didn't care about, but it's kind of creepy to leave anything in his possession now. Besides, if he stays in jail, he has to get someone to remove everything, I imagine." Knowing her friend wasn't convinced, Brooke avoided looking at her.

Even the dreary and unseasonably cold and windy day didn't dampen Brooke's newfound mood as Chloe maneuvered the streets to Ty's home. The lawns had turned a greenish yellow, partially covered by the fallen leaves, which had lost their brightness and curled at the edges. Maybe the end of autumn was also the end of her problems.

Chloe motored up the graveled drive and pulled up close to the house. "Do you want me to come in with you?"

"Actually, I have an idea. I'll take you to my studio and show you what I need to bring along, so we can get some work done. I'm in the mood to get back to normal," Brooke explained.

"I'm happy to help you as much as I can. With your work and getting back to normal, I mean," Chloe said. "You still need to be careful, so don't expect to work at your normal pace. I have a feeling I'm going to have to hold you back because your ambition might get the best of you."

Brooke couldn't help but laugh at her friend's concern as they walked the overgrown path from the house to her studio. The path crossed the adjoining property lines. Leftover berries and dried flowers from perennials, which recently boasted a spectrum of colors, protruded from the brown weeds that had taken over in the past two years since Brooke left the house.

The rest of the short walk to the neighboring property was in silence as they bent their heads against the wind. At their destination, Brooke pulled open the screen door. A sudden gale of wind wrenched the handle from her light grip. "I haven't watched the weather channel for probably a week. Are we in for a storm today?"

"I haven't kept up on the weather lately, either, but it sure looks like we're in for something," Chloe commented. As they spoke, dark clouds rolled in from the west. "Well, let's get inside and get this done since we're here."

Brooke showed her agreement and shuttled them into the warmth of her studio. "Let's see… There are so many miscellaneous things we'll have to bring." She looked around for a starting place. "I guess the best scenario would be to bring the stained glasses I'm in the middle of. Those would be on my work table over there." With a refreshed mind on where she left, Brooke decided what materials she needed packed up. "If you want to, you can make a pile by the door of those glasses, and next to my table you can see the materials I set out for the next steps. I think they'll keep us busy for a while." Brooke realized that Chloe knew exactly what to look for. Brooke had learned the skill from her a number of years ago.

"That's not a problem, so if you want to go back to his house and gather your things, we can get this done a bit faster."

"Good idea. I won't be long, and then I'll come back to make sure you found everything. If you have a question, just call my cell phone. There's a phone on the ledge over there," Brooke told her with a nod toward the north wall.

"Gottcha. Now, get going." Chloe's command fell short of laughter as Brooke did an about face and hurried back to the house.

The wind rushed her into the front entry. Brooke turned around and shut the door with her back against the centered glass. The sudden silence without the disturbing weather left her alone. A different aura enveloped the house. Instinctively, she glanced around the entry, curious as to the disruption of the search. She focused on the gun cabinet.

The unlatched glass door caught her attention, along with two empty gun holds. The vacant spots belonged to the guns Ty most often used for practice. Black dust coated the door handle and the frame's edges. Smears of the dark powder streaked the typically pristine glass. She knew Ty had taken both guns to the firing range the day of her injury. Hadn't he returned home at some time and put the guns away? Who had them, if he hadn't returned the weapons?

Brooke's head swirled with confusion. Thoughts she had been able to avoid with everything else going on, forced their way to the front of her conscience. The control she'd attained since the shooting deserted her.

She had to get it back. Control was what she wanted. Control of the situation was what she needed. Her legs grew weak and trembled as she instinctively went to the gun cabinet. Brooke reached out and gingerly touched the handle. She pushed gently to close the door and shut out the demons that rushed from the two empty red velvet rests.

Brooke walked backward, away from the cabinet. Her gaze stayed on the glass door to make sure it wouldn't open and reveal any hideous truth she closed up with the remaining weapons.

She grimaced as her injured shoulder bumped the frame of the opening to the kitchen. Her hand flew up to cover her shoulder as she turned to face the room where she, Ty, and Marla had shared dinner as recently as a couple weeks ago. Brooke randomly attended Ty's therapy sessions to assist with his rehab after the stroke. She wasn't completely heartless and it was the least she could do. He had the stroke after he signed the divorce papers. Again, the room had a cold feel. The heater worked fine, but the atmosphere held no warmth.

Brooke slowly walked through the kitchen, examined it as if the structures, furniture, and appliances were extraordinary components she hadn't taken the time to get familiar with before. She lowered her protective hand and ran her fingertips along the edge of the Formica countertop. Before the divorce, they'd contemplated exchanging it for a granite slab of mixed browns and grays. Ty claimed he'd saved money for it, to surprise her.

She stopped at the end of the counter and examined the familiar items arranged against the wall. Ty hadn't removed them after she'd left. She didn't want them. They'd stay in their places. She touched the face of one Mammy doll they'd picked up on a trip to New Orleans five or six years ago. Nestled next to her sat others and a couple worn, white ceramic vases holding dried sunflower heads. The yellow flowers complimented the cornflower blue rimmed cabinetry. They represented warmth and sunshine. The color blue now looked as cold as a frigid winter sky. Even the stainless refrigerator next to the arrangement had an icy glare. Ty hadn't changed a thing.

Brooke shivered in spite of the warm sweater she hugged to herself. Her gaze roved the countertop and stopped at the table. Apples filled a willow basket at one end of the rectangular furniture. She had popped in at an orchard on her way to check on Ty's therapy session last week. It was the first she had come over in quite a while. With an abundance of apples, more than she could eat, it was easy to leave a few behind. She didn't notice if any were gone. She only saw the bright and cheerful red had dulled. Possibly, she imagined it, but nothing held the former comfort of the kitchen.

A blind that hung the full length of a French door leading into the garage was at an angle as if the door had slammed and caused it to swing to the side and hook an edge over a lower hinge. She walked over and straightened the window treatment. Again, she saw the black dust coated on the handle and the wooden frame near the latch.

Brooke touched the black, sooty powder and hoped it could reveal answers or at least clues to who had shot her and why. She hadn't returned to her former home to retrieve forgotten articles. There weren't any. She wanted answers. Where were they? Reenergized by the fear and confusion of the whole incident, Brooke turned and looked around the kitchen with a different focus.

Brooke ignored the miniscule layer of dust accenting the countertop. She did see a counter laden with a half-empty jar of salsa and a torn bag of chips with the crumbles tumbled from the crinkly, plastic bag. She remembered the debate she had with Ty and Marla between having wine or strawberry margaritas. The wine won solely on tradition.

The ghostly faces of Ty and Marla laughed and talked while they made up stories relating to their dinner choice. Brooke saw herself seated a distance away to observe the drama before the divorce. On this revisit, she saw Ty and Marla's eyes meet and catch many times. Why hadn't she seen this before? The steaming food, which after a time disappeared from the plates, didn't bring any warmth to the current kitchen.

The longer Brooke watched the former scene, the colder she got. She needed to leave this room. There was nothing here for her.

The next thing she knew, she stood in Ty's study. This was where he kept his house and investment paperwork, his piles of *Outdoor Life* and *Field and Stream* subscriptions, blueprints of many of the houses he'd helped refinish, and plans and ideas of his own which he wanted to incorporate into this house at some later day when he hoped he could enter the construction field again. Hopes and dreams of the past and present were neatly stacked and organized on a desk table he'd made before his stroke.

The desk was of red cedar. The top was planed smooth with rounded edges on every side. It was a simple rectangle of five feet by three feet. Ty's computer, a stack of scratch paper, and two pens neatly lined the center of the desk. Behind the closed laptop sat a photo of Ty and herself in a summer garden scene. Contentment radiated from their smiles. Nine years ago. Brooke thought they still looked the same, except for the exuberant smile.

She pulled on two small drawers on the right side. It held pens, paperclips, collected business cards, and other miscellaneous small items, which would clutter the top. The second drawer held copied disks of building plans and hunting trips Ty considered. The rest of the right side and the left were simply shelves to hold the blueprints, financial diagrams and forms, and a collection of the most looked at books, which elaborated on his hobbies. Everything was in place.

Brooke hesitated and then opened the center drawer, finding nothing. The next drawer replicated the former. Brooke began to look with more purpose. Her pace quickened, and she was sure to find what she didn't want if she kept going. Forgetting the organization, which was an integral part of this house's makeup, Brooke plunged her right hand into the depths of the shelf below the last drawer.

She dragged the softly folded blueprints to the edge and let them tumble to the floor. Brooke grabbed the top rolls and furtively ripped the seals and shook them loose. Nothing but the chalky blue lines with numbers and random phrases in code covered the pages. She tossed those aside, grabbed more of the fallen prints and continued to unfold the diagrams.

Not caring about the chaos she created in her ex-husband's sanctuary, she dove into the next shelf and pulled out old bank statements and quarterly investment papers. Brooke scanned the sheets. During their marriage, she never was in the habit of keeping up on the exact progress of their finances, but the numbers seemed a bit out of the ordinary. She had no business to know about his current situation, but the paperwork went far back into their marriage.

Brooke knew they hadn't had a problem paying their bills, but she began to wonder where the extra money now came from when Ty had a fixed income from disability for the last two years. He was better at finances than the credit she gave him. It was an easy explanation. No red flags appeared, yet.

Again, she reached into the depths of the lowest shelf. This alcove held the last few *USA Today* newspapers Ty probably read with his morning coffee. Missing the bottom paper, Brooke reached in further to pull it out. The last page stuck to the shelf and released with a light tug.

This page initially looked like it held dried paint of brown, green, and black smears. As the paints had dried, they'd leaked through the thin newspaper and settled as insufficient glue onto the shelf.

Brooke leaned closer to examine the paint-like substances. She touched the paint and it readily came off onto her fingertips. Bringing it to her nose, she didn't notice a scent. She rubbed the crumbling colors together and watched them turn to powder and float to the cream-colored carpet.

Brooke's eyes refocused and grew wide as she realized what she'd found. Her heart sped to nowhere as her arms began to tremble. Brooke lowered herself all the way to the floor with her entire weight on her right arm. She peaked into the lower shelf. Against the back wall of the desk, three small jars were crammed into the corner. She didn't need to pull the jars forward. She knew what they were.

She glanced around the room to make sure she was still alone.

Ty was in jail.

Marla was in jail.

Scott couldn't come near her. Maybe that was better, though. She hadn't gotten the chance to really get to know him. Yet, she knew she thought about him too much.

Sitting back on her heels, Brooke placed her right hand on her thigh and stretched her fingers as she slowly pushed them down her jeans. Her hand dampened as she considered what she'd found. The colored powders turned into a dry crème and rubbed off in streaks. A war had begun and this was the shooter's paint choice. A hunter uses the same cover-up.

Brooke's mind jumped back to the study as she heard the front door shut. Her painted hand flew up, with remnants of her discovery still smeared on it.

"Brooke, are you okay? I thought you'd be ready by now," Chloe called from the entry.

Furtively making a decision, Brooke called out, "Fine, I'm fine. I, uh, was just trying to find a few sweaters I haven't taken out for the cold, yet."

"Do you need some help? I'm done in your studio."

Before Chloe could find Brooke nowhere near her closet or dresser, Brooke thought to say, "I'm nearly done. Actually, if you'd like to put together a quick cup of tea before we go, that would be nice." Brooke stalled, knowing what else she had to do.

She too quickly dipped her head to the lower shelf to retrieve the face-paint jars and stung her chin on the edge of the partially open upper drawer. Without the use of an extra hand to press against the pain, Brooke continued to reach into the shelf and pull the evidence into her lap.

At the same time when she shoved the jars between her legs as she sat on the floor, Chloe appeared at the door to the study. "Brooke, what're you doing?"

"I, uh, got sidetracked," Brooke looked toward her friend, trying to cover her nervousness. Discounting her former explanation for taking so long, Brooke added, "I'm sorry. I needed to check…"

"It's okay. I'm in no hurry," Chloe responded as if she understood what Brooke was going through and relieved her from making up a story.

Brooke lowered her head and took a deep breath. She glanced at the stains on her jeans. "I'll finish up quickly, and then we can leave."

"I'll leave you alone and get the tea going."

As soon as Chloe turned her back to the study, Brooke dug the jars from between her thighs where she'd squeezed them so tightly that the lids left marks on her jeans. Hugging them to her chest with one hand, she rose from the floor and began to turn toward the door just as Chloe reappeared.

Glancing at Brooke's tightly clasped hand to her chest, Chloe asked, "What type of tea did you want?"

Prefacing her answer with an explanation, she stuttered, "Uh, these are just some things I would like to take with me." Brooke hoped for no questions. "Maybe we should wait until we get to your house for the tea. I think I'd like to get out of here as soon as I get my things. I doubt there's any tea in the cupboards, anyway."

Respecting her unspoken request, Chloe said, "Sure. That's probably best. I'll wait in the entry.

The speed of her heartbeat forced a tear to trickle down her cheek. Brooke bent forward to let her encumbered hand wipe the moisture off her face. She kept her head bent, hugging the paint jars to her breast, as this unexpected shower escaped her tightly closed eyes. Her shoulders trembled painfully. With her head still down, she fixed on the jars in her grip.

Could Ty have used these? This face-paint, or camouflage, was in every hunter's home. Everyone knew this was his favorite room of the house, so someone may have put these here. "He may not have loved me the way he should or the way I wanted during our marriage, but I don't think he hated me," Brooke whispered to the empty room.

With little thought to her next move, Brooke motored down the hall to her former bedroom. Her mind continued to swing in and out of rational thought. She wondered if Ty had shot her, or if it was someone else. Is this why the police didn't want her to see Scott?

"Oh, my God. I can't believe I can consider such a monstrosity," Brooke whispered again. She shook her head to dispel the despairing thoughts and sniffed her tears back as she steered to a storage closet.

She pulled out a mid-sized satchel to disguise her lack of gathered nonexistent items. She dumped the paint cans in it and pulled the zipper tight. She had thought the divorce would take care of her submissive side. Apparently, she needed one more catastrophic incident to finish the job.

Brooke went to the hall bathroom and threw a handful of lukewarm water across her face. She didn't want Chloe to see the shades of pain and confusion.

"Chloe, I'm ready to get my things from the studio now."

"All taken care of. I had time to get everything into my car while you collected your things."

Brooke's nerves nearly tumbled out along with her speech. "I need to make sure you didn't forget anything. I'd hate to have to come near this house so soon, if we left anything behind."

Showing no offense to the reprimand, Chloe countered softly, "If I missed anything, I'm sure I'll have the materials at my store, Brooke."

Making eye contact, Brooke wanted to say something. She wanted to tell Chloe the questions she'd formulated but couldn't. She wanted to tell Chloe what she'd found but couldn't find the words. Dare she even think it? Should she verbalize the puzzlement this whole situation raised?

Brooke caught Chloe waiting for a response. "Oh, yeah. What was I thinking? I got all my materials from you, so of course you'll have more if we need them." She attempted to hide her embarrassment and shook off the last twenty minutes. "Chloe, let's get back to your house, eat something really naughty and gooey and hot, and...and sit by the fire and pretend winter isn't right around the corner. How does that sound?"

"I'm the one who's supposed read minds, but you read mine this time. Let me carry your bag," Chloe insisted as Brooke struggled with the one useful arm and the bag that banged against her knee as she crossed the entry.

Relieved by the offer, Brooke let the bag drop to the floor. Pausing, she took the biggest breath she ever remembered needing, smiled wearily, and said, "Thank you. Thanks for everything."

"My pleasure, and you don't have to keep thanking me. I'm your friend, and I'm going to keep acting like one." Chloe opened the door and motioned Brooke out.

* * * *

After a short drive, which Brooke found relaxing, Chloe announced, "Brooke, we're here."

Jerking forward as her eyes snapped open, Brooke mumbled, "The paint is in my bag."

"What? Brooke we're at my house, now."

"Oh, yeah. I knew that." Brooke thought quickly as she acknowledged their arrival. "I didn't check, but did you bring my paints?"

"Yes, they're all in the trunk with everything else. We'll unload it tomorrow, though. It's too cold out and getting dark already. Besides, we have plans for a warm and filling night. Let's get you out of the car, and we'll have fun."

"I'm not an invalid. My legs didn't get shot. I can probably run to the door as fast as you."

"Actually, you might beat me because I'm going to carry your bag in."

"Good, I wasn't really in the mood to go for a run," Brooke confessed as she pushed the car door open and the cold wind whistled up her sleeve. Without another word, she maneuvered out of the car and rushed to the back door. Huddled by the entry, Brooke waited for Chloe before opening it. "Hurry. Hurry, before my hand freezes to the doorknob," Brooke hollered into the wind.

"I'm coming. I'm coming," Chloe shouted back as she raced to the porch.

Brooke wasted no more time and threw the door open. Both tumbled in and quickly shut the door to keep out the weather.

"Brook, I'll put your bag in your room. Why don't you get into something comfortable while I heat dinner up?"

"I agree to get my warm and fuzzy robe on, but I want to help you with dinner. I can't let you do everything. I feel I'll wear out my welcome real fast, if I don't do something."

"There's not much to do. I already have something gooey and soon to be hot prepared." Chloe offered, "You change your clothes, and when you're done you can start the tea while I change mine. We'll make this kind of a pajama party tonight. Sound good?"

"Yes, I'll be back in a flash." Brooke turned down the hall as Chloe headed for the kitchen.

Making good time, Brooke returned to an empty kitchen. "I'm in the living room trying to get this fire going," she heard from the next room.

"Did you do everything already? I was supposed to help."

"Dinner's in the oven and I started a pot of water for the tea. I wasn't overworked. Oh good, there it goes," Chloe said triumphantly as the kindling lighted. She rose from the hearth and turned to face Brooke. "Goodness, Brooke. I didn't think. Let me help you with that." Brooke had one arm in her robe, but didn't have any success placing the other sleeve over her injured shoulder. The robe dragged on the floor as Brooke stood close, looking like a lost lamb.

"At least I didn't have to worry about my bra," Brooke chided. "I didn't put one on this morning because I couldn't figure out how. Plus, the strap would rest on the wound. I'll have to invest in a strapless, I guess, but I didn't think it'd be necessary for the rest of tonight."

"See, you're still thinking clearly!" Chloe informed her as she delicately draped the robe onto Brooke's shoulder. "Don't be afraid to yell for me when you need help in the morning. I probably won't think of everything, so remind me."

"I haven't thought of it all, either. I forget that I need both hands for so many things until I run into something." Feeling warm and ready to relax, Brooke looked toward the fire. The last time she'd sat by a fire was the night before at Scott's home. It was warm and comfortable, too, but in a different way. "I'm glad you made a fire, Chloe."

"I'm sure I wanted it as much as you so don't give me any credit there."

The room became silent except for the crackling from the bark of the logs. Brooke was about to seat herself when the teakettle sang a high tune. “I’m still up so I’ll get that.”

Chloe rummaged around in a nearby closet looking for TV trays, and then followed Brooke. “I’m not taking your ‘tea’ job way from you, but my stuffed shells should be ready, too. We’ll eat by the fire because that’s what type of night this is.”

During dinner, they talked about the weather, movies, and which morning they would slip into the coffee house down the road. In silent agreement, Brooke and Chloe didn’t mention the stop at Ty’s house.

Brooke hoped that not talking or thinking about the paints or unusual financial information would make them insignificant.

Chapter 16

Brooke's eyes fluttered open to an extraordinarily bright room. It wasn't like sunlight, but rather something a change in the weather brings. Looking through the small slit under the window shade, everything appeared white.

She didn't appreciate the odd feeling, so Brooke pushed herself out from under the layer of cotton blankets, leaned to the window, and pulled back the curtain. It wasn't her imagination. A sheen of sparkling snow contoured Chloe's backyard. About an inch of fluffy snow lay over a bench and the birdbath along with a few tufts of frozen green, which still popped up along the ground.

She always felt childish when the first snow of winter came, although the feeling left quickly this year. She envisioned the time to bundle up and go outside only to toss around a few traditional snowballs. Her predicament dampened the fun.

Checking the clock Chloe had plugged in and set on the bedside table, Brooke saw she'd slept an entire night plus some. She decided to head for the kitchen in search of her friend.

"Good morning."

"It's barely morning anymore, but good morning to you, too. I feel as if I missed all the fun of morning, the newspaper searching, the coffee, and all those things before getting busy," Brooke complained.

"I hate to remind you, but I think at least your next couple of weeks will be an extended morning most of the time," Chloe informed her.

Raising her hand to push lively strands of hair away from her view, Brooke responded, "You're probably right, but I do need to decide what I'm going to do about the stained glass for Scott's project."

"I have coffee ready, so why don't you sit down, enjoy a cup, and we'll discuss business."

"I'm glad we didn't talk about any of it last night, but I'll start to get restless if I don't have a plan to go by soon. For my work and everything else I have to think about right now," Brooke admitted as she returned to the same seat she'd occupied yesterday.

"I agree. You needed a good night's rest in order to get a clear picture of everything. Plus it was fun doing things friends do together."

"Yes, and I'd suggest a snowball fight this morning, but I don't think it'll be as fun as usual."

A light jazz station played from the kitchen radio. A mix of saxophone and clarinet kept the kitchen from falling into silence. When the radio announcer changed tunes, Brooke looked up and said, "I think it's time for me to talk about what happened and what I should do next."

Chloe remained silent.

"First, I don't know if I even know everything that happened or if what I'm thinking is accurate. Does that make sense?" Brooke didn't wait for an answer to the rhetorical question. "All I know is that I was going to take a chance at getting to know Scott outside of work and then the next thing I'm doing is trying to figure out who shot me." Brooke stopped here, slightly embarrassed at her comment about Scott. "Did you know that I liked him more than I wanted to?"

"Yes, Brooke, I had felt the vibrations between the two of you."

"My head aches from thinking about everything. I want to organize it in my mind and make sense of the last few days...of the last few months, actually."

"Would you like to start with you and Scott, first? I'll talk with you about whatever you want. I'll tell you how I honestly see the situation, so make sure you only ask me questions which you really want to get an answer for."

"I know. I know you won't lie to me or simply say what I want to hear. That wouldn't do me any good." Brooke reached across the table to fill their cups. "Do you understand why I'm afraid of a relationship with Scott?"

"I have an idea."

"Well, I know I wouldn't let Scott treat me as unfairly as Ty did, so that's not the problem. I thought I just had to make sure that he's as nice as he seems to be before I think about dating him. Now I have to wonder if there really should be a restraining order to keep him away. I doubt it, but 'what if'?"

Brooke sat back as the phone rang, reminding her of the world outside which continued regardless of what she was going through.

Chloe held up her hand to indicate she needed to answer. "Hello… Yes, she's right here."

Brooke's eyes widened in question as to who knew she was there and would be calling her. "Hello." Brooke sat silently as she listened to her caller. "I want to be there. I will be there," was all Brooke contributed to the five-minute call.

She looked at the face of the remote phone for the off button to stall the information.

"What did she want?"

"That was the District Attorney's secretary."

Chloe nodded.

"She wanted to let me know Ty and Marla's arraignment will be in two days. I don't have to be there, but I want to. Also, if there's enough evidence to keep them in jail and continue with a trial for the shooting, maybe the police won't think it's necessary to keep Scott away from me." Brooke made a quick decision. "I'm sure I can drive, if not I'll call a cab. I know you have to have your store open."

"Don't worry about me. I'll make sure you get there. I don't know if that'll be enough to get rid of any suspicion on Scott, but we can hope. I have my doubts about him being involved, but the police must have some other idea, and they know more than we do right now."

"They're supposed to keep me informed, so why don't I know why they suspect Scott?" This was a real question. A question Brooke wanted an answer to.

Shaking the curls that wandered over her eyes, Brooke needed to change course and plunge into the other issue she needed to figure out. "Chloe, I have to talk to Scott. I have to finish the work I promised him, and I can't do it without contact with him."

"That's the easy part."

Brooke straightened up and furrowed her brows. She demanded, "Well, tell me. Tell me what makes it easy. I could really handle something easy right now."

"We know you're restricted from talking to or seeing Scott."

"Yes, yes. Hurry and tell me," Brooke interrupted.

"As far as we know, there's not a restriction against me having contact with him."

"You mean it? I…I had thought of that, but I didn't want to trouble you or get you involved."

"Trouble? I feel terrible because you won't have the thrill of doing the whole project on your own. I know the Renaissance scenes you're painting on the glasses are a dream of yours from way back."

"I'll still be able to do the painting. I'll probably need help when I assemble the glasses." Still adjusting to the one positive piece of news they'd created this morning, Brooke came up with another risky idea. "Maybe I could run into Scott when you meet with him?"

"Hold on. Don't get too crazy, yet. There are fines when you break police orders. Although, we can figure out what pattern the police use for 'guarding' you and work with that."

"Chloe, I could kiss you! I promise I won't get either one of us in trouble. I need to hear his voice so badly."

With a smile, Chloe warned, "We'll need to wait a few days or more, so we know what we can get away with and I can't promise you anything."

"I know. At least I have something to look forward to."

Chloe sipped her coffee and asked, "What's his number?"

Brooke put her fingertips to her forehead. "His number? It's…uh. I know this… 555-2563. I almost thought I wouldn't remember. It's easier looking at a phone, but that's right."

Chloe reached across the table for the phone stationed near Brooke. After a number of rings, Chloe began to speak, "Hi, Scott. This is Chloe Heathlan. Brooke asked me to call and tell you that she, and I'll still be working on your project. Give me a call back and we can discuss how we'll keep making progress on the stained glass." Chloe hung up and shrugged.

"That was silly of me. I thought I'd hear his voice at least." Brooke sighed as she realized the call was one-sided.

"I'm sure he'll call back." As the change of emotions drained Brooke's energy, Chloe suggested, "How would you like to work on the glass after we get dressed? I need to open my store in fifteen minutes and we can work right there."

"Deal," Brooke agreed as she rose from the table, ready to get the day going.

Brooke met Chloe twenty minutes later in her store, attached at the front of the house. Chloe hauled in the supplies for the glass they'd left in the car the night before. "This is the last of what we brought from your studio, Brooke," Chloe announced as she set a box of paints on the worktable in the back.

Brooke's mind stumbled over the memory of the other "paints" she still had hidden in the satchel. Not ready to reveal that finding, yet, she decided to leave them in the bag.

"Oh, you're way ahead of me," Brooke commented. "It took me longer to get dressed than usual, but I'm getting the hang of using one arm."

"I was going to ask if you needed help, but I knew you'd want to try it on your own." Changing subjects, Chloe asked, "What stage are you working on?"

"Fortunately, I had cut a lot of the glass shapes I need for the next half dozen windows prior to this last weekend, so I'm good to go with a lot of painting right now. I do have another stack of glass that needs assembling with the 'came' and copper accents. If you're interested and have time, you can work on those."

"I'll finish opening this morning because Tuesdays are typically busy, but I definitely want to help. This is a terrific project, mixing stained glass with the structures of a landscape. To tell you the truth, I was a little envious when you decided to present your idea to Mr. Marshall. I'm glad you got the job and now I get to help! Don't mistake my meaning, though. I don't like the reason you need my help."

"I know that. You're the best of friends, and I'll owe you after all you're doing for me. It's too bad I didn't listen to you when you told me not to walk on that trail," Brooke added.

"Don't worry about it now. Sometimes I still surprise myself with what I know. I won't say anything else about the walk except if it didn't happen then, it would've happened at some other time."

Brooke stiffened as she bent her waist over the worktable, arranging her glass and painting tools. Chloe never talked about or offered her psychic abilities unless someone specifically asked for input into their future. Most of the people who contacted her wanted to know positive things about their love lives or finances. During many readings, Chloe left out the negative insights to keep listeners from unnecessary depression.

Brooke's intense curiosity about the details of her shooting didn't lead her to intentions of finding out the future ahead of time. She didn't think her nerves could handle any more big surprises until a forced confrontation with them.

Instead of dwelling on the unknown, Brooke sat at the worktable while she envisioned the next scene she wanted to paint on the glass. Originally, she planned to work on a series of smaller panes covered with chubby cherubs tangled up in vines, but her mood led her to one of the larger scenes.

She pulled out her charcoal templates and dug for the one styled after herself and Scott. If nothing else, work on this painting would make her feel closer to him in addition to making progress on the project. The scene portrayed a voluptuous goddess with full hips and breasts discreetly half-visible through the tangle of vines. One arm reached but didn't touch the masculine form who desired her.

Eager to start, she still decided to pull out the glass she wanted Chloe to mold together. As she set the materials for Chloe's work on the other end of the table, the business phone began to ring, and the first customers hurried in from the snow.

With a smile at the normalcy of the day unfolding in spite of her turmoil, Brooke began to open the paints. She started with the lightest color and pulled the scene from her mind's fantasy. A fantasy that included Scott and little else.

She thought it'd be difficult to concentrate on the painting's subject, yet Brooke began to sense an unexpected pleasure as she painted the naked bodies.

Even if only she could see it, the painting captured characteristics of Scott, which she never failed to appreciate. She remembered his powerful hands, his soft brown eyes, and his commanding stance. The man and woman became heavenly figures with the light touch of her paintbrush and dabs of a sponge.

Not sure of how much time passed, Brooke leaned back to stretch her aching back as she finished with the first layer of paint. Chloe popped back a couple times to check on her, but kept busy with her store and the phone all morning. Brooke didn't mind. She welcomed the time alone with something to occupy her thoughts other than the shooting and all the repercussions that surrounded it.

In the next step, Brooke needed to cook or heat the painted glass before she put on the next color. She went to the back room of the store to set the ovens and then returned to the worktable. She studied her work and planned the next color's coordinates while waiting for Chloe to have another break in business to help her place the glasses in the nearly ready ovens.

"Oh, my! What happened to your arm?"

Brooke looked up in surprise as a comfortably plump woman with short, curly orange hair peered at her. The woman appeared amazed as she stared through multicolored glasses, too small for her face.

Never having considered how she would deal with stares or questions from people she didn't know, Brooke surprised herself with a quick response. "I needed to come up with an excuse to skip the ski hills this winter." Brooke glanced at the building snow on the window's ledge and silently thanked it for providing a quick but false explanation.

Changing her attention to Brooke's work, she asked, "What're you working on here? It looks awfully complicated."

Brooke couldn't help but give her a little information. "I'm doing these for a landscaper."

"Well, how in the world are they going to fit into landscaping? Isn't that usually done with trees and other plants?"

"It'll be placed in the hardscape structures. It's a new idea that's working so far," Brooke explained.

The woman tapped her forefinger to her chin in thought. "That wouldn't be the Maple Haven Bed and Breakfast, would it? It's a beautiful place being remodeled."

This got a little too close to home, so Brooke simply nodded.

Brooke could see the thought processes circle behind the flagrant eyeglasses. The woman looked at Brooke with sudden recognition. "Are you the one who was shot this weekend?" Barely taking a breath, the woman added, "My guess is that it was the nurse. Women get very jealous and it would be too obvious if your husband, or is it ex-husband, would shoot you. Ya know, women do use guns."

Brooke became uncomfortable with the one-sided discussion just as the orange-haired woman put an end to it. “I’ll let you work and get the supplies I came for.”

Noon had come and gone before Chloe headed her way.

“Looks like you got a lot accomplished today,” Chloe commented as she admired all the newly painted glass set around the table. “I’m sorry I wasn’t able to help so far, but with the snow continuing I don’t expect a lot more action up front this afternoon.”

“That’s not a problem at all. I enjoyed getting back to my work and feeling like I can still do something. I will need help putting these in the ovens, which I heated already, please.”

“Of course. Why don’t we get them going, and then we can take a break for lunch?” With both hands, Chloe picked up one end of the large and newly painted glass while Brooke only used her right hand. Carefully maneuvering, they managed to place the six pieces of glass into the ovens without incident.

“Speaking of food, when are you going to the grocery store next?”

“I planned on today, but it depends on the road conditions now. Although, the store is only a mile or so and it might be an adventure to go out in the first snow, if there aren’t too many others thinking the same.”

“As long as it’s a safe adventure.”

“I think we have a plan. After my store closes, we’ll head out.”

Brooke nodded and then mentioned the orange-haired woman’s acknowledgment of her shoulder.

“Oh, that was Shelby. She knows everything that happens around here. I’m surprised she didn’t know who you were before she even got all the way to the worktable. Don’t worry about her, though. She’s just the one who wants to figure out a town mystery before anyone else, including the police.”

“Why would she know who I was just by seeing my shoulder?” The answer came to Brooke before she finished formulating the question.

“As I am sure you know, articles in the newspaper and coverage on TV.” Chloe paused.

“Was it awful? I mean, what kind of things did the reports say?” Brooke’s hands had a slight tremble to them as she cleaned her paintbrushes.

“You already know everything they entailed,” Chloe began.

Seeing Brooke's expectant look, she elaborated. "The Sunday paper was very vague because the only thing which was known at that time was the fact that there was a shooting of a young woman on a walking trail. There weren't any names or details. Monday and today's paper are more informed."

Brooke didn't say anything and waited for more. "They stated the police had some leads. Names were mentioned."

Brooke didn't want to know, but the question came out. "Was the arrest mentioned?"

"Yes, but the articles didn't mention what evidence was used to make the decision. I have to tell you the article also said there are three suspects."

"Three? Only Ty and Marla were arrested. It didn't say who the other one was, did it?"

"No." Chloe grabbed a couple sodas from the refrigerator and passed one to Brooke.

"They can't be suspecting Scott, can they?"

"Like I said, no other names were given, but with the police not allowing any contact between the two of you, that would be my guess." As Brooke's lip began to tremble, Chloe jumped up and skirted the table to hold her friend. "Brooke, it only makes sense the authorities would wonder about him, but it doesn't mean he did anything. They're just being cautious."

Brooke let Chloe hold her for a brief moment, and then edged away from her saying, "You're right." She popped the top of the soda can and listened to the fizz. "I'm sure the newspaper isn't the place for me to find answers, anyway."

"Brooke, all I can say is everyone has more than one side. Consider this, would people who knew you and Ty think you would ever get a divorce?"

Chloe went back to her seat as Brooke got a hold of herself. "You're right again. Our friends were surprised. Well, at least they acted surprised."

The kitchen became quiet except for the creaks in the wall brought on by the shifting winds outside. Brooke tapped her can on the table and then blurted, "Chloe, I just lied."

With a surprised look, Chloe stopped her soda can in midair.

"I hate not telling the truth, but my side of the friends, probably including you, didn't think Ty and I would've lasted as long as we did."

"Maybe this will be a decision-making time for you. Let yourself move on," Chloe offered.

"Everything feels as if it has changed, so what's the difference if there's another change?" Brooke answered with a shrug.

"Which reminds me. I didn't get a chance to tell you, but Scott did call today."

"He did?"

"Remember, he's not supposed to contact you, but there's no restriction on him calling me. He has a good aura, so I'm comfortable with speaking with him."

"Did he ask about me?"

Chloe smiled. "First, he mentioned your work. I think that was mostly an excuse to call, but he did ask how you're doing. He sounded concerned about you and only mildly interested in the part about your work."

"Did you tell him that you'll help me with the glass?"

"Yep, I told him we'll keep up with the schedule. I also told him he can pick up a few pieces next week."

"You mean he'll come here? Will I have to leave when he shows up? I'm almost nervous to see him again. I wouldn't blame him if he wants to get this project done, so he won't have to deal with me after all this."

"Take a breath, Brooke." Chloe laughed as Brooke tumbled her thoughts into the conversation. "Scott was also shocked that I suggested he come out here, but he certainly was in favor of the request. I don't think it'd be so bad, if he comes here and accidentally has the opportunity to say 'hi.'"

Brooke absently moved her soda to the side and sank back into the chair. "Things are really messy now."

"I guess it's to be expected because this wasn't a simple crime."

Brooke cringed, influencing Chloe to add quickly, "And we don't know who did this. It could be some random incident, not even someone we know."

Brook didn't completely believe this theory, but she wanted to. "I hope that's the case."

Chloe jumped up as she glanced at the clock. "I need to get back to my store for a couple hours, and then we'll make a dash to the grocery store. Okay?"

"Yes, of course. I think I'll take a little catnap. All my energy hasn't returned, yet. Would you wake me up when you're ready to go?"

Chloe bobbed her head as Brooke headed for the couch where she could watch the snowfall. Lying down, she recalled her dream and fought the lengthened blinks until they won.

Chapter 17

Brooke awoke to a dull thumping sound. "I gathered a pile of winter clothes for our journey," Chloe announced as she dropped her armload of apparel to a table. "I have winter jackets, mittens, scarves, boots, and colorful knit hats for the ears. The snow is so pretty with the streetlights shining on it that I have the crazy urge to go out even more than earlier. Are you still game?"

Adjusting her eyes to the dimmed lighting, Brooke pushed herself up to get a better look out the living room window. "It looks beautiful from in here."

"Oh, have you changed your mind? We don't have to go. I just thought it'd be something fun to do."

"No, no I want to go, too," Brooke confirmed as she shook the grogginess from her head. "I need to get out. I don't want the cooped up winter feeling to start already. Which jacket is mine to use?" Brooke pawed through the pile partially slipping from the table. Pulling out a lavender and crème colored knit hat, she stuck it on her head. A tail fell down her back, which prompted a giggle. "I look like an elf with this on."

"Mine doesn't look any better," Chloe agreed as she placed a mint green and raspberry hat over her bun, causing her hair to fall loose to the side of her head. Chloe separated the pile and helped Brooke with hers. "We look like abominable snowmen that are ready for the mountains now."

Looking out the window again, Brooke informed, "We're ready for the street, anyway. It doesn't look like plows have touched the roads yet. I'd guess there are four or five inches out there."

"I can handle that. So, let's get going."

They left the house and headed for Chloe's car. Huge snowflakes quickly stuck to their hats and other articles. Most of the traffic headed in the opposite direction as people were on their way home from work.

Chloe entered the street as the car's back end took the turn at a slide. "I did that on purpose," Chloe jested. "Just makes the ride a little more fun. I'll be careful, though."

Brooke became transfixed by the yellowish street lanterns, which glowed under a covering of new snow. It reminded her of her life. Everything was changing, but the foundation remained the same. If only that could be altered, too.

"Brooke, is there anything in particular you want to get?" Chloe's question brought Brooke back to the present as they turned into the moderately full parking lot.

"I haven't really thought about it, but I'm sure I'll find something. Plus I want to make dinner tomorrow."

"I didn't think we'd have to park this far from the door. Must be people stopping after work just like we're doing," Chloe commented as she picked a spot between two other cars already gaining an inch of snow cover since parked.

Brooke usually enjoyed running into people while shopping, but the memory of today's encounter left her with a need for anonymity.

"Let's get inside and see what we can find," Chloe encouraged as they followed other fresh prints to the door.

Once inside, Brooke attempted to keep focused on the stocked aisles and cases. She didn't want to invite conversation from other shoppers. She and Chloe discussed the meals for the rest of the week, assuming Brooke would be with her at least that long. Occasionally, Brooke couldn't help but glance around her, checking to see if she knew anyone in the same aisle. She recognized a few, but no one who required a hello. She convinced herself that the handful of them staring at her didn't mean anything.

"How're you tonight?" A clerk behind the checkout counter greeted them.

"We're playing in the snow and having a good time with it. And how're you?" Chloe responded.

"Just fine, thanks." The clerk smiled back. "Did you find everything?" The clerk looked at both of them as she asked about their shopping experience. Her gaze turned into a stare as her eyes rested on Brooke.

Brooke's jacket hung open, which exposed her arm and the sling wrapped over it as she dug into her purse to contribute her share of the bill.

Feeling uneasy, Brooke rushed to answer with the hope to avert the clerk's eyes. "We found everything and then some."

With her hands no longer scanning items, the clerk questioned, "Are you Mrs. Bellin?"

Chloe took a breath and turned to Brooke. She knew what was coming. Brooke simply answered, "Yes, I used to be."

Obviously not understanding the turmoil she caused in Brooke's stomach, the clerk exclaimed, "I thought that was you!" Returning to calculating the purchases, she went on, "I read all about your shooting. I can't believe this happened here in Creek Willow. I bet it was painful."

The clerk paused and looking directly at Brooke, bent over the counter and asked, "Are you going to testify against your husband? I don't know what I'd do. I heard the trial is in two days."

Brooke had no intentions of answering as her mouth fell open. She looked at Chloe and wondered how to handle this outburst. Brooke was thankful there wasn't anyone else in line, but she was amazed at the girl's audacity.

Chloe stepped in here. "Honey, uh, Sheila," she said, taking note of the nametag, "the former Mrs. Bellin is tired and there's not a trial in two days. It's an arraignment, and there isn't proof as to the one at fault, yet."

"Oh, so the newspaper made it all up. Wouldn't you know? I thought it was pretty fast to figure out such an awful crime." She glanced at the total. "It's sixty-two fifty-three, please."

"Brooke, why don't you warm the car up? I'll finish paying and meet you out there."

Brooke appreciated the escape and slid behind Chloe to head for the door with her gaze on the floor. She wasn't going to chance making eye contact with anyone else.

The outside of the store wasn't affected by the altercation. The sticky flakes of snow still cascaded around her and glittered with the lights. Looking up to the sky, Brooke felt a mental chill. Whispering to the ice crystals, Brooke pleaded, "What's happening to my world? Scott, I want you so badly. I need to see you soon. I fear you won't pick up your glass next week or else I'll have to be gone when you arrive. I even hope to see you in court. Just to see you would make me feel better."

Brooke didn't want to get caught talking to the night air, so she ended her discussion, put her head down, and shuffled her boots to the car.

* * * *

Scott's pencil scratched nonsense, and then erased the effect. It happened again. Nothing got done.

He pushed the rumpled stack of blueprints to the top of his drafting desk. 10:32 pm. The watch ticked at its usual pace, but the night wouldn't go away. He knew the arraignment was tomorrow morning. It'd be his chance to see Brooke in front of the legal hands who forbid him to do just that. Brooke would certainly be there. She wasn't required to attend, but Scott knew she wouldn't miss it. He hadn't quite convinced himself to keep away from her.

Chapter 18

7:53 a.m. Brooke arrived at the entrance of the chosen courtroom. Everyone else in the room seated themselves close to the probable action. A mousy blond dressed in gray pants with an almost matching blazer took a small space in the front row. She crossed her legs and her back hunched forward, waiting for information. A pen clicked in a pattern on the legal pad resting on her leg. Her press ID hung around a pale neck. She was the only one on the right side of the courtroom.

A small group of elderly men dressed in khakis and sweaters, still sporting the lines from months of remaining folded, assumed the middle row behind the defendant's side. They were attentive and appeared ready for action.

Two young women sat close together on the left side. Their attire was casual at best and they stuffed worn backpacks under the bench. They continually whispered to one another with excited expressions poorly concealed as they checked out the uniformed and suited men entering from various doors.

Brooke stood alone at the entrance wondering which side to sit on. Chloe had dropped her off after a pleading request to give her this time by herself. Was she for or against her ex-husband?

The prosecuting attorney turned to check on the viewers of this morning's free show. Noticing Brooke pausing at the door, he nodded to indicate she should sit behind his table.

Brooke made eye contact, but didn't move. To sit behind District Attorney Sabin would mean she supported Ty and Marla's guilt. As a few other stragglers entered, Brooke chose the last bench on the left side. She hoped she'd blend in and not make a statement either way. Fortunately, a couple and two other suits chose the right side. The attendance was in better balance.

"All rise."

The air froze as Judge Casper entered. He looked God-like with his immaculate robe flowing behind him only to reveal his dusty and creased oxfords. All eyes from the audience moved at his speed.

"Please be seated."

Simple words. Simple commands. So much meaning.

Brooke hugged herself tight as a chill filled with apprehension riveted from the pit of her stomach to her extremities as if the closing of the large and creaky wooden doors threw the morning's cold air over her. The demands of a gavel silenced the courtroom except for the scuffling of paperwork from the front desks.

Brooke wasn't familiar with legal procedures. She had never contemplated needing to know the steps. The only information that guided her was what the District Attorney's secretary had briefly given away. Today's arraignment was to verify if there was enough probable cause through evidence to hold the accused. That would be her ex-husband, Ty. Marla's arraignment would follow his. Brooke didn't understand the separation, since it was the same alleged crime, but again she never had much interest in legal matters. All of a sudden, it became critical that she study up on what happened in this vacuous, brick building. She also had a twinge of regret for sending Chloe home. Chloe may have helped her understand the ramifications of today's proceeding more clearly.

Today wouldn't be the outcome of the whole scenario. Brooke concluded she was smart enough to figure out the main ruling, so she focused on the uniforms who walked Ty to the left desk.

Brooke was aghast at how Ty looked. It was obvious he attempted to hold his head high, but she saw a droop to that façade. His face was pale with dark rings halfway around his eyes, which she could detect even while sitting so far back. She was almost sure he was wearing the same clothes as when he visited her in the hospital. But he hadn't used the cane, which now accentuated his limp. Brooke wondered if he'd kept up with his therapy.

District Attorney Sabin stared straight ahead as the defense attorney opened his case. Brooke had to strain to hear what he proclaimed. It sounded foreign. She didn't understand the litany because her mind warped the words into another dialect. She forced herself to focus and follow the reasoning.

"...of course his fingerprints were on the alleged weapon. It's his gun. Everyone else's fingerprints are on it, too. There's not a single thread of proof, which will show that Mr. Bellin was the last to use the gun.

"Furthermore, Mr. Bellin was signed in at the rifle range during the time of the shooting. Also, the unused gun cleaning cloths were found in his garage." The defense attorney paused here for emphasis. "Don't you think the gun cleaning cloths would have been used to wipe off his fingerprints, if he had shot his ex-wife? No, the cloths were found clean and unused."

Attorneys had a tendency to pause and let the information sink into the listeners' mind. Brooke was grateful for this. Everything she heard told a brand new story. She wasn't informed of the recoveries of the investigation. She needed these broken sentences to absorb the terrifying slew of information loaded on her.

"Let's assume Mr. Bellin was able to drag himself into the woods full of shrubbery, broken branches, and other debris littering the forest floor, set up his tripod as the investigation claims, get a shot off at his ex-wife, and miss! Miss? How could a veteran hunter miss a target approximately seventy-five feet away while using a 30.06 rifle with a high powered scope?" He ended this with a violent turn to his client as he slapped his hand on the stack of files that rested on the table.

"Yes, Mr. Bellin had a life insurance policy of three hundred thousand dollars on Ms. Bellin, which wasn't cancelled after their divorce. His aim would've been better than missing his target of the heart by five inches, if he had intended to collect it.

"Ty Bellin has informed me of the reason for the large policy. In conjunction with Brooke, they bought equal policies for both of them. He wanted her well taken care of if his health failed. Brooke had wanted the same for her husband of fourteen years. She wanted him to be able to continue with his therapy and extensive healthcare if she passed." He sounded so sincere.

"Objection for the purpose of assuming the thoughts of a third party," District Attorney Sabin proclaimed.

"Sustained. I will not consider the last statement by the defense," interrupted the judge.

Brooke's heart thumped and reeled unnaturally as the temperature in the room came to a boil. The last statement by the defense was true. She began to consider whether the outcome would follow suit. She wanted to leave the room and not subject herself to the painful words so carefully picked and tossed up for judgment.

"I have one last statement, Your Honor."

"Proceed."

Returning to a calm and formal tone, the defense attorney continued. "Mr. Bellin was not the one caught removing evidence from the scene in the form of a white bag of apples.

"I rest the defense with the claim that there is insufficient evidence to proceed with a case against the defendant, Ty Bellin, under the charge of attempted murder."

Brooke stiffened as she heard the actual charge for the first time. It echoed back and forth against the cavernous walls of the room where Ty would be innocent unless proven guilty. Unless... The defense attorney was adamant about Ty's innocence and made it believable to her ears.

As papers returned to shuffling and the next round got ready to commence, Brooke startled herself by remembering another subject for the first time since she'd entered the courthouse. Allowing herself to slightly turn her neck and take a peek at the audience, she checked to see if anyone had snuck in since she had sat down. It didn't surprise her, but she didn't see Scott.

Brooke half-hoped Scott wanted to see the proceeding. The other half of her was glad he wasn't listening. She wasn't sure what she felt at this point, and even getting a glimpse of Scott wouldn't guaranty comfort under these circumstances. Also, she didn't want to get him in more trouble by breaking the questionable restraining order right in front of a room littered with every type of legal personnel she could think of.

As Brooke faced the front again, she caught District Attorney Sabin glance her way. He didn't appear to be upset that she sat on the opposing counsel's side of the courtroom.

Attorney Sabin stood erect and silent at his table for a supplementary half minute before he began his contradictions to the defense. "Your Honor, I have organized a list of evidence similar to what the defense claims is insubstantial. The difference is I will prove what the defense is attempting to disregard.

"Let's begin with the gun used at the scene. A bullet with enough recognizable grooves revealed that a 30.06 is the make of the weapon used. This led our investigation to begin with Ms. Brooke Bellin's known surroundings and acquaintances. In Mr. Bellin's home we found a gun matching that description."

"Objection. There are probably a thousand guns of that make within a twenty mile radius," the defense interjected.

"Overruled. This is a preliminary hearing and I need to hear what both sides have to offer. Support your evidence and continue, Counsel." Brooke felt the judge didn't portray any biases.

"Thank you. Yesterday my team revealed Mr. Ty Bellin's fingerprints on the recently fired weapon. A weapon fired from a tripod in the woods, substantiated by the three equilateral grooves embedded in the ground approximately seventy-five feet from the scene. It's standard that persons with disabilities, such as Mr. Bellin's, typically use tripods." Judge Casper scribbled a note on his legal pad.

"Concerning the clean gun cloths…of course, Mr. Bellin was not afforded the opportunity to clean the gun before the investigation of his home. He needed to make an appearance at the hospital, not figuring the police would be so prompt to check his home."

Flipping his paperwork, Sabin continued, "Yes, Mr. Bellin was at the firing range. He was not the one who signed his name and time on the registrar, though. The lab will check the handwriting. If the time is not exact, that will make a huge difference.

"Let's turn to the emotional stability of Mr. Ty Bellin." District Attorney Sabin provoked a thoughtful look as he rubbed his chin. "Is it likely that he hurried to the state park, secured his location, which he assumed would be the best to murder his ex-wife, and took a shot at her heart? With intense anger, upset, and full of revenge, do you believe a man can shoot with the accuracy of a sharpshooter through tangles of tree limbs and brush and hit his target one hundred percent? That's an unlikely hypothesis." It was Sabin's turn to slam his fist on the desk.

He continued in a loud, distinct voice. "With a three hundred thousand dollar life insurance policy waiting to be handed over, of course Mr. Bellin wanted to murder his ex-wife." Silence. Sabin let his conclusion sink in as if he were already at trial.

Calmly, he dug his hands into the refuge of often-used pockets and walked slowly the length of the prosecutorial territory. District Attorney Sabin lowered his voice and made a final claim. “Mr. Ty Bellin was nervous and hurried. He missed his mark and only injured Ms. Bellin.

“I’ll request a two million dollar bail to make sure Ty Bellin doesn’t finish the job,” the prosecutor requested with finality.

District Attorney Sabin folded his request and returned to his chair. The attendees of the proceeding began to whisper and debate the issues. Judge Casper adjusted his glasses and peered intently at his shorthand of notes.

The evidence stunned Brooke. It was more than she wanted to know and it only confused her. She wanted the criminal apprehended, but it would be easier to stomach if it were someone she didn’t know. Both sides were convincing, so which one was right?

Brooke raised her sunken chin and took note of the courtroom. The reporter busily scribbled her notes and repeatedly checked her cell phone. The pencil tapping probably accompanied her adrenalin for a front-page story.

The two casual college girls huddled together, undoubtedly whispering about their fortune in witnessing a prelim for an attempted murder that starred powerful men in suits, noticeably attractive to more than a few women. As they attempted to be serious, they dug in their knapsacks pulling out lipstick and cell phones.

The older men were nearly silent, with thoughtful expressions. Other random people who came for whatever reason, Brooke overlooked. She had seen enough of the varied reactions, and they gave her no clue as to what would happen. Ready to find out, she nearly held her breath.

After a handful of minutes, the court became silent, inviting the conclusion. Judge Casper shuffled his papers one more time, and then looked up. He briefly looked at the defense attorney and ultimately rested his gaze on District Attorney Sabin.

With an exasperated sigh, the judge began. “Counselors, you have both represented me with a lot of evidence to consider. It appears the investigation is not complete.

“Ah…I have a problem with the timing. By this I direct my discussion to District Attorney Sabin.” The judge cast his stone brown eyes at Sabin until he had his attention exclusively.

"I'm surprised and a little disappointed in your presentation today, Counselor. I would expect more proof of the alleged evidence you exhibited today. First, I appreciate the fact that the weapon is a 30.06 and Mr. Bellin owns this type of gun. And yes, his prints are on it. Not too surprising. The difficulty with accepting this as proof is you found out about the make of the gun, *after* you had him arrested. Not only that, but the fingerprint analysis was not finished until yesterday afternoon. There were a myriad of fingerprints on this weapon.

"Also, the *possibility*, of the firing range's registrar being tampered with is not a conclusive report to submit. It's pure speculation."

Changing his direction of attention to the defense, Judge Casper continued. "I see an extensive buildup of evidence without a direction at this point. By this, I mean the evidence is not complete without the corresponding tests and evaluations completed. There is no reason to have a particular individual singled out until the evidence has been sufficiently assessed by the forensic team."

Taking a breath, Judge Casper shook his head as he pulled his reading glasses to the bench. "And the apples. I don't understand what apples have to do with attempted murder. Unless you're assuming a William Tell's son scene, I don't see the relevance of apples being out of the ordinary during the fall.

"In conclusion, Mr. Ty Bellin, you are free to go." Judge Casper had one more thing to say. "But I do suggest you stay in the area. I'm sure you're concerned that the offender is apprehended without further harm to Ms. Bellin."

Pushing himself out of his chair, Ty stood and addressed the judge. "Yes, Your Honor, I certainly am."

The judge did not respond. He only stared at Ty while he shook the defense attorney's hand.

District Attorney Sabin didn't look at the defense attorney as he carefully stacked his materials and placed them back in his briefcase. Shrugging and pulling at the front of his jacket, he turned and headed for Brooke.

Brooke sat frozen to the far back seat she'd meticulously chosen, not sure if she should run out before Ty passed her or to wait for him. She hadn't contemplated what to do no matter the outcome of the arraignment.

This wasn't a procedure that placed or removed guilt from Ty's position. There was no sense of relief, only a fear for the unknown which instantly covered her.

District Attorney Sabin saved Brooke from making a decision when he appeared in front of her and knelt down to speak. "Ms. Bellin, you are aware that Mr. Bellin is allowed back into the community?" Brooke only looked at him, inviting a more complete explanation. "Also, you're allowed to see or not see Mr. Bellin under your own discretion.

"My advice, though, is to stay away from him. I'm not saying he did it, but until the gray areas are thoroughly accounted for he'll still be considered a suspect along with Scott Marshall and Marla Vrahn."

Brooke widened her eyes as if she were watching the climax of a horror story. More frightened now than she gave herself credit for since the day she walked the nature trail, she recalled a wakeup in the hospital with lights and monitors, blinks and beeps, all in control of her life. "I don't understand. I'm supposed to stay away from them although Ty and Marla can come and go as they please. Scott Marshall hasn't even been arrested or charged with anything and there's a restraining order. That doesn't sound right. Are there other people I should beware of?" The district attorney didn't offer the help she expected.

Beginning to lose a thread of control, Brooke shook as she continued, "Are there others who are considered suspects, but haven't been named, yet? How can I go home, if whoever did it knows where I live? What am I supposed to do now?"

"I understand your confusion, Ms. Bellin. I suggest you return to your friend's house at least for today. This will give you some time to calm down and make some rational decisions." District Attorney Sabin's knees cracked as he returned to standing, and asked, "Do you have a ride?"

"Yes," Brooke half-lied. She hadn't phoned Chloe yet to pick her up. Brooke didn't know how long she'd have to wait, but she didn't want a police escort, either.

Patting the back of the bench, Sabin finished with, "If you have any questions or concerns, feel free to call my office." As if that would help. Sabin turned and headed for a set of doors to release him from the armpit of the law.

Brooke pulled out her cell phone and remained seated before the next arraignment for Marla began. She didn't want to be here for this one, but she still needed a few minutes to regain her equanimity.

As she dialed Chloe's number, she saw Ty excuse himself from his attorney. He hurried down another aisle, and headed for the same doors as District Attorney Sabin.

Chapter 19

Sabin walked through the doors. As soon as they completely shut behind him, he checked the lobby for other officials. Moving to the side, he watched as the connected officers, investigators, and the defense attorney headed for the exits. As the uniforms and creased suits became smaller and separated through the swinging doors, District Attorney Sabin cast his eyes on the figure seated on a bench halfway down the dim hall.

Ty looked at ease as he sat with his knees relaxed in a wide spread and his arms cast over the back of the four foot bench. With an upward slant to his lips, he carelessly looked to the front and then up to the ceiling.

"Bellin," Sabin said as he confronted the seated figure. "You made it this far. I did my part, and now the rest is up to you."

"I appreciate your consideration of my welfare. I'm going to assume it was caused due to a savvy move on your part, not because of sloppy preparation."

"There's only so much I can do. I'm not the only one involved in the investigation of this case. I've done my part." Sabin's lips grew tight.

"No, your part is ongoing, if you want to keep your job," Ty reminded him.

"You're wrong there. I win either way. Don't you think the tide has turned here? Don't bother answering me. If you attempted to kill your ex-wife, who'd believe anything you say about the District Attorney who incarcerated you?" Sabin glowered at Ty while checking his periphery angles to make sure no one approached the heated, but quiet confrontation.

"What I know about you will never disappear. I better not end up in some filthy hole with nothing but men looking at my ass." With this last threat, Ty rose from the bench and systematically used his cane, emphasizing his disability. As if nothing had taken place other than a traffic ticket, Ty didn't look back while he sauntered to the exit.

Sabin checked his watch. The next preliminary was in ten minutes. He would have to follow through as planned. Marla Vrahn's charge was as an accessory to attempted murder.

* * * *

Scott walked the lawn and checked the landscaping at the Maple Haven Bed and Breakfast project. A few of his men worked on the hardscape, but with the recent snow, there wasn't going to be any turf work done for the rest of this winter.

Glad he wasn't entirely alone, he randomly exchanged jokes with the few workers to keep him from thinking the world had erupted and left him the only survivor. Since the restraining order kept him away from Brooke, the police had searched his home and office. As far as he knew, they'd found nothing because there was nothing to find.

Scott had made himself a hearty breakfast early this morning for two reasons. First, he was hungry and most of all he wanted to give himself maximum time to decide on whether to go to the arraignment and hopefully see Brooke. He also reconsidered because of the order, and he didn't know if Brooke would attend, although he figured she would. After pushing the omelet made from leftovers in the refrigerator and the crisp bacon around the plate a dozen different ways before it disappeared, Scott decided not to watch the proceeding. He didn't think he'd be able to see Brooke without talking to her and wanting to hold her, which was forbidden.

He needed to clear his mind for the day and get some work done. Scott tempered the disappointment with the call in which Chloe told him there would be finished glass to pick up in a few days. He hoped Brooke wanted to see him. It wasn't like she had twenty-four-hour security to keep them apart.

Chapter 20

"I'm going to check and see if the newspaper's on the porch yet," Brooke spontaneously announced while jumping away from the table.

She and Chloe had risen early and started the morning with fresh ground coffee, which left a tasteful and warm scent throughout the kitchen. Yesterday, after Chloe had retrieved Brooke from the courthouse, Brooke hadn't made a single comment about the proceeding. Even when the news came on at night, she wanted it turned off. She didn't intend to relive the day's trauma along with thousands of viewers who were now keeping track of her tragedy.

Looking at the clock above the stove, Chloe got out of her chair while agreeing, "The newspaper should be here by now. Let me get it."

"Nonsense. My legs work fine," Brooke insisted. "It's time I see it in writing. The whole thing is hard to believe as it is." She disappeared through the living room.

Brooke could only think of how she would react when reading the results in a public paper. Without any comments about what happened, she gave no indication of how she felt or what she wanted to do. She didn't show the slightest interest in the preliminary results for Marla.

As Chloe waited for Brooke's response to the objective news report, Brooke came shuffling back into the kitchen with the newspaper hugged under her arm. Leaning forward, Brooke dumped the paper onto the table. She admitted, "I'm afraid to look. I carried it under my arm, so I couldn't catch a glimpse of the first page until I was back here with you."

Chloe smiled sympathetically. "I'm not going anywhere, Brooke. Whenever you're ready, we'll read it together."

Brooke slipped back onto her chair with her leg bent underneath to give her a controlling position over the newspaper's facts. Staring briefly at the folded paper, she took a deep breath, laid the paper out, and plunged into the inevitable.

"Here it is at the top of page one." Brooke read the headline, "'Scoring Fifty Percent in the Attempted Murder' they wrote." Brooke looked up to see a quizzical expression cross Chloe's face. Brooke needed to know what it meant, so she hurried on. "'Yesterday morning at the Wisla County courthouse two preliminary hearings were held. These were for the attempted murder of Brooke Bellin involving two alleged suspects. Ms. Bellin's ex-husband, Ty Bellin, was released on insufficient evidence after a fiery exchange between District Attorney Sabin and defense counsel, Attorney Rusch.'" Brooke tightened her grip on the flimsy edge of the paper. "'…coming back with a victory in the second round, Sabin was able to keep Marla Vrahn behind bars for conspiracy to attempted murder.'" Brooke's hand trembled as she read the last sentence.

"Brooke, maybe you shouldn't read the rest right now," Chloe suggested.

Brooke did stop here as she attempted to recapture her voice, which was restricted as her throat tightened on each word she read. Lowering the paper, she spoke to Chloe. "I didn't know Marla was put back in jail. I couldn't stay to watch her. I called you to get me before her preliminary started. I wonder what the police have on her that was different from what they presented for Ty's arraignment."

"I'm sorry this is so hard on you, and I don't blame you for not wanting to stay longer yesterday."

"I think I've read enough," Brooke decided as she refolded the paper and pushed it to the side. She continued to voice her thoughts. "I didn't know Ty hated me so much, no matter how many times he..." Brooke wasn't able to say the adulterous explanation out loud.

Brooke looked down at her hands, set on the table, as she twined her fingers tightly. "I find it hard to believe Ty would have it in him, but what do I know?"

"Everyone has another side, Brooke. I think you found your other side," Chloe informed her.

Before responding, Brooke stared into her eyes and saw Chloe as her friend, not an accuser. "I knew I wanted something different than what Ty and I had, but even after the divorce, I didn't believe a man existed for me.

A man who would treat me and make me feel the way I started to believe Scott could. It was an accident to find him." Cocking her head to the side, she continued, "I didn't even meet Scott until nearly two years after the divorce. How could Ty still feel resentment toward me?

"If I could erase these last few days and give everyone involved their lives back, I would."

Chloe made a correction to Brooke's last statement. "Brooke, you didn't take anyone's life from themselves. Don't worry about anyone involved, but yourself. Once you find out who really hurt you, you'll be glad they're caught."

The pipes in the wall creaked as the heat kicked in. Brooke looked around her, observing the comfortable warmth, scents, and colors of the kitchen. "I'll just have to make it up to anyone involved who shouldn't be."

"Honey, you don't have to do a thing. They're responsible for themselves, and Ty, Marla, and Scott will have to adjust on their own to whatever the law finds out. They're adults and capable of this."

With a sigh, Brooke agreed. "You're always right, Chloe. I thought I became friends with Marla, but I don't really know what she's like other than the therapy sessions, a few meals together, and we walked the trails a couple times. It was quite a while ago that we've done anything together."

Chloe interrupted, "Marla knew about your favorite trails?"

"Yeah, she joined me two or three times. Everyone can use them because it's a public park."

Chloe nodded as if things had begun to register in her critical mind. "I didn't know you did so many things with Marla. I was under the impression you only saw her when you stopped by during some of the therapies."

"No, we did other things which would make me suspect her less. I thought we'd become friends." Brooke paused before she continued with her assessment. "Although, there were times I would get to the therapy session a few minutes late. I was finishing my own work and hurrying in at the last minute. Sometimes I would find Ty and Marla very close. I guess I dismissed it because they had the right to do whatever they wanted. I have a hard time believing things unless they're in black and white. Plus, he wasn't my husband anymore. It didn't really matter.

"I tried to reduce the sessions I attended, but as soon as I missed a couple, Ty would call and claim that my help was beneficial to his progress. I guess I acted as an assistant to Marla."

"Brooke, you also have to realize Marla has only been held on conspiracy. That would mean someone else is involved, if the police are right about her. I don't intend to scare you, but whether it is Ty, Scott, or someone you don't know, the person is still out there."

"I hardly believe it's Ty, and I know Scott wouldn't do this." Brooke hesitated, and then continued, "Scott and I had surprises for each other. We didn't get to show them until he came to see me at the hospital, but I know it wasn't him." Brooke could feel her cheeks getting hot as she looked at Chloe with a command to tell her what really happened.

"I know you want answers to end this whole thing and right now would be a good time to do it, but I don't have the answers. I wish I did," Chloe reported. Brooke realized she wasn't ready for more evidence and details. She hadn't even wanted to finish the article.

Shaking her head, Brooke sipped her coffee. "Yeah, I don't know how much more I can handle right now." With a deep breath she looked up decidedly and changed the subject. "I do know I need to get some stained glass done before Scott comes over to get what we promised him. This also means I need to get to my studio. I need a few more things."

"We can go this afternoon, but don't I have what you need?"

"Actually, it's some of the colored glass you had to order, so I'd rather not wait for another order. I can just run over to the studio where I have some. I didn't realize we'd get this far, or I would've brought it all right away." Brooke hoped Chloe wouldn't question her theory, and added, "Maybe I should go by myself this time. You might be ready to get rid of me for awhile." Rethinking her last statement, Brooke said, "Actually, I need to stay at home soon. I don't want you to think you've acquired a roommate."

"Nonsense, I haven't had to rely on the coffee shop for my social fix." Chloe became serious. "Brooke, I'm happy to have you here. Also, Ty might pop over to your apartment at any time. I don't think it's a good idea to be with him alone right now. Whether he…either way he probably isn't in the best of moods." Brooke knew Chloe questioned Ty's part in the shooting, but tried to be objective.

"I miss my apartment and studio," Brooke muttered into her cup.

Brooke's forlorn look mirrored in her coffee as Chloe decided, "Let's go now. Don't bother getting dressed. Throw your coat over the pajamas and we'll take a run to your studio. We should empty out all your materials, so you don't have to go there again, and then Ty can't watch you work from a window or catch you off guard. I'll put a note on the business door saying I'll be open an hour late."

Brooke couldn't help but smile at the suggestion. "Thank you, again. I think it'll put me in a better mood. I've procrastinated about finding another studio since the divorce. One that wasn't so close to Ty's house. I always liked my little shop, but it's definitely time. Past time, actually."

"Quit thanking me, and let's get going." Chloe chuckled. "I don't want my customers to think I'm closing down."

Chloe chatted about the change of season in the landscape as she and Brooke headed to her studio. Brooke heard the words, but didn't retain the conversation as she drew a different picture of the surroundings. The gray sky penetrated the land to give it the same washed out color. Even the snow appeared gray where it had remained stuck to the north side of hills and tree lines. Was this how her future was going to be painted?

"Chloe, I need to check his house, since we're headed next door." Brooke had to tell her this, since Chloe insisted on going. I'd like to go in alone, if you don't mind. I won't take long. If Ty's home, I'm not afraid of him."

"I'll be right outside. I'll give you fifteen minutes, and then I'm coming in." Worry creased Chloe's brow as Brooke insisted on entering his home without invitation as they arrived.

"I'll hurry," she reiterated as she carefully opened the car door and walked quickly to the entrance.

Brooke put her hand around the door handle, thinking of how long the last few days felt since she had entered his house. Now she detected an apprehension growing, which she hadn't given herself time to feel while in a rush to get here.

The unlocked door opened with the customary creak during the first foot of movement. She knew Ty had to be here. Sensibly, where else would he go after his release? She didn't know what to expect when she talked to him. Brooke also admitted to herself that, along with personal items, she had removed herself from this house long ago. She wanted to realize her position with Ty. If he'd shot her, she wanted an explanation.

Her shoes clicked on the tile entry as she entered with trepidation. She couldn't avoid the confrontation, so Brooke called out, "Ty, where are you?"

No response. Brooke proceeded to the kitchen, mainly because it was the closest. A few dirty dishes lay scattered along the countertop, but otherwise, everything was in place as she had seen it on her last visit.

Not wanting to change her mind and turn to run, Brooke quickly checked the empty living room. The most likely room left to check would be Ty's study. He spent a lot of time reading and using his computer.

As she paused at the entrance of the study, Ty looked up from the crossword puzzle, which appeared daily in *The Sounder*. The tension in the air multiplied so quickly Brooke swore she could see it threading and twisting in knots as their eyes met.

"Well, Brooke, you've decided to come home to me."

Brooke stared, not knowing how to respond. Ty didn't wait. "You aren't afraid of me, are you? They dismissed me because I wasn't the one who shot you. That should release some of your fear." Brooke swore he could sense the blood spinning in circles through her tightened body.

It never occurred to Brooke to be afraid. She still thought of him as she'd known him for the last fifteen years. She had a difficult time thinking things had really changed even through this surrealistic trauma. The low throbbing in her shoulder reminded her.

"Don't worry, Brooke," Ty drawled. "I'll do the thinking for you." He set the paper at his side. Sarcasm tainted his next comment. "I'm used to this from many years of detouring you from living in your fanatical world of everyone being good and nice."

Brooke swallowed after Ty's callous remark. She hadn't considered a confrontation. Actually, she hadn't made any preparations as to how Ty would react upon seeing her and what he'd say. His attitude left her mute.

"Brooke, I'm still the one who's 'nice' and will treat you as you deserve. You don't look too sure about this. Don't you have anything to say to your ex-husband who had to spend a couple days in jail, away from his beautiful wife as she lay in the hospital needing him to comfort her?" Ty pushed himself up from his recliner. Stony eyes did not portray the care about which he spoke.

Brooke took a step back as she formulated a response. Without correcting him that she was his ex-wife, she said, “Ty, I know you didn’t do it. I didn’t think you were the one. Not for a minute.” Brooke recognized the excuses she planned to lay out to keep him from coming closer to her. It crossed her mind that it was a mistake to come here.

“I know, Brooke.” Her name slid through his barely opened lips. Reaching out a hand, he continued, “Come here. Let me touch you. I need to know you’re still alive and with me again.”

Thinking frantically for an exit, Brooke blurted, “Please don’t hug me. My shoulder, it still hurts and the pain has spread.” Brooke felt relief flush her cheeks as she saw Ty back up from his intentions to hold her.

“Wouldn’t you feel better with a little loving?” With this statement, Ty deliberately caressed her right arm as he came closer again. Brooke felt the warmth of his breath as he leaned into her neck and placed light kisses while nudging her collar away from his target.

She froze, distaste forming a sticky film in her mouth. “Ty, I…I love you, but I’m not up to this right now.” Brooke forced herself to play along. Chloe was right. He did have another side. It hadn’t occurred to her that he’d come on to her and make her feel like maggots crawled on her skin.

Ty released her with a last touch of his finger running along her cheek. “I understand. You’ve been through a lot.”

Brooke felt a brief moment of relief as she backed up a couple steps. She thought seeing Ty would release her anxiety, but a prominent rattle of doubts careened around the facts and inferences raised at the arraignment. Now she had to figure a way to get back to Chloe without Ty becoming angry.

Changing the subject, Ty asked, “Where’re your things? I’m sure you wouldn’t mind staying with me for a while for protection. How about we have breakfast together to celebrate getting back to normal?”

He didn’t have a clue. “I already had breakfast.” Thinking quickly, she added, “I have all my work at Chloe’s.”

“I don’t think you should continue with the B& B job because, from what I understand, the police think Mr. Marshall is the one who shot you, Brooke. There probably won’t be a job when the police are done with him.”

Ty exaggerated a sigh while rubbing the back of his neck. "Brooke, how would you like me to take you to Chloe's to bring your things back? You should be with me at a time like this."

He wouldn't give up. "Uh, Ty, Chloe is waiting for me. She brought me here." What else could she say?

A glimmer of anger flashed across Ty's deep-set eyes and disappeared just as fast. "Brooke." He kept using her name. "Brooke, you're probably very confused and tired right now, so you should listen to what I tell you and it's the right thing to do.

"We can visit Marla on the way back, if you want."

Brooke couldn't believe what he suggested. "Visit Marla? You don't believe she had anything to do with this?"

"How could she? She was with me. We were at the firing range when you were shot." The blatant words were a stinging reminder, as if Brooke continually needed to recall the event.

Ty began to walk toward her again, closing the small distance that remained between them. The slight remnants of the stroke he suffered over two years ago were undetectable in his movements. Brooke slid her feet back a couple inches, trying not to make it obvious that her nerves were rebounding against his comments.

"Brooke, must I remind you there isn't any real evidence against me or Marla?"

Brooke glanced at the clock on Ty's desk. She'd entered the house seventeen minutes ago. Hopefully, Chloe would keep her resolution and check on her soon.

* * * *

Chloe stepped out of her car, staring at the entry to Ty's home. She willed the door to open with Brooke keeping to their plan of a short stay before she had to intervene. Chloe wished she could spontaneously call on her psychic abilities to see the likely confrontation inside the house, but it didn't happen that easily. Instead, she slowly walked to the house, nearly on tiptoe to avoid making excessive noise.

Intending to eavesdrop, Chloe stopped at the entry door. Leaning one ear closer to the door, she tried to hear anything unusual. She heard clips of a conversation. The voices held at a normal level. She'd wait a few more minutes before knocking.

"Brooke, did you hear me? There's no evidence. What if there isn't any evidence against anyone? You need me to protect you."

Brooke shivered as Ty paused and another smirk creased his face. "What about your studio? Don't you want to get back to your stained glass? I know it means a lot to you. Continue with smaller jobs. This job for Mr. Scott Marshall," he mocked the name, "is too big, anyway. You've been working too much, and you don't need to. I have money, if you need some."

Brooke covered her injured shoulder with the other hand, as if she needed to protect it. With a quizzical look, she said, "I'm on a fixed income of sorts now, and I want to do this job. Besides, the work I need to do is at Chloe's right now. It's hard to transfer it at the stage we're at." Not knowing why, possibly to appease him, she added, "It might take a couple days for me to be able to bring the work here, back to my studio."

"Well, darling Brooke, you can still be here, in a real home. Go to Chloe's when you need to work." Ty looked at Brooke as if she wouldn't be able to counter his logic this time.

She did run out of reasons and excuses. "I found your face paints," Brooke spontaneously told him. Her eyes widened and her breath caught somewhere between her lungs and the point of exhale. Was this it? Was this the accusation to cause Ty to finish the job, even if he hadn't started it? Brooke had a habit of adding the 'if' in her questions.

She expected the "evidence" she'd found to ignite Ty's carefully controlled anger. Instead, she saw the smirk he acquired with ease. "What paints, Brooke? You're the one with all the paints for your silly glass projects."

He turned on her with a different style. The Ty she'd known for so long had changed in a matter of days. Instead of calm and easygoing, still always sure of himself, he cajoled her and ridiculed her art.

She'd started it, so it was up to her to continue. She would have to reveal she had snooped and rummaged through his desk. Brooke didn't want to give Ty extra time to build anger or revenge for her doubt in him. Trying not to stumble over her claim, she added, "I found your paints hidden at the bottom of your desk."

"What does this mean? Nothing. I'm a hunter. Of course, I have camouflage paints. I can keep them wherever I want. There's no law against keeping them in my house, is there?"

Did he want her to say what she meant? Would he force her to say what he had to know already? She didn't know where else to take the discussion and wanted to leave. Did she have to blatantly accuse him for him to react? Ty had too much in control. She hadn't made him nervous, but rather he appeared to be strengthened in his self-assurance. He had no fear. He had no guilt. He had control. Brooke lost her confidence.

"I think I should go. Chloe is waiting for me." As Brooke dropped the subject and turned toward the door, Ty's hand shot past her shoulder and pushed against the weathered wood. He blocked her exit plan.

Chapter 21

District Attorney Sabin shut the door to his office and returned to his desk where Officer Kaehne had refused the offer to have a seat. "You need to change the note," Sabin informed him.

"Hey, I got it for you. I don't want any more to do with it. Do it yourself." Officer Kaehne kept his hands in his pants pockets, so the DA wouldn't see the trembling of his hands.

District Attorney Sabin shook his head. "Did you forget who the boss is here? It's awfully handy having a secure job when your wife likes to spend and kids have to keep up with their friends with the iPods, computer games, and ridiculous clothes which aren't worth what you pay at a Goodwill store." Officer Kaehne stared. District Attorney Sabin saved him from an immediate response with a cool and remindful comment. "I thought you were hell bent on getting Marshall in a bit of a pickle over this. You're going to help me, and I'll return the favor."

Officer Denny Kaehne sighed exasperatedly with the thought of weaseling his way out of his end of the deal. He'd never liked Scott Marshall. Ever since the day Marshall had taken his girlfriend years ago. Kaehne had wanted to see him fall. Kaehne would never admit Maggie had never been his. There wasn't any heart wrenching love gone wrong or a crushing breakup. It didn't matter that Maggie and Marshall had broken up only a few months into the relationship. Marshall simply represented the kind of man Denny could hate.

Marshall was always the one smiling with glowing white teeth as a defensive tackle while sacking the quarter back. Why hadn't he chosen one of the cheerleaders who'd proudly displayed oozing and disgusting admiration as they showed as much tight and firm skin they could get away with? Instead, Marshall focused on the quiet sideliner, Maggie. She was probably more of a challenge, bundled in sweaters and jeans attached to a chastity belt compliments of her family's beliefs. But he, Denny Kaehne, was the one who should've gotten the faded jeans down to her ankles and made her his property. That never happened.

Officer Kaehne loved his wife, kids, and home, but he couldn't let go of his first big loss. He would have liked to give himself credit for learning and becoming more mature in the last twenty-two years. District Attorney Sabin's plan slid off the deep end, and he didn't include Kaehne in the reasoning or underlying catalyst for such an in-depth scheme. Who cared if Bellin wanted to kill his ex-wife and chickened out or didn't have the ability to shoot straight? If the nurse had a part in the shooting, let her rot, too. Those would be big headlines, so what was with putting the blame on Marshall? At least Kaehne didn't care about him. The only thing Kaehne wished for Marshall would be to fall flat on his pretty face someday, but not quite this badly.

Play the game, follow the rules and he could keep his secure job and the life he'd built over the crater his high school years had dug for him. "Whatever you say, Boss."

"Where do you have the original note?"

"Don't worry. I'll bring it in with me tomorrow." This response would keep Sabin from excessive badgering. Officer Kaehne felt he had a tangible amount of control with the white apple bag and attached note in his custody. He'd discarded the apples because they'd begun to rot and dispense a sour smell. The forensic team had already examined a specimen and the rest weren't needed.

District Attorney Sabin had ordered him to be in charge of the white bag because Sabin had a special need for it. Officer Kaehne had thought it was an odd practice, but as Sabin said, he was the boss. By the time Kaehne realized how deep he was in on the unethical practice, he didn't know how to get out.

"Actually, I think you need to take a lunch break at home, or wherever else you stashed it, and get it to me today. I need to be on top of this and there aren't many reasons to delay an arrest for an attempted murder. The evidence doesn't get any fresher," Sabin told him.

Officer Kaehne sensed the district attorney's control. Sabin prolifically manipulated statements and evidence. He considered it part of his job. Sometimes the things you need or want get in the way of integrity. At times, currency and testimonies were interchangeable. He never forgot who slandered and who helped because someday, odds are, they would need him.

* * * *

A soft knock bounced off the door. Both stopped breathing. The knock repeated only louder. Ty held still as the door slowly creaked open.

He didn't miss a beat. His hand dropped softly to Brooke's shoulder. He remained close and gave her a peck on the cheek. Just in time for Chloe to view the concerned ex-husband.

"Oh, I'm sorry if I'm interrupting something, Brooke. I was just wondering how much longer. I should probably get back to the store." Chloe used this as an excuse with an almost sincere smile.

"Ah, yeah. I'm sorry I'm taking so long. I, ah, forgot one thing. I'll grab it quickly and I'll be right out." Brooke hadn't collected a single item, yet. She hadn't gotten past the tennis match of volleys Ty tossed at her.

"I'll let her go soon. I'll be happy when she returns to safety. We were discussing how soon she could get her things back here. Besides, I need my therapist back." Ty offered with a bucket of charm thrown in.

As if fooled, Chloe agreed, "Okay. Hurry, hurry. I'll be in the car."

Brooke gave Chloe a shaky smile and turned back to Ty. "I'll call for another therapist to come out here."

"I want you to do it. You know where I am and what I need. I thought you cared because I'm sure it'll be a setback to have someone new running my therapy."

"That's not fair. You know I've always cared. I…I'll come back and help you. With the new therapist." Brooke broke their eye contact as she looked for help floating in the air. It wasn't there. "I have to go."

"I thought you had some things to collect for your last night." Ty kept insisting she would return.

"Forget it. It's nothing important." Brooke reopened the door. Under her breath, she added, "And it might have been a mistake."

"Excuse me."

"Nothing. I was only thinking of who I need to call for a therapist." Brooke stepped to safety on the other side of the door. "I'll call you later today or tomorrow. I have to go now. Bye."

"I'll be waiting for your call." Ty said no more, but she understood his inference.

Brooke gasped the fresh and chilled air she gladly walked into. The tension escaped her shoulders. She didn't notice the change until her sore shoulder throbbed in protest as the muscles relaxed and pulled down. Straightening herself, Brooke hurried down the sidewalk and eased herself into the warm and waiting car.

"Everything okay?" Chloe didn't comment on Brooke's missing items she'd used as a reason to return to Ty's home.

"Yeah, everything's fine."

Chloe followed Brooke's example and said nothing more. The atmosphere turned as quickly as a cloud passing over the sun. Gray thoughts blanketed her conscience. The black and white world she'd lived in for most of her life felt smothered with uncertainty, and when you don't know the questions to confront, how can you find answers?

"Brooke, what's wrong? What happened over there?" Chloe surreptitiously glanced toward Brooke as she made a right turn. Brooke's cheek supported a liquid shine.

Wiping the evidence with the back of her hand, Brooke responded, "I don't know. I don't know. I'm not even sure where to start." She stopped here again.

When Brooke closed up, Chloe suggested, "We're just about home. When we get there, I have to open my doors, but I also want to talk to you. And I think you need to talk, too."

Brooke sniffled back the increasing tears and agreed.

Sitting again at Chloe's kitchen table, the laughter and cheerful former scene from a few hours ago vanished. Brooke composed herself while Chloe dressed for work, opened her store, and took care of a spontaneous customer.

When Chloe returned, she hurried to the table with a can of soda for each and attempted to open the conversation lightly. "It's a little early for a real drink, so I thought we could start with these." Chloe kneeled on her chair and confronted Brooke. "What happened, Brooke? What upset you so much?" Brooke spontaneously held her chin high and erased the tears as she innocently stared at her friend.

"I'm okay now. It was nothing. I was emotional for no reason in particular."

"Normally I'd let you get away with holding it in, but not this time or else you'll eventually explode. I know there's something going on and I need to know you've figured it out, too."

"What do you mean 'you know'?" Brooke responded startled.

"You tell me." As Chloe urged Brooke to realize the changes in her life, she cocked her head toward the door leading to her business. "I think I hear someone coming in. Just when I want to have a slow day. Think about what's going on because I'll be back and I know you need to get something off your mind."

As Chloe left the room, Brooke seriously recounted the time with Ty. She thought about his actions, the multiple expressions he conveyed, and came up with nothing concrete.

Brooke glanced around the kitchen for a visible phone book. Samples of Chloe's stained glass garnished random spots on the walls and enhanced the sink light, the door light, and every other excuse for light Chloe created. A line of late season herbs hung off the ledge of the sink window. On previous warm days with the sash open, an Italian breeze circulated through the room. A warm comfort seeped into Brooke's chilled bones. Looking further down the counter, she saw a row of multicolored glass jars for holding dried beans, flour, sugar, and herbs, which held a phone book against the red brick backsplash.

Brooke contemplated where to start since she hadn't looked into therapists since Ty's stroke. She picked the most logical place, the organization Marla came from.

"You've already covered for her? Sure, I can be there tomorrow. Thank you so much for your help." As Brooke ended the discussion, Chloe returned and rested against the doorframe.

"Where're you going tomorrow?"

"I need to familiarize the new therapist. I can take a cab. I should've brought my car back today, but I didn't think of it until we got back."

"That's not what I meant, but I gather with another person present nothing will happen."

The calm feeling Brooke had fought for dissipated slowly as her breath left a strangled feeling within her. "Chloe, I'm only doing what I promised.

Ty does need another therapist. He's been doing so well this past year and I haven't gone to nearly as many of the therapies as I used to at the beginning. I would feel responsible if I didn't do this for him."

Chloe placed herself at the head of the table, and said, "Brooke, I know this is hard. I know you feel responsible. It's in your nature, but you have to take into account what's really going on." She didn't wait for Brooke to object. "No matter who aimed their gun at you, no one other than Marla is in custody right now. You can't expect to continue life as if nothing happened." With a softer tone, "I'm only saying this for your own good."

"What do you know that I don't know? I'm just not getting it."

Holding Brooke's attention with their eyes connected, Chloe responded, "Like I said before, you know all the details. The hard part is to sort through them and see where they lead you. To answer your question, the only thing which comes to me that may help you concerns a mix up with the evidence."

At this unexpected disclosure, Brooke urged, "You think the police are making mistakes? Should Marla not be in jail? Are you suggesting Ty should be? Or someone else who hasn't been mentioned in the investigation, yet?" Brooke purposefully left out the remaining name that came to mind.

Chapter 22

Brooke and Chloe weaved up the driveway to the studio early the next morning. Chloe had insisted they didn't park in Ty's drive. As she maneuvered the last curve, Chloe slammed on her brakes. The turn faced the studio along with Ty's adjacent property to expose a view of long since tended gardens turning brown and white with snow. The studio was the reason for the sudden stop, though. It had changed from the creamy-white, wooden structure, complete with a small stone chimney and multiple paned windows, to an incomplete shell.

A smoldering shell.

Brooke's gasp alleviated the silence in the car. She peered through eyes instantly creating new streams of tears. Streams of emotion she visited too often lately. Chloe glanced at her friend and let her foot off the brake to ease the car up the last fifty feet of the drive. The house remained complete. Positioned far enough away to avoid a probable wind, not a flake of ash or soot stuck to the exterior.

Brooke didn't say anything as she riveted her stare to the studio after opening the passenger door. Locked in a moment of despair, Brooke turned her head quickly to see anger darken Chloe's eyes as she exclaimed, "What in God's name is going on? Brooke we should just leave."

"Please, turn around and go to Ty's. He has to know what happened."

With an exasperated expression, Chloe did as instructed. "You shouldn't confront him now."

Not paying attention to Chloe's suggestion, Brooke scooted out of the car and ran to the front door, charging in. "Ty. Ty, where are you?"

"Devastating isn't it?" Ty conceded nonchalantly as he appeared from nowhere. "I didn't realize my ex-wife was making enemies while I slept." At least he got their status correct this time.

Brooke shook her head in utter disbelief. She hastily examined an unscathed Ty, and then said with a quavering tone, "Why didn't you call me? What happened?"

"I didn't call because I knew you'd be here this morning and you need your rest. I took care of it at about five a.m. when I woke up to make a head call."

"What happened?" Brooke repeated, ignoring his male attitude.

"The police want to know who your enemies are. I'm surprised they haven't contacted you, yet." Ty walked closer to where Brooke had rooted herself. "Darling, who's doing this to you? You must have some idea. A jealous artist who wants your new job? Maybe someone who wants your life? A boy-toy who knows he can't have you?"

Brooke shivered at the cold words so easily tumbling from his mouth. Glancing at the wall clock, she hoped the new therapist would show up ten minutes ahead of appointment. She dared to look back at the man who changed daily from her ex-husband to…to someone she didn't recognize. Brooke replied, ignoring the last question, "I'm clueless. I don't understand why or how or who would do any of this." Before she could continue, there was a soft knock on the door behind Brooke's back.

A rush of relief gave Brooke the nerve to unfreeze herself from the spot in which Ty held her. "Can I come in? Are you both okay?" Concerned, Chloe appeared to forcefully included Ty in her sincerity.

Smiling brightly, Ty said, "Hi, yes we're fine. Brooke probably told you she wanted a new studio, anyway."

Chloe cocked an eyebrow toward Brooke just as she began to open her mouth in protest. "The therapist isn't here yet?" Chloe didn't wait for the obvious answer. "Brooke, let's take a look at your studio." She grabbed Brooke's uninjured arm and led her out the door. Chloe shuttled her down the path to the charred sanctuary where Brooke had been happiest.

"I'll say it again. I don't think you should come here anymore. Not until the police have done their job." Brooke held her shaking hand to her forehead and agreed with a mere bob of her chin.

As they neared the remains of the studio, Brooke began to cough. Sobs choked her throat as the air currents lifted the ashes along with smoke, which curled and threw a haze over the morning sun and followed her no matter which way she turned.

"There's nothing left. It's all gone," Brooke managed to say as she studied the leftovers. "That, over there. That was where my work table was." She blinked her eyes in an attempt to see through the tears caused by the demise of her studio and nearly all she existed for during this peculiar time in her life.

Chloe stood close as Brooke continued, "Now I see what kept me alive and hopeful and able to continue my life. It was my work, if you want to call it that. I didn't consider the stained glass work. I loved it."

Kneeling on the path, Brooke reached out for a blackened hinge to gingerly test the metal and observe if it held the heat from its destruction. It was a simple hinge that had opened the door to the biggest and best part of her life. The door that had led her to her worktable was nearly undetectable underneath the rubble. Around it lay melted shingles and burnt two-by-fours. The two-by-fours were probably the remnants of her work table where she first diagramed her ideas for Scott.

The sun countered the near freezing air and warmed the hinge. Brooke brought the hinge to her cheek and smeared the soot from the corner of her dried lips, up her cheekbone, and rested it at a curl of hair at her temple.

Chloe knelt down with Brooke as she resumed sorting through what puzzled her tender psyche for, admittedly, longer than she realized. "It's dead. Yes, my past is dead." Quickly looking into Chloe's face to find acceptance, Brooke explained, "The perfect life I conditioned myself to believe in is dead. It never was. When Ty wasn't the husband I thought I married, I would excuse myself and come to my studio. Here, I could pretend and fantasize that everything was the way it was supposed to be or at least, the way I wanted it to be. When we divorced, I still used this studio, trying to pretend my life was just as good as I had previously fooled myself to believe."

Seeing a quizzical expression cross Chloe's face, Brooke managed a critical laugh at herself. "Don't you see, Chloe? I turned everything inside out so I could exist here. Everything I just said was actually the opposite of reality. I know that now. I admit it. Nothing was right here. After the divorce, I shouldn't have kept using this studio. It's actually on a separate parcel of land, but still attached to my old house property. I should've moved on."

"I'll help you do that, and I think you've finally realized that you need to. That's a good thing," Chloe said encouragingly.

Brooke talked on, as if Chloe hadn't said a word. "I was happy to be alone. Didn't want to meet anyone, and then I accidentally met Scott. And I admit this, too. I fell in love with Scott Marshall. I've never let him know.

"And now he's the one who can't come near me. That's insane."

Brooke abruptly stopped recounting the tale as she stood in response to a lead from Chloe. She wiped under her swollen eyes, removing some and smearing the rest of the chalk-like soot. She laughed softly, with less energy. "You must think I'm nuts by now. I can't make up my mind about my own life and I'm the one living it. Maybe I can let go now that my studio is gone."

"I didn't take it as a truthful comment, about you wishing for a new studio, but it may be a good thing now. At least your current projects are at my house. You didn't lose everything." Chloe offered a positive twist to the destruction. Growing serious for a moment, Chloe said, "I want to get you back to my house. Ty can take care of himself. After all this, he shouldn't expect anything from you."

"I know. You're right, but I have to be here for the therapist."

"Brooke…"

"I won't stay long. I'll only fill her in on where Ty is with his therapy. Let's pick up my car when we leave, and then I'll go directly to your house. I promise."

Before Chloe could make another attempt to haul Brooke away, they heard the sound of an approaching car.

"It's probably the therapist now." Brooke turned toward the driveway.

Chloe wrapped her arm around Brooke's waist as they both spotted the silent red and blues hidden behind the windshield of the car rounding the curve of the drive.

Chapter 23

Walking into his apartment, Officer Denny Kaehne threw his jacket over the back of one of the four marked-up and scarred kitchen chairs. His wife had left for work earlier in the morning along with his kids to drop them at school. He needed this time to himself. Thank God, for a break with time to ferret out his decision.

Deftly unlatching the buckle of his gun holster, he carefully laid it across a space on the table next to the cereal bowl dried with this morning's milk.

He pulled the chair away from the table, causing the jacket to slip to the floor. "Shit," Denny muttered as he bent over, picked the jacket up, and took more care to position it securely on the chair back. He plunked himself onto the chair and thumped his elbows on the table. Lowering his head, he rested his forehead on the palms of his shaking hands. He held this position for a moment until he began to run his fingers through his spiked and lacquered hair. Tossing his head back, he claimed, "I may not be at the top of the ladder yet, but this is going too far."

Even as Denny admitted this to himself, he directed his stare to the coat closet near the door he'd just entered. If he opened the closet, he'd end up being part of something he didn't anticipate or want. He always worked toward a good connection to the top men of law in his community. He was greatly interested in this attempted homicide case, but the procedure was way out of line. He wanted to keep his job, but District Attorney Sabin had a leash on him. He wished he had realized it when he accepted responsibility for that damn bag of apples.

"This is wrong, this is wrong," Kaehne repeated, attempting to convince himself as he heaved out of the chair and took the few steps to the closet. Opening the hollow door, he stared down at the white paper bag with the attached note carefully folded and set in the back corner of the tight compartment.

Officer Kaehne gingerly grabbed the white bag as if it might blow up with his touch. Back to his position at the table, he placed the bag in front of him, smoothing the wrinkles out and obsessively pressing down the crinkled edges as he stared at the tattered note attached.

I picked the sweetest apples for the sweetest man, Brooke.

"What a bunch of crap," Denny muttered. Holding the raffia ends that tied the note to the bag handle, he slowly pulled and watched the loops of the bow disappear. He slid the bag to the back of the table and placed the note in its spot.

Again, he contemplated. What should the note say now? This is where he needed to prove his ability to analyze and rework a handwriting sample.

Chapter 24

"Just what you need," Chloe murmured as she stood close to Brooke.

"I couldn't expect the police to not want to talk to me after this, I guess," Brooke decided. She folded her one arm across her chest as they waited for the unmarked squad car to approach. Willing to hold off the inevitable, Brooke stood her ground as the detectives rummaged between the seats before opening the doors.

With her feet fidgeting and Chloe's embrace tightening around her, Brooke didn't take her eyes off Detectives Gaynor and Rell as they directed their stroll her way.

"This is probably not the best place for you to be, but we assumed we'd find you here," Detective Gaynor commented as he approached the two women. "We first checked Ms. Heathlan's business and home. We saw the note on the front door stating she'd be back in an hour. We then surmised she drove you here to see the remains from the fire."

Before any questions were posed, Brooke stated, "You know more than I do about this. I only came here to help Ty with his new therapist and then I saw this." Brooke turned to the remains of her studio and waved her hand toward it.

"You weren't called by the police? Or Mr. Bellin? No one called you here to see this?" Detective Rell cocked his head to the side in amazement.

"Like I said, I only found out by coming over here."

The questions started. "You didn't get any threats, phone calls, letters, or an email suggesting something of yours was going to be destroyed?"

With a shaky response, Brooke answered, "No, should I have?"

Prefacing his answer, Detective Gaynor explained, "This morning when we met with the firefighters, they named the cause as arson starting in the fireplace, which was probably an attempt to make it look like an accident.

Typically, if someone wants to destroy another's property or belongings which have meaning to them, a warning is first conveyed."

Brooke looked past the detective to the house. Furrowing her brows in a thinking manner, she tried to recall a conversation or statement, which began to float elusively through her mind. She couldn't grasp where it came from.

At the same time Brooke searched her mind, another car crept up the drive and distracted her concentration.

As Brooke looked beyond the detectives because of the car, Detective Rell asked, "Were you expecting someone, Ms. Bellin?"

Attempting to shake the deliberation from her mind, Brooke looked back to the detectives with a blank stare. She had lost her train of thought and wanted it back. She knew there was something she needed to remember.

"Ms. Bellin?"

"Ah, yeah, it must be Ty's new therapist. I came here to help her get acquainted with the therapy room and what he's been doing."

"Ms. Bellin," Detective Gaynor paused until he had her complete attention. "Ms. Bellin, we strongly advise you to have as little contact with Mr. Bellin's home as possible right now." He clarified the hint by adding, "This includes Mr. Bellin."

Chloe had been quiet through the whole exchange between her friend and the detectives. Relaxing her grip on Brooke, Chloe spoke up, "They're right, Brooke."

Confused by this collaboration against Ty, Brooke slowly looked at the faces intently watching her. "But Ty was released."

"Your ex-husband was released on technicalities and an unfinished investigation. He shouldn't have been arrested immediately. Not until the evidence was evaluated properly." Brooke widened her eyes at this information. Detective Gaynor told her more, "We're still watching him. Also, the local police have a different view on the case than we do."

"What do you mean?" Brooke became agitated as she watched the therapist park her car on the far side of the squad.

"We have a few quirks to work out with them, and no one is discounted, yet."

"You mean to tell us you and the local police don't work well together?" Chloe broke in here before Brooke had a chance. It was a ridiculous notion of the law not working together when someone's future was in peril. Brooke knew Chloe could read between the lines effectively.

"Ms. Heathlan, we all work by the same code of ethics."

Unlike Brooke, Chloe challenged his evasiveness. "That's not an answer. If you guys are having a personal or professional, if I dare use the term, difference, how is Brooke supposed to feel safe?"

"We're doing our best. We strongly suggest she stay clear of any of the past or current suspects."

"Who are the suspects now?" Brooke felt a bit of relief at Chloe's attempt to obtain a clear understanding of where the investigation stood.

"We can't place the blame on any one person right now. We still have Ms. Vrahn in custody. Until the forensic team has completed their analysis, we're at a standstill." Detective Gaynor added, "We'll let you know when we hear any results."

Reentering the conversation, Brooke asked, "I'm the one this whole investigation is about, so why can't I know who's involved? Ty must still be a suspect since you don't want me to be around him."

"The district attorney informed us that he made it clear to you after the arraignment to keep away from your ex-husband along with the rest of the possible suspects." Brooke didn't remember the exact conversation, so she took Detective Gaynor's word for it.

Detective Rell kicked a stone lying near his foot as he looked down to study the cracks between the bricks of the walkway. Deciding that she wasn't hearing anything new, Brooke turned and hurried to catch up with the therapist.

"Brooke," Chloe called after her.

Brooke turned while continuing backward up the path and yelled back, "I have to help. I promised." With this, she turned again and greeted the therapist at the door.

"Ms. Bellin, we'll give you fifteen minutes, and then we need you back here," Detective Rell yelled after her. She waived her arm in agreement and disappeared into the house.

* * * *

Turning back to Chloe, Detective Gaynor said, "We'll give her these few minutes because we're right here, and I doubt Mr. Bellin will do anything with all of us around. After this, though, she has to stay away. For her own safety."

With a thoughtful expression painted on his face, Detective Rell confronted Chloe. "You and Brooke seem to be close."

"Yes, we've been friends for a long time beginning when Brooke learned the art of stained glass. She took lessons from me."

"You're more than teacher and student now, I presume?" Detective Gaynor again took over.

"Much more. Granted, we don't have a lot of in-depth, personal discussions. Much of what we know about each other isn't spoken. We just know."

"Must be a woman thing," Gaynor said with a chuckle.

With the serious expression kept firm, Chloe retorted, "No, it's a real 'thing.'"

"Do you have something to tell us without Ms. Bellin here?" Detective Gaynor resumed his professional attitude.

Chloe tightened her lips and deepened her thought for a stretched and silent minute. "First, I have a question for you. Let's see if you agree with what I think."

Chapter 25

"Sorry I'm late for work this morning." Scott caught Justin, a rookie employee, rushing from his truck onto the job sight at Maple Haven Bed and Breakfast.

"Don't make a habit of it. We have a lot of finishing work to do and I'll be picking up a load of the stained glass tomorrow or the next day and I want everyone to be awake when placing them in the structures." Scott let him off easy because he had a lot more on his mind than an occasional late employee.

"Thanks, Boss. I actually did have a reason, if you want to hear it," Justin told him. .

"Shoot."

"On my way to work I had to wait for a stream of fire engines and police cars. I could see smoke probably four or five miles east of here. Apparently there was a road blocked, and the traffic was detoured for a mile and a half." Scott immediately became alert as he clued in on the distance and placement. Justin offered, "I can stay late today, if you need me to. It won't be a problem."

As if something more important occurred to him, Scott absently responded, "No, it's not necessary today. I'll let you know in the next couple of days if I need you for overtime. Right now, help Jeff with the roof of the center gazebo. I'll check back in a bit. I have to make a run for some things I forgot about." With a quick slap on Justin's back, Scott scooted off the plywood bench he used as an outside office and headed for his pickup.

Scott had nearly forgotten about the just finished reprimand as he whipped open his truck door and hurtled his stone dust and sweat covered body inside. Four or five miles east of here. Near Brooke's studio. He barely considered the restraining order the court had slipped over his wrist as he mentally calculated the distance to her studio along with the scrap of information he knew about the fire.

Scott hadn't had contact with Brooke since the night she'd left his home. Brooke, a perfect woman he knew he could love. He had to assure himself the fire didn't involve her, otherwise he had to…

Had to what? Who was he kidding? He couldn't run up to the studio. What if she was near it? Granted, he could probably see from the road. If her studio was fine, he would go back to work. If the fire was at her property, what would he do then? Drive up to see if she needed comforting and to tell her everything would be all right? Brooke might not be there, anyway.

Scott eased his foot off the metal platform under his foot that sped him and his heart to Brooke. "Watch the speed limit," he mentally added. He couldn't turn around at this point, halfway there already. Besides, he hadn't talked to or seen Brooke in what seemed like forever. Scott tried to avoid it, but the thought of possibly catching a glimpse of her dark, silky hair or her tender, yet strong body adrenalized his heart, not to mention his Levi's.

He'd spent too much energy on containing his emotions since Brooke had come home from the hospital. With the surprise and sudden news of the fire, Scott's emotional guard deserted him. He had no choice when the pheromones leapt and squeezed along the unfamiliar path to make his skin tingle with sexual need. He had barely taken the first step for this need, so it was a ridiculous notion to think of Brooke like this.

Angrily, Scott punched at the stereo and tried to locate a station devoid of emotional ballads. Apparently soft rock, soft country, soft everything dominated the morning airwaves. He switched to AM talk radio as an alternative.

"…Can we trust our legal system in this day when there isn't any personal service and everything is controlled by computers or authorities who don't care?" the dramatically high-pitched voice demanded from station 103.1 AM.

The voice lowered its pitch. "Where's the proof? In the machine? In the computer?

"I don't need to answer this question for you who have fallen victim to technology. Should we let it run our lives?" A muffled cough sounded through the speakers.

"There are a lot of gray areas as we stumble through the clouds the justice system and politics are allowing to seep into our decision making of what is right and wrong. Do you agree?

"Call me. Get on the phone and let me know if the black and white of technology should be in charge of decisions in the judicial and political arena," the announcer vehemently demanded of his listeners.

"That's right," Scott murmured in agreement. "Who can make a rule to keep me away from Brooke? The written rule is wrong in this scenario. If nothing else, I certainly would never harm her." After agreeing with the disc jockey, Scott nearly convinced himself to inquire about her after he checked her studio.

A commercial for a local laundry store telling its listeners to keep their act and clothes clean calmed Scott's sudden need for rebellion. He returned to his original intention of driving past Brooke's studio.

As Ty Bellin's house, adjacent to the studio property, came into sight first, Scott sat higher in his seat and strained his eyes as far to the right as he could without making it obvious he wanted to check if it had been part of the fire. He drove a few miles an hour slower so he wouldn't miss anything. He didn't want to repeat this endeavor.

Looking toward the house perched on the hill, Scott didn't detect anything abnormal. The house stood tall and complete from his view. As his truck moved further along the edge of the property, he did see three things worth noting. He saw people in front of the residence, smoke rising in the background, and the absence of Brooke.

Chapter 26

Catching a quick glimpse of the side and a sliver of the front of the house, Scott saw the two detectives he'd previously spoken with at the hospital. He witnessed Chloe talking with them, but he didn't see Brooke in the picture. The dark sedan next to Chloe's car must be an unmarked squad.

Allowing himself to turn his head for a better view, Scott still didn't see Brooke. He did notice the other thing that made his heart beat like a frantic drum. Hazy smoke floated a short distance behind the group in curling waves. The smoke was nearly invisible, and he had to focus to catch the innocuous streams of gray.

With a sudden rumbling of gravel beneath his wheels, Scott brought his sight back to the road as his truck veered toward a ditch filled with broken branches, gravel spray, and tall grass bent over from the previous snow. He quickly jerked the wheel back to the asphalt and exhaled deeply, not realizing until then that he held his breath.

Scott knew he would have to turn around and drive by again. Coming from the other direction would give him a better view of where the smoke came from.

What a joke on his heart. Brooke's studio resided directly underneath the shadow of smoke. Brooke wasn't with the group next to the house.

Scott cursed himself for getting involved. As soon as he allowed his heart to take control, he had no say in its momentum. From bad to worse, Scott conjured a picture of Brooke's charred body lying in the remains of her studio. His heart ballooned with love and longing but was caged temporarily with the restraining order. At this pace, he felt his heart would explode.

Scott pulled into the next driveway, spun his wheels around, and backed out onto the road facing the way he had come. With a little too much energy, he squeaked his tires into fast motion and came upon the site again. This time he quickly glimpsed the rubble of stone and charred wood remaining from Brooke's studio. The same three people stood by the house. Scott didn't hear an ambulance, but if Brooke wasn't with Chloe and the detectives, where was she?

He couldn't bring himself to admit the next thought. If Brooke had been in the studio, an ambulance would've been here by now. Maybe one came and left already, he just didn't know about it.

Scott heavily considered turning into the house driveway to find out the details. As he fought the right and wrong of stopping, he decided that the only right thing to do would be to stop and question the detectives. If he had to go to jail because of it, he'd been in worse predicaments.

Scott pulled up to the detectives as close as possible without running them over. They both turned to the oncoming vehicle with surprised expressions.

He jumped from his truck and charged up to Detective Gaynor and Detective Rell, and shouted, "Where is she? Did anything happen to her? Tell me where she is." He clenched his fists, turning the knuckles white.

"Whoa, hold on there, Mr. Marshall." Detective Gaynor raised his arms straight out with palms flexed as Detective Rell reached for his gun.

Chloe ran up to Scott. "Scott, she's okay. She wasn't in the fire." Scott turned to her, still tense and loaded with adrenalin. He saw a look of warning from Chloe as she quickly filled him in and the detectives moved to block the path to the Ty's home. "She's at my house. I made her stay there."

Gaynor looked at Chloe and cut in. "That's right, she's fine. We need you to leave the premises."

"Leave? What the hell for? She's not here and I want to know what's going on." Scott turned on the detective. "I talked to my attorney and he said the restraining order was filed by her ex as a legal guardian. What the hell does she have a guardian for and what right does he, or anyone else have in making decisions for her?"

"Mr. Marshall, calm down."

"I'll calm down when I get some answers."

"We're working on them. We'll get this mess straightened out."

Anger coated his words, as Scott breathed heavily and said, "That's what everyone is telling me, 'We'll straighten this out' and I haven't seen a bit of progress since Brooke left the hospital."

Detective Rell glanced toward the house, then returned his attention to the confrontation, saying, “There has been progress. We can’t give you the details yet.”

“Hang in there. Be patient,” Detective Gaynor warned Scott.

Scott scowled, glared at the detectives, and turned back to his truck. As he stepped into the cab, he craned his neck out the window and told the detectives, “There’s no way I’m staying away from Brooke much longer. And there’s no way whoever shot her is going to get away with it.” After the last word, he sprayed gravel as he reversed his truck to the road.

Too quickly arriving at the job, Scott didn’t turn in. He headed for a few minutes of down time to think of what to do next. He was going to see Brooke. He was going to keep her safe. A plan, he needed a plan and his mind was beginning to work. He accelerated his truck and took the next right turn.

Chapter 27

Still standing in the driveway, Chloe spoke first after Scott left. "Is there a reason District Attorney Saban 'let' Ty go?"

Detective Gaynor lowered his head in disgust. He didn't like being part of a twisted investigation that he sensed from the beginning. The local authorities left a murky trail as they worked the attempted homicide case and he was sure other loose ends would eventually be revealed. Gaynor answered with his own question. "That's the question you have for us?"

"I'm sure I could think of more, but that's the first one to come to mind," Chloe answered. Her garb of dark colors with an ankle length skirt covering the tops of a pair of English boots, gave her the look of a quiet and soft-spoken, middle-aged woman, but it didn't detour her from being outspoken. She stood her ground and waited for an answer.

"There's a lot of investigation to be covered, yet," Detective Rell began as he looked to his partner for confirmation.

"That doesn't answer my question. There's more to it, isn't there?"

Not treading on fellow workers from the police profession, Detective Gaynor answered, "Actually, it is an answer. Many follow-up checks on evidence already in custody are happening. The forensic team is at work. Then a conclusion will be determined before more action on suspects."

Releasing his breath slowly, Detective Rell appeared relieved he didn't have to come up with an answer for Chloe. Detective Gaynor supplied a smooth cover-up of what they really thought of the police department's investigation practices. Lowering his head slightly once again, Rell looked over to Gaynor.

The expression Detective Gaynor displayed showed nothing. The stern expression and pencil-thin line where his lips held tight revealed he didn't appreciate being harassed about the department's abilities.

The silence impressed the lack of satisfaction on Chloe's part. "I have a proposition for you."

Gaynor's eyebrows twitched with annoyance. Attempting to alter the conversation, he looked at his watch and commented, "She has five more minutes otherwise, Rell, I want you to go in and get her."

Chloe looked toward Detective Rell. "Why don't you go in there a few minutes early to see if everything is copasetic?"

Detective Rell shot a look at his partner. Gaynor wasn't in the habit of taking orders from civilians, but under the circumstances it was a relevant request. A line of thought crossed his forehead. He matched Rell's waiting stare and nodded. "Yeah, why don't you see what's going on? Ms. Bellin might need assistance in excusing herself."

Detective Rell cocked his head to the side and retreated to the main door.

After the door shut behind Rell, Gaynor turned back to Chloe, ready to put the discontentment to sleep with a softer approach not intended for his partner to witness. "Ms. Heathlan, we're doing all we can. We want to find the perpetrator as much as you do." Her forehead crinkled with displeasure, and Gaynor gave up the easy touch. "What do you want me to say? I can't discuss the inner workings of the police department with everyone who doesn't fully understand our tactics and how we work."

"I want you to tell me the truth. I know there's more to it. I'm good at reading between the lines." Again giving him a stare, which could crack a marble statue, Chloe looked directly into his eyes. "I can help you more than you think." Gaynor detected a line with bait attached at this comment.

His face contorted with a wary interest. "What do you mean 'you can help us more than we think?' Are you withholding information? We don't buy evidence, if you're suggesting this. Also, if you're withholding possible evidence, *you* can be arrested. " As an afterthought, he added, "And there aren't any lines to read between."

"No? I think there is. I'm not selling anything. I have an ability quite out of the ordinary, but some police departments welcome such help."

Standing back an extra step, Detective Gaynor briefly acknowledged Chloe's attire and her mannerisms. "What, are you some kind of psychic or something?" Expecting her to laugh at this suggestion, Gaynor immediately knew he hit on what she implied. "Unbelievable." He couldn't come up with any way to better articulate his astonishment and initial uncertainty and what to do about this unusual revelation.

Chloe pulled Detective Gaynor from the deep thoughts he habitually fell into when confronted with an extraordinary circumstance. "Well, believe it."

"Okay, try me. Tell me something to convince me you pull vibes from the air and can figure this case out," Detective Gaynor demanded. His sarcasm didn't resonate the way he intended. He'd heard of psychics who helped legal departments locate clues, but he hadn't personally worked with any, and he didn't want to appear too eager.

"I can tell you trust me but don't want to."

"If that's the beginning of your psychic news, it wasn't very good. Your time is running out."

Chloe half-smiled, looked around the porch near the door where they waited for Detective Rell and Brooke, and revealed a hint. "Detective Gaynor, I can't specifically tell you who shot Brooke, but I have an important scrap of information to help find out."

"Go on." Gaynor fixed his stare on Chloe.

"There are two pieces of falsified writings. What I mean is, they have either been altered or were never factual."

"Do you know what kind of writings they are?" Detective Gaynor became interested. Anything to help clarify the mud the police officers threw into the mix.

Chloe grimaced, shaking her head. As she took a breath to explain what she knew, the front door opened and Detective Rell escorted a weary and red-eyed Brooke.

Chloe ran over to Brooke and grabbed her hand. "Brooke, is everything okay? What happened inside?"

Brooke's voice trembled in a low tone. "The nurse will work out fine. She's experienced with cases similar to Ty's."

"No, what happened? Why are you all shook-up? You don't get upset like this for nothing."

Brooke looked up, blinking her eyes to gather the tiny tears on her lashes. "Ty thinks the burning of my studio is probably a good thing because he doesn't want me to keep working. He says I should return to him and he'll take care of me."

"Brooke," Chloe discreetly began while still holding her hand, "you're not his anymore. When will he get that through his thick head?"

"It's okay. He only meant to comfort me since my studio is gone. It already happened and it's a done deal." Sucking in a great deal of air as her tremble lightened, Brooke added, "I'll still finish my big project, though." She looked down at her shoes. "Scott's project."

"What happened?" Gaynor repeated to Detective Rell.

"Nothing physical. Ms. Bellin showed the nurse the usual procedure. Mr. Bellin seemed to delight in letting his ex-wife know he could keep her busy since she didn't have a studio anymore."

"Did he actually say he's glad it burned?" Detective Gaynor asked.

"No, but I got the feeling."

Brooke's gaze bounced back and forth while the detectives discussed her as if she hadn't left the house.

"We'll discuss this back in our office. Now we need to escort these ladies from the premises." Detective Gaynor left the details for later review.

The women took the clue and began to walk toward the cars. Brooke angled toward Chloe's vehicle. Detective Rell followed Brooke as she dragged behind Chloe and Detective Gaynor.

Chloe tugged on Gaynor's sleeve. "Detective, Brooke doesn't know anything about what I just told you, so don't ask her about it. I don't want to upset her more. This whole ordeal is nothing more than a ride on an ice covered road. One minute you think you're in control and the next you're facing the wrong direction."

"I want to talk to you about this again. Soon," Gaynor added quickly as Brooke and Detective Rell caught up. Addressing Chloe and Brooke, Gaynor told them, "We'll follow your car to Ms. Heathlan's residence, and then we'll be back to speak with you later today."

"Detective Gaynor, we have to stop and pick up my car along the way."

As Gaynor nodded, he informed, "We'll get a few things straightened out about things you should know." He made a mental list of what he could safely tell them and of how Chloe's fortune telling would affect his next step.

Chapter 28

Chloe wheeled into her drive, followed by Brooke. She stationed her VW behind Chloe's eclectic mix of statues near the drive, which curved around the back of Glass Arts. As they retreated from their respective cars, the detectives watched them enter Chloe's home through an entrance to her kitchen. The detectives rolled away as the door shut out the chilly breeze.

Brooke didn't wait for an invitation, but rather sat heavily at the kitchen table. Chloe came close to her and put a hand on her shoulder. "Brooke, I'll be back in a flash. I have to open my doors, so I can stay in business." Brooke looked up without an effort at a smile and nodded her consent.

Chloe moved with urgency to unlock the front door. Flipping the "open" sign over, she glanced around and shook her head at the lack of time she'd spent on the floor of her obsession. With a mental note that everything seemed in place and she could resume business with the jingle of the worn bells hanging from a hook on the door, Chloe quickly returned to the kitchen.

From a first glance, Brooke held her head straight, appearing to deliberate the morning's events with a controlled mind. As Chloe rounded the table, she saw the tears roll in a haphazard stream over Brooke's structured cheeks. The late morning light stripped any remaining color Brooke had attained from the hours spent in the sun through the summer and autumn. The only color came from her redlined, dull green eyes.

Chloe wrapped her arms around Brooke's shoulders, being careful not to squeeze the healing wound on her left side. She pressed her cheek to the dampness covering Brooke's skin and held her in silence for a moment.

Breathing in a stuttered flow of air, Brooke opened the conversation. "I'm okay." Nothing else.

"Brooke, you're so strong and I'm here for you to say whatever you need to." Knowing Brooke wasn't as she said, Chloe added, "I know you're thinking 'what's next?' This is a horrible and vindictive act against you again, and it will end." Not wanting Brooke to think she knew how and when the attacks would stop because of her unique ability to see the future, Chloe explained, "The detectives are on the right track and they'll...*they will* be the winners."

Brooke showed no reaction to these desperate comments.

"Oh, I'm sorry, Brooke. I don't know what to say. This is such an unreal situation. But it's true. I'm here for you and the detectives are going to find whoever is tormenting you."

"I know. I know you're all trying to help me through this. It does feel traumatic. The shooting and now the fire. But I think the hardest part is what it's doing to my emotions." Brooke lifted her face to look at Chloe. "I know I'm a mess."

"Nothing a nice warm towel soaked in chamomile can't remedy," Chloe readily offered.

Brooke reached out her right hand and grasped the loose sleeve delicately covering Chloe's slender arm. "Chloe, I don't know what to think or what to do. I'm in turmoil as to who, other than you, I can even turn to."

Brooke began to analyze the people intimately involved in her life. "One minute Ty wants to hold me and comfort me, acting as if he wants me as his wife again. The next he portrays happiness at what happened to me. I must be misunderstanding what he thinks because I can't imagine his switching of nature is truly taking place. He must feel one way or the other."

She let go of Chloe's sleeve, and added, "This morning Ty told me he's going hunting next weekend. I know he planned this hunt quite a while ago, but I'm surprised he didn't cancel it. I'm shocked he can even think about it right now."

She continued to spill contradictions onto the table. "And Scott. Scott has been a saint to me. I can't imagine him involved in anything corrupt, yet I really haven't known him for too long nor am I familiar with what his whole life consists of. And there's the restraining order. Why? The DA avoided any direct answer when I asked him about it. He said he'd check into it. He hasn't done anything as far as I know."

"Did you ever call any other attorneys?"

"That day. I forgot to tell you, but I called three or four lawyers and when I mentioned what was going on, they all backed off." Brooke drummed her fingertips on the table. "It almost seemed like they were afraid of the DA."

A thought came to Chloe, similar to the one about the falsified writings. "Brooke, maybe something's up with the district attorney's work ethics. That may be a stretch, but you never know."

Brooke's fingers stopped their music. "That didn't occur to me. Do you think the detectives, since they're from out of town, have thought of that?"

With a flash of insight, Chloe said, "I think they're objective, so it's possible."

Holding up a hand to keep Brooke's questions for the end of her sermon, Chloe skipped back to Scott as a topic. "And Scott, he has a resounding aura. With him, it's up to you to lead the path." She purposefully didn't mention Scott's heated exchange from earlier.

"What do you mean? Now, whenever you mention a 'path,' I instinctively think I had better listen. The last time you told me to change paths, I didn't follow your advice, and look what happened."

"Don't take my comment so literarily. This time I just think Scott is similarly confused and will leave the leading to you until he's sure not to cause you any harm. Just be yourself. This is one time I believe in listening to your heart because the logic of the whole situation leads you in whatever avenue you happen to be in the mood for. In other words, it may get you lost."

"Are you giving me a reading right now?" Brooke tilted her eyes to Chloe and emitted a small laugh.

"No dear, this isn't a reading. It's just life. You'd probably tell me the same things, if our roles were reversed," Chloe informed. As the mood lightened, she told her, "I need to check my messages since I opened late today. Do you need anything? Are you going to be alright?"

"Chloe, you're so good to me." Brooke stood up and wrapped her healthy arm around Chloe's shoulder this time. "Thank you. I think I'll walk down to the coffee house and get us a dose of espresso, and then I'll leave you alone to work for a while. I should probably get to work, too."

"I like your idea. Not about working, but I do have a lot of catching up to do. A little caffeine may help me get inline quicker," Chloe agreed as Brooke reached for her coat and purse.

"I probably need to get out for a few minutes, if nothing else. I'll be back quickly." Brooke carefully slipped her coat on and left from the back door.

Chloe began with her messages. The red circle blinked repeatedly, telling her she had missed a handful of phone calls. Getting ready with her pen and stack of scrap paper, she rested her hand with the pen on the table that stationed her communication gear.

As the first two calls informed her of clients looking for particular stained glass apparatus, she wrote down what she needed to check on before she returned their calls. As she finished scribbling her last reminder, the next voice made her stop writing.

Chloe hurriedly rewound the unfinished message to hear it with accuracy. "That's what it said," she whispered with urgency as a beep sounded and the next message started.

She slipped a quick look at the antiquated clock ticking on the wall above her phone station. Granted, the clock hung with a slight cant to the right and the pendulum no longer swung, but it kept accurate time.

Scott Marshall would arrive in fifteen minutes to pick up the finished glass Brooke had stacked neatly in the supply room. Chloe knew it would be best for Scott to pick up the glass and leave before Brooke returned, but she also felt if Brooke would get to see him for a few minutes, it might raise her spirits a bit.

She stood up and raised her fingers to tap her mouth as she contemplated whether or not to make sure they met.

A heavy rap resounded on the wooden back door.

Startled from her thinking, Chloe jumped and turned to get the door. "I guess my decision has been made for me. Whatever happens, happens," She murmured while reaching for the handle.

Pulling the door open, Chloe stood face to chest with a ruggedly handsome and tired looking landscaper. "Scott, come in." As Scott nodded appreciation at the invite and stepped into her kitchen, Chloe explained, "I was just listening to your message. We just got back a short time ago."

"Yeah, I figured." Scott didn't mention the former show he put on. "How's Brooke doing after hearing about the fire?"

"She's fine physically. It does scare her a bit that she was attacked again." As Chloe stepped back so Scott could enter and leave room to close the door, he glanced past her obviously checking to see if he could catch a glimpse of Brooke. Answering the unasked, Chloe said, "Brooke went down the street to get us a coffee."

Scott didn't show any of the aggression he had fallen into earlier. "Oh. I only need to pick up the glass." He stopped for a moment. "I hoped I could have a word with her. About the work, I mean. I know I'm not supposed to see her, but you'd be here to make sure nothing happened."

"I was thinking about it when you knocked on the door. The biggest problem with seeing her is the detectives are going to be stopping by, and I don't know what time. I wouldn't want the two of you to be seen together."

"That wouldn't be a good thing," Scott agreed with a sigh. He apparently accepted the fact that he needed to follow the rules until the legal restraint had its chance in court. Chloe could only imagine the resentment building in him at this point "Well, I suppose I'll just get the glass."

"They're in the supply room, this way." Chloe turned to lead him. With a resigned expression, Scott followed.

Chloe wound her way through the supply room and stopped at the back. Directing Scott to a stack of meticulously covered random shapes of flat articles, Chloe said, "Here're the finished ones." Chloe bent down and began pulling the relevant items off a low shelf.

Scott picked up the top glass and pulled the wrapping from it. Gazing at the naked figure painted on the smoky glass, Scott commented in nearly a whisper, "They're perfect. So like Brooke to paint something so beautiful."

With respect to the emotion in his tone, Chloe agreed, "Yes, Brooke has a way with transferring intense feeling into her art."

As if he were here strictly for work, Scott rewrapped the glass and bent forward to collect a stack.

Fortunately, Scott had a strong hold on the next stack of glass as a voice chimed her arrival.

"Chloe, I lost control and got us more than coffee." Brooke talked as she traveled toward the sounds she detected in the supply room. "They had so many warm and sweet smelling treats that I couldn't help myself..." She lost her voice as she stepped into the supply room, nearly bumping into the backside of Scott.

"Oh," was the only thing Brooke could say as a gasp of surprise escaped.

Scott turned quickly still grasping the glass he had just lifted. "Brooke."

They simply stared at each other. Brooke didn't know whether to run and hide from him or to have him drop everything and fall into her embrace.

While looking at the storeroom clock, Chloe was the first to voice a complete sentence. "You must've been meant to run into each other today. Actually, I'm glad it happened. You both need it."

A smile crept over Brooke's lips as she watched Scott's mouth return the gesture.

"Not to turn a joyous reunion sour, but it'll have to be fast. Don't forget, the detectives will be here eventually."

Brooke bowed her head at the last remark as Scott rested the edge of the glass back on the shelf. His eyes never left her.

With an excited shrug, Chloe instructed, "You two stay here for a few minutes. I'll go out front and watch for the detectives. I'll warn you if I see them."

Still left with little vocabulary, Brooke and Scott nodded their agreement and appreciation as Chloe moved quickly to leave them. She cautiously added, "Move fast if I tell you they're approaching. And Scott, make sure they don't see you leave. You parked your truck in the back, right?"

"Yes, thankfully."

Chloe acknowledged his comment and hurried to the front of the store.

Scott averted his eyes only for a moment as he returned the stack of glass to its original place on the shelf. Tentatively holding a hand out, he simply whispered, "Brooke." After another shorter pause, he gained momentum. "I didn't think I was going to get to see you. This was the only way I could think of. To come over for the glass with the hope you would be here."

Brooke took his extended hand. She had many times fantasized that she would feel his strength through a touch. Looking down at their connection, she nervously fingered his palm. "Scott, I'm very confused." She made an uncomfortable gesture with her shoulders. She wanted to say so much, to tell him how she felt and how her interest in him had grown. Why couldn't she verbalize her feelings for him when given the chance? All the thoughts and discussions she imagined and obsessed about while falling asleep at night became muddled, and she didn't know where to start.

Scott put his free hand on her shoulder. "I wanted, *still* want to be the one to help you through this. Tell me what I can do."

Brooke felt trapped in silence. Where were the words? She grew frustrated with herself and knew their time had a limit. She didn't want to waste another second. As if she had to push a button to open the trap, Brooke found her way. She didn't know which trap door she opened but out tumbled, "Scott, I like you. I like you more than I should or can admit. This is all such a mess, and I don't know how I can do this. Maybe it's an unrealistic fantasy of mine, having no chance of coming true. How can I move from one life, completely erase it without any repercussions, and step into the perfect world I dared to imagine? I wanted to ask you something, too."

With a soft, yet serious tone, Scott responded, "Shh…Brooke, one thing at a time. You put too much pressure on yourself. The only control you have over the crime against you is to keep yourself safe." Taking a quick look at his wristwatch, Scott quickly added, "This isn't how I imagined our reunion, but how can I expect the shooting, investigation, and now the fire not to affect our time?"

Brooke interrupted him, "That's not what I meant to say." Struggling to say the right thing, she found new tears to emphasize her statement. "I wanted to say the perfect thing, but I don't know what it is." Looking over Scott's head at the shelves loaded with the craft that brought them together, she tried to right her speech and stop the tears. "I just wanted to tell you how much I miss you, but everything seems to have changed."

With a perplexed deepening of his light brown eyes, Scott told her, "Brooke, I miss you, too. I miss everything about what we had and what I wish for in the future. I haven't changed. You believe me don't you?"

Brooke focused on his eyes. "Yes, I don't believe anything they say about you."

"Who's saying what about me?" Scott combed his hand through his hair as he waited for Brooke to clarify her statement. She realized he knew less than she did, which wasn't much.

"I don't know all the details, but when the police finally tell me what they're doing and what they think they know, I won't be able to believe anything against you."

Before Brooke got up the nerve to ask him the "something," the bell on the front door jingled. Brooke and Scott froze. They tensed and waited for Chloe to clue them in on who'd entered. Brooke released Scott's hand, held through their entire discussion, and let him guide her to the side of the supply room.

Scott furtively looked along the wall near the door. "Brooke, do you know where the light switch is? It may be to our advantage to turn it off."

Coming to life, Brooke crept a couple feet further from Scott's gaze and reached for an old switch loosely attached to the wall. As the light silently faded, Brooke commented, "The switch is in an odd place. Chloe always complains about it, but it's not high on the list of things to change right now."

Scott reached out and brought Brooke close to him again. This time he pulled her chest to his and held her. No more words. He held her tightly while resting his lips on her forehead.

Brooke felt the heat of Scott's body penetrate her sweater. She felt the rush of his breath slow as a minute passed without a signal from Chloe. "I think we're okay." Changing the subject, Scott admitted, "I do have to get the glass in my truck and should be gone before the detectives arrive."

"Definitely. That's a good idea." Brooke knew she had to agree to his logic.

"I want to spend more time with you. I'll try to return later, after the detectives leave. Is this alright with you?"

"Yes, please do. I miss you so much." She longed for a repeat of the last minute. That minute could expand into hours and she'd still want more. "You better call first to make sure no one sees you."

"Definitely." Scott returned his look to the plates of glass. "I better load these."

Brooke nodded as he turned to reach for the stack of glass he'd originally started with. As Brooke moved to help, Scott ordered, "Don't help me. I want this to last a few extra minutes before I have to leave."

She smiled in response and let Scott do the work. She stood at the door to open and close it for him, trying to keep the cold outside.

As Scott turned from his truck to get the last load, Brooke heard a vehicle pull up to the front of Glass Arts. Leaning out the door, she saw it was a dark sedan.

Scott looked to the front. "Brooke, the two men in the car don't look like typical artists. I can't see them clearly, but I have a feeling I don't want to hang around any longer."

Brooke's expression switched gears. "Quick, Scott, you better go. It's probably the detectives, and I don't want them to see you with me." She knew he understood her meaning after the brief rekindling.

Scott made a move to mount his truck and disappear. Brooke stood at the door to assure his departure. It should have been a quick move, but Scott remained in the seat rummaging through the tossed items at his side. The faint sound of jingling bells tinkled as the business door opened.

Brooke craned her neck to discern the holdup. At this time, Scott shoved his door open and jumped out, running back to Brooke. "Brooke, my keys. They must be inside." Skipping over half the steps on the porch, Scott squeezed past Brooke. The light was still out. She hoped he didn't need it, hoped the keys were in plain sight.

Scott searched the tables for his keys, coming up with nothing. Brooke realized Scott needed extra time, so she kept an eye toward the door leading to the showroom. She heard heavy footsteps of more than one set of shoes.

* * * *

Chloe had a customer to provide an extension of time until she acknowledged the detectives and began to talk creatively in a louder voice aimed to the back.

Finding an opportune moment, Chloe said to the customer, "Let me check in back to see if I have more of the size of copper you need."

Just as Chloe attempted to excuse herself, Detective Gaynor interrupted, "Ms. Heathlan, do you mind if we have a look around?" The question held the tone of a sure answer.

Chloe stopped with her hand on the doorknob of the supply room. She hoped Brooke was the only one behind the door.

Chapter 29

As Brooke listened to Chloe and her customers, she forgot about her unasked question and turned to Scott. “Scott, the people who came in have to be the detectives. Chloe’s acting differently. We can’t be found together.” Brooke didn’t need to refer to the restraining order and the consequences of breaking it.

“If I leave now, they’ll see me or at least know we were together.”

Brooke shook her hands in front of herself to release building nerves. “We have to think of something. Fast. Where can I hide?” Brooke scanned the supply room. Only shelves and three uncovered tables filled the back room. Nothing to close herself in and hide.

“Brooke. Brooke, take a breath. If I have to stay here because of my truck, then you have to disappear.” The clock barely changed as Scott whispered a plan.

* * * *

Chloe fumbled with the previously working doorknob. Looking over her shoulder to the detectives who stood behind her, she explained, “This is an old doorknob and I sometimes have trouble with it.”

“Need some help?” Detective Rell questioned.

“No, no I have it.” Every second counted, but Chloe’s time expired. She hoped Brooke and Scott had read the signs and knew to evacuate or come up with a plan.

Chloe slowly opened the door as if she needed to avoid knocking into something. “This is my supply room, if you want to take a look.” At this point, Chloe turned around and looked herself. Scanning the room, she didn’t see anyone. Not sure if she should be relieved yet, she walked in and blocked as much of the detectives' view as she could with her swaying skirt and waving her arms in a wide gesture to reveal the back room.

Breathing out relief at the empty room, Chloe began to talk rapidly. "This is where I store my…"

"Where's Ms. Bellin right now?" Detective Gaynor interrupted with obvious disinterest in what the room held.

"Uh…I believe…"

The door to the outside swung open. With the power of a confident male, Scott stepped from the porch and reentered the building as if he belonged. The detectives exchanged glances.

Fortunately, the detectives were more in favor of Scott than the involved police officers. Detective Gaynor redirected his question. "Where's Ms. Bellin?"

"Chloe arranged for Brooke to be at the coffee house while I picked up her work. We're following the rules, Detective," Scott matter-of-factly informed him. Against his customary character, Scott submissively added, "I wouldn't want to make this any harder on Brooke than it is already. I'll play by the rules." Chloe watched Scott as he didn't take his stare off the detectives.

* * * *

Scott picked up the last load of glass and continued with it to his truck. As the detectives evacuated the supply room with Chloe close behind, Scott contemplated Brooke's unasked question. She had thrown her jacket on, vanishing down the street to head for the coffee house a second time.

He didn't want to assume that everything was okay between them, but with such a short reunion, it was hard to tell. "Hopefully Brooke knew I wanted to see her and today wasn't an accident," he told the cab of his truck as he slipped in after he completed his pickup.

Having forgotten about his keys again, Scott stopped the truck door from closing and returned to the cold to retrace his steps. He walked up and down the trail he'd left to the back door while angling his eyes differently with each return. Just as additional frustration enveloped him, he saw the metal ring attached to his keys underneath the first step of the porch. Apparently, they'd fallen from his pocket and bounced off the bottom step.

As he kneeled down to retrieve his keys, he glanced down the street to see if Brooke was on her way back. He wanted her so badly, but maybe it was better for now that he wouldn't have another incomplete, two-minute visit.

He returned to considering an attempt to stop by tonight with genuine curiosity about her question. He started his truck and proceeded to back out to the street, bothered by the unfinished conversation.

Chapter 30

"Did you change it?" District Attorney Sabin didn't bother with a greeting.

Officer Kaehne threw the note in question on Sabin's desk.

Sabin scrutinized that his office door was closed and no one would break in with an urgent message. He put his hand over the small square of paper attached to the white apple bag as he stared expectantly at the officer.

Officer Kaehne didn't answer, but rather scowled and turned his head to the window.

Ignoring the apparent dislike of Kaehne's task, Attorney Sabin asked, "You checked to make sure the paper used was the same kind as the original, right?"

Officer Kaehne clipped a short answer, "I analyzed it."

"What about the dirt smears?"

"Those, too."

Digging for all the pertinent information, Sabin didn't forget anything. "The ink?"

"The ink is from a simple Bic medium point black pen. I traced the letters necessary and filled the rest in with the computer."

Sabin knew Officer Kaehne excelled in this field, yet he waited for further assurance. "I checked everything. It's as good as it's going to get."

Releasing his tension, District Attorney Sabin pushed back in his chair with a couple of inches of his stomach stretched over a worn belt. "Good job, Officer. I knew I could count on you. You're moving up fast in the ranks with your knowledge and cooperation. Glad we 'stole' you from the Chicago PD." The tainted compliment made no impression on the young officer.

Officer Kaehne ignored the comment and asked, "Can I go now?"

"Uh, one more thing." Before Officer Kaehne interrupted, Sabin announced, "If you're on the stand, which you probably will be, you didn't have the bag of apples and the note at your apartment. Agreed?"

"Whatever you say, Boss." His dark eyes matched the district attorney's stare. The door clicked heavily as Officer Denny Kaehne departed.

Sabin pulled himself forward in time with the banging of the windowed door. Crossing his hands over one another, he leaned toward his calendar, jammed with notes along with scribbles and changes that were common on a daily basis. He wanted to put some time between Officer Kaehne's visit and his next task. He hadn't put this matter on his written list. Sabin didn't worry about forgetting to include this mission as soon as possible.

Looking at the clock, he figured a good twenty minutes should pass before he visited the evidence room. It was unlikely the evidence room and Kaehne's attendance would be connected, but no sense in alerting anyone in the office who might be bored with their work and looking for anything odd to jumpstart an idle mind.

Scribbles and names on his calendar reminded him of phone calls to make to attorneys, paralegals, and various officers on a dozen other cases. Sabin scheduled time for research that he only trusted himself to do, all before a short appearance in court at three. The list wasn't too draining, but once it became active the time would slip away like the butter on a cob of corn.

Sabin picked up the grimy handle of his desk phone and made the first call. Unbelievable as it was, even district attorneys had to hold. As he waited impatiently four and a half minutes, the delay gave him unnecessary time to sweat out the details of his unlisted task. Grateful even for the nasally voice to cut his thoughts, he did his business and made the next call on the list.

The supposed five-minute calls brought him into the next hour, so he pushed aside his list, picked up the scrap of dirt-encrusted paper Officer Kaehne had left with him, and headed out of his office.

"I'll be back in fifteen," District Attorney Sabin barked over his shoulder to the secretary occupied with answering calls and repeatedly informing the callers of his absence for the rest of the day in accordance with orders from that morning.

"Where can I find you, if there's an emergency?" The secretary asked as her head popped up from the most recent note she penned.

"I'm not the first one on a murder scene, so I'm sure they can wait 'til I return," Sabin remarked with irritation.

The secretary let it go. Sabin didn't look back to see her dismiss his remark, but headed for the brown elevator doors a hundred feet down the hall.

He pushed the button marked for the basement. The elevator gave a slight jerk and swiftly rumbled down the four floors. Sabin checked his watch. Nearing noon, the evidence room dispatcher would close the room and head for lunch. This would actually be the best time to be alone in the restricted area.

"Just in time, Jake." Sabin changed to an amiable tone as he confronted the dispatcher. "I hoped to catch you before recess. I need to take a look at the Bellin case evidence."

"You've got five minutes until I leave for lunch," Jake smirked as he looked at Sabin. District attorneys didn't have to follow all the rules. "Unless you want to make sure no one else comes in while I'm gone, then I'll make an exception."

"I'll take the deal. I'd rather have peace and quiet, anyway."

"Good. Just sign your prescription here, and I'll be out of your way for thirty or maybe forty minutes after I bring the evidence out," Jake instructed as he tapped on the register. He turned to a padlocked gate standing between him and the secured evidence. Pulling a dull key from the chain on his belt, he unlocked the gate, entered, and shut it behind himself. Only Jake had access to this room.

Sabin rubbed his chin and glanced around the entry as he waited for the dispatcher to return. Peering at Jake's computer, he noticed Jake didn't logout. This would make it even easier for him to add the evidence to the list already compiled and as an added bonus, the origin of the information would be on the dispatcher's computer. Perfect.

Jake clanged the gate open again and came out wheeling a dolly loaded with cardboard boxes labeled as evidence in black marker. "This is everything as of now. I'll put it by the table, and you can go at it. If you leave before I get back, lock the door behind you, okay? It'll be my ass if this room is unlocked with no one in it. I still have to follow some rules."

"Definitely. Thanks for setting me up."

"You bet." Glancing at the register, Jake repeated, "Don't forget to sign in. It's another rule I abide by." Jake grabbed his coat as he watched the district attorney scribble his name and time on the next available line.

"Now get out of here. I have work to do," Sabin mocked.

"I'm gone." Jake left through the same door Sabin had used.

Hunching up his shoulders and preparing for battle, Sabin went to the evidence table. Knowing he couldn't waste time if he wanted to accomplish everything in one visit to reduce scrutiny and purpose of dragging the files out, he pulled the boxes from the floor and spread them on the table.

Sabin studied the labels, which revealed the contents of each box. The top box contained victim body evidence, then interview dialogue, hospital records, and additional boxes for individual suspects, and crime scene physical evidence. He stopped his search here.

As Sabin sat at the designated office chair, he arranged all the boxes in a semi-circle around the edge of the table. He wanted them to appear as if he needed the room in front of him. Also, he wanted to obscure the angle of the security cameras. Opening a flapped lid, Sabin began to pull out the plastic bags and copied notes. Halfway through the familiar findings Sabin looked around the room.

"Stupid move," Sabin thought. "No one's here. I shouldn't appear to be checking for anyone." He returned to checking the different bags of evidence until he felt confident.

Keeping focused on his project, Sabin slipped his hand inside his coat pocket. He pulled out a pen and began to scrawl nonsense on the legal pad set between the boxes.

He again reached into his coat pocket. This time he retrieved the plastic bag labeled as crime scene evidence. Evidence found near the victim. Evidence in the shape of a dirty white bag attached to a small square of paper.

Chapter 31

"I see her coming down the street," Chloe said as she peered out a window.

"Quite the chilly day for a walk for someone recovering from a gunshot wound," Detective Gaynor mentioned.

Chloe raised her eyes in surprise. "Scott Marshall needed to pick up her work, so she volunteered to leave. We're trying to follow orders. Actually, I think the walk may be good for her. She's always liked being outside."

Gaynor raised his shoulders in retreat. Chloe returned her gaze to the window and watched Brooke step carefully on the hastily shoveled sidewalk while balancing a carton holding two cups of steaming java. She had another bag tucked under the same arm.

"I have to finish with the customers out front. Detectives, if you want to wait for Brooke in my kitchen she'll be here in a moment. Just go through that door, the one to your left. Have a seat at the table, and I'll send Brooke in."

Detective Gaynor tipped his head to her and maneuvered behind his partner between stacks of materials as they headed to the kitchen.

At the same time, Chloe grabbed the article she'd found in the storeroom and then stepped back into her showroom to assist her clients who busied themselves amongst the racks of colored glass. "Sorry about the wait." She didn't mention what took her so long. "I did find the perfect piece to fit with your project." Chloe held out the bubbled, lavender glass for the customers to view.

As their eyes sparkled with excitement, Chloe glanced out the always-available windows to check on Brooke's progress. Not seeing her, Chloe knew she had to intercept Brooke in the storage room to caution her about the meeting the detectives waited for.

"Do you have more of this style of glass?" The blond and stylish woman questioned.

Perfect. "I'm sure I have more in the back. Do you know how many plates of the glass in this size you'll need?"

"We're new to this craft, so we may need your help in figuring how much we'll use," the also stylish brunette offered as an unneeded delay.

"I surely can do that for you," Chloe said as she cocked her ear toward the storage room and heard the back door creak as it opened wide with a bluster of cold air seeping into the front.

Chloe began to get nervous and attempted to conjure up an excuse to run to the back room again as the blond pulled their plans from a glittery, beaded bag loosely hung at her shoulder.

As Chloe was torn in two directions, the blond announced, "Here, this is what we came up with." She unfolded the penciled drawing with an expectant look at Chloe.

Chloe relaxed her anxious position and figured Brooke would have to handle the meeting on her own. "Let's see what you have there." As she reached for the crude drawing, the storage room door peeked open.

Always the fast thinker, Chloe perked up as she caught a glimpse of Brooke's coat sleeve attached to the handle. "Brooke, I'm glad you're back. *We* have some clients here who need help with planning a project."

"We have…Oh, yes!" Chloe noted that Brooke sensed something was up, as she added, "I'm sorry I'm late. Just had to run and get hot coffees to warm up."

Chloe walked over to Brooke with the customers' plan. Leaning in close to Brooke, Chloe whispered, "The detectives are waiting in the kitchen to talk with you." As Brooke's head jerked up and her eyes widened, Chloe spoke in a louder tone, "Brooke, why don't you come over to the desk and help me with this?"

"Be glad to," Brooke said as she looked around for a place to deposit the coffees and bag which likely contained more scones.

On the way to the drafting table, Chloe discreetly informed, "The detectives are probably getting impatient, so help me with this and then you won't have to face them alone."

Brooke nodded and bent over the drawing. Serendipitously, it was a simple plan for a stained glass hanging from a hook in front of a window.

The customers told them it would be a gift to their grandmother, which gave away the fact that they were sisters.

Brooke and Chloe could have suggested a thousand ideas and improvements to delight the women, but simplicity and speed were the forefront endeavor this time. At any minute, Chloe expected the detectives to barge back into the showroom.

"Brooke, I think we have this covered. If you want to go to the back and continue what you were doing before, I'll meet you in a few minutes." As an afterthought, Chloe added, "Don't go any further until I get there. I want to see where you're at."

Brooke nodded. With a nervous smile, she patted the drawing and turned to exit the showroom with the coffees and paper bag.

Back in the storage room, Brooke stopped to organize her thoughts. She knew the detectives were going to talk to her soon, but a strange feeling invaded her mind. The chaotic atmosphere of the morning kept her mind off the shooting and the details of it. Now it all came at her like a thick fog. The fear and gravity of the incident suffocated her.

She breathed deeply and noticed one of the Styrofoam cups of coffee dented against her coat and caused a stain to soak into the nylon. She rolled her eyes and continued to the door to Chloe's kitchen.

As Brooke eased the door open and entered, the voices from the showroom diminished. Detectives Gaynor and Rell sat at the table. Gaynor, who faced the opposite wall, leaned back on his chair with his legs spread under the table. He tipped his head back to see Brooke enter. Rell only needed to change his look from his folded hands as he lifted his head up.

"I didn't know you'd be here when I got back. I just left for coffee. I'd have brought you some also, but I didn't know." Brooke paused. "I already said that, didn't I? You can have these, if you like."

Detective Gaynor interrupted Brooke's explanation, "No, we're fine. You went out in the cold to get those, so you deserve one yourself."

Brooke's shoulders relaxed as she detected a trace of kindness in his remark. "Thank you. I think I do need one of these." The earlier coffee, long forgotten, needed replacement after the multiple episodes in the first half of the day. "I'll make a pot of coffee, anyway. I'm sure you're just being kind. It won't be anything special. Just a regular brew, but on days like this it's still good."

Brooke turned quickly to the adjacent counter housing the coffee pot. Before she thought out more idle conversation, Detective Gaynor began, "Ms. Bellin, we have a lot of information we need to discuss with you today. Some is factual, but a lot is circumstantial."

"Are these things you discovered after our last talk?"

"Actually, most of the hard evidence is the same."

"Why…?" Brooke attempted to interrupt.

"Hold on. Like I said, a lot of the hard evidence hasn't changed, but many non-tangible details have been added, which are clouding our view toward the previous evidence."

"I…I think I would like to wait until Chloe can be with me to talk about this."

"Would you prefer an attorney?" Detective Rell offered.

"No, I do want to talk about this and know what's happening, but I think it'll be better with her here." The detectives returned a questioning look at her. "I'm not sure I always understand things the way you might intend them to be understood." Seeing puzzlement form creases on Gaynor's forehead, Brooke tried again to explain. "I…I don't always draw the right inferences. I take things at face value. I just want to make sure I understand everything correctly, and if I forget something Chloe can remember it for me." Brooke wrinkled her forehead and bit her lower lip as she waited to see if the detectives understood her. It wasn't a complete story. She did want Chloe available for clarification on the investigation's details, convinced they would be overwhelming. Possibly Chloe would know details the detectives might be keeping to themselves.

Brooke began to pour coffee as she feared the exclusion of her friend in the conversation. The detectives didn't respond, but rather shifted in their chairs.

The door to the storage room swung open as Chloe feigned innocence at her timing. "That was quite a delightful sale, so I deserve a break." Chloe smiled comfortably at her guests and walked to the counter to unload the hot ceramic cups from Brooke as she attempted to add the purchased coffee to her grip. "Let me help you, Brooke. Remember, you only have one steady arm."

True relief relaxed Brooke's muscles as she accepted the help. "The detectives want to update me on the accident." This was the best way Brooke could describe nearly being killed.

"Yes, dear, I sent them back here to wait for you." Facing the detectives, Chloe asked, "Do you mind if I sit in?"

"Brooke mentioned that she wants you here," Detective Gaynor answered. While Chloe slid into a chair, he added, "We aren't here to scare you or to offer false promises on the investigation. We think it's important you know what's going on. It's important we work together on this."

With complete attention, Brooke nodded. Putting her hands flat on the table, she said affirmatively, "Tell me the truth. Tell me what you know. I'm ready for this part of the year to be closed."

Chapter 32

To officially start the meeting, Detectives Gaynor and Rell opened their scuffed and marred folders. They each pulled relevant documents from thick volumes of typed, handwritten, and copied papers and set them in an apparently chronological order.

Brooke fastened her attention to each document as they lined up. She noted crisp forms thrown over tattered notes, and then covered by more. “I created this much information in such a quick crime?” She surprised herself by voicing her thoughts.

Chloe adjusted in her ladder-back chair as she sipped her coffee and kept her eyes focused on the notes.

“Ms. Bellin, you have to keep in mind that someone tried to murder you. You do realize it‘s an extremely serious crime?” Brooke matched Detective’s Gaynor’s stare as she exhibited understanding. The pause lasted longer than necessary to exemplify the weight of the crime. “We’re not here to scare you, but Marla Vrahn is the only suspect incarcerated at this time. And we believe there’s more to it than just her part.”

Brooke glanced toward Chloe for the impossible help to voice her thoughts. Knowing Chloe only wanted to listen as a backup participant, Brooke summed up her jumbled thoughts and said, “I’m not sure what to ask you. Certainly, there’s been progress, but I can’t see it. Are you saying Marla should be in jail, but she’s not the only one?”

The detectives exchanged looks. Rell nodded toward Gaynor, which prompted him to proceed with the issue of the visit. “We’re not going to go over every detail, just the conflict that has arisen.”

“Does this include anything about the restraining order on Scott Marshall?” Brooke hadn’t given up on correcting this issue.

“That’s a small part of it.”

“I don’t think it’s small. Will you be able to cancel it?”

Detective Gaynor flipped through a couple notes. "The order has been added to our investigation, but it takes time and there'll be a separate hearing for that, too."

"I still haven't been told how it happened. I certainly didn't file for it." Brooke stiffened in her chair.

"Ah, apparently your ex-husband filed for it, legally, we're informed. The paperwork is being examined."

With a strong voice devoid of the previous anxiety, Brooke questioned, "What's the other conflict we're going to discuss?"

Chapter 33

"We have two separate set of reports," Detective Rell began. "One set which we have compiled and one from the police department." Brooke listened, emotionless. Rell glanced at his partner. "What we're most concerned about is the differences in the two compilations."

Chloe's brows edged together a fraction, displaying her rapt attention. Brooke's countenance didn't alter. She adopted this new attitude in order to not crumble at what she knew would be unexpected. Brooke wasn't sure if she reacted to her apprehension and concerns in a statistically normal manner, but it was the only way she could stomach the whole ordeal. She sat firm in her chair and waited for more.

Eying her, Detective Gaynor told his partner, "Start with the police department's version."

Pulling the top form from the pile in front of him, Detective Rell tapped his forefinger on the form as he turned it to face Brooke. "I'll start with the few things the local police and we have in common. I'm sure you're aware that there are three main suspects being Marla Vrahn, Ty Bellin, and Scott Marshall." Brooke's shadowed stare twitched as the only notice she gave to indicate hearing the list of names. "The fourth possible suspect, Mr. Bellin's friend Roger Detris, was deleted from the list due to background check and positive alibis. You're aware he was also at the shooting range with Vrahn and…"

"Yes."

He accepted the quick answer and moved on. "Briefly, about Ms. Vrahn, the police and detective department agree on the evidence confiscated from her apartment during a search, made legal by permission through her landlord. The most convincing crime we can attribute to her is accessory. We're not worried about her part at this time. She'll remain in custody. What we do need to sort out is the conflicting evidence reports about Mr. Bellin and Mr. Marshall." Brooke's fingers stroked the sides of her Styrofoam cup.

Chloe also watched the detectives, but she included furtive peeks toward Brooke.

Detective Rell glanced at both women, and then returned to his stack of collected information. He tightened his lips and searched for the next account. "Ms. Bellin, your ex-husband, Ty Bellin, previous to his initial court date, had an undisclosed meeting with the District Attorney. No other law officers present. Were you aware of this meeting?"

Allowing a motion of her still features, Brooke spoke with little animation. "He didn't mention it to me. I wasn't with him when he was at the municipal building and haven't had any discussions with him." She didn't mention the few times she forced herself to risk seeing him because that didn't count as a conversation in her mind.

"This is an unconventional action by the D.A. He didn't record or document this meeting. Also, the only record of this meeting came from a temp secretary who was interviewed by us, not the local police."

Brooke didn't ask what this indicated. She trusted the detectives would tell her what she'd need to know.

Flowing with the fast pace of information acceptance, Detective Rell plunged on. "At the preliminary hearing, Mr. Bellin was released on what we would like to think of as poor preparation on the District Attorney's part.

"What the D.A. attempted to use as evidence was not evaluated and verified by the forensic team. He had to have known his conduct with the alleged evidence wouldn't be acceptable.

"This leaves us wondering why the District Attorney would tarnish his reputation with such sloppy work along with release of a suspect," Detective Rell summed up. "Gaynor, why don't you take over our part in the investigation of Mr. Bellin?"

Detective Gaynor paused, giving time for a reaction from Brooke. There was none. He advanced the discussion as he pulled a thick folder from the top of the pile. "We started with the same evidence as the District Attorney. The difference is that we waited until the forensics team had done their work.

"In our view, Ms. Bellin, your ex-husband should still be in jail." Again, Brooke didn't alter her facial features.

At this information, Chloe didn't change her expression, either. Brooke remained rigid in her chair. She tightened her thigh as Chloe rested her hand on it. Brooke's hands remained clasped around the near empty coffee container.

"Ms. Bellin, we suggest that you continue to stay away from Mr. Bellin at this time. Maybe, you should file a restraining order against him. We understand you've communicated with him and been with him for periods of time. Don't do it. Don't see him."

"I'm not afraid of him," Brooke whispered.

Detective Gaynor lifted his eyebrows. "It's unknown whether he'll attempt the same alleged crime again, but for now don't take the chance." He trapped Brooke's stare in tandem with his last statement.

An uncomfortable silence chilled the room. Brooke calmly accepted the facts. "Ms. Bellin, are you following us?"

"Yes, I understand." Brooke blinked slowly and resumed her stance. "What else?"

Chloe's mouth fell open, and she quickly closed it. Brooke felt a quick, supportive rub to her knee.

"On to the remaining suspect," Detective Rell announced. "Scott Marshall. Stereotypically, he could easily be the shooter. The police department is attempting to expand on this with several points of interest.

"The obvious lies in the fact that Marshall was at the scene close to the time of the shooting. He could have called 911 hoping you wouldn't live to see the ambulance or he regretted the action."

Reacting in place of Brooke's chosen silence, Chloe cleared her throat after the analysis.

"Please remember, Miss Heathlan, my part in this discussion is to relate the evidence procured by the police department and to explain how they're interpreting and using it," Detective Rell explained. "You may add to or question anything at anytime. That's our purpose for being here today."

"Yes, of course. Please continue," Chloe politely responded.

"Ah, where was I? I was just about to list the other items the police have numbered against Mr. Marshall. The evidence room is holding Mr. Marshall's shirt which is soaked with…clues from the scene." Brooke appreciated Detective Rell's careful choice of words at this juncture. "They also have other tagged items with traces from the scene found on them.

"The white paper bag with an attached note Mr. Marshall took from the scene was found at his home." Looking up from his list, he explained, "It appears the police think the note is relevant as to why Mr. Marshall is suspected. They're going for the idea that he doesn't like not being first on your list, angry about an unexpected breakup, or possibly mad over what the note read." Detective Rell took a breath here.

Brooke offered no explanation to discredit the pile of alleged information against Scott. She swallowed, waiting to hear everything and remained quiet.

Chapter 34

The detectives both shifted in their seats and passed a concerned look.

Brooke had been nearly silent throughout the meeting. The accusations against Scott, the man who caused her chest to tighten with confusion and excitement, didn't alter the safety zone of detachment she experimented with at this meeting. Her experiment was more successful than she'd predicted.

Brooke's mind swirled with rebuttals and counterclaims to the police work, but lost them in the mix of thoughts. She willed herself to *please* say something in Scott's defense. The anxiety hadn't surfaced during the accusations toward Ty.

Brooke looked around the table at watchful eyes and participants who waited for her explanation. Maybe she could counter the theories. It didn't happen. The thoughts were stuck in the mud created by her silence.

"Brooke, did you know about these allegations?" Chloe prodded.

With a slow and forced turn to her friend, Brooke simply stated, "No. Not until now."

"Do you…?" Chloe stopped abruptly as Brooke frowned and looked back at the detectives.

Detective Gaynor picked up the dialogue. "As for what we think about Scott Marshall's involvement, of course we checked him out as a suspect. It's routine to investigate everyone who was at the scene, friends, family, and anyone else who might be involved or have pertinent information." Gaynor watched Brooke as he related the rest of the discussion.

"We, of course, are still watching him and everyone else we have investigated. Marshall is not at the top of our list, contrary to the police officers' investigation. This is where the conflict lies.

"Our evidence still points to your ex-husband." At this statement, a small gasp of alarm escaped Brooke. She felt a squeeze on her thigh as

Gaynor continued, “The one thing we haven’t had access to, yet, is the note you left on the bag of apples Marshall took from the scene. Apparently the police are relating this to Marshall’s involvement.”

Brooke found motion and lowered her head to stare at the dented Styrofoam still in her hands. “That was private.”

Pushing exhausted air from his mouth, Gaynor commented, “We’ll find out when the evidence is tagged and released for us to view. Ms. Bellin, I know this is a tough situation to be in and to think clearly at all times. If and when you have something to add to this discussion, please don’t hesitate to contact one of us.”

Detectives Gaynor and Rell began to reassemble their notes. Gaynor glanced at Rell, gave a small shake of his head and rose from the table.

Brooke noticed his frustration as Detective Rell said, “Ms. Bellin, if you aren’t comfortable talking with us, there are, uh, women or other detectives who can take your statements.”

Brooke could feel the men’s eyes on her as they clung to a final hope that she would tell them something to fill the gap in the investigation. She did have something to say. Something she knew was important. “Thank you,” she murmured with a twist of her lips. It was time to take things into her own hands. She had a few ideas.

They remained alone in the chilled kitchen after the detectives’ exit, which left a swarm of cold air. Chloe swiveled in her chair to face Brooke. “Brooke. Brooke, are you okay? What happened to you during this confrontation?”

Brooke’s shoulders sunk unevenly low. Only her injured shoulder remained higher in order to avoid the pain and pressure an unnatural posture would impose. Absently, she reached her one hand to Chloe’s hands, both positioned on her knee at this time. “I…I don’t know what happened. Or actually, what didn’t happen.”

“This wasn’t an everyday scene. We can’t be too surprised at an unusual reaction.” Chloe smiled and squeezed Brooke’s hand. “If you think about it, this day’s been quite filled with activity and surprises. You’ve been out in the cold a couple times today to search the town for hot coffee, the visit from Scott heaped a load of emotion on you, and then the detectives. And the day is only rounding up to the early evening.”

Noting Chloe's rendition of the day, Brooke didn't bother a counter of additional details. She simply stated, "Yeah, I guess it was a draining day."

"Definitely. I know what we should do tonight. I'm sure we've had enough coffee, so for dinner I have roasted red pepper soup, which only needs a heat up with a toss of feta cheese. I'll make grilled cheese sandwiches for dunking. And we can watch a movie, or even better play a game of Scrabble. What do you think?"

"I like your idea. A movie or something certainly would clear my mind of everything else for a while."

Checking the wall-clock, Chloe said, "I need to officially close the shop for the evening, so why don't you stir up some hot cocoa or tea. When I get back we'll start on the dinner."

With a fresh smile, Brooke agreed. She remained in her seat until Chloe left the room. Listening to the door click shut, Brooke tapped her fingers on the table. She reached through the thinning mud her thoughts had been stuck in all day and scraped together ideas about what she hadn't had a chance to finish today.

Chapter 35

For as much as the day had drained her, Brooke's adrenalin kept her fingers tapping. She needed to do this right now, while Chloe was in her shop. She had intended on doing it in the morning, but with constant scene changes, it never happened.

Chloe wouldn't object, but Brooke didn't want Chloe to have to worry about her, especially after the detectives just told her to stay away from Ty. He wouldn't be in town, anyway. It was personal, and Brooke could handle it on her own.

She looked at the phone, which sat quietly on the counter. With a furtive glance toward the door, and then back to the phone, Brooke jumped out of her seat.

Looking at the phone that she now held in her hand, her mind jumbled the numbers she hadn't dialed recently. He usually called her. Brooke pleaded with the ceiling to recall the simple digits as she attempted a mix of numbers.

Wrong numbers. A nonexistent line. At least she hadn't reached someone she didn't know. One more try.

The phone rang. "Hello."

The gravelly, deep voice startled Brooke, even though she'd made the call.

"Hello," Scott repeated.

"Uh, hi. Scott, it's me." Brooke waited to hear if he'd be receptive to the forbidden call.

"Brooke, hi," he repeated. "Can you hold a minute?"

"Sure," she agreed as she watched the door. Brooke heard some clanging and paper shuffling on the other end of the line.

Scott didn't explain his brief absence when he returned to the phone. "Brooke, I'm so glad to hear from you. I'm sorry, but I can't make it back to

Chloe's. I got busy and didn't know how long the detectives would be with you. It's probably too risky to try again." Not letting her break-in, Scott added, "I want to see you more than ever, but I also don't want to cause you any problems right now."

Brooke felt a flush of heat warm her cheeks from the sheer pleasure of hearing Scott's welcome tone. Her fingers relaxed on the rough surface of the table. "I could talk to you for hours, but I only have a few minutes. I doubt there'll be a good time for you to come back here tonight, anyway. I wanted to call you the other day, and then talk to you this morning, but there wasn't any time.

"I tried to mention this before we separated this morning. About you coming to my apartment. This is kind of short notice, but this weekend my ex-husband is going to be out of town hunting, so he can't spy on me or check on me. I want to stay at my apartment."

"I'm sure you miss it."

"Yes. Yes, I miss a lot of things since, since…what happened." Brooke paused briefly. With her gaze still fixed on the door, she hurried into her reason for the call. "I know we aren't supposed to be near each other, but I was wondering if you would like to come over to my place for awhile this weekend?"

Brooke hoped for a quick, affirmative response, but she only heard a low sigh. "What makes you think we can do this without trouble?"

"Well, I won't let the police know I'll be at home. They have no reason to check it out."

"What about the fire? Have they finished the investigation?"

"Uh, yes, but I'm planning on going to my apartment, which is at least six or seven miles from my old studio." She didn't go into detail. Her time ran short. She continued to watch the door and listen for Chloe's footsteps. "Please, just meet me at my place on Friday evening, if you can." Footsteps clicked on the hardwood.

"I want to see you, Brooke."

"Please. I have to go. I'll be there on Friday." Brooke rushed to reestablish her plea. She didn't get to say everything and ended the call without an answer as she forced herself to disconnect with the best part of her day by shoving the phone back in its cradle just before Chloe returned.

"Have you decided what you want to do this evening?"

Not having given a thought to it, Brooke answered, “A game of Scrabble would be fun.” She didn’t really enjoy playing games, but it would make a good diversion to the phone call she’d ended.

“Great. I’ll whip us up an overdose of hot chocolate mixed with extra chocolate plus more chocolate, seeing as you didn’t get to that yet. It’ll give us the energy to come up with some crazy words. What do you think?”

“Sorry I didn’t get our drinks together, but I think you have a super idea,” Brooke responded with a chuckle. “Where do you keep the board?”

“That’s a good question.” As Chloe rummaged in the kitchen for the ingredients to her concoction, she said, “The game is in my cabinet close to the fireplace.”

As Brooke walked into the sitting room, she noticed a cabinet against the same wall as the fireplace. A dark, grayish-green structure covered the wall. She couldn’t put a name to the odd color. She had never noticed it before, even though she had traveled through Chloe’s home innumerable times.

Confronting the doors of the cabinet, Brooke noticed faded, black painted pictures haphazardly scattered upside-down and sideways on the front. She tilted her head different directions to discern the identity of the paintings.

Some of the figures had dots and sparkles scattered through swirls similar to pictures of galaxies. Focusing on neighboring paintings, Brooke noticed small faces with contorted features. Other creepy figures exhibited cats with an ear absent, frogs with protruding warts, and lizard-like animals. The heavily designed circular figures could pass as snowflakes, but the black paint gave them an eerie appearance.

Brooke cocked her head as her eyebrows rose. She reached for the twiggy styled knobs. The doors creaked as she pulled them open. A light, sparkly dust swirled forward and settled on her shoes.

The cabinet had a series of shelves, none piled with articles Brooke recognized. Jars of different colored powders, crystals and beads, and what looked like spaghetti lined half the shelves. Small boxes sported labels in a foreign language. Decks of different types of cards with pictures of ancient wizards were stacked exactly the same distance from each other along the middle shelf. The stainless mixing bowls didn’t seem to fit. Yet, Brooke didn’t know what the rest of the contents were for, so maybe they did.

"Did you find it?" Chloe asked as she entered the room. Mugs of steaming, thick, hot chocolate kept both her hands busy.

Startled from her reverie at the contents, Brooke involuntarily swung around in reaction to Chloe's entrance. "Uh, I just opened the cabinet." Returning her search to the shelves, Brooke scanned the remaining ones. At the bottom, tucked against the side of the cabinet were a couple game-like boxes. "Is it down here?" Brooke knelt down and looked back at Chloe.

Chloe glanced up as she set the mugs on the coffee table. "Yes, it should be in that pile." Slowing her movements and gliding to Brooke's side, Chloe apologized, "Brooke, I'm sorry. I shouldn't have told you to get the game."

With a nervous laugh, Brooke said, "I have to do something around here, too. You're letting me invade your home, and I don't want to be a burden."

"Nonsense, you're most welcome here. I should've warned you about my ingredients cupboard, as I like to call it."

Brooke stared at Chloe wondering what the cupboard's contents meant. Probably something to do with Chloe's psychic abilities, which she didn't want to be overly involved in experiencing. The one time Brooke asked for Chloe's help, she had ignored the warning.

If Brooke had heeded the warning, she wouldn't be standing and looking at Chloe with an arm wrapped to protect a gunshot wound. She respected and truly believed Chloe had a gift, but the intangibility and the pull of the future into the present baffled Brooke.

She tried to ignore the contents. Brooke stalled by wiping the dust from the game's tattered and sunk-in cover. Removing the lid and settling it under the coffee table, Brooke kneeled on the floor to take her side of the table. She attempted to dismiss her findings. "I found the game, so it's not a big deal. Everyone has a cabinet or closet they store odds-and-ends in."

Brooke avoided eye contact as Chloe studied her face. Sitting on the edge of the couch opposite Brooke, Chloe said, "Brooke, I can tell what you saw upset you and I can't leave you in such a position. I'm sure you think I deal with the psychic world more than you realized. I also know you're not comfortable with this side of life, but don't let my cabinet worry you.

"Most of the contents have nothing to do with my psychic endeavors. I'm not into brewing caldrons of magical potions or casting spells." Brooke raised her head to listen to Chloe's explanation. "The powders are simply different incenses, the beads and crystals are for a little sparkle to add to my jars of potpourri, and everything except the cards is for different types of art projects."

Relieved, Brooke said, "Oh, I guess I was surprised." As an apology for her doubts, she explained, "I wasn't worried you would turn me into a lizard or turn my hair green." Brooke then slapped her one hand onto the table. "Let's have a shot of chocolate and get this game going."

Short, inconsequential words arose first. Gradually building into longer words, Brooke used five letters to spell "house."

"Did you plan that word?" Chloe asked.

Quite often, especially lately, Brooke contemplated what Chloe knew. Brooke refused to ask, but rather told Chloe about her choice. "Well, I had the letters, so I made the word." Knowing she did have to tell Chloe part of her plans, she added, "I've been thinking about my home. I haven't had the chance to tell you, but Ty will be gone on a hunting trip this weekend. Just outside of town. I want to stay at my apartment." Brooke felt a twinge of apprehension as she remembered she said the same thing to Scott. She didn't plan to reveal the invitation she'd offered him.

"When did you find out?"

"When I was at his house and you and the detectives waited outside for me." She hurried to explain the late revelation. "So much was going on, and I hadn't made up my mind until earlier today. This is the first time we've been able to talk without others around."

"Brooke, slow down." Chloe returned to the subject of Brooke's apartment. "I can certainly understand why you want to be in your own home." Chloe studied her letters while Brooke replaced the ones she used and added points to the scorecard.

Vertically, from the 's' in the word 'house,' Chloe reverted back to a small word, 'see.'

"I 'see' I am still ahead of you in points, Chloe," Brooke commented with a smirk.

"I see things, too," Chloe responded as she cautiously chose the next two letter blocks to add to her collection.

Brooke didn't acknowledge the possible hint. She slowly ran her fingers over the tops of her letter blocks and attempted to come up with the most advantageous combination. "I see that I can only make the word 'doubt.'"

"Are you sure that's right?"

"Why? What's wrong with it?"

"I see you should not cause yourself doubt." Chloe's words meant nothing to Brooke.

"I'm not following you, Chloe." Brooke squinted as she looked across the game board at her friend's expression.

Chloe scrutinized her letter blocks as she switched them in multiple patterns. Brooke returned her focus to the board as Chloe commented, "Brooke, if you doubt your 'house' plan, maybe you should reconsider."

Brooke didn't miss the inference this time. She put her hands in her lap and leaned over the table. "Chloe, I need to be in my own place for a while again." She left out the invited guest. "Besides, Ty will be with Roger. There's no chance he'll be around or visiting my apartment. I doubt Ty would do anything to me, and I won't be alone with him at any time. I have no reason to go to his house again, and he doesn't have a key to my apartment."

"Sounds like you have this all thought out." Chloe sighed resolutely. Brooke's determination to be at her home for the weekend was upper-most in her plans.

Chapter 36

"I'm sure they're listening to our discussion," Ty barked.

"This is supposed to be private," Marla hissed back.

"How else do you think they get evidence that has no way of being found out?" Ty edged forward on his chair to shorten the distance of the metal table between them. They knew the guards had stationed themselves outside the door. The ten by eight foot room was supposedly soundproof, but rights slipped away from the allegedly guilty without them even knowing. Not easily seen ceiling cameras focused on them.

Covering the square footage quickly, Marla inspected the room. "I don't see anything."

Not able to make Marla realize the intensity of her predicament, Ty switched gears. "Did they tell you when you'll get out?"

With indignation Marla said, "Tell me? I've only talked to an attorney once. All he did was ask me questions about Brooke getting shot. He didn't give me any information about what's going on or how I can get out of here."

"You didn't tell him anything, did you?" Ty threw the weighted question on the table.

"Of course not." With her anger at a tolerable level, Marla added, "The lawyer told me the police are going to search my home, if they already didn't."

"You must've suspected that."

"Yes, but first, there isn't anything to find. Not much, anyway. And secondly…"

"What do you mean 'not much'?" Ty rose from his seat and leaned further into the table.

"Well, my shoes were in the house. I suppose there could've been dirt on them. Ty cocked his head and Marla quickly explained, "I've been to the walking trails before, so naturally there's dirt on them."

Ty relaxed with this clarification. "What's the second thing?"

"Well, I can't remember. You interrupted my thought." Marla folded her hands over her nose and mouth and shut her eyes. She suddenly came up with, "I didn't okay the search."

"So."

"So? That means it's illegal. If they find anything, they can't use it against me."

"What, did you learn that at nursing school?"

Ignoring his sarcasm, Marla said, "I was never told that there was a warrant to search my house, and no one asked me if they could do it."

"You might have a point there." Ty pursed his lips and looked up. "You better be right. I have a way out of this, but it won't help you any. You tossed the shotgun shells, right?"

Marla looked at him blankly. "From the firing range? So what if I used your gun there."

"Stupid… Well, if you didn't, they'll only point to you, and then you've screwed yourself."

Defending her part, she demanded, "You better get me out of here. I don't deserve this."

Ty reminded her, "I don't think you've done anything wrong and I'm sure the local police are on Marshall's trail by now." It was a paltry excuse for reassurance, but Ty had more than Marla's welfare on his mind.

* * * *

Brooke's tennis shoes weren't bright white when she arrived, but now they were definitely shaded with a powdery gray, which camouflaged their age. The snow continued to melt as it touched the still warm destruction and left darkened patches of wet ashes. The dry parts floated as she stepped among the charred timbers. Most of the frame remained standing, although it leaned in incongruous angles. Parts of the ceiling and walls had fallen from their posts to create piles of burnt-smelling, crumbled wood. Choosing to stand in what had been her workroom, she stared down at the floor.

At first, it all looked like a jumble of firewood. The studio had existed of much more than the frame and its walls. She kneeled down and poked at an object reflecting the light from the overcast sky. Edges of the glass Brooke had ordered for her landscaping project with Scott turned from enchanted colors to blackened glass. The colors were indistinguishable at first sight. Covered in the leftovers of the fire, they all looked the same.

A tear began to descend Brooke's cheek. As it slid over her cheekbone and quickly dipped down the rest of her face, she swiped it away with the back of her hand. "This is all replaceable," she found herself repeating.

The part that wasn't replaceable was the memories. Brooke wandered to the next room to see that the fireplace had caved in on both sides, and a thin line of stone stood tall to represent the chimney. She recalled meeting Scott in this room and discussing his job. Brooke thought she could almost smell his male, raw scent. The same spice had distracted her when they studied the plans for her stained glass.

She shook her head at the memories. She next thought of when Ty had planned and remodeled the old shed for her to use as a studio during their first year of marriage. This probably should have been the initial thing she recalled.

Not caring anymore whether her shoes were washable, Brooke shoved the stones that had fallen from the chimney with the toe of her shoe. The mix of ashes clung to the tip. She looked into the fireplace and saw the grate had collapsed with the heat. She also saw three round balls covered in soot. Snatches of red peeped through the incomplete cover of ashes.

Curious as to the identity of the objects that appeared to be unaffected by the fire, Brooke tested the strength of the remaining chimney form with her hand as she braced herself to take a closer look. With her other hand she reached for one of the balls.

She recognized the form and released her grip to fling it to the floor. With a thud, the apple hit and stayed in place. A chunk of wet soot fell to the side and revealed more of the apple. Brooke always thought of apples as a cheerful reminder of a cool, yet sunny and colorful autumn. But not this time.

"Who put this here?" Brooke queried as she backed up from her position and wiped her hands down the front of her jeans. "They couldn't have been here during the fire. They'd be unrecognizable then."

Brooke looked around her, expecting the someone to be watching her. Only the ashes settled on the wet soot and crystallized snow lay in patches around the studio. An occasional gust of cold air rustled the leftover leaves still hanging from the towering oaks.

Brooke turned around to look at everything. Hugging her zipped jacket closer to her, she searched the sky, her brown, wasted garden that she used to tend daily, and the mess of burnings at her feet. She raised her view to the flat, gray clouds as tears criss-crossed her cheeks.

"This isn't fair. I'm going to have to figure this out myself." Remembering the catalyst for her tears, she abruptly turned and grabbed the same apple she had thrown.

Feverishly, she wiped the rest of the soot from the dull, red coat of fruit. "It's not the same. It's not the same." Brooke needed to know if these were from the only bag of Jonathan apples she had bought. The kind she had given to Scott. She tentatively bit into the one she held. Expecting the normal resistance of a crisp apple, her teeth came down hard and sliced the inner side of her lip. The apple caved in without a crunch and Brooke felt a mouthful of mush that she immediately spit to the floor.

"It's not the same," she repeated. "It can't be from the apples I gave Scott. I know it can't be," Brooke finished in a whisper as a trickle of blood seeped down her chin and her knees sank to the darkened floor. She bent forward and huddled herself into a mess of black smears and sticky tears.

Chapter 37

The steady crunch of snow came closer and forced Brooke to raise her head and attempt to wipe the mixture of emotion and grime she knew covered her face.

"Brooke, I went to your apartment, but..." Scott stopped at the crest of the slope at the north side of the studio. His smile flattened when he saw her folded in the mess of her destroyed property. Regaining motion, Scott plunged through the few inches of snow.

"Brooke, Brooke, are you all right?" Scott reached her side and settled his hands around her waist to help her up as she struggled to right herself.

Brooke didn't dare look into his eyes. She continued to wipe her face with the sleeve of her coat. "I'm such a mess. I came down here to see my studio up close. I didn't know you were coming. I found..."

"Brooke, I'm here. I'll help you." He hugged her close.

"Oh, let go," Brooke squeaked against his chest.

"What?" Scott loosened his grip and looked down at her mass of dark curls against his chest.

"My shoulder. It's pushed against you too hard."

"Oh, I'm so sorry. Here I want to help you and I only make it worse." Scott released his grip. Putting his hand under her chin, he gently lifted her face. He began with an encouraging smile.

Brooke sniffed to hide her apparent emotions. She directed her look at Scott's warm-looking lips while she braved her own smile.

The smile quickly turned upside-down as she averted her look to the surrounding chaos of her studio that once was her getaway to passion and dreams.

He broke her trance, saying, "Brooke, you've got to be cold. Your pants are wet and you have soot all over the rest of yourself." His gaze traveled the unusual spectacle Brooke portrayed, pausing at the blood sticking to her chin. "We'll clean your chin, too."

Feeling silly at how she'd bit her mouth, Brooke didn't offer an explanation. Holding her coat closed at the neck, she suggested, "Yes, I suppose we should get to my place."

Not sure what to say next, she pretended deep concentration on picking her way out of the studio.

After covering fifty feet or so, Brooke chanced a look at Scott to see him watching his feet. Whether the snow and slippery spots or the tethered emotions affected Brooke, she chose to walk slower. With better balance attained, she again glanced up to Scott.

"Scott, I wasn't sure you were going to come and see me. I didn't even know if you understood what I tried to tell you when we talked."

"I took a chance that you weren't disguising any of the conversation and that what you said was what you meant."

"Yes, more than anything."

They arrived at her apartment in separate vehicles. Scott parked first and jumped out of his truck to escort Brooke to the front door. With a gentle hold around her waist, he opened the door and ushered Brooke in ahead of himself. Surprisingly, the warm air rushing her front and circling her body caused a chill to vibrate up her back.

"Brooke, you should take a shower to warm up."

She acknowledged the obvious suggestion.

She wanted the weekend, the night, or however long his visit, to be special. She thought of all the fantasies she had created about kissing his lips and exploring the parts of his body she had yet to see and feel. Something held her back.

Brooke focused on his comment. Finding a fragment of hospitality, she offered, "Would you like something to drink while I clean up?" Why wasn't she asking him to join her? An ideal opportunity to make her fantasies of passion real. Previously, she hadn't thought anything could block these urges when given the chance.

He interrupted her confusion, "No, no, Brooke. Uh, you take care of yourself, and I'll wait for you." Scott paused. "Right here. I'll wait right here. Or at least I'll find a seat and wait," he added with a tender touch to her arm.

With welcome relief, Brooke sighed. "Thank you. I won't be long." She walked backward a couple of steps, and then turned while pushing her hair away from her face. Brooke quickened her step to the bathroom. It wasn't that she didn't want Scott. He was the most gorgeous, kind, sensitive, and caring man she knew. She just didn't feel right at this particular moment. She had waited so long to be with him, and now her mind wouldn't allow her to enjoy the reunion the way she anticipated.

* * * *

Scott shoved his hands in his front pocket as he watched Brooke scurry away to clean the afternoon's debris. As she disappeared through a door, he wandered into the living room.

He saw Brooke everywhere. Soft shades of plum swam across the couch and loveseat and into the lampshades. Another run of sage accented the valences topping the long windows open to a snow-covered square of lawn. A soft rug of a dusty brown covered a portion of scuffed hardwood in front of a small, river stone fireplace.

"I'm not ready, if she's not ready," Scott murmured to himself. "But I'll make her comfortable, if I can." With this initiative, Scott kneeled in front of the fireplace. Reaching to his left, he collected a stack of old newspapers and kindling.

He looked for the larger logs and assumed they'd be along the same wall. Nothing in sight, so he leaned back further until he needed to swing his free arm back to catch his fall. Scott released a smile and muttered, "I need to take care of Brooke tonight not the other way around."

He regained his balance and heaved himself off the floor. Turning around, he didn't see any logs stowed in any part of the room. The next obvious location would be outside the French doors.

As dusk turned to dark, Scott checked next to the doors for a light switch. He noticed the plate accenting the toggle. So Brooke. Depending on what angle he viewed it, the cut-glass wall plate changed between colors of plum and lavender. "Perfect. She's perfect." He flipped the switch.

He continued outside in search of fuel for the fire. The air took on the night's stiff chill as the rest of the sun visibly sank behind a hedge of trees. He walked across the veranda and noticed a path leading to the back of the apartment where the outside lights couldn't follow. The reflection of the slivered moon on the snow led his way.

Scott noticed he wasn't alone outside when he spotted a pair of slow-traveling headlights.

Chapter 38

Scott appreciated the extra light, although surprised at the extended time it gave him. A few yards from the side of the apartment, three stacks of meticulously sized logs made a natural wall. It appeared each stack had a use, small logs to help start a fire and medium and large logs to encourage extended flames.

After Scott located the firewood, he looked out toward the vehicle lights, which slowly traveled past the lot to reach the far side. The shrubs and bushes along the edge of the road and a steep incline of terraced land hid the make of the vehicle.

He waited until the lights accelerated and left the area before he piled a combination of the logs into the curve of his arm. As a few clumps of crusted snow mixed with loose bark settled on his shirt, Scott straightened up from his chore and took a last look down the road. The lights didn't return.

He stepped backward, turned, and followed his prints back to the door.

* * * *

Brooke entered the living room wrapped in a cherry red, velour robe that hung to her ankles. Her damp hair allowed her curls to twist and curve around her neck and cheeks, reddened from a diligent scrub.

She remembered this scene from one of her too frequent fantasies. Scott stoked the smaller logs to encourage their contribution to the warmth of the fire. She remained at the entry and watched the outline of his body as he confidently stacked the wood.

His body. The topic of her dreams, of her wishes. The strength and power Scott exhibited left Brooke's heart sore for the feelings she knew existed but remained hidden. Her imagination led her to believe this reunion, the time she'd craved since their separation, would be nothing but smiles, hugs, kisses, and loving.

The kindness and caring were obvious. The loving didn't have a place in the mood of this evening.

After Brooke formed this opinion, she silently walked to Scott and stopped behind him. Lightly touching his shoulder, she whispered, "Scott." It was enough.

Scott swiveled on his knee to face her. Still on the floor, he reached his hands to her waist and pulled her to him. Burying his face in the softness of her robe, he imitated her feelings by simply saying, "Brooke."

She needed more of his touch. Her legs shook as she lowered herself to meet him in front of the hearth and to hold him as he did her. With arms securing their embrace, they remained together only to listen to the igniting of the flames.

She felt the warmth build and kneeled back, still facing him.

"Brooke, are you okay?"

Appreciative of the evident concern, she smiled with her response. "I will be. Just you being with me again, makes me feel safe."

"Before we forget about the time, are you sure your ex-husband is out of town? I don't care about running into him. I can take care of that, but the restraining order puts a crook in us being together."

Understanding his apprehension, Brooke assured, "I talked to Roger, Ty's friend who he'll be with this weekend. They were loading Roger's truck, intending to leave around two."

"Okay. I'm not worried about myself, but I don't want you to have to deal with anymore confrontations or stressful situations." As Brooke remained focused on Scott's explanation, he added, "You've been through enough today alone."

"Thank you." Not only did she thank Scott for his consideration, but for everything.

Silence arrested the moment as they watched the fire gain momentum. She wanted nothing more than the company for herself, yet Brooke noncommittally suggested a few things to do. "Scott, would you like to watch a movie or do something else? Anything besides a game."

"You don't like games?"

"No, I sometimes enjoy them, but not right now." Brooke didn't feel the need to mention the Scrabble game she'd recently played.

"No, this is good." Scott watched another set of lights brighten, and then dim through the French doors as he spoke. "Actually, I'm thinking that I shouldn't stay too long."

Brooke's head sunk down as he related his decision. "Is it because you're so busy or you aren't comfortable?"

"I did want to make time to be with you, so that's not really the problem." Brooke felt the air from an exasperated sigh. "I just don't know if it's the best idea for me to be in your apartment, especially with all that's going on right now."

Brooke couldn't even formulate her objections as she anticipated the perfect weekend to never happen. "Oh, I understand." What a lie. She didn't understand.

Upsetting events, news, and stories overflowed Brooke's reservoir of control. It became too much. This pushed the tears over the edge.

Scott placed his hand to the side of Brooke's chin and brought his body closer to her. "Brooke, it's not that I don't want to stay. I was going to suggest my place, but you wanted to be in your own home. Actually, we could be found at either, so I guess that doesn't matter too much."

She sighed with frustration and tried to wipe the evidence of tears on her sleeve. "It's almost as if we're the criminals." Scott reached for a handful of tissues on the nearby end table. Pausing to make use of the offer, Brooke changed her course. "Enough of me feeling sorry for myself. I want us to enjoy whatever time we have, so would you like to stay for a drink and maybe something to eat?"

"If that'll make you smile, and not a fake one, I will," Scott said with his own grin that Brooke took for encouragement.

Not able to ignore the request, she allowed one last sniff and wipe of her eyes with the damp tissues to make room for a smile. "Okay, you win." Getting herself off the floor, she said, "I'll be right back."

"Do you need help?" Scott asked as Brooke whirled around to head for the kitchen. Waving her hand to pass on the offer, she disappeared on her mission.

Scott returned his gaze to the fire. Watching the flames change shapes and color as the wood heated up and popped in symbiotic rhythm, he couldn't shake the uneasiness of their get-together. Scott twisted his body to look out the doors. The moon had disappeared behind clouds and no headlights filled the gap this time. Still, he needed to take another look.

As he neared the French doors, he could feel the cold from the glass. He calculated the distance the house was from the road and the time it would take a driver to enter the driveway and end up at the door. There was a myriad of reasons why someone might stop by. He knew he could get out of the house. There were doors and windows in all directions, but his truck was in the driveway. And he wouldn't leave Brooke to handle it on her own.

As he came up with a decision, Brooke returned with her hands full. A plate of circular and rectangular, seed-covered crackers abutting an array of different shades of cheese occupied her right hand. The other hand held a mixed drink. She set them on the same table where tissues crowded the edge, as she told him, "I have to run back and get the other drink. I guess I couldn't manage everything in one trip." Scott stopped his rationalization and turned her way. Before he could offer to extend a hand again, Brooke repeated a more sincere smile and hurried back for the other drink.

Back in the living room, she handed Scott his beverage as he rose from the floor. "Don't worry. I'm not trying to poison you. It's only a whiskey and coke. I probably should've asked what you wanted, but I decided to see if my intuition was any good."

Scott laughed at her admittance.

"Was I wrong?"

"Close enough. It's been awhile since I've had one. I usually just grab a quick beer. This is a good choice for tonight, though." Scott pulled Brooke close to him once more.

He lowered his forehead to touch hers and nuzzled her cheek. Brooke moved closer, as if the fire hadn't put enough warmth into the room. Wrapping his free arm around her waist, he slipped his hand lower to feel the firm curve of her behind. He adjusted his hips to rest even with hers. With a slight sway, he moved back and forth with her.

Brooke enjoyed the silence. She also wanted to talk and didn't know for how long they would be together or when the next time would occur. She wanted to make the most of this night, and there were so many things to cover.

"Scott, would you like music? We can dance better, if we're both hearing the same tune."

"I like it just the way it is. I think we're moving quite well together, don't you?"

"I thought so, but I just wanted to make sure you felt the same." Brooke held her glass out to the side and rested her head on his chest. She could hear the steady, rhythmic beat of his heart. The only thing she wished for at this moment.

Her stomach let out a low growl. "Let's eat the treats you brought out for us. It sounds like you're ready for them," Scott commented. "I think I am, too."

Reluctantly pulling away from the safety and warmth he supplied, Brooke agreed, "You're right. I haven't had a chance to eat since this morning. I hadn't really noticed until now when my stomach started talking to us."

As Brooke attempted to sit on the opposite side of the coffee table where the tray of snacks rested, Scott pulled her to his side. "There's enough room for you to sit next to me."

They both thoughtfully picked their combination of crackers and cheese. As the food tempted their hunger, the tray emptied faster. "You prepare a mean snack, Brooke."

"Thanks. It was spur of the moment, and I haven't gone shopping in a while, so I couldn't do what I would've liked to."

Emptying his plate, Scott followed with, "Are you staying here tonight? All weekend? We didn't get to talk much about this weekend. I only hoped I got the right message before I came over."

"I plan on staying here until Sunday morning." Brooke stopped eating and looked at Scott, waiting for his reaction.

"Do you have to stay here?"

Brooke looked at him with surprise. "What do you mean? Why shouldn't I?"

Scott sighed heavily as Brooke considered his reasoning. "I don't want to worry you, but I'll be worried if you stay here alone."

Brooke straightened up at this unexpected turn in the conversation. He hurried to finish his thought. "It's not that I don't want to spend the night with you, and I planned on it when I came over, but…I'm probably overreacting."

"What? What happened? Did I…"

"No, you didn't do anything." Scott turned to face Brooke and wiped his hand on his pants before swinging his arm around her. "When I went outside to get wood, I saw a set of headlights traveling excessively slow as they passed your house." Brooke remained still as her eyes widened with concern. "Maybe I'm being overly cautious, but what if your ex is trying to trick you? Or what if it's the police watching what you do? I don't think they have the highest regard for me."

"Why would you think that?"

"I haven't had much time to talk with you, so I don't know how much we know of the same things at this point in the investigation. Were you informed about the latest search of my house?"

"I know they looked around when they first told me not to stay with you, but I haven't heard anything since."

"Well, the police did come over again. I didn't care because I've got nothing to hide, but the other day when I was thinking about you, I wanted to read the note again that you had attached to the bag of apples. It was gone."

Interrupting him, Brooke exclaimed, "Why would they take that? It has nothing to do with anything." The detectives had mentioned it when they visited.

"I know, I know. I told the detectives at the first interview that we had a bit more than a working relationship. I'm sure my statements were passed on to the police."

Brooke's innocence overwhelmed her. "The note was meant just for you. They have no right to take such personal things." The tears were ever ready on this day with any nudge from the unexpected, but she wasn't going to let them take over again. Squeezing her eyes tight for a moment, Brooke waited for the saltwater to recede before she returned to her first concern. "If you aren't going to stay with me, how long will I have you tonight?"

"Just in case anyone is watching, my visit should appear to be a friendly visit. Actually, I'm not even supposed to do that, but I guess it's better than being found in bed with you, or whatever we decide to do together," He quickly added. Then Scott answered her question. "Maybe another hour or so, or however long it takes me to convince you not to stay here by yourself."

Finding an opportunity to make light of the serious discussion, Brooke falsely joked, "That'll be all night, then. I want to stay in my own home. I have that right. I can't let anyone scare me away from here. At least for the weekend."

"Brooke, I can't stay. It's just not safe. For either of us. Once this is all over, you can live here as you should."

Brooke leaned away from Scott and began to pick a loose thread from the inside hem of her robe. Not looking up from the lengthening thread, Brooke suggested, "Can't we pretend for a while that we'll be together 'til morning?"

Scott gave his answer with a kiss to Brooke's rose-colored lips. She could feel the tension ebb from her body as if water trickled down her arms and legs followed by a chill of excitement she hadn't felt for so long.

"Oh God, Scott," Brooke murmured into his lips as his tongue began to search for hers.

Right now, she didn't need anything else. Brooke had dreamed of Scott's kisses, powerful and consuming. The real thing was better than the fantasy. She sensed his shoulder-length, sandy colored hair, darker with the loss of sun, fall forward to tickle the side of her neck.

Sheer male power surrounded her, and his warm breath on her skin caused her need to heighten. Previously, her fantasies had to satiate her cravings, but nothing could truly take the place of Scott's body so close to her own. The sensation his mouth created surged to where she grew wet with anticipation.

Brooke wrapped an arm around Scott's firm back while her injured arm reached for his waist. She pulled herself closer in a primitive exhibition of possession. Her lips tugged on his. She parted her lips as an offer for Scott to plunge his tongue without restrictions.

Scott stroked her back and held her tight. His kiss strengthened, and then his lips traveled across her chin and to the spot on her neck that his hair caressed, leaving her to gasp. Brooke felt the need of his lips to leave his marks all over her neck and everywhere he could place his mouth. She tossed her head to the side to offer more.

He hesitated between touches.

Then he softened his kisses until he pulled away. The sudden release startled her. Reaching for him, she wanted more.

Scott placed his fingertips on her ravaged lips to intercept her search. Brooke's eyes questioned the motion. "Baby, I can't do anything more."

"I thought…"

With pain and obvious longing, Scott looked into her eyes. "No, it's not you. It's just not right."

"I don't understand," Brooke whispered with a quiver ending her statement.

"Brooke, believe me. I want you more than anything, but now's not the right time." Scott tightened his grip as it lowered to her waist. "I'm nervous as hell. We aren't supposed to be together, and I don't want to have a memory of making love to you for the first time while I'm looking over my back.

"I don't care if I get caught with my pants down, but not you. You're a lady and don't deserve the humiliation. You deserve better than this."

"But I want this. I want you." Brooke stopped here. *Say it. Say it,* she urged herself.

He didn't know she had more to say. "I want us to be free with our emotions and whatever we want to do with them. When this is all over, it will happen."

"When this is all over," Brooke reiterated. "When *what* is over? When will *it* be over?" A strain of frustration crept in her tone. *Why couldn't she say it?*

"Come here, Brooke," Scott said as he reached for her and cradled her against his warm and strong chest.

Brooke let him take her close. She needed it. She needed more, too. The best was to reciprocate the hold. As she reached her hands around to sink them into the thick knit of Scott's sweater that remained on, she felt the heat from the fire at his back.

Why haven't I said it? I want to. She wanted to be happy with whatever they'd have tonight. "Are you getting too warm so close to the fire?"

"No, baby, you're the only thing keeping me warm right now." He turned his head to check the fire. Even the stretch of his neck was all man. "I'll put a few more logs on and bring in another load before I leave. I don't want you to get cold tonight. Unless you've decided to return to Chloe's for the rest of the evening?"

Closing her eyes with a half-smile, Brooke said, "No, I'll stay here. I appreciate your concern, but I'll be fine." *Maybe if you tell him, he will stay.*

"I've been here nearly an hour and a half already. I'll get you set up, and I probably should get going." With a reluctant expression in the twist of his lips, Scott pulled away.

Brooke suddenly reached her hand to Scott. "Scott, wait." She paused here, trying to figure out what to say. "I don't want you to go." *That wasn't it. He's said it. Does he know how I really feel? But I can't say it. I haven't said it. When will I say it?*

Scott took Brooke's hand and gave it a tender squeeze. She remained silent. Grabbing his jacket from the couch, he went out the French doors.

I know what I need to do before I tell him.

* * * *

He took a deep breath and slowly let it out as he stopped outside the doors. Scott spread his legs in a wide stretch, shoved his hands in the jacket's pockets, and looked around. It was getting late enough that the traffic had diminished to a random few, but none crawled slowly by as before.

The lack of headlights didn't let him forget about the odd lights from earlier. He felt alone in Brooke's yard right now, but that gave him little confidence for the rest of the night that she'd be here by herself.

Shaking his shoulders to get himself on the move, Scott went to the woodpile and loaded his arms. There was enough fuel for the fire tonight, but a second load couldn't hurt. He'd try to return tomorrow, but his schedule was never static and things changed by the minute.

Brooke was sitting on the couch when Scott brought in the second armload. She rose from her seat as he dumped the wood in the bin next to the fireplace. Pressing against him, she began to wipe the woodchips and bark from his sleeves. "Thank you, Scott. I really didn't need that much, but it's nice of you to bring it in."

"I wanted to do it for you. I know, I know. You can do it yourself, but you still aren't supposed to lift this much. Besides, I like feeling useful at times."

A genuine smile lit Brooke's face as she tugged at the zippered edges of his jacket. "I want to beg you to stay, but you're probably right. Not right that it'll be dangerous, but I understand your apprehension." She let go and touched her hands to his chest. "I'll be fine here tonight. No boogeyman will get me, and I'll keep the doors locked. You better leave before I change my mind and lock them before you escape."

Relieved at Brooke's newfound optimism, Scott's tension eased, at least about them and their relationship, incomplete as it was. One more firm hug and he vanished behind the solid door of the foyer.

Scott studied his hand on the steering wheel as he flipped the key vigorously to start his truck. He gripped the steering wheel with his hand that only seconds ago touched feminine warmth and now only a cold, hard object had its attention.

With more aggression than necessary, Scott turned his truck around and roared to the end of Brooke's driveway where he stopped to check the dark street. He looked back toward her apartment. He should go back and protect her. Although, if he got caught, then he couldn't help her in any manner.

"That's it. I can't stay, but I can't leave." Scott craned his neck to judge the depth of the side of the paved road. "The road's a public place and I pay plenty of taxes." With this resolution, he pulled onto the road and immediately swung to the side.

Scott cracked his window and left the motor running. He jerked the seat back as far as it would go and attempted to stretch his long legs to the extent that the cab would allow. Still getting comfortable, he adjusted the collar of his jacket for ease of movement, checked the position of the mirrors, and pushed his back against the seat. He had a clear view of the patio around Brooke's apartment.

He watched the illumination waver in the windows of the living room, from bright to dim and back to bright again. Either Brooke added logs to the fire or they were simply adjusting themselves as they burned. Otherwise, the lights in the apartment remained the same. "I wonder when she's going to bed." He mused aloud to help keep his eyes alert as the warmth of the truck reminded him of the length of this day.

Scott again checked his mirrors as a late driver's headlights shined inside the cab. The motion of the lights slowed as they approached, and then curved around his parking spot. He watched as the car resumed its previous speed and disappeared around the next bend.

"That's probably what I saw when I gathered wood earlier. Although, there wasn't a vehicle parked here for a driver to go around," Scott analyzed. The previous lights still concerned him.

He checked his watch only to find he'd left Brooke's house fifty minutes ago. Rubbing his eyes, Scott looked around his truck for entertainment. The passenger seat sported a thick pile of folders containing the specs for his active assignments. Another pile of papers that slipped to the floor consisted of take-out menus along with wrappers from ordered food, advertisement bulletins announcing the shrubbery specials he entertained to finish off the Maple Haven account, and a loose copy of yesterday's local paper.

Noting that Brooke's lights hadn't been extinguished, Scott fought himself against returning to her home and her warm body where he could easily imagine falling asleep while he cradled himself against her. With a sigh of exasperation, he reached for the newspaper and caught the edge of it between his fingertips.

The crinkle of the paper in the silence of a cold night helped rouse him long enough to flip through the pages and catch a third page title: *New Evidence, New Suspect.*

Red and watery with exhaustion, Scott's eyes managed to open wide as he straightened up and popped on the overhead light in order to read the small print. He wasted no time in scanning the article.

In an effort to move forward in the case of Brooke Bellin's unfortunate brush with an attempted murder, the police have put forth extensive hours of investigation to build a case against a more probable suspect. The police have not disclosed the name of this person. Their only comment was to inform us of a note they located which gives the alleged perpetrator reason for the action...

"Jesus Christ," Scott exclaimed through a rush of sudden fast breaths. "A note? That's got to be the one they took from my closet. How can it make me a suspect? Do they think she meant it as a joke?"

Scott began to hypothesize aloud. "I know she wants to love me. She wouldn't kiss me or act the way she does, if she didn't. I've told her that I love her. Maybe not in those exact words. I can't remember." Scott realized he hadn't heard the same admittance in words from Brooke. "She hasn't said it to me. That doesn't mean anything. Maybe she thought she did. Maybe I didn't give her the chance."

Throwing the paper back to the floor of the truck, Scott slouched in his seat with a hand stroking his tightly trimmed beard as he contemplated the article and his relationship with Brooke. "This is insane. If the police thought I was guilty, they would've arrested me already. They certainly know where I work."

It took him fifteen minutes to come to this conclusion as he again checked his watch and flipped the button on the overhead light. He'd repeatedly turned his truck on and off for the past hour. He turned it off again and rolled up the windows in an attempt to trap the heat for a longer time.

The faint light of the moon soothed his weary eyes. It mesmerized him as he intently watched frosted shapes take form on the windshield. The cab stayed warm enough. It was the right warmth to relax his eyelids. He'd close them only for a moment.

During that moment, the moon crossed the sky. The frosted flakes covered the extremity of the truck. The cab grew cool. He shifted for comfort and slammed his knee against the dashboard.

Scott coughed his lungs awake, pushed against the armrest to straighten up and recall where he was and what his intentions were. "Damn, I fell asleep." He condemned himself against his fight to stay awake. Glancing swiftly to Brooke's residence, he was relieved to see that her lights still glowed in the pre-dawn darkness. "I don't know what's so great about her not going to bed, but I guess nothing has happened since the lights are the same."

Scott glanced both ways on the road he'd conveniently inhabited for the last couple of hours. He shifted in his seat to analyze Brooke's apartment one last time, and then turned the keys that still dangled in the ignition. His truck imitated its owner's cough and rumbled in place. The engine stabilized and Scott aimed it toward his home where he needed to get ready for another day of work.

Brooke's house lights never changed. They only diminished from his rearview mirror as he left with a beat-up heart and an involuntary rigidness in his groin. He was sure of her safety after his watch.

Chapter 39

Brooke rolled over and slapped her hand at the sound coming from the end table. The phone jingled in its cradle, signaling the early morning. The screen illuminated the word 'restricted.'

Normally not answering such calls, Brooke assumed it couldn't be a telemarketer because the sun had yet to make its appearance.

"Hello."

"Hi," Scott responded. He nonchalantly asked, "Did you sleep well?"

Brooke sat up more alert at the pleasant, yet early wakeup. "Uh, yeah. I think I did." Looking around the room, she saw the leftover glow of the fire. "I must've. I didn't make it to bed, but rather fell asleep on the couch. I'd probably still be asleep, but the phone rang," she added lightheartedly.

"Sorry about that. I know it's early, but I've got to get ready for work and wanted to check…to say good morning." Quickly, he added, "I didn't want to leave my number on your phone in case the police would take offense to it."

"Good idea. I wouldn't have thought of that." As Brooke became more awake, she recalled the intense, but unfinished feelings of the previous evening. Before Scott hung up, she needed to know his plans. "Scott…"

"Brooke…" he said simultaneously. As they laughed at their eagerness, Scott caught his voice first. "Go ahead. You first."

With a flush of insecurity, Brooke asked, "Scott, I was wondering… Well, are you going to be able to come over again today?"

With a serious tone, he answered, "Right now, I don't know."

"Okay. Well, I'll probably go back to Chloe's for awhile to work on the glass." Hoping it would make a difference, Brooke informed, "I'll be back here at about four o'clock."

"Four. I'll see what I can do. I won't call again, though. I don't want to leave any tracks."

With lambent hope skittering over her skin, Brooke subtly mentioned, "I won't wait up, but I'll be here."

"Be careful."

"Be careful, be careful of what?" she said as she looked around her, out the windows, at the fire she'd started after returning from a productive day of work on the glass art with Chloe, and then at the clock.

With her legs curled under her as she rested against the arm of the same couch she'd slept on earlier, Brooke wrung her hands and tried to make a decision as to her next move. To help herself motivate, she rose to stoke the logs Scott had carried in for her but didn't replenish the burning pile.

The clock on the mantel, lit up by the burst of flames from the fire, told her the time had passed to expect a visit. Of course, Scott would've arrived before eleven thirty.

Setting the iron poker back in its holder, Brooke stopped and breathed in deeply. She held in her disappointment and slowly exhaled as she began to close the night. She drifted among the candles that melted away the hours of the eve and extinguished each. As each flame went out, she wet her fingertip to touch the wick and eliminate the drifting smoke.

Brooke made her rounds back to the couch where her fleece blanket, dotted with sheep over a background of cobalt blue, lay rumpled on the cushions. Picking it up, she hugged the softness to her chest and ultimately allowed herself a moment of despondency as she summoned up the intensity of yesterday's short time with Scott.

They had made love with their lips, with their touches. A tingle spread through her core, proving the need to have more than a memory from yesterday. She wanted it to be like she imagined from further back on her calendar.

"Silly, silly. It wasn't that long ago, and I'll certainly survive another day or however long it takes us to be together. I'm going to make sure it happens, that I'm completely available," Brooke chastised herself as she shook the blanket flat in order to fold it properly. Chloe would've warned her if she weren't safe with Scott.

She stooped toward the table to turn off the lamp, the last illumination of the room. At the same time, a soft knock on the door startled Brooke and caused her to knock her hand into the stem of a lamp. She quickly caught it with the same hand as it tottered on the end table. The crescendo of the beat from her heart left no energy to move.

Another patient knock sounded.

Regaining her self-control, Brooke righted the lamp and slowly headed for the entry door.

"Are you what I'm supposed to be careful of?" Brooke asked softly as she opened the door to see Scott waiting with his back to her while he watched the surrounding area.

Scott jerked his broad shoulders around as if surprised she opened the door. A smile of questionable anticipation accompanied him as he stepped forward.

"Brook, I almost didn't come."

"Shhh… You did come. It doesn't matter."

They devoured each other with their eyes. It took Brooke an extended moment to become aware of the cold air exchanging space with heat from inside the apartment. "Of course, come in. I want you in here with me, not standing in the cold."

"I hoped you'd ask." Brooke flushed as she bent her head. She allowed herself to acknowledge the need she'd buried and avoided throughout the night. She barely moved as Scott ushered himself through the half-open door. His wide chest brushed her shoulder and slid her robe to the side, exposing the upper curve of her breast. Scott lingered between the door and its frame as he caught a glimpse of the breathing flesh.

Instinctively, Brooke reached for the lapel of her cherry-red robe, yet left her hand resting in its softness as she realized that she wanted Scott to have access to all of her. She watched him until he raised his eyes to match hers.

"You smell like a garden," Scott said as he took in a deep breath of the honeysuckle soap and powders she'd lavishly applied to her body. He shook his head and finished his step indoors. "You better pull that closed. You'll get cold standing in the doorway." Brooke held her breath as he gently grasped each fold along the opening of the robe. Instead of covering her bare skin, his hands drifted down the material as his soft brown eyes repeated their last search.

Pushing out a breath of air, he let go and reached his hand back to shut the door.

All of a sudden self-conscious, Brooke pulled her robe closed. She assured herself it was okay to be in her robe. It was late, and she had no forewarning of Scott's unscheduled arrival. Their footsteps echoed against the entry walls as Brooke led the way to the living room.

"Brooke, I'm sorry it's so late. I had to make sure no one watched me."

"I know." Not able to hide her relief, Brooke added, "I had given up hope a while ago." After a pause, she confessed, "No, not really. No matter how late it got, as long as I was awake, I know I would've kept hoping that you'd show."

Slightly abashed as they stood facing each other, Brooke attempted to cover her anxiety. "Would you like anything to drink? Coffee? No, that's right, you don't drink coffee. Something else?"

"No, I don't need anything."

Quickly thinking of something else to talk about in order to vanquish the silence, she told him, "Chloe and I finished a lot of the stained glass pieces this afternoon. The pieces for the bridges, the ones for three of the pergolas, and now half of the arbor collection are finished. We scheduled…"

"Brooke, Brooke, that's great. I'm not worried about your progress. I know you'll keep on schedule. Besides, my crew can't assemble them in this weather. I'll arrange to have them picked up and stored until they're able to add the glass to the structures."

"Okay, you're right."

As she furtively searched for another subject, Scott changed her direction. "I appreciate your update. I should be more concerned about it, but actually, I'm more concerned about you. That's why I decided to take another chance and come over."

These words returned a slight amount of comfort as Brooke realized they still stood as if it'd be a quick parting. "Scott, please, sit down."

Scott looked at the dying fire. "Looks like you need another log on the fire."

"I was going to sleep, so I had let it die down, but if you rather sit up for awhile, that's a good idea."

"I'm still nervous about being here, so I don't think I could sleep even if I tried. I'll get you another load of wood."

"That's not necessary. You brought plenty in yesterday."

"Quite all right. Before I sit down, I'm going to make sure you're warm." As Scott let himself out the French doors, he confided, "Brooke I do want to keep you warm in other ways, too." With that last remark, he entered the chill of the darkness outside and left Brooke with the second genuine smile since she'd opened the house to him on this night.

Once outside, Scott automatically searched the road for unusually slow headlights. It was dark except for the light from the house. He walked to the far end of the woodpile this time in search of perfectly dried wood. As his next step slipped, he grabbed the edge of the stacked wood to steady himself.

It felt like a mushy substance that he skidded on. As he lifted his boot to check the sole, his gaze wandered to the ground. With only a faint light, Scott couldn't distinguish the color of the bumpy pile next to where he stepped.

He leaned over and stuck his finger in the pile only to come up with rotten apple.

* * * *

With a return of energy, Brooke rushed to the kitchen and retrieved a couple glasses of ice water. She deduced they'd talk for a while and the previous apprehension had already drained the moisture from her mouth. Returning to the living room, Brooke swiftly set the glasses on the table and hurried to the doors as Scott, with an enormous armload of wood, was unsuccessfully reaching behind his back in an attempt to secure the door.

"I'll get that," Brooke said and relieved him of his burden.

She walked up behind him, enjoying the familiar scene as he tended the fire and returned it to a blaze of crackling logs.

Turning from his task and still on his knees, Scott reached up and settled his masculine grip around Brooke's waist. "I had to see you tonight." She barely heard what he said as she melted in his powerful hands. He drew her closer. Close enough for him to settle his face in the folds of her robe.

A pleasantly painful ache sprang from the accelerated warmth at the juncture of Brooke's thighs. She was aware that he could create this feeling in her, but it had been so long since she let it guide her. Still, she didn't want to rush into the ecstasy she knew would follow.

Capturing Scott's face in her hands, Brooke gently pushed him back to allow herself to sink to the floor with him. Down on her knees, and then leaning back on the heels of her feet, Brooke caught his gaze. Her lips didn't part, but the corners rose in a shy, yet seductive smile.

"You're doing it to me again."

"What am I doing?" Brooke tilted her curls to the side.

"You have a look."

"Everyone has a look."

"Not like the one you give me."

Brooke gave no implication of understanding his statement.

Breathing in deeply, Scott briefly explained, "The curve of your mouth. The look in your eyes with them half lowered while watching me. It all makes me want to take you without a thought."

A responsive smile that separated her lips showed her approval. "I so want you to make love to me. Even with everything that's going on, I feel ready." As the words left her mouth, Scott closed the space between them, claiming her body against his. Brooke whispered, "It won't have to be secret for long."

Scott pulled her legs from underneath and lowered Brooke to the floor. She gladly accepted this position and showed her need as she arched her back and exposed her taught nipples that crept out from under the edges of her robe.

"I shouldn't be doing this. I shouldn't be doing this," Scott murmured raggedly with anticipation. He tugged at his belt and undid his pants, shoving them off onto the floor. Getting on his knees, he stripped his sweater off and threw it to the side.

At the same time, Brooke shimmied out of her robe. It was an invitation and he accepted by placing his hand over her breast, covering all the flesh and caressing her nipple between his fingers. He spread her heated thighs open with his knee and free hand.

Warm passion dripped uncontrollably as Scott lowered his face between her smooth thighs. Brooke gasped as she felt the vibration from his lips as they searched her inner thigh. She could barely contain herself and then he lightly tongued her only to return to the side of her wetness. She tilted her pelvis, wanting his mouth to taste her again.

"Give me more, Brooke. Give me more." His hand searched for her other breast where it met her smaller grasp, lent to help him stimulate the lust he'd developed in her. She moved her body against his mouth as if he was already inside her.

Wanting to reciprocate the pleasure, Brooke curved her waist to reach for Scott's erection. Keeping his mouth on her, he moved his hips sideways. She lightly rubbed his scrotum taught, and then circled and stroked his sex. As it grew strong in her hand, he nipped lightly at her folds of sensitive skin.

With a teasingly slow circle of his tongue, Brooke hardened in return. He lifted up and returned his lips to her warm mouth, where she tasted the flavor he feasted on.

"I can't help it, Brooke," Scott said in exasperation with his hot breath against her cheek. At the same time, he pulled away from her massaging hand and pushed his hips between her thighs.

Again, misunderstanding what he was getting at, Brooke responded, "I want this as much as you, Scott. Please, please don't stop."

"No, baby, I have no intentions of stopping this time." He rocked his hips to open her wider, to let him in, as he murmured, "I won't hurt you. I'll never hurt you."

Closing his eyes tight, Scott dropped his hips lower to her writhing body below him. Brooke felt small beads of heat trickle down the side of her belly. He eased into her and plunged deep, tightened and pushed deeper. Immediately he slowed as he detected the resistance surrounding his excitement.

"I won't hurt you, baby," Scott repeated, audibly this time.

"You're not hurting me. I want to completely feel you in me," Brooke gasped as Scott completed his entry. She felt him reach her sweet spot. Her body shook as she tried to pull him in further.

Scott eased back, and then traveled the same route as Brooke raised her hips to meet his need. She rotated her pelvis and wouldn't lower her body with the rhythm, but rather kept urging him to sink deeper and erase the pain accumulated from their restricted time.

Still far inside her, she felt Scott's body tighten while he bent forward and kissed her breasts with wet lips. She grabbed his shoulder and dug barely noticeable nails into his muscles while the hand of the healing arm rested softly on the opposite side.

She lifted her chin and kissed Scott's forehead as his mouth searched her soft flesh. She felt the power and tenderness in his touches and knew she couldn't control what was probably the ticking of the clock, the metallic sound she heard from a corner of the room. She encouraged him to stroke her inside long and hard and wanted him as close to a climax as herself.

"Brooke, sweetheart, are you ready?"

Brooke attributed Scott's timing to nervousness. She made herself easily ready for him. "You make me ready the instant you touch me. Can't you tell?"

Scott let out a low, fierce growl as an answer. She circled her legs around his waist, matching his energy as he shoved his hand beneath her and held her backside off the floor.

Her breathing grew faster. Her core tightened as he gave slow, hard thrusts and his pelvis repeatedly rubbed against hers.

"Scott, Scott, I can't stop the feeling anymore. I have to..."

"Go ahead, baby. Don't hold back. I want to hear what you feel."

Brooke didn't let him pull back as her muscles clenched around him. Her cheek pushed against his chest, flattening the soft spatter of hair. She saw his bicep flex as he shocked her senses with a deepening of his penetration.

She gasped and cried out his name as exhilaration surged through her center. Grabbing his arm, she squeezed with each volt of the orgasm.

Scott shifted his pelvis, intensifying the sensation. She licked her salty lips and tightened her stomach to hold on to the last shiver of ecstasy.

She became aware of a pulse between her legs as her body weakened and she breathed in the musky sexual incense their bodies created.

She looked up at Scott and saw his eyes close tightly. In a flash, he pulled his manhood out and poured his steamy fluid onto her heaving belly. A deep and raspy groan accompanied his release.

He gradually opened his eyes while his body remained still for a moment.

Brooke smiled as she smeared her fingers where he left his climax. She glanced up and saw him watching. In a whisper, she assured, "I'm glad we didn't wait any longer."

He lowered his gaze to connect with Brooke's stare. His eyes were sexy, half covered with heavy eyelids. "I'll be better prepared next time. I really didn't think we'd..."

"Shhh..." Nothing worried her.

7\

Chapter 40

Scott collapsed onto Brooke's chest, avoiding her shoulder. She adored the heat and weight of his body. She snuggled her face against his neck as wispy lengths of his hair fell over her cheek. "Scott, don't get off me, yet," she murmured beneath his ear.

As if it was a signal, his body tensed. He waited a brief moment, and then gently lifted off her. He ran his fingertips across her heated belly and focused his eyes on hers. Even though the fire sparked various shades of orange light, it had nothing to do with the shades of brown that waved around Scott's irises. "Brooke," she knew what was coming. "I have to go."

She waited for more, waited for Scott to say that he was kidding.

"I feel cheap, but I have a bad feeling that if I stay… Well, we might get an unpleasant interruption." Scott watched as Brooke attempted to hide her disappointment. It didn't work too well.

Instead of responding, Brooke simply encompassed his shoulders with her arm and again, pushed her face into his neck. He allowed this one last comfort, and then he wrapped his manly arm across her back and pulled her to a sitting position.

"I know. You're probably right. I should be thankful that you care enough to try to see me for now. I am," Brooke said.

Scott pulled away and began to gather his tossed sweater and other clothing. He handed Brooke the robe she had started the night in. As she tied the front of it, he watched the same dangling thread she'd pulled on earlier.

Scott took a hold of the string and began to wrap it around his index finger before speaking. "Brooke, how can you… I mean, with everything…"

"I'm not following you." It was easy for Brooke to know his first decision ahead of time, but she was baffled this time. His tone forebode more unpleasant news.

"What I'm trying to say is that you shouldn't be seeing me."

"What?" Brooke's hands shot up to her mouth with her forearms secured together over her chest. After making love with such passion less than five minutes ago, she willed his words to be different. They weren't.

"Brooke, it's not that I don't want to be with you. I do, and I've told you that I do. Yet, now's not the time." Scott hurriedly finished his explanation before Brooke could question his decision. "As long as you know and believe that I wasn't the one who…who hurt you, we'll be okay when it's all over."

There was the saying "when it's all over" again. When would it be gone?

With a quick glance to the floor, to the snapping fire, and then back to Scott, Brooke looked him in his magnetic eyes and said, "Yes, I believe you."

He caressed her chin with a soft touch. "I won't call you until I think it's safe. As long as no one knows about this, we'll make it."

Brooke could only nod in agreement. All of a sudden instead of this weekend starting a good thing, it appeared to act as a quick tease. She didn't understand why Scott needed assurance that she didn't blame him. There wouldn't be any talk about it soon.

Chapter 41

"What do you have on your agenda today?" Chloe asked as she poured the morning coffee.

A couple days had passed since the complicated weekend. Brooke avoided any possible contact with Ty and had returned to Chloe's relatively early on Sunday. She kept herself busy by starting a new section of the stained glass for Maple Haven. That was her Sunday project. Today was different.

"I have an appointment this morning."

"Oh, did I forget or didn't I know about it?"

"I don't think I ever had a chance to mention it," Brooke informed her.

Chloe sipped her coffee and didn't push for details.

Brooke was nervous to talk about the reserved time she had set up, but she also wanted confirmation that it was the right thing to do. She needed an agreement to her decision. "Okay, okay. I can't stand not talking to you about this. I had a fabulous weekend at my place and it gave me a lot of time to think about my appointment. I still think I'm right about showing up for it this morning." Brooke purposefully left out the details of the weekend.

Chloe cocked her head and held her cup slightly below her chin. At attention, she sat quietly, waiting for Brooke to expound on her schedule.

"I'm meeting a real estate agent." There, she'd revealed her secret.

"Oh, you've decided to buy yourself a small home instead of renting? A small bungalow with room for a new studio would be fabulous." Chloe didn't understand, or at least she covered it well. "Which one are you talking to this morning?" With a light giggle, Chloe added, "I think I can excuse you from work for a while as long as you bring me back a double espresso with a topping of froth."

Dropping her head, Brooke chuckled. She looked back at her friend, and said, "You must've known that we set the meeting up at the coffee house?"

"Really? I hadn't thought about it that deeply, but how convenient. I'm not surprised they're willing to travel to such a hospitable place considering the market right now."

"Oh no, Chloe. This is about an additional thing I have to take care of." Brooke still had a hard time admitting her decision, and saying it aloud was even worse.

"I didn't mean to pry. I assumed you were thinking a new home of your own would be a nice way to get, uh, your life back into perspective. You know, a fresh start away from anything related to the shooting. And with a new art studio, so you wouldn't have to rebuild so close to Ty's home."

"I can't deny that. I'm sure it's hard for you to share your space continually, too."

Chloe shook her head to negate such an idea. She remained quiet as Brooke rounded up the nerve to reveal her morning rendezvous.

"Okay, here goes. I actually have two reasons to meet with the agent from Camden Real Estate. First, you're right about me wanting my own place, but it's contingent on another sale." Here she paused, wondering how she could force the words to the surface. "It's time for the house Ty's in, the house we still own together, to be sold."

Chloe raised her brows along with her eyes surfacing like two full moons over a dark lake of coffee. If they looked anything alike, Chloe and Brooke could have been looking into mirrors. Brooke was just as surprised that she finally told her secret. Not a real secret, she didn't have time to consider telling or not since she had called the real estate agency.

"Since the divorce, I've given him so much time to find another place. A place he could be comfortable in and have room for his therapy equipment. I don't think he's tried to find anything, and his therapy doesn't appear to be necessary anymore. He's quite recovered from the stroke, which was over two years ago." Brooke paused for a sip of coffee. "And my studio is gone, so I've nothing to hold me to that piece of property next door, either."

Brooke took a breath and gave Chloe an opportunity to comment. "I don't blame you for choosing that route." She didn't add any advice.

Brooke didn't feel the relief she'd expected with having a force behind her, no matter how small. She didn't have any doubts. Maybe that's why she didn't have a different feeling after Chloe sided with her. "I'm ready," Brooke claimed with a tone of surety.

* * * *

Brooke tapped the side of her ceramic cup as she waited. She wasn't sure if it was the extra shot of espresso or her nerves that kept her constantly alert for any movement near the door of the coffee cafe. She'd arrived ten minutes early, and now, ten minutes after the meeting hour, she still sat alone. Not surprising. She repeatedly heard that real estate agents didn't keep accurate time.

Brooke conveniently sat at the same table that she and Chloe had shared when she gave her warning. Brooke vividly recalled her ignorance in not listening. This time she would adhere to the advice real estate agent Camden was sure to impart.

Sitting stiffly on the wooden chair, she leaned forward as if that would give her an advantage on her viewpoint of the door. Brooke noticed an ache rising up her spine. She twisted in her seat to relieve the rigidity and attempted to internalize the comfort and ambience of the café surrounding her.

Her eyes scanned the mismatched and distressed, multicolored tables and chairs. The cornices over the many mullioned windows were patterned with soft browns and raspberry colors. The coffee bar attributed warmth from a lacquered, dark cherry wood. Brass railings encased the numerous coffee dips that scattered the front edge of the bar.

It didn't work. Brooke barely noticed the clinking cups and spoons mixed with the tune of a soft jazz saxophone to entertain the diners. She took a deep breath of the scented air in a last attempt to relax.

Realistically, she couldn't be surprised at her apprehension. It wasn't a common activity she intended to accomplish today. As Brooke reviewed her conscience, the tarnished bell hanging over the door gave a paltry signal of the incoming cold air along with a man in a long, black, wool overcoat.

Brooke began to rise from her chair as Jeff Camden caught sight of her and motioned her to remain seated. He smoothly wove a path through the scattered furniture without attracting attention from the other chattering customers.

Brooke's fear that she would appear conspicuous solely because of her purpose was glad to stay in her seat at the edge of the room. Other customers paid little attention to real estate agent Camden's entrance.

"Hi, Brooke. How're you doing?" The ease of Camden's voice comforted her. He sported a graying mustache and matching shortly trimmed hair. Brooke felt a fatherly presence even though he was only five to ten years older than she was.

She gave the typical answer. "I'm fine, thank you."

Camden nodded politely and sat across from her. Before spreading the forms out, he began, "I understand the house you want to sell has two names on the title. That of you and your husba…rather ex-husband. Is he in agreement with this decision because his signature will also be needed?"

Pushing the overload of coffee to the side, Brooke clasped her hands and laid her arms on the table. "It was our written agreement when we got divorced. I didn't follow through with trying to sell until now. He doesn't have a choice."

As if she wasn't a spontaneous client, Jeff Camden asked, "So you've talked with him about proceeding with the sale now?"

Brooke calculated her answer and responded, "Not yet."

Camden raised his eyebrows. "He doesn't know about this meeting? Are you sure he's ready to sell?"

"Well," Brooke began as she contemplated how to get around this question. "I've given him nearly two years. Our verbal agreement was that he would be in charge of the sale."

"That's quite generous of you. I don't hear such stories often. Maybe you should explain what that means to the possibility of him agreeing to a sale right now," Camden requested after her unorthodox answer.

She looked down and spread her hands out, attempting to regain her control and finish the story she had mentally prepared. It wasn't necessary for him to know the details of her decision. If she did all the footwork, it would be easier to get Ty's signature.

"I'm sure he wants to move on as much as I want the house sold," Brooke suggested as she met Jeff Camden's eyes.

"Right now I'll assume you'll be able to get his signature. Will you be looking to buy another house? Did you want to move out of this town?"

Brooke tilted her head. "I'm not sure what you're getting at, Mr. Camden. I intend on staying in town. I don't know what Ty intends to do."

Pushing himself back in the chair, and then coming forward to the table again, Camden said in a low tone, "I'm aware of the current news. I'm sorry, I thought that with the shooting, you might be interested in leaving town."

"The shooting has nothing to do with it," Brooke quickly told him.

Throwing his hands up, Camden said, "Forgive me for my presumption. It's none of my business. We'll go from here."

Brooke couldn't help but add, "I don't know who shot at me. Nothing has been proven yet, and I still have a hard time thinking that my ex-husband could've done it. He may not have been perfect, but…I can't consider that right now. Besides, his nurse, Marla Vrahn, is the one in jail."

Brooke noticed him adjust in his chair as an awkward silence began. Speaking slowly, Jeff Camden offered, "Brooke, I didn't mean to bring up your personal life. I'm sure your situation is difficult at this point." Pausing with consideration, Camden informed, "I'll have the papers implemented. If you have a legal agreement that the house will be sold, I can have the papers presented to Mr. Bellin."

Collecting herself with a shaky breath, Brooke answered, "As soon as possible."

"Tomorrow. It can be done tomorrow." Camden watched Brooke's expression.

"That's fast. Um…yeah, go ahead." Brooke ran her hand across her mouth to wipe away the imaginary crumbs from never ordered food. "Yes, do it. Will I be informed when Ty receives the…" Her voice dried and left the air weighted with the end. The end of the discussion. The end of the last connection to her former life.

Thinking of the sudden and incomplete ending with Scott over what she had anticipated as a fulfilling weekend, Brooke made another decision. It didn't matter if she had a man in her life. She'd rather have no one if it was the only way to erase the stress she endured.

That was a lie. She still needed Scott.

Stopping her cultivating mind, Jeff Camden answered the unfinished question, "My secretary or I'll call you as soon as it's verified that your ex-husband has agreed to the sale." He gave her a warm smile of encouragement for her decision.

The timing was right. The inference was bad.

* * * *

Scott walked out of the hardware store positioned kitty-corner from the coffee café. Adjusting his bag of miscellaneous parts for a repair on his crew's table saw, he couldn't help but to glance toward the café that he knew Brooke frequented.

The snow-covered ground brightened the sky without the help of the sun. Looking through his perpetually worn sunglasses, Scott couldn't see inside the windows of the café as the glare of the snow bounced back at him. He still felt closer to Brooke, just being close to something she liked.

Scott made a mental note to call Chloe to find out if there'd be any stained glass ready to pick up soon. He realized he'd just picked up a load last week, but it was a way to see Brooke accidentally.

Walking to his truck, Scott took a last look at the café as the door jingled open. A man in a business coat patiently held the door for the next person to exit.

Scott's feet slid to a stop as he misjudged his next step on the shoveled path along the sidewalk. With his foot anchored in the snow bank, Scott let the snow tumble into the cuff of his boot. He watched the unmistakable dark-hair of his Brooke scatter its ends across her shoulders when she entered the icy breeze of the late morning.

Scott's first thought was that he'd picked the best time to run his errands. He couldn't speak with Brooke, but to see her was a rare treat he didn't have to manipulate into the day's accomplishments.

The contented smile vanished as Scott witnessed the unknown man place his hand at Brooke's lower back and guide her to the parking lot. He could see them talk, but was startled when the distinguished-looking man leaned into Brooke's profile with his face obstructed by her blowing hair.

Oblivious to the snow melting in his boot and the sting of the wind on one side of his face, Scott remained in place as nerves began to jitter and flatten his heart against the wall of his chest where he felt it pound with anxiety.

Scott watched as Brooke and the unidentified man paused at the entrance of the parking lot, spoke a few words, and then continued together to his car. She got in, and he shut the door for her.

Chapter 42

Brooke settled into the leather seat of Jeff Camden's car. "You're right. This is better than walking." Camden smiled at her as he started his car. "Took me a minute to figure out that you offered me a ride. It was hard to hear over the wind."

"I thought I could get you to agree after a few minutes outside. I'll get you safely to your friend's house."

* * * *

Back at his office, Scott tossed the bag of parts onto his desk along with his intentions to get right at that project. Pulling his chair from its place, he reached over the partially organized stacks resting on the desk to turn the radio on.

Scott ignored the topic of dissention on the talk radio show. He simply wanted noise to help him not think about what he wished he hadn't seen.

There. He started to think about it already. He knew he would succumb to an analysis of what happened. Scott was well aware of his own patterns. He never liked to leave things unfinished or not thought out completely, but he typically was able to come up with a provable answer. He wasn't so sure this time.

Scott absently sat in the chair, put a foot on the edge of the desk, and pushed against the spring at the base of the seat to leave him somewhere between half sitting and lying in the chair. Tears weren't his style. Instead, he focused on the frost that grew around the perimeter of the window straight ahead.

What he saw had nothing to do with the view beyond his office. He repeatedly visualized the hand at Brooke's back, the stranger's face near her cheek, and the car door that closed her away from him.

“Maybe that was a new officer on her case,” Scott told the empty room. “He acted too friendly for that and she didn’t urge me to stay overnight this weekend.

“Get a grip, Scott,” he told himself. “She’s allowed to have friends. Don’t worry about it unless she gives a reason to.”

Scott gave himself a couple more minutes of idle thought before getting busy. He did make one promise to himself. He needed to slow down with Brooke because he knew he could fall too fast and too hard. He wanted proof that she was thinking about the future with him, not just a temporary and safe relationship.

He didn’t like the touch of jealousy he felt, either. He would add that to his list of things to work on.

Chapter 43

Watching the copper curve and hug the edge of the glass gave Brooke comfort in the ease of the fit. They blended well. They fit each other.

The coppery effect surrounded the shadowed glass as if they belonged together. The arms of the male encased the soft and curvaceous body of his angel in two colors entangled and burnt into the glass. Only two colors left the details imaginary.

Brooke tossed her hair to the side as she bent closer to her creation. The normal peace her work gave her slipped in and out of focus. She was on schedule and pleased with what she'd accomplished this week, but occasionally her thoughts traveled to the other issues in her life.

She hadn't heard from the authorities recently on the progress of her case. She hadn't heard from the real estate agent, or from Scott since their weekend interlude.

Brooke couldn't put her conflicts into an order of importance. They were all related yet separate. There was a measure of hurt attached to each one, which left her to wonder.

"Hey there, Brooke. How's your work coming?"

Brooke, startled by the interruption of her mind's discussion, jerked her arm as she turned toward the voice. At the same time, a box of supplies scattered to the floor.

Chloe scrambled to the ensuing mess, attempting to catch the falling pieces. "Oh, I'm so sorry. I thought you would've heard me open the door," she claimed.

"No, I guess I was in deep concentration." Brooke joined her on the floor to assemble the escaped rolls of wires from the box. "Not a big deal. I didn't knock over anything breakable."

As they crawled around the floor to round up the remaining rolls, Chloe sat back on her heels. "Brooke, I got a call a few minutes ago."

"Oh," Brooke responded, stopping a minute to glance up from the floor. When she saw the look of concern on Chloe's face, Brooke dipped her head and pretended to look for more materials, although they were collected.

"Brooke, Ty called." Brooke slowly sat up and focused on what Chloe had to say. She continued, "He's coming over in about half an hour."

Brooke put her hand to the back of her neck to counteract the creeping tension. "Did he say what he wanted?"

Before Chloe could answer, the phone rang. "I'll let the machine answer."

"No, get the phone. I'm interrupting your business more than I wanted to already."

"I'll be right back." Chloe went for the phone near the door. After a brief moment to listen to the caller, she said, "It's for you."

Brooke's hand trembled as she extended it.

"It's not Ty."

With a small smile of gratitude, Brooke answered the call.

Chloe busied herself and returned the wires to their home. She examined Brooke's work while she spoke on the phone.

"That was my real estate agent. Uh, Jeff Camden." Brooke didn't expect complete surprise from her dear friend, but in return Chloe showed no surprise at all and remained quiet, giving Brooke an opportunity to expand on the situation if she chose.

"You look like you expected this. That is, for me to want the house sold, and actually follow through with it." Brooke was ready for a comment from her friend's keen insight into events.

"Ty received a call this morning about his part in the sale. I'm sure that's why he's coming over," Brooke finished. She didn't comment on the tardiness of the agent to confront Ty, nearly a week later than promised.

"You've gone through a lot of changes, issues, and realizations this year, which can understandably affect your view on the future," Chloe commented on Brooke's first statement.

Brooke interrupted. "No really, Chloe." She slapped her hands on her thighs. "What do you think? I'm confused, I'm frustrated, and most of all I feel nothing is stable. Everything in my life is changing. I don't have my studio for my work, I can barely spend time in my apartment, and my ex-husband will not accept that I'm not part of his life. His awful life, and he has…has odd mood swings toward me. He still treats me like he owns me. That's got to end.

"Oh, and I shouldn't forget the man who I accidentally let myself get involved with. Yeah, I saw him the weekend I was at home. Part of it was wonderful to be with him again and the other part was rushed and secret and left me feeling as if it was all about the sex and nothing else."

Brooke's hand went back to squeeze the pain out of her neck. "I'm not sure what to do next. Should I run away and start over? Should I stay here and try different tactics to get my life back in order? Or should I continue to do what I'm doing?"

"Oh Brooke, I want to give you answers to all your questions, but I don't have them. I only warned you about the trail you traveled because it dealt with your safety." Brooke nodded at the acquiescence and waited for more.

"I can tell you that you are and will be safe with whatever route you travel this time. I can't be sure on the final results because you're in control of that. Am I making any sense?"

Relaxing her position, Brooke answered, "I understand what you're telling me. The scant glance to the future is enough for me. At least I know I won't get shot at again. That's part of your forecast, right?"

"I don't see any guns involved this time. You know I'll be your friend through it all, don't you?" Brooke heaved an audible sigh and smiled. "And not to change the subject, but Ty will be here soon. Do you want me to stay close, go away, or stay on the other side of the door and jump in if necessary?" Chloe asked. Brooke accepted the small attempt at humor to relieve some of the intensity of the conversation.

Getting up from the floor, Brooke said, "No, no, I'll be alright. Just do whatever you were doing before he called. I knew this encounter was inevitable. It's about the only thing on my 'list of things to do' that I can control. "

"Okay, I'll be up front." Chloe copied Brooke's movement from the floor, and then backed up to the door and disappeared.

Brooke took a deep breath and glanced at the work she had suspended. She was certainly thinking in a different vein and to pick up where she stopped wasn't going to happen right now. "Time for a shot of hot cocoa, I think."

Brooke stared at the mugs in the cupboard as her hand rested on a gold flecked and oddly shaped specimen and then proceeded to pull two down. "I might as well be polite and offer him a drink, too."

She watched the milk turn in perfect circles as it heated on the tray in the microwave. Not wanting to hypothesize what Ty would say when he arrived, Brooke detached her gaze from the milk and checked the cupboards for the cocoa mix in addition to unnecessarily wiping the counter clean of nothing visible.

A knock on the door caused Brooke to freeze in mid-stir. She thought she was ready for this. She'd anticipated the meeting, but it'd be different when it really happened.

Taking a deep, shaky breath, Brooke slowly and very carefully set the spoon on the counter she had just cleaned. "Open the door, Brooke. Let him in," she commanded herself.

Attempting to hold her head high and falsely show confidence, she opened the door.

Brooke stared into the face of a man she thought she once knew.

"Don't look so surprised. You knew I'd be coming."

"You're right." Brooke stepped away from the door. "Come in." Ty acted as if he'd won a round already.

"What's this?" Ty opened the discussion as he threw a folded paper to the table. Digging further in his pocket, he brought a hand-sized electronic device into view. Casually turning it over in his hand, he looked at Brooke until he had her rapt attention. Apparently, he gave the device more relevance than the pending sales document.

He placed it on the table, closer to himself.

Without an answer from Brooke, Ty implicated a different tactic. "Which one would you like to discuss first?"

Brooke involuntarily lowered her brows. "What do you mean? I have only one thing to talk to you about."

"I doubt that."

Ty's coolness and nonchalance toward the real estate contract startled Brooke. That's what the document he threw on the table must be. She was sure of that.

Brooke hadn't prepared herself for things to go astray so quickly during their meeting. She assumed the right words would come to her with their history and the current issues ensuing, but Ty threw a crook in what she falsely expected. "I…I don't think I have anything else to talk about with you." She wanted to be in control, but it was vanishing quickly.

Tapping his finger on the device, Ty asked, "Do you know what this is?"

Brooke followed the movement with her eyes, and faltered, "No." Her mouth ran dry with ignorance.

The hot cocoa remained on the counter. Hospitality didn't fit into this scene.

Ty smirked as he pulled out a chair and sat near his surprise. He made himself comfortable as he spread his legs in front of the seat. His blue eyes glinted in the streams of light from the overhead table fixture. Brooke waited for him to speak, but he remained waiting for her to do the same.

Biting her lip and feeling the dryness, Brooke wanted to get this over so she started again. "Let's talk about the papers."

Ty snagged the papers from the table. Tapping the document on the table's edge, he questioned, "What's this all about?"

Stunned at the question of the obvious, Brooke looked at him still calmly seated. "Those are the real estate papers, aren't they?"

"Yes, Brooke," Ty said, drawling her name out and emphasizing the k. "I understand what they are, but what do you think you're doing by abandoning me? I need you to keep me on track with my therapy, and you need me to protect you. What if someone attempted your life again?"

"How can you say that?" This wasn't progressing at all as she anticipated.

"What? That you're abandoning me, that you're good at therapy, or that you might get a gun aimed at your pretty face again?" Ty sneered as he asked the last question.

"This isn't funny." Taking a deep breath, Brooke felt overwhelmed with the magnitude of their discussion and chose not to hold back anymore. "I'm not abandoning you. You did that to me a long time ago. Don't you remember the blond, and might I mention, long hair on your shirts after work? What about the phone calls that slipped into my hand when you thought I wouldn't be around? And the new perfumes you claimed you tested at the mall even though you never seemed to find the right one to actually buy and bring home for me?

"You still haven't let go since the divorce. I'm sure it's partly my fault by helping with the therapy, but it's time. When the house is sold, you won't have any reason to contact me."

Ty's demeanor remained intact. Brooke stamped her foot as she continued, "You had the stroke. I felt so bad for you. I wanted to help, so I held off on saying anything about you not selling the house.

"Apparently, the only way for you to realize that we aren't together anymore, is to sell it. I found a different home two years ago, now it's your turn." Brooke paused here, waiting for Ty to explain away her rationalization and make her feel foolish at the same time.

"Ah, Brooke, you haven't figured it out yet. You have always been so naïve, but I thought you were smart enough to understand."

"Understand what? I haven't a clue as to what you're talking about." Brooke's face flushed as her voice rose.

"It's my nature, Brooke. I knew you'd put up with it, but I didn't think you were such a believer in a perfect marriage." Standing up and stretching as if he was preparing for an in-depth explanation, Ty towered over Brooke as she felt herself sink into a tightened posture with an attempt to insulate herself from whatever was to come.

"Although, I will have to admit, our marriage was pretty close to being perfect. Perfect in the way I wanted it, anyway."

Brooke cringed more as the words assaulted her. She didn't ask for further explanation, but it came anyway.

"Yeah, the women you insist I had, were another bonus from the deal between me and the district attorney."

Brooke's faced crumpled as she muttered, "Your deal? What kind of deal, and what does it have to do with us? With us right now?"

Talking in tangents, Ty answered, "How do you think we could afford the house we live in? I was a good finishing carpenter, but they don't make the money we spent. And your work, you probably spent it on your garden or more glass supplies."

It was Brooke's turn to sink into a kitchen chair. With her head down, she asked, "So, you're saying we have nothing? Wasn't the house ours?"

Ty cocked his head to the side with a chuckle. "No, I'm saying I have money. I'm saying that I've been able to pay for everything. If you still don't get it, then I've told you enough.

"Let's move on to the next item of importance," he said, as if they'd resolved a plan for the house sale.

The conversation overwhelmed Brooke. Her foot fidgeted under the table. She couldn't imagine what else Ty would bring up. She was sorry he'd come over.

Interrupting her thoughts, Ty presented the second subject. "Again I ask you, do you know what this is?" His hand covered the other object on the table.

Losing enthusiasm and energy to hold back emotion, Brooke simply said, "No, Ty, I said I don't know what that is. Why don't you enlighten me?"

He began with another of his sardonic smirks, "This is a trail-cam, Brooke. Do you know what this is used for?" Brooke's quizzical expression answered him. "I can take videos with this." Picking the trail-cam up and juggling it in one hand, Ty continued in a taunting manner. "It's programmed to begin taping when objects, such as pheasants and other woods animals, move in front of it."

Brooke squinted, waiting for a relevant explanation. "Of course, that's what this piece of technology is designed for, but it doesn't only work in the woods. I can set it up anywhere and moving objects will turn it on." Ty paused here.

Brooke began to acknowledge the diversity of his surprise. The weekend flickered through Brooke's conscience

"Do you want to see what I videoed most recently? Keep in mind that I didn't take this with me during the hunting weekend." Ty walked toward the entrance to Chloe's living room where the television sat quiet and dark in its corner. Brooke could see the edge of it as her eyes followed his movement.

Ty hunted without his trail-cam, yet he said he used it. It videotaped moving objects. The camera wouldn't have distinguished what kind of moving objects.

With a rush of fear, Brooke jumped from her seat. "I don't believe you have anything that matters on your camera, and I don't want to see it." She stood rigid as she waited for Ty's reaction.

"Oh, it matters, all right. When you see it, you'll change your mind about selling the house." Ty crossed the living room and scanned the electronic devices attached to the television.

Brooke's curiosity, outweighed by apprehension of the possibility that her illicit weekend was portrayed on film, forced her to follow Ty into the living room. She had to do something to keep him from playing it. Better yet, to get the film erased even if she didn't know what it might show. He had no business being in her private life.

"You can have everything in the house. I have nothing left. My studio is gone. I don't want anything. It means nothing to me. I just want out." As she spoke, Ty located the plug-in on the television. Brooke felt a dampness connect her skin to the soft threads of her sweater. Barely controlling the tremble in her voice, she pleaded, "Don't play the tape."

Ty looked up from his mission. "Are you afraid of a little entertainment? Don't you want to know how *my* weekend was?"

He dropped the wire that dangled from the trail-cam. With the apparatus in one hand, he reached out and grabbed Brooke's arm with the other. "Do you think I'm going to let you walk out of my life? You've made it so easy for me." He kept his voice low with a grumble of anger seasoning the words. "I really don't want to start over."

"Ty, why do you even care anymore? You have Marla. You can sell the house or buy it for yourself. I'll get out of your life."

Needles of pain pricked her arm and sent spears of the same to her shoulder as Ty jerked her healing arm. The black lines in his blue eyes thickened, leaving no room for warmth as his anger intensified. "Good question, Brooke. Without me, you are nothing. And Marla, she's trash and is going to get a roommate with stripes. Don't you remember what she did to you? I'll build you a new…"

"Ouch, Ty, you're hurting my arm." Tears spurt from Brooke's swollen eyes as her demeanor faltered.

Ty released her arm and gave a final warning, "You know what's on this video. I want to watch it less than you do, but I'll let you find out its content by what happens next. Don't bother calling…your boyfriend."

Brooke's mouth popped open as she sucked in air to fill the sudden vacuous space in her lungs. She had no retort. Her mind was as overfilled as her lungs felt empty.

Chapter44

"Did everything go as planned? Chloe floated in from the business end of her home. "Was he receptive to getting the house sold? I didn't hear a ruckus, so I figured you didn't need me."

Brooke returned to a seat at the kitchen table. She positioned her arms over her chest, intimating that the room was cold, or that she needed to shield herself from something.

"I see you have two cups of cocoa on the counter growing cold. Did the meeting go faster than you expected?" Chloe turned and focused on Brooke. "Brooke, what happened this time? Are you alright?"

Snapping her head to attention, Brooke slowly responded, "Nothing. Nothing happened." Tension sucked the sound out of the room. After a few moments, she added, "That's it. Absolutely nothing happened the way I expected."

Chloe left the cocoa on the counter, just as Brooke had, and eased herself into the chair closest to her friend. Brooke shivered with Chloe's warm hand resting on her arm.

"Brooke, can I help? Are you going to be alright?" Chloe paused with her litany of questions as Brooke looked to her vacantly. "I'm sorry. I don't mean to pressure you, but it's obvious that something isn't right."

Without answering the questions, Brooke responded, "I'm not feeling well." Chloe's hand dropped to the table as Brooke rose from her chair. She turned and walked toward the bathroom.

The mirror reflected red and green eyes with puffed and swollen lids. Brooke shut her eyes and dunked her head to the faucet with a splash of warm water. As she contemplated her next action, Brooke gingerly stepped back to the kitchen.

Not intending to sit, she stood blocking the gray light from the kitchen window. A ghostly glow emanated around her. Parting her dried lips,

Brooke whispered, "Dead." Chloe began to lift from her chair, but remained suspended as Brooke continued. "He's dead to me."

"Oh, baby..."

"He said that Marla did it."

"Ty has proof?" Skepticism edged Chloe's voice.

Startled with the suggestion, Brooke focused on Chloe's intent features. "I didn't think of that."

"What do you mean?" Chloe shook her head in confusion. "Isn't that what we're talking about?"

Brooke began to pace the floor. As she left the outline of the gray light, she saw color flood her skin and felt her cheeks burn. "Chloe, Ty said he had a video of something. I thought it was of Scott and me. Last weekend. I wouldn't let him show it to me." She stopped in mid-step. "Maybe I was wrong, and it was of...of the shooting."

Chloe quickly theorized, "Wouldn't he have said something sooner, if he videoed the shooting? It would've cleared him. But...and he could only have videoed it, if he knew it was going to happen."

"Maybe that's why he didn't turn the tape over to the police."

"So we're back to step one, meaning he's involved."

Brooke leaned against the sink and tapped her fingers on the dull, chrome edge. Her energy ebbed with her thoughts. "I don't know. I'm so confused at this point that I can't think straight anymore. He said Marla did it, but how does he know?" Her body trembled as she turned to face Chloe.

Chloe jumped up and wrapped her arms around Brooke. "The police will figure this out. It's their job."

"Ooh, not so tight on my shoulder." Chloe loosened her grip as Brooke gingerly rubbed near the wound. Switching back into gear, she wearily added, "We'll find out soon. There's some type of court proceeding in about a week, although I haven't heard from the police or detectives for a while."

Pulling away from her friend, Chloe smiled encouragingly. "It'll come out in the end.

"By the way, is your shoulder okay? I thought it was getting better."

"Yeah, it is. I bumped it earlier, that's all."

Moving the discussion in another direction, Chloe asked, "Do you have any plans for the rest of the day?"

"Actually, I have come up with something that needs tending to all of a sudden." Brooke spontaneously decided her next move.

Chapter 45

She stood inside the entry of Hunters' Outfitters, the local sporting goods store. Trying to keep her mind from escaping its intentions, Brooke took an overview of the overwhelming animal and weapon displays around her. Australia, the Arctic, African plains, along with the nearly inaccessible kettles of Russia were represented by their native, hunted animals.

The raised claws grabbed at the viewers. The taxidermy eyes stared past Brooke. Yet, the fur looked soft and in need of a warm touch. The planted animals so resembled the confusion surrounding the man who'd caused her to come here. Ty had just as many personalities as these hunted animals. Inclusively, they all need to survive or they'll be hung up to view.

Brooke shuddered against the chill that sprang up with this primitive thought. She turned down the aisle with the smaller, less offensive taxidermies and headed for a counter to look for a salesperson.

An air vent above the initial counter blew hot air over Brooke's shoulders, yet she couldn't shake the cold running its path through her body as she stared at a glass case full of gun shells. She did a quick turn to the next counter.

The nearest end began with scopes for mounting on guns. Brooke quickened her pace and passed binoculars and then telescopes. Noticing the correlation to her search, she slowed down and followed the turn in the case.

The display graduated to video cameras.

"Ma'am, I'll be right with you," a young clerk dressed in camouflage announced.

"Yes, thank you," Brooke responded with a quick upward glance from the case. To hide her nervousness, she lowered her gaze back to the cameras.

The objects under the glass began to melt into each other and then push away and become their own again as Brooke fluttered her damp lashes.

Most of the apparatus were black or an army green. Some could fit in her pocket, easily discreet.

Ignoring the fact that she marked up the glass, Brooke ran her finger over the case to direct her vision to each of the items underneath. She didn't know the differences between them all, but it gave her a few moments to keep her eyes lowered while she attempted to clear them before the clerk returned.

"What can I help you with?"

Brooke's head snapped up as her eyes instantly dried. "Uh, I am…I'm looking for trail-cams?" It sounded like a question instead of a statement.

With a welcoming smile, the clerk with a badge tagging him as Jack waved his hand to the far end of the counter. "You're real close. What kind are you looking for?"

"Kind? There's more than one?"

"They all do the basics of taking pictures, but there are different levels of technology. Are you looking for still pictures or videos? We'll start with that," Jack offered as help.

"Well, I haven't really thought about it. Um…Let's start with pictures," Brooke decided, realizing that pictures or videos would capture the same meaning in her circumstance. As she forced her thoughts to have direction, the questions formed. "With pictures, how long between each one does the camera take?"

"You can set them for different intervals. Typically, a hunter sets it somewhere between thirty and sixty seconds. What are you hunting for?"

Brooke's eyes snapped wide-open. "Me? I'm…looking at these for my boyfriend. I want it to be a surprise, so I didn't want to ask him any questions." She got back to his other questions, which became clearer as her mind focused on its mission. "Does a battery last long, and do you have to be within a certain distance to make them work?"

Eager to impart his knowledge, Jack explained, "A battery lasts about three months and you don't have to be anywhere near the tree it's attached to. That's the beauty of these cameras. You can be somewhere else in the woods, you can be sleeping, you can be anywhere and the camera will photograph what you're missing."

Brooke heard enough.

The clerk continued, excitedly jumping into more unnecessary details. "See the straps attached at the sides of each of the trail-cams?" Not waiting for acknowledgment, Jack continued, "They can be strapped onto many different sizes of trees and set for a viewing range and size of animal that will trigger the camera."

Brooke pulled her head back at this comment. "So, you can take pictures of only certain things and leave others out?"

Cutting short his explanation, Jack answered, "Sort of. You can set the camera for size of animal that will trigger the photos. If you aren't concerned with the activity of birds and squirrels, then you set the weight that will trigger a picture to something larger. Make sense so far?"

"Uh, yeah. I think I know enough." Brooke hesitated while the clerk apparently waited for a choice on her purchase. Coming up with an excuse, she said, "I'm going to think about this for a few days. I, uh, don't need to get it today. But thank you for your help," she added, hoping to dismiss his attention as she analyzed her thoughts that began to crowd her predicament.

"If you have any more questions, I'm always here."

"Yes, thank you again," Brooke murmured as she absently turned from the counter.

Brooke wandered through the aisles while heading for the entrance. Her mind zoomed back and forth between the facts the clerk had recited just as she kept her eyes continually averted from the captured animals sneering from their attachments on the walls. She couldn't change the probability that Ty had successfully viewed her and Scott together. Not sure how his jealous side would react to such pictures, Brooke maintained that the detectives advised her well as far as to stay away from him. If Ty did have anything to do with the shooting, he might finish this time.

Bowing her head in thought, and to avoid the surroundings, Brooke pulled her coat tighter around her. Turning down the last avenue, she collided with a man bent over to examine a lower shelf of fletching.

"Oh, I'm sorry. I wasn't…"

"Brooke, hi."

Brooke shook her head and blinked her mind into the current scene as the man she'd run into rose up next to her.

Chapter 46

"Brooke, I never suspected I would run into you here."

With relief in recognizing his friendly face, yet nervous for her reason in being here, Brooke cast her stare away as she responded, "Roger, it's good to see you."

Retracting his smile to a serious look with a matching tone, Roger asked, "How're you doing, Brooke?"

The quick change of attitude caused Brooke to forget the surroundings and focus on the exchange. "I'm good." He cocked his head. Brooke detected a hint of guilt from his expression.

"That's not very convincing," Roger informed her. "Brooke, I ran into Ty after our hunt." He watched her reaction closely as she closed her arms around herself again and lowered her chin.

After a moment, Brooke returned her attention to Roger and tried to disguise her anxiety with a simple acknowledgement. "That's nice."

"Do you have a little time?" Roger came closer and trapped Brooke's eyes in his meaningful stare. "I'd like to talk with you." Not waiting for her to decline, he moved on quickly. "There's a pub a couple doors down. I'll take you out for lunch. How 'bout it?"

Taking the chance to look away as her comfort level sank, Brooke mumbled, "Uh, I do have a lot to do today."

"Brooke, I think it's a good idea that we talk."

Ignoring his implication, she countered, "I'm not really hungry right now…"

"We don't have to eat. We'll get a drink. Or a soda. Doesn't matter."

Taking a second look and noticing Roger's earnest expression, Brooke caved. "Well, I suppose I have a few minutes," she admitted with an extra pull at her coat.

"Come on," Roger said, as he affectionately wrapped his hand around her elbow to lead the way.

"Owe." Brooke automatically pulled away as Roger unknowingly touched the tender spot left by Ty.

"Oh, sorry, sorry. I thought I wasn't touching your shoulder."

"You weren't," Brooke automatically responded. With her usual cover-up, she added, "You didn't do anything. That was just a natural reaction." With her brows furrowed in contemplation, Brooke followed his lead.

"I'll just have a coffee. Black, please."

Roger refocused his stare to the waitress before he ordered an anytime breakfast.

As the waitress resumed her flow down the aisle of tables, Roger turned his attention back to Brooke. "Is your arm healing on schedule?"

Stirring the black coffee with the handle end of the spoon, Brooke answered, "Yeah, actually my shoulder is doing well. I just can't sleep on it or lift things above shoulder level, yet." She nodded in rhythm to the circling spoon. "It's fine. I'm doing good." Here she stopped and looked at Roger, waiting to hear why he really wanted to speak with her.

Still attempting casual conversation, Roger mentioned, "It hurts all the way to your elbow sometimes?"

"No," Brooke answered too quickly.

Roger jumped in for an explanation. "What's wrong with your elbow?"

Brooke swallowed the steam along with a dose of mediocre coffee to stall for a story. She wasn't good at making things up on the spot. "Ty and I bumped into each other. We turned around at the same time," with a nervous laugh, "and cracked elbows." That was close to the truth.

Obviously not convinced, Roger slid nearer to the edge of his seat and made sure he had Brooke's attention on the other side. "Brooke, I'm sure you're wondering what I really need to talk about." Without hesitation he continued, "You probably know more of what's going on with your case than I do, but I've accidentally run into a few inconsistencies."

Brooke's attention level urged Roger on. He began with another question. "Do you know if the police or whoever is working on your case has figured out the details to the time of the shooting?"

Puzzled again, Brooke slowly answered, "The time of the shooting has never been a problem as far as I know."

"You're right. I should rephrase that. What I meant was the time schedule of the suspects." Brooke wasn't following the tangents he tried to lead her on. "Have the authorities affirmed the times Ty and Marla gave for their attendance at the shooting range when…you, uh, when you were hurt?"

"I didn't know there was a discrepancy about their times." Brooke looked into her cup as she hurriedly drained the brew while recalling the recent meeting with the detectives. She searched the bottom of the cup as her brows drew together. Without looking up, she queried, "Why do you ask? How do you know so much?"

"Of course, I've been questioned by the local police and the detectives from Milwaukee. But that's not what got me curious about their progress." Brooke looked up with interest. "The police and detectives don't seem to be following the same facts."

Taking a deep breath, Roger laid out his theories. "Nothing seems out of the ordinary with the detectives' investigation that I've heard. But I have friends on the police force. None that are on this case, but the information isn't exactly top secret."

"So what are you saying?"

"It sounds like some of the evidence the police have contradicts some of the facts." Roger paused as the waitress brought his breakfast and poured their cups full again. Brooke sank in her seat as she anticipated hearing the additional problems arising from her injury.

"Some of the evidence sounds basic, but there are a few things I'm not sure about," Roger explained. "After the hunting weekend with Ty and talking with him yesterday, I wonder if I can help. I wonder if I can help you."

With a thought coming to mind, Brooke pushed herself up in the chair. "Why are you all of a sudden playing detective? Did Ty put you up to this? Is he trying to get some information from me through you?" Brooke took a breath and stared at Roger. "Did he tell you that I insisted on going forward with the sale of the house?"

Brooke's adrenalin surged as the whole shooting and everything and everyone involved rushed in and out of the synapses of her brain. "And this is my decision. I made it on my own. Many times, I almost went through with it. Now I will. The house sale has nothing to do with the shooting. I don't know who did it or why. I can't imagine why. Who could hate me so much?"

Roger looked around the pub, obviously interested if anyone looked their way. He reached his hand across the table. Brooke refused any comfort at this point and snatched her hand away from his. "No, no, I don't need anyone. It seems I'm not supposed to trust anyone right now.

"Oh, and I forgot to say that my dear friend Chloe has nothing to do with my decision either. And I bet there's someone else you're wondering . Mr. Marshall. I call him Scott. Yes, I'm allowed to do that. He's sort of my boyfriend, but he has nothing to do with my decision. Nothing, nothing. I'm sure after this whole mess is over and I finish the stained glass for his job, he'll want nothing to do with me, anyway."

Brooke took a turn to check peripherally the dining area for observers, and then reversed her attention back to her companion. Roger twisted his mouth and rested his fork on the side of the plate.

"Sorry. I didn't mean to embarrass you."

"It'd take a lot more than that, Brooke." Roger adjusted in his seat. "Brooke, I have to tell you this. Mr. Marshall is in jail."

Chapter 47

Brooke remained still. Too still. Tears glossed her eyes, a constant feature, lately. She fiddled with her coffee cup and then took a slow drink. As her hands shook while purposefully placing the cup in the exact spot it came from, Brooke said, "What did he…" Shaking her head she finished, "Why is Scott in jail?"

"As I said, I talked with Ty and he told me that Mr. Marshall broke a restraining order."

Brooke held her breath as she thought her mind around this fact. "Did he tell you anything else?" She regretted this question right away.

"Actually, he didn't sound like himself." Roger didn't appear concerned with Scott being in jail, but rather his conversation with Ty.

Brooke was thankful Roger didn't dwell on Scott's situation. She'd check into it after she returned to Chloe's. She wondered why she agreed to talk with him because the only other subject could be Ty, and she couldn't think of anything good about him as a topic, either. "Well, I imagine when someone finds out they have to find a new home they aren't in their favorite mood."

"Brooke, he didn't say a thing to me about selling the house." After a silent pause in which Brooke couldn't help but show astonishment, Roger added, "He said he was looking forward to when you felt comfortable to rebuild your studio next door."

"I think I need another shot of coffee," Brooke muttered, not knowing what else to say.

Brooke's thoughts careened around Ty's manipulations and the fact that he'd waited two years to come after her and make demands on her return to his life. The only thing that had changed since their divorce was that she'd attempted to allow another man into her life.

Roger filled his fork with a glob of the slightly greasy egg mixture from his plate, motioned to the waitress for more coffee, and then proceeded to eat.

"Now that we're both uncomfortable, what else do you have?" She didn't intend to sound harsh, but needed to find out the urgency of this talk.

"I'm sorry I'm throwing all this at you. I had wanted to think the information through more thoroughly before I approached you, but we ran into each other, and I figured I better jump at the chance." He took another bite. "Ty and I talked quite a bit while on the hunt."

With her surprise subsiding, Brooke wanted to know what other secrets would kill any feelings left for her ex-husband as a person. "Isn't that what men usually do when they get back to camp?"

With an appreciative snicker, Roger responded, "Yeah, that's what us men do." Quickly getting serious again, he moved on. "Brooke, Ty mentioned a handful of things that add up and make me wonder a bit." Her fingers circled the rim of her cup. "Uh, he was adamant about paying for my part of the trip. I didn't let him do it, but he kept saying he had plenty of money and wasn't worried about it.

"I just assumed that with his investments and disability pay, he had saved a lot. Then he went on, kind of laughing about it, saying him and the district attorney had some kind of connection. He seemed to infer that he wasn't worried about your case, either.

"Now, I could take that as Ty thinking the police had everything under control, but with the authorities constantly changing their views and with no one in jail for this case except for Marla and other things I've been privy to, something doesn't seem right." Roger paused for a swallow of coffee.

"Keep going," Brooke offered.

"Before I continue, just know that I'm not trying to dig into your personal life." He waited for an acknowledgement. Brooke's urgent look was enough.

"Like I said, there are one or two things I wouldn't think much of, but there's too many inconsistencies to ignore. The apples in your garbage can in the garage match the kind you had in a bag at the scene, and the gun cleaning pads, also in the garage, were the kind Ty uses for his Winchester. That's not unusual except he never fired that gun at the range."

Brooke soaked in the details, but said nothing.

"I'm kind of jumping around, but I don't want to forget anything and have to bother you again with this," he said apologetically. "As far as Marla, the dirt on her shoes and at her apartment match the scene. The next thing I have to say ties Marla and Ty to the scene. It's the entry time Marla wrote in the registry at the shooting range. I've always been particular about time, and what Marla recorded wasn't accurate."

Naturally, ready to defend the nurse Brooke thought was a friend, she countered, "What, did she accidentally write the wrong hour?"

"Uh, no. She penciled in that we arrived about twenty-five or thirty minutes earlier than the actual time."

"Okay," Brooke whispered as she became aware of what Roger insinuated.

"One last thing Brooke," Roger began as Brooke stood up.

"Can you excuse me for a minute? I'm sure I had too much coffee," she told him before she left the table and headed for the bathroom.

Staring at herself in the smudged mirror of the diner bathroom, Brooke reluctantly allowed herself to face reality. The apples at the scene were the only ones of that kind she had bought. Add all the other items Roger tallied, and she realized the police dismissed her shooter. Either that or the police had an awful sense of communication.

Fumbling in her purse for lip balm to moisturize her dry lips, Brooke saw her eyes in the mirror. They imaged the fear and knowledge of the facts that weren't so unknown anymore. With shaking hands, Brooke drew the stick of Vaseline across her colorless lips, averted her eyes from the distraught expression she displayed, and then followed the maze of tables back to Roger.

She cautiously returned to her seat. Beginning without a preamble, she said, "Roger, I do appreciate the effort you're taking to straighten me out." She ignored the raised eyebrows as Roger poked his fork around the emptying plate. "You probably think that I should've realized the assumptions which come from what you've just told me, but I guess I find it hard to think aversely of anyone. Unless it's shoved in my face, I guess. When I hear everything itemized in this manner from someone, you, who most likely has little interest in being involved in such a thing, I have to be realistic."

Refreshing his mouth with a gulp of coffee, Roger told her, "I'm glad this is making sense to you, Brooke. I don't intend to condemn anyone, but the facts bother me even if it's about a long time friend like Ty.

"I do have one more relevant item I think you need to hear."

"Okay. I can handle another detail," Brooke forced herself to say.

"This piece of evidence contradicts most of the other things I've been talking about."

Brooke lowered her head in disbelief. Her thoughts and analysis of the information were leading in a one-way direction through the conversation up to this point. The idea of twisting her momentum caused her unexpected fatigue as she slumped into the cold vinyl of her seat.

"Maybe I can't handle it, but go ahead."

Chapter 48

"The police have a note you wrote which was attached to a white bag previously full of apples, which you brought to the scene."

Brooke let out an unexpected sigh of relief. "I did write a note, but I don't see how that has anything to do with accusing anyone of shooting me."

"The police have a different view on that."

Anger crept into Brooke's response. "Yeah, I should've sold the house and not left it up to Ty. Then he wouldn't have any reason to contact me. Ever again. But I felt sorry for him. For Ty." She wasn't done. "God knows I loved my glass art studio, but that was too close to his territory, too. And then Ty begged me to help with his therapy after his stroke. He's greatly improved physically and can probably go back to work, if he wants to. Apparently, he has enough money either way. He doesn't need me anymore. And the note, as embarrassing as it may be, was the truth." Brooke stopped to take a breath.

"Brooke, that doesn't make sense." Roger watched her as he pushed his empty plate to the side.

"I'm sorry. I know Ty's your friend and I shouldn't talk so badly about him."

Shaking his head, Roger explained, "No. Brooke, that's not it. Not long ago I would've been completely surprised at your attitude toward him, but a lot has happened in the last couple of weeks. What doesn't make sense is the note."

"You know what the note says? I think it's pretty obvious," Brooke explained, cocking her head to the side.

"I was told what you wrote, but your explanation doesn't match your writing. Maybe I misunderstood or it was changed along the grapevine."

With a nervous edge to her voice, Brooke abashedly looked down at the few drips of coffee that bubbled on the tabletop and asked, "What did you hear?"

"Actually, I don't remember the exact words."

Realizing something was askew in the translation of the simple note Brooke had left on the bag of apples for Scott, she prodded again, "As I said, I'm single and allowed to have a boyfriend, although I'm sure I've screwed that up somehow."

"Not many men would consider the note encouraging."

The coffee cup grew cold, yet there wasn't room for more in the empty ceramic as Brooke choked out a response. "The note? Was it that hard to understand? I know men aren't supposed to think the same way women do, but I'm not sure how it could be misinterpreted."

"When you broke it off with him, Scott Marshall, that gave him a reason to be a suspect," Roger said

Brooke jerked straight up in her chair. Her lips quavered as she muttered, "Broke up with him? I…I don't understand where that came from. I probably should've for his sake, but I've been selfish with my own needs.

"I may not deserve him or ever completely have him after all the trouble I've caused, but I didn't end what was barely started."

Roger nodded as the waitress picked up his plate and offered another round of coffee. Brooke paid no attention to the unwanted refill.

"Now I'm confused," Roger admitted. "Your note said something about ending what shouldn't have been started. Like I said, I don't remember the exact words, but it wasn't a love note."

Chapter 49

"Scott's attorney wants to talk with you."

"What?"

"He called while you were out," Chloe explained.

"Did Scott think he couldn't call himself?" Brooke hadn't removed her coat when she returned to Chloe's and was already confronted with more unexpected news. "You always answer the phone, so he wouldn't have to worry about talking with me."

Chloe walked closer to where Brooke planted herself, near the entry door. "Scott was only allowed one call." The incredulousness of the situation rearranged Brooke's expression, so Chloe spoke quickly. "Scott's attorney called and said Scott broke the restraining order. His attorney also said he needed to talk to you about some note or letter that was in question. The attorney said it might keep Scott in jail longer than abusing a restraining order."

"The note? The note again." It was Chloe's turn to raise her eyebrows as Brooke gasped in frustration.

Without an offer of explanation, Brooke whirled around and hurried out the door saying, "I have an errand. I'll be back soon." The door slammed in-between the two and ended the unfinished conversation.

Cupping her hand over her forehead, she kept her eyes focused straight ahead as she careened her car over the well-known road through the maples and pines. The beauty of the snow clumped on their branches was lost in her thoughts of distress.

"What's happening? What's happening to my life?" Talking to herself, hoping to make sense of the recent changes, Brooke enumerated the issues that ripened with each encounter early in the day. "I don't understand why Roger stressed Ty's offer of generosity. It has to be because of all the help

Roger gave him after his stroke. What's wrong with Ty wanting to return the favor?"

Switching persons of interest, Brooke continued her self-explanation. "Scott is probably tired of me and my problems by now. We can't be together, and yet I convince him to spend time with me last weekend and he was apparently found out. I'm sure Ty videoed Scott and me." Brooke slammed her hand against the steering wheel and breathed out heavily in disgust and fear of what was next.

"I'm probably getting dehydrated with all the tears I've spilled." She wiped the back of her hand across the wet lids mainly to see the road winding in front of her because she was past caring about her appearance.

This was all too much at once. *No matter what happens, it's easier on TV. Everything is resolved in two hours. Or the main person ends up dead, and then it's still over for them. Why is nothing being done for me?* The changes in the last few months rose to the surface of Brooke's conscience and chilled her, as there was no stopping her thoughts.

I haven't heard from the police lately. I'm sure they haven't forgotten about me, but I'm not aware of any progress. I guess I'll find out about that next week at the proceeding.

Proceeding? I don't even know why there is a proceeding. Marla's still in jail. Ty, I don't know what to think about him anymore. He won't acknowledge my need to sell the house, yet some people think he shot me.

Shot me. Yeah, I was shot. I went from a single woman who may have found love to losing everything I've been working for this year. My studio, my expanding career with the stained glass, and probably the hard-to-find perfect man, Scott. Maybe I was supposed to stay who I was, a lonesome divorcee. Shaking her head as she skirted a wide corner still a few miles from her destination, Brooke swallowed dryness in an attempt to distract herself. It didn't work.

I don't know. I don't know. I don't know Ty anymore. Do I even know Scott or have I ever? If he's who I've learned him to be, why's he in jail? I thought he'd get out right away for simply being accused of violating the restraining order.

As Brooke neared her destination, she slowed down to look for the familiar car. Unfortunately, she saw it parked in the drive. She pulled over to the side of the road where a handful of evergreens camouflaged her vehicle.

"Now what do I do?" She had to say this aloud, hoping an answer would come her way. "Do I go in the house with Ty there, or come back later? I have to find out what's really going on.

"Answer me, answer me!" Brooke screamed inside her closed car as she slammed her fists on the steering wheel again. The vibration of the hit cursed up her arm and ignited in her shoulder.

"Oh, damn," Brooke cried out as her frustration drained her energy. She softly rubbed her shoulder and became silent.

Forcing herself to gain control and formulate a plan, Brooke looked between the separations of a few branches toward the house and saw Ty walk toward his car. With a burst of nervous energy, she put her car in reverse and backed up two hundred feet to a crossroad where she swung the car north and lost herself in the twists of the country road. She wanted to give Ty time to leave and not see her in the process.

This wasn't Brooke's usual route when she left his house. As she continued driving, every quarter mile a home sprung up out of a meadow or platform of trees that had lost their layer of snow to the winds. The properties had a peaceful vacancy, leaving the inhabitants to Brooke's imagination.

What did a house know? She cruised past white paned windows against siding fashioned to look like cedar shakes. Neatly organized shrubs linear across the front of the enclosed porch and you have a classic look portraying a probable classic family. That's how Brooke had envisioned her former home.

Her former home was where she had spent exhaustive hours combining the perfect plants in the yard and mentally draining her creativity with colors and styles for the façade. That's what it was, a façade. Nothing was right anymore. Ty was hiding something.

Brooke wanted to give Ty at least ten minutes, but not much longer, to disappear. She'd make her venture quick. When five minutes expired, she turned the car in one of the perfectly plowed drives and reversed her direction.

Following the turns of the pavement, Brooke accelerated steadily. Too much to consider. Where and what was she going to look for when she got to his house?

Her speedometer crept up.

Was Ty hiding money?

There were a few slick spots on the road's curves.

Maybe Ty had forgotten something and gone back into the house. "What else do I need to consider?" Brooke whispered just as she felt her car's backend slide to the outside of the twist in the road. "Oh, oh, hang on." The slide jolted her. With adrenaline already pounding through her veins, she didn't need this. She lifted her foot from the accelerator and automatically swung the steering wheel to counter the slide.

"Okay, I need to slow down first. I don't need to get back any faster than when I left." Saying it aloud made it a command to heed the road's condition. Brooke let her breath out as the car righted itself.

Two more minutes and she would be back at the driveway. She lost her train of thought other than to go in the house and check if she could find anything out of the norm that she had previously missed. There must be something.

Pulling up to the drive, she first noticed Ty's car had left. Brooke turned into the drive, ready to leave as easily as she might need.

A moment later, she fumbled with the house door latch as her nerves recharged. The door silently opened, welcoming her back.

"I have to check Ty's personal areas." Brooke voiced her intentions. She started with the smallest and easiest to check.

Digging in drawers by his nightstand, she found the usual. Her hands stumbled over an old watch with a broken band. Ty had accomplished that when he'd chopped firewood four or five years ago. A block of wood had flown up from his chainsaw and hit his wrist. A stack of old birthday, Valentine, and anniversary cards she'd given him and scattered change lay throughout. He should've gotten rid of the cards.

This was no time for reminiscing. Brooke jerked the sticky drawer back in place and moved on to the next two. More discarded items along with the half-used notebook Ty used to carry when it was difficult for him to speak after his stroke were in these drawers. She was tempted to page through it to recall their conversations from an easier time, early in their divorce. What a contradiction. The early part was supposed to be the hard time.

She was amazed she considered the after-stroke time easy. Compared to now, it was. Brooke shoved the notebook in its place, lifted herself from the floor and headed to Ty's office.

She should've started here so as not to waste time. She partially hoped she didn't find anything.

Brooke looked at her watch. She wasted too much time with contemplations. Heading for his desk, she eyed the bottom drawer. Insurance papers, tax forms, and miscellaneous long-term paperwork resided here. The drawer was used once a month or less. What had she missed when she checked here last time?

She kneeled on the floor and pulled the drawer open. Flipping through the papers, she deemed it all normal. The next two drawers were the same.

As she hurriedly rummaged through another group of papers, she began to think it a waste of time. She stood up still holding some of what was in the last drawer when a packet of smaller sized notes flew to the floor. "Darn it," Brooke muttered as she bent over. She attempted to gather the papers in the order they fell and reached for the few that had slipped under the bottom drawer, in-between the legs of the desk. She used her fingertips to detect the papers when her hand hit a cardboard box.

Brooke stuck her face to the floor. Ignoring the missed cobwebs that gathered under the desk's frame, she pulled the aged, gray box forward.

Her hands trembled as she lifted the cover, attempting not to rip the rigid cardboard. Stacks of old pay stubs horizontally lined the left side of the box. They meant nothing to her search, but she remembered the days when Ty cheerfully went to work, gave her kisses to last the day, and the sun shined. *Don't forget, he didn't always come home after work.*

As Brooke's hands held the sides of the box, she noticed her watch. Turning her wrist, she checked the time. It was already twelve minutes since she entered the house. She needed to keep moving because she'd allotted herself only fifteen minutes.

Hastily re-covering the box, she tucked it away. Brooke moved herself to the chair and surveyed the rest of the office, looking for a hint of where to look next with the remaining few minutes.

The desk had very little clutter on its surface, only a couple of pens, a stack of sticky-notes unused, Ty's computer, and another stack of receipts. She probably should've checked his computer first, although his password was with him in his head.

Brooke absently flipped through the receipts with the notion that she wouldn't find anything. The receipts were all the same, only bearing different dates that appeared to be monthly. They were of a simple number, seven thousand.

"Seven thousand? Where did these come from? There must be a couple years' worth of receipts." The nervous feeling multiplied as Brooke trembled in the heated room while glancing around her and to the door. She'd already been here sixteen minutes.

She needed to stabilize her thinking. "Okay, take a few and get out of here before Ty returns." Looking behind her at the imagined sounds and occasional creaks from the frame of the house, Brooke slipped the middle of the stack into her coat pocket. From the swivel-seated desk chair she had conveniently rested on, she turned and jumped up to head for the door.

On her way to the entry, Brooke stopped suddenly and glanced into the living room, at the loveseat, at the cold fireplace. With a nervous shake of her pocketed hand, she turned and entered the room, only lit by the overcast afternoon.

She focused on the grayish-white and black ashes resting on the iron grate. Brooke's first thought was the magnificent blaze at her apartment on the evening Scott had returned to her. She recalled his hazel eyes. When he looked down at her, she could only see half of them. They still made her tremble with anticipation. Her mind skipped to remembering the male scent of Scott's skin.

With a mental slap on the wrist, Brooke backed out of the room, keeping in mind this was no time for such memories.

She chastised herself for parking her car in the driveway. Brooke had every right to be here. She was still part owner, even if it wasn't acknowledged with her physical presence. It would be a lot different if she found something to implicate Ty.

Extending her welcome, she hurriedly maneuvered to the front door. She peeped through the crack as she opened it. The drive was vacant except for her car. Slightly relaxed, she absently locked the door and continued on course.

Brooke backed her car into the turnaround area. As she looked down to shift, Ty rolled into the drive. "Oh," Brooke gasped. "Oh, what am I going to do? I shouldn't have stayed so long." She instinctively put her car in park. She knew it was too late to avoid him.

A thin smile formed on Ty's lips as he pulled ahead of Brooke's car. Faster than a blink, he headed for her. "Brooke. Brooke, so good to see you," she heard through the closed window.

Brooke managed a smile in return as he arrived and tapped on her window. Forcing herself to lower the window, she came up with a quick plan. "Hi, Ty. I, uh, was told to make sure your doors were locked."

"How thoughtful." He fell for it while he glanced at the driveway and her car's position. "Are you going to keep me company for a few days?"

Astounded that he would dare to request this of her, Brooke's voice stuttered. "I don't think that would be right."

"No? I think it's right." Ty paused. She said nothing in return, so he helped her out. "Shouldn't you be safe after such a traumatic event?"

Brooke didn't want to enrage him, but she stuck to her intention. "I'd rather be alone until it's all over."

"Well, you must know that Marla and Mr. Marshall are in the hot seat." She attempted to cover her surprise, but the raised eyebrows gave it away.

With satisfaction, he began to tell Brooke a story. "Marla and Marshall's fingerprints are on the gun. Marla had dirt from the trail in her apartment. And didn't she give the wrong time at the shooting range?" Ty continued as Brooke shifted uncomfortably. "She told me she was going to shoot at a different set of targets, so I didn't see her for most of the time we were there. Perfect planning on her part, I'd say."

"I should be going." Brooke didn't know what else to say as Ty added his own version to the facts.

"Sure, Brooke. We'll take a vacation alone after all this." Brooke put the car in drive as Ty leaned into the window, forcing her to listen to his last revelation. "And don't forget, Brooke, that I'd never allow Marla to have me, and Mr. Marshall knows he can't have you. There's proof. I think they had it in for you." Ty moved back from the window and motioned her release with a sardonic wink and wave of his hand.

Chapter 50

"She won't," Ty affirmed.

"What do you mean 'she won't'?" District Attorney Sabin countered.

"Like I said, she won't go through with it. I saw her only an hour ago, and she didn't even mention it."

"Maybe she's afraid of you."

"No, I know her and she's too dependent on me. She would've sold the house years ago, if she really were going to do it. Besides, I put the fear in her in a different way."

Sabin remained quiet, as Ty explained, "I assured her that Vrahn and Marshall should be the ones in jail, as they are."

District Attorney Sabin chuckled, closely followed by the return of his office demeanor. "Bellin, we have to talk."

"Isn't that what we're doing?"

"Don't be a wiseass. I'm going to make you a deal, and then we're finished," Sabin commanded.

Not hiding his smirk, Ty said, "What grand finale do you have in mind?"

"First, I've kept you out of jail. That's worth more than any amount of money." Ty appeared indifferent to the comment. Convinced of his offer, Sabin continued, "You want me out of your life as much as I never want to see your face again. I'm confident of the conviction of Vrahn and Marshall, releasing you to go away.

"It wasn't easy and it's a tricky situation, but I think that what you did compared to my, shall we say issues, more than clears me of any obligation to you in the future." Sabin pinned his stare on Ty.

Ty curled up his lip as if in thought. Then the sardonic smile returned. "Okay. Say I agree with you. How am I going to tell Brooke that I don't have enough money to move out of the house? She thought I had an early pension."

"That's your problem. You received enough to invest, if you chose to."

Curling his hand under his chin and dipping his head down, Ty contemplated the offer. He didn't want to remind Sabin that evidence, specifically against a district attorney, wouldn't evaporate. When assured that he'd stay out of jail, Ty would forcibly resume District Attorney Sabin's payments.

Unwrapping another topic, Ty demanded, "What about Marla? She thinks she's getting out."

"Ha, where does she get that from?"

"She said the evidence was obtained illegally. That she didn't okay the search and there wasn't a warrant."

"She's watched too many detective shows because it was legal. Her landlord, owner of the property, gave us the right to search, and that's all we need in such a case."

"I think you need to get her out," Ty demanded.

"Not a chance. You better be happy you're not in there."

Ty tightened his lips into a thin line. Before having a chance to make a retort, there was a knock and Officer Kaehne barged in.

Sabin turned to the door. "Kaehne, I'm busy."

"Sorry, but I…"

"I'm going, anyway. I've heard enough." Ty used the interruption for an escape. He got all the information he was going to get.

"Don't forget what I said," District Attorney Sabin yelled after Ty as he skirted the door and it swung shut behind him.

"Shit, I hope I made my point," Sabin mumbled as Kaehne stood nervously in front of the desk.

"Is there a problem?" Officer Kaehne asked before he announced his reason for the interruption.

"Ah no, no. What do you need?"

With a slight hesitation, Kaehne said, "I want to talk about the note."

"What's wrong with it?"

"Nothing. Nothing, but I don't feel right about it."

"You don't have a choice." Sabin rifled through documents on his desk without looking at the officer.

"What if we get found out?" Officer Kaehne didn't wait for a reply, but began to speak urgently. "It looks good, but don't you think Ms. Bellin will say something? And I don't know about accusing an innocent man. I can handle not getting the bad guy, but…"

"But what? You're position is to follow my orders." Shaken with the possible lack of cooperation with Ty and his officer, District Attorney Sabin stopped and took a breath. He tried a different tactic. With an uncharacteristic warm smile, he said, "Listen, we're not doing anything wrong here. Marshall did do it and we simply needed another bit of concrete evidence. Time is running thin, and we needed to take a shortcut."

Seeing a look of disbelief in Kaehne's eyes, Sabin added, "You have a real good job, Kaehne." He let it soak in. "It would be a shame if I have to make a call to one from a long list of qualified applicants."

Officer Kaehne shook his head, tapped his fingers on the edge of the desk, and turned and left the thick air in the office.

Chapter 51

"I can't wait until this is over."

"I don't blame you. Soon," Chloe responded after Brooke recounted her findings throughout the day.

"I had a busy day in the store, so I didn't plan much for dinner."

"I should've been in charge of that," Brooke interjected.

"Nonsense. You had a busy day out of the store, so we're even. I do have an idea," Chloe announced as she perked up. Chloe threw open the refrigerator door and dug in the bins for ingredients to a spontaneous idea. "Let's have grilled cheese with a layer of shaved smoked ham, a thin slice of onion…" She saw Brooke wrinkle her nose. "Yes, onion. It's good for your complexion."

"That does sound kind of good. I guess I'm getting hungry. I don't think I ate today with all that was going on," Brooke commented. "I'll help."

"It's not much work, so why don't you stoke the fire for me and wait in the living room."

Relieved with the effortless order, Brooke got up from the kitchen chair, gave Chloe a tight squeeze, and moved to a seat by the fireplace. The fire was wonderfully warm with random snaps as oxygen escaped the bark of the birch limbs Chloe commonly used to start fires.

Brooke didn't conjure up the same sensations she had seen while staring at Ty's darkened fireplace earlier. Recalling her mission, she poked at the fire and delighted in the sparks swimming up the chimney.

Chloe arrived carrying two mugs topped with mounds of quickly melting whipped cream. "I took the liberty of adding a touch of peppermint schnapps. Just for flavor of course." Chloe giggled. "Honey, I think you need to loosen up a bit, so I thought I'd help."

"Thanks, Chloe. I appreciate it," Brooke responded as she reached for the mugs, trying to avoid any spills.

"The sandwiches are almost…" Chloe turned toward the sound of her phone and interrupted herself. "I thought I was done with that sound for the day. Hold on, I'll be right back."

With the frying pan in her hand and the phone tucked under her chin, Chloe peered around the corner from the kitchen. "Brooke, it's for you…Ty."

Brooke froze with her back to Chloe as she held the fire poker in-between the logs she adjusted. Catching her breath, Brooke carefully set the poker in its stand and turned. "What does he want?" Chloe shrugged. "I just talked to him… Sorry, I'll take the phone." Brooke didn't want to put her friend in the middle.

She took the phone and held it to her chest, giving Chloe time to return to her preparations. "Hello."

"Brooke." The tone was wrong. She didn't answer. "Brooke, did you send them to check on me?"

"Uh Ty, I don't know what you're talking about," she answered honestly.

"Well, tell me, Brooke. What are the detectives doing back at our home digging around?" Ty controlled his voice, yet a harsh hint of sarcasm surfaced. "Do they think they'll find something new?"

He didn't wait for her nonexistent response. "Brooke, dear wife of mine, what did you tell them?"

Defending herself, Brooke chose her words carefully as she looked toward the kitchen to note if Chloe heard the conversation. "Ty, I'm not your wife anymore, and I…I haven't talked with the detectives in quite awhile. I don't know why they're back at your house."

Ty released an exaggerated sigh. "I know you wouldn't lie to me." The phone clicked, and the silence echoed through the receiver.

Brooke sank into the sofa with the phone held in her sweating palms and her shoulders hunched while she stared at nothing.

Chloe silently entered the room with the grilled sandwiches on colorful plates. Stopping for a moment a few feet from Brooke, Chloe softly spoke, "Did something new happen?"

Without answering the question, Brooke said, "I'm tired. I'm tired of it all and I can't wait until it's done and over with. At least Scott's preliminary hearing is soon." Looking at Chloe, she changed topics, "I bet those sandwiches are great."

Taking that as an invitation, Chloe smiled and hurriedly set the plates next to the cups of cocoa and took a seat next to her wounded friend. Without repeating her concern, Chloe suggested, "Let's enjoy my creation and the cozy fire, shall we?"

With a smile of agreement, Brooke reached for the plate nearest her.

Later, Brooke turned out the light and stumbled to the makeshift bed Chloe had set up for her. An idea that nagged at her sporadically throughout the evening came fully to life. Sitting on the edge of the bed, she reached for her cell phone and made the call.

Responding to the dispatcher's greeting, Brooke said, "May I speak with Detective Gaynor?"

Chapter 52

The couple dozen interested citizens whispered and concocted their own plots along with premature conclusions. Shoes clicked on the hardwood. Paper shuffled from the front, resembling an important agenda. The attorneys sipped their water after lengthy opening arguments. It was fifty-fifty unless a listener had prejudices one way or the other.

Brooke held a rigid pose on the front bench. She sat stiffly as if cold, yet her feet sweltered in the black pumps she had wiped the dust from this morning. She had intended to appear respectable as she witnessed Scott's preliminary hearing for alleged attempted murder. The restraining order violation hadn't even had its time in court before he was also charged for the crime against herself.

She had passed on any viable information she had gathered concerning the shooting, the face paints and large, unexplained checks. Brooke talked to Detective Gaynor a few days ago, and then he repeated the raid on Ty's home. She hadn't heard from the detectives on their intentions or if they found anything. Her heart, battered and beat, felt swollen with pain.

District Attorney Sabin stood, adjusted his glasses, and diligently flipped through a stack of forms. The courtroom returned to silence as they waited for the onslaught of questioning. Satisfied with the information he scanned, Sabin turned his attention to his witness, Officer Denny Kaehne.

After Officer Kaehne attested to his assignment on the case of the attempted murder of Brooke Bellin and to his credibility as a Creek Willow police officer, District Attorney Sabin jumped right in with questions. "Officer Kaehne, let's begin with the evidence you discovered and were witness to at the Kettle Moraine State Forest, the scene of the attempted murder on Brooke Bellin." He paused here to emphasize the charge for the court.

Going through the preamble of the assigning of Officer Kaehne to the case, District Attorney Sabin then asked, “Who made the 911 call?”

“The call was made by the defendant, Scott Marshall.”

“How long after the shooting was the call made?”

“The call was within thirty minutes of the shooting.” Brook glanced at the detectives sitting farther down the bench from her.

“Remember that fact.” Sabin commanded everyone in the courtroom. “Moving on to the evidence at the scene, was there any evidence that Scott Marshall was at the scene?”

“Yes sir, there was,” Officer Kaehne said confidently.

“Can you list for me what evidence purported that Scott Marshall was at the scene?”

“Simply put, his footprints surrounded the crime scene. He was also present when the paramedics and I arrived.”

“Don’t you think Mr. Marshall would have left before the authorities arrived, if he had any part in the shooting?”

“Objection. Speculative,” the defense attorney shouted.

“Sustained.”

Unruffled, District Attorney Sabin rerouted his directive. “Officer Kaehne, was Brooke Bellin obviously alive and conscious when you arrived?”

“Yes, she was.” Concrete facts were easy. Sabin would make it as easy on his officer as he could.

Helping the jury, Sabin surmised, “Then Ms. Bellin possibly saw the perpetrator, and Mr. Scott Marshall thought better of leaving and wanted to appear helpful by dialing 911, yes?”

“Objection. Leading the witness,” Defense Attorney Childs, not completely new to the game, appeared to know where Sabin was going with this.

“Sustained,” agreed the judge. Sabin still got his point across.

With an air of confidence, District Attorney Sabin changed tactics. He began to fire questions. “Were Scott Marshall’s fingerprints on the weapon determined to be involved?”

“Yes.”

“Did Scott Marshall’s footprints that surrounded the victim allow any angle to be available for the shot?”

Defense Attorney Childs stood to object as Officer Kaehne rapidly responded, "Yes."

"Getting back to the time," District Attorney Sabin said as a reminder, "Did the allowance of thirty minutes before the 911 call give Marshall the time to come up with a story…"

"Objection!"

"…and time to note Ms. Brooke Bellin was still alive?"

Judge Sims stood tall and narrow, but the rap of his gavel probably deafened the attendees.

"Sabin! You have questioned very little already that has not been a stretch from the broad privileges of this court. Contain yourself or I will."

"My apologies, Your Honor," Sabin meekly responded.

Leveling the heat, District Attorney Sabin lifted the corner of his mouth to his assistant and then turned to the witness. "Officer Kaehne, we have made it clear that Scott Marshall was at the scene for quite awhile, at least thirty minutes after the shooting."

Judge Sims narrowed a straight stare in Sabin's direction.

Appearing to change topics, Sabin confidently asked, "Through your research, what lifesaving certifications does Mr. Marshall hold?"

Another easy question. Officer Kaehne told the court, "The defendant is certified for mouth-to-mouth and for CPR."

"Did he perform any of these operations on Ms. Bellin with the time he had?" Another jab about the time.

"Not to my knowledge."

Sabin walked a loop around his table, glancing at Brooke as he came near. She fisted her hand and placed it over her mouth. The district attorney returned to face the witness and persisted down the same path with his questioning.

Sabin threw in a few more questions to set Scott up, and then he changed directions. "Concerning the evidence gathered following the crime scene, what did Scott Marshall take from the scene, even though it's not practice for anyone other than an investigating officer to remove any physical attributes?"

"He removed a white paper bag containing apples," Officer Kaehne answered.

"Why would he want a bag of 'apples'?" Sabin nodded toward the jury with the rhetorical question, following up by asking, "What was attached to the bag of apples?"

"A note," Kaehne answered while rubbing his hands together.

"Why don't you inform the court what the note said," the District Attorney suggested.

With the briefest, yet noticeable pause, Officer Kaehne spoke quickly as he read from a legal document. "The note reads 'I'm sorry. I cannot do this anymore. The apples are the last sweet thing I can give you. Brooke.'" Spontaneous gasps of amazement sprung up throughout the courtroom.

Brooke's mouth fell open as her hands clenched the edge of the bench on the side of each of her thighs. She craned her neck toward the detectives, mouthing the words, "That's a lie!"

Sabin crossed the floor back and forth in order to view surreptitiously the reaction of the people of the court. He caught Detective Gaynor nod toward an expectant Brooke.

District Attorney Sabin softened his voice. "Oh, so apparently Ms. Bellin ended her affair with the man who shot her?"

"Objection! That requires the officer to know the mind of a participant who is not on the witness stand."

"Sustained. Sabin, in my office," Judge Sims bellowed.

* * * *

Brooke removed her hand, laying it stiffly in her lap. Posture still tight, she attempted to get the detectives attention. When Detective Gaynor saw her motion to him, she furtively pled with her eyes for an explanation.

Detective Gaynor caught her eye and responded with another confident nod.

Didn't the detectives understand? Weren't they going to do anything? The District Attorney was mutilating Scott's credibility. He had been in jail longer than the one who should be, and Sabin had every innocent factor turned against him. That's not what the note said. Why wasn't anyone, especially Scott, doing anything about it?

Scott sat at the defense table. He sat up straight in his assigned seat, an attempt at a proud posture. Brooke sucked in the tears that wanted to escape for the humiliation, frustration, and injustice of the whole process forced on him.

She didn't need to consult Chloe's innate ability to know the only thing Scott had any amount of guilt for was to love a woman whose ex-husband twisted his needs for his own convenience. The anger at the injustice began to boil and froth in her fingertips and shoot up her arms. The only thing that calmed her was to look at Scott's back and see the sadness in the slight droop of his manly shoulders. It was worse for him.

Or was it worse for herself? She absolutely knew she couldn't have a relationship with anyone in prison. If Scott went to prison, whether he actually was guilty or not, she would have to move on without him. There was no doubt in her mind about this. She couldn't imagine a relationship from a prison cell.

* * * *

"Sabin, what the hell are you doing out there?" The words of the Honorable Judge Sims echoed in his cramped office. Not leaving time for an answer, he insisted, "I know you have the habit of expanding the boundaries, but this is *out* of bounds."

District Attorney Sabin opened his mouth to retort, but Judge Sims wasn't ready to listen. "If you want to claim to know what all the absent persons from the stand are or have been thinking, then you better be prepared to present them in person, or else I will find you in contempt and it won't be cheap." Sims gave him a cold, sharp look, and then turned to regain his authority in the courtroom.

"What else have you got?" The judge barked at Sabin when he returned to the prosecutor's table.

Acknowledging the judge's question, District Attorney Sabin turned to Officer Kaehne, still seated under oath. "Just a few more questions, Officer Kaehne. Is it possible that Scott Marshall was at the scene at the preordained time of the shot, left to create an alibi, and then returned again to make the call to 911?"

"According to the timeline, that is possible."

"Thank you. That's all I have." Sabin sat in the vinyl seat at his disposal, satisfied with his last revelation.

Chapter 53

"We'll take a twenty minute recess," Judge Sims announced as his gavel resounded against the paneled walls.

With the noise that erupted as the court cleared and everyone began to discuss the morning's questions, Brooke jumped up, her nerves raising goose bumps beneath her blouse. Immediately turning to the detectives who prepared to exit, Brooke vehemently demanded, "What's going on? Why…why are these false statements being allowed?"

Surreptitiously casting a glance to the nearby people, Detective Gaynor quietly requested, "Brooke, come with us." Without accepting an acknowledgment, Detective Gaynor and Detective Rell turned and proceeded to the prominent hall doors.

Brooke had no choice but to follow. She had to remind them of the inaccurate statements for which she'd previously supplied the truth.

Saying nothing as she remained close to their lead, Detective Gaynor stopped at a door to a small conference room. He held it open and motioned for Brooke to enter. As the door shut behind her, she repeated, "What's going on? This hearing is beginning with lies. All lies."

"Briefly, that is our plan," Detective Gaynor began to explain. Brooke gave him a puzzled look, wanting details. "I cannot tell you everything. It's much more than your case, not that it isn't a major factor or important, but we need the prosecutor to set up our case."

"I don't understand. By deceiving the court? By making a mockery of the truth?"

"Actually, yes. That's part of it," Detective Rell agreed.

"What...?"

"Listen, Ms. Bellin, we cannot and don't have the time to run through the details. You have to trust us," Gaynor told her.

Brooke put her fingertips to her forehead and shook the loose curls hanging over her shoulders.

"Come on," Detective Rell gently persuaded and put his hand on her shoulder. "We need to get back. By the end of today or tomorrow morning you'll understand our role in this."

"We'd rather you didn't have to witness any of this, but it's uncommon for the victim in such a case to be absent. It'll be over soon," Detective Gaynor reassured.

Brooke found herself speechless under the uncanny manner the detectives confidently allowed games to be played in court.

Chapter 54

"When you're investigating a case, do you just..." Defense Attorney Childs waved his hand across his waist level, "...uh, decide to investigate in a manner you feel fits the situation?"

Officer Kaehne frowned, as he haltingly answered, "No, the police force is trained in standard procedures according to the crime."

Starting in a low voice, Childs asked, "Is that how you noted Scott Marshall's prints at the scene?"

"Ah, yes. His prints were readily visible, and it's my job to note evidence suggesting another person, other than the victim, at the crime scene."

"Did you note Brooke Bellin's prints at the crime scene?"

"Yes."

Childs voice raised a level. "What can be learned about her prints?"

Thinking it a useless question, Officer Kaehne gave a standard answer, "Ms. Bellin's prints will show where she came from, where she was headed, what position she was at during the shooting, and if there was a struggle."

Raising his voice again, Attorney Childs queried, "What about the prints seventy-five yards from the impact?"

Officer Kaehne shifted in his seat. "I was not in charge of the distant evidence."

"Fair enough." Childs easily condescended. He didn't leave the issue alone. "You are aware that the police report signed by you indicates footprints of Marla Vrahn and Ty Bellin at the seventy-five yard point?"

"I believe I okayed the investigation of another officer. That's procedural."

Shooting another tangent into the questioning, Attorney Childs requested, "Officer Kaehne, after you have attested to the evidence at a scene, for the sake of the jury to understand the investigatory procedure, do you, at a later date when all evidence is gathered, analyze the connection between said evidence?"

"Yes, along with other officers present and the district attorney."

"So you and other officers and the district attorney did not find it more than coincidental that Ty Bellin, along with his very close nurse, Marla Vrahn, left footprints entwined together at seventy-five yards from impact?"

Kaehne's hands became sweaty as he rubbed them on his thighs. "I don't believe I had a part in that analysis."

"Didn't you just inform the court that you and the other authorities make these decisions together?" Attorney Childs voice rose, and his eyebrows lifted in confusion.

Searching for an intelligent answer to keep himself out of a corner, Officer Kaehne offered, "Some decisions of obvious proportions are not necessarily passed around to all the investigators of a scene."

Adding a touch of excitement, Childs quickly countered, "It's only important to hash out whose prints are directly at the scene?" Doubling his chances, he added, "Even though the forensic team claims the shot was not at close range?"

"No. I mean, yes. We decided the further prints were not related."

"So then you did help make the decision?"

Officer Kaehne's mouth fell open as he headed for the corner he didn't want to get backed into while on stand. Defense Attorney Childs brought his voice back to the original level to say, "Forgive me. We already covered that. I'll move on.

"Officer Kaehne, whose fingerprints were found on the gun attributed to the shooting? There was more than one set, true?"

"Yes, Marla Vrahn, Ty Bellin, and Scott Marshall had prints on the gun." Kaehne settled in his seat. Again, the concrete facts were the easiest.

"Was it discernable that Scott Marshall's fingerprints were on the trigger?"

"Objection!" District Attorney Sabin bellowed from the so far silent prosecutorial side. "It is irrelevant as to prints on the trigger due to the inability to discern *any* clear prints on said position."

"Overruled."

"Were Scott Marshall's prints clearly on the trigger of the gun?" Childs repeated.

"No, but..."

"That answers my question," Attorney Childs interrupted. "Let's move on to the timing. Are there any witnesses or physical evidence to indicate that Scott Marshall arrived at the scene, left, and then returned?"

Officer Kaehne thought a moment before answering. "Yes, an employee of Scott Marshall will testify according to the time Mr. Marshall was at a work site before the incident."

"Great, we'll know the possible time Scott Marshall could have arrived at the scene," Defense Attorney Childs broke in. "What about when he left? What about when he returned again?"

"It's entirely possible Mr. Marshall did not leave and return, but there was definitely the opportunity to do so."

"I understand. It's circumstantial." Childs took a drink from the paper cup of water at his disposal while he ran his forefinger down his notepad set on the table. Returning his attention to the witness, the attorney stated, "I'd like to discuss the note. This is the note that the prosecution's evidence portrays that Brooke Bellin wrote. It allegedly states she wanted to end her involvement with the defendant." Defense Attorney Childs systematically recounted the journey of the note to the evidence room. "Was the note ever reexamined in the evidence room, always with the presence of the security guard, of course?"

"I don't know for sure. Most evidence is examined more than once," Officer Kaehne responded. He attempted to remain objective. Disgusted with his part in the unethical procedures, Kaehne shook his head.

Childs then averted his eyes from the witness. Honorable Judge Sims was at attention. "Will you please read to the court from Exhibit fifty-eight," he handed the document to the judge, "what the note in question said?"

Officer Denny Kaehne relayed the note most recently supplied from the evidence room.

"Now we can assume that Ms. Brooke Bellin is breaking up or cutting her relationship with the defendant, Mr. Scott Marshall." It wasn't a question, so Officer Kaehne remained quiet. "I'll move on to the apples." Defense Attorney Childs circled back to his table with a quick glance toward Detectives Gaynor and Rell.

"The apples in the white bag with the note attached, which were discovered at Scott Marshall's home, were Jonathan apples. Ty Bellin did not have any Jonathan apples at home except for the apple core in the garage garbage can. Can you tell us whose dental records matched the bites from this apple in the garbage?"

"The bites on the apple matched the dental records of Ty Bellin," Kaehne replied.

"Was this one of the apples from the white bag at the scene of the crime?"

"Objection! Speculative. Those apples can be obtained anywhere," District Attorney Sabin reprimanded.

"Sustained."

Attorney Childs turned back to the defense table, directed a confident look to Scott, and then returned his attention to Judge Sims. "I have no further questions."

The prosecutor called other officers involved in the investigation. Their main contribution was a pact that Brooke and Scott's footprints were the only prints salvageable. Additional expert witnesses verified the gun and the time of injury. The experts hedged on agreement about the distance of the shot, but District Attorney Sabin recounted that Scott Marshall had been up to four hundred feet from the victim, which gave him every opportunity to be the shooter.

Chapter 55

"How'd it go today?" Chloe set a cup of coffee in front of Brooke as a preamble to dinner. "You might want something a little stronger, but I thought I would start you with coffee." She sat across the kitchen table from Brooke and waited for the day's summary.

Dropping her head back and closing her eyes to position herself to think of where to start, Brooke came up with, "The prosecutor did a good job on convincing the jury that Scott shot me." Chloe reached across the table and squeezed her hand. "Actually, I don't know if that's completely accurate, but I sure felt that way when I left."

"Well, it's only the first day of the hearing, Brooke. I'm sure Attorney Childs will do his best to turn the tide."

Pulling her hands into her lap, Brooke sighed. "I still don't believe Scott could've done that to me. Even though I've told the DA he would never do that to me, Sabin seems convinced that I'm wrong."

"That's his job. It's easy for me to say, but tomorrow may be different. Isn't the defense attorney calling witnesses tomorrow again?"

"Yeah, I think Attorney Sabin is done with his. I haven't recently talked with Attorney Childs, so I haven't a clue as to his strategy or what he knows."

"What about Ty?"

Brooke mirrored her court stance as she stiffened upon hearing his name. "I haven't talked with him lately." Brooke lowered her face to the steaming java and let the moisture warm her skin. After a lengthy pause, she concluded, "My heart is dead relevant to Ty. Scott probably feels that way about me. I'm so alone right now. I can't be with someone who's in prison. Even if he's falsely accused. It just wouldn't work."

Chapter 56

"What time did you, Ty Bellin, and Marla Vrahn sign in at the shooting range on the day of the shooting of Brooke Bellin?" Defense Attorney Childs continued his examination of Roger Detris.

"We arrived at 5:20," Roger stated.

"Why are you so confident of the time?"

"I've always been a time merchant. Uh, I'm very aware of time, and I had looked at my watch when we arrived. It's a habit."

"Who signed the three of you in at the shooting range and at what time did the register implicate?"

"Marla Vrahn signed us in at 4:35."

"Why didn't you correct the time, say if you consider yourself such a 'time merchant'?"

"I didn't think it was a big deal. I didn't know Brooke was going to get shot."

"Thank you. I have no further questions," Attorney Childs said to dismiss Roger Detris from his questioning.

After District Attorney Sabin took a few minutes to cross-examine Roger, Attorney Childs called on Bart Hellner, Attorney Sabin's accountant.

"What is the relevance of the District Attorney's accountant?" Judge Sims queried.

"Your Honor, I'm building a platform of reasonable doubt for the charge of alleged attempted homicide against my client, Scott Marshall."

"As you know, Counselor, there is a broader allowance of evidence in a preliminary hearing, so I'll allow this witness. Be careful where you go with this as it may not be allowed in a further trial, if there is one."

Childs nodded appreciatively to the judge. "In that case Your Honor, I would like to dismiss this witness and proceed to the next, Mr. Ty Bellin."

For whatever reason, Brooke noticed a pleased expression briefly appear on the defense attorney's face. He regularly turned her way to reveal his impressions.

After a brief recess, Defense Attorney Childs called Ty Bellin to the stand. Childs questioned Ty about his alibi. Ty claimed ignorance of the time discrepancy. Ty asserted that his footprints at the state park were from a former diversion during a walk he had taken. Of course, his fingerprints were on the gun. It was his.

Childs covered the rest of the evidence of the crime. Then he approached the more personal aspects of Ty and Brooke's relationship.

"Mr. Bellin, what type of involvement would you say you have with your ex-wife, Brooke Bellin?"

Ty curved his lips in an enchanting smile. "My wife, Brooke, is beautiful, talented, and the love of my life." Defense Attorney Childs opened his mouth for the next question, yet Ty had more to say. "I've always been there to help her, so naturally I was devastated when I needed her to take care of me after a stroke. I wasn't sure she could handle me alone."

Childs glanced quickly toward Brooke. She remained intent on the proceedings, wondering how Childs would tie the mentioning of the accountant and Ty's testimony to anything that would clear Scott.

"Uh, Mr. Bellin, I'm under the impression that you and Ms. Bellin are divorced?"

"Well, in legal context we're not married." After a confident smile, Ty added, "She still needs me."

Prompted for the next question, Childs asked, "You claim she still needs you, so how does that make her unable to handle you in return?"

Ty's smile crept away as a sad and concerned mask appeared. "Well, I don't like to publicize our issues, but Brooke, uh, she's a bit unstable at times."

Attorney Childs jumped in, "Mr. Bellin, are there records of your wife having any mental instability?"

Ty was quick to rebound. "There's a small issue of which I became her guardian a few years back. As I said, we never liked to publicize it, so we worked through it together." He had the stage and wasn't leaving. "Brooke has a habit of becoming insecure. When she gets this unnecessary temperament, if I don't intervene, she will try to get the attention of other men. Sometimes I miss the clues and she's successful with a man who has no values and takes advantage of her." Eyes and mouths popped open, becoming wide throughout the courtroom.

"When Brooke has enough or 'becomes herself' again, she drops the interested man." Summing up his point, Ty added, "That's what's going on with Mr. Marshall. The note proves it."

"So Mr. Bellin, that's how you also obtained the restraining order between Mr. Marshall and Ms. Bellin?" Ty answered affirmatively.

"I have a copy of the document declaring you as Ms. Bellin's guardian. Can you tell me what state Dr. Cortes practices in?"

Ty appeared extremely happy with himself. "It's not a state, but rather Dr. Cortes practices in the Virgin Islands." Brooke watched the mock surprise on Attorney Child's face as he turned and shared his opinion with the court. This encouraged Ty. "We had an extended vacation when she needed help."

Addressing Judge Sims, Attorney Childs requested, "I want all statements relating to Brooke Bellin's mental instability stricken from the record. Nothing was offered during discovery to support the validity of a doctor from a US territory. Supposedly, this doctor claims Ms. Bellin has a mental aberration, and it cannot be allowed."

Judge Sims thought a moment, and then heaved a sigh along with his answer. "I agree with your pleading, counselor, but Mr. Bellin is only relating his version of their marriage as you asked him to." Observing the court, Sims announced, "This preliminary hearing is for the alleged charge of attempted murder, yet I'm willing to include the charge of obstructing the restraining order to save court time."

Turning to face Ty on the witness stand, Judge Sims became stern with his instructions. "Mr. Bellin, unless you can prove the validity of this Dr. Cortes and your guardianship, I am dismissing the restraining order as of the end of this hearing. Without the status of Ms. Bellin's guardian, you cannot petition for a restraining order between two other people. There's nothing to prove that this Dr. Cortes is licensed with the Board of Psychiatry in the United States. And Attorney Childs, the testimony stands. Let's move on."

Brooke silently cheered for the first win of the day.

Childs quickly began his next line of attack. "Mr. Bellin, what was your annual income before your stroke?"

"I grossed fifty to sixty thousand."

"What about after your stroke?"

Ty coughed and put on a thoughtful expression. "It's hard to say. I do receive a pension and as of late I'm able to do some side work."

"What do you make now, Mr. Bellin?" Attorney Childs repeated.

"Uh, about forty thousand."

Returning to a comfort zone, Defense Attorney Childs confronted an obvious discrepancy. "Mr. Bellin, what is your home worth?"

"I don't know. I haven't checked the market lately."

"Would you say one hundred thousand? Two hundred? Five hundred thousand?"

With an obviously prideful breath, Ty answered, "I don't think it's that much, but rather around three-fifty."

"Do you have a mortgage?"

"Yes."

Defense Attorney Childs continued this line of questioning until he unfurled a loan of two hundred and eighty thousand reduced to seventy-two thousand in merely five years. "Where do you get the money for such large payments?"

"Objection!" District Attorney Sabin jumped to his feet. "The witness already revealed his sources of income and what does this have to do with the charge on Scott Marshall?"

"Sustained."

Childs circled the defense table and checked on Brooke. She sat as still as a picture. He swiveled his attention back to Ty Bellin.

Perfect. "Do you have a life insurance policy on Ms. Brooke Bellin?"

"No, we always assumed I would die first." Liar. Brooke refolded her hands across her lap.

"So you need the checks you regularly receive?" Not waiting for an answer, Attorney Childs requested, "At this time I would like to enter these check stubs into evidence." He presented a stack of check stubs to the court.

Judge Sims reached his hand out. "I'd like to see those." As he perused the papers, his face turned shades of pink to a deeper red. His voice boomed as he yelled, "What is this supposed to be? A joke? Checks for thousands from District Attorney Sabin to this witness, Ty Bellin."

Before the defense attorney uttered another statement, Judge Sims sensed disorder begin to rumble. "Close all the doors. No one leaves or enters," he shouted to the security officers at the doors. "Counselors, I want you in my office. Now!"

Gasps of surprise resounded throughout the courtroom. The newspaper photographer snapped his first shot of Ty, followed by other members of the court and the front row of spectators.

Ty's cool and caring façade faded.

* * * *

The court reporter waited for more. Defense Attorney Childs rushed his next statement. "Your Honor, I'm proving that there's reasonable doubt against the charge on my client." Attorney Childs barely took a breath before supplementing his statement. "Furthermore, I am displaying the deal between District Attorney Sabin and Mr. Ty Bellin that will ultimately lead to the fact that Ty Bellin needs Sabin's money, District Attorney Sabin is dealing in unlawful ventures to receive this money, and how it is that Ty Bellin is not at the defense table right now instead of my client, Scott Marshall."

The whispering and chattering court stopped in midstream. Eyes focused on Defense Attorney Childs, wanting to know where his last statement would take the case.

Attorney Childs stood motionless and slightly stunned at his own well-formed explanation. He couldn't turn back now. The facts he worked on to unravel through the examination of Ty Bellin surreptitiously revealed themselves in the court of law, and he now needed the backup he set up backstage.

"There will be no more statements. In my office!" Judge Sims bellowed.

District Attorney Sabin wiped his forehead, glanced to his assistant, and then shuffled to the judge's quarters. Defense Attorney Childs motioned to his paralegal and to detectives Gaynor and Rell to follow. The judge's door close behind the group.

Brooke shifted on the bench and looked at Scott. He kept his back to the visitors' benches. She loudly whispered, "Scott. Scott, please turn around. It's me."

After a moment's recollection, Scott turned to meet Brooke's gaze. Brooke couldn't form any words as his eyes mesmerized her. She managed a nervous smile, and then he turned away.

The smile vanished. Brooke's nerves sprung and she began to shake. She needed comfort, someone to sound off her confusion by the whole morning's testimonies. Chloe had appointments at work all morning and wouldn't arrive until the afternoon. Brooke did not want to be alone.

Chapter 57

The members of the courtroom began to discuss their views as they waited for the court officials to return. Loud voices from the judge's chamber occasionally rose above the din. Twenty minutes passed.

Judge Sims returned from his office, shutting the door behind him. Standing before the court, he announced, "We're going to take a recess for the rest of the day and will return to session tomorrow at eight a.m." He rapped his gavel and returned to his office, offering no explanation.

Brooke slumped with fatigue. Her eyes were the only part of her that remained alert, waiting for Scott to turn her way once again. And he did. The beautiful light brown eyes distinctly displayed confusion. She felt his pain, but couldn't do anything to help. Security escorted Scott through the side door again. She would see him tomorrow morning. Members of the proceeding remained up front while security singularly allowed the viewers to leave.

* * * *

"Scott Marshall was set up to take the fall," Defense Attorney Childs announced.

"You better have evidence to back up that accusation or I *will* order a mistrial and you'll be at the court's mercy because of the wild demonstrations exhibited," Judge Sims warned.

"I've got more than enough along with the evidence collected by the detectives," Childs added.

"This is preposterous. I'll have your license for this outrageous conduct. I've done nothing wrong," District Attorney Sabin threatened as his sagging features reddened.

Childs turned to Sabin, his voice livid as he claimed, "I have a list of witnesses that don't belong in this trial, but they'll confirm why they're living outside the bars for a hefty price charged by you." He tripped the trigger and Childs wasn't done.

Still focusing his discussion at Attorney Sabin, Childs rhetorically asked, "And what does this have to do with Ty Bellin? You have the habit of regular payments, large payments of seven thousand, which you give to Mr. Bellin.

"The next question is why do you give him this money? Mr. Bellin happens to know that you take bribes and instead of turning you in, he cashed in on it."

Detectives Gaynor and Rell remained quiet. Their briefcases bulged with the evidence. Judge Sims crossed his arms tightly over his chest and listened intently.

Attorney Childs had more. "There are a lot of facts to take you down and we recently acquired the cooperation of the rookie officer, Kaehne, who you pulled into this as a necessary part of keeping his job.

"The next big question you might ask is, where does this tie into the attempted murder of Brooke Bellin? Easy." Turning to the detectives, Attorney Childs requested, "Detectives, will you please play the videos so kindly taped by Jake Hershner, dispatcher of the evidence room, and another by Mr. Bellin."

District Attorney Sabin turned to his assistant, whispering, "Do you know anything about a video?" Detective Rell plugged the video-cam into his laptop.

"The only video I heard of is the one Bellin said he took of his ex-wife and Marshall," the assistant whispered.

Hearing the assistant's explanation, Detective Gaynor broke in, "We have that video plus one taken previous to it. Ty Bellin must've wanted to critique his aim."

Chapter 58

As the first video ended, Defense Attorney Childs stopped the tape along with the incessant clicking that accompanied it. "You don't need to see the scene between Ms. Bellin and Mr. Marshall. That's irrelevant to our purpose. The second video will reveal tampering of evidence, compliments of this county's district attorney. That would be you, Mr. Sabin."

"Don't play it." District Attorney Sabin became agitated, with a sheen of moisture rising on his forehead. "Don't play it." His voice wore down to a pleading inflection.

As Sabin made his request, the attending officers moved in and slid handcuffs around the sweating wrists of the District Attorney.

Judge Sims directed another officer. "Arrest Ty Bellin."

The officer returned to the courtroom where Ty remained at the witness stand with other officers on guard. Seeing the officer head his way, Ty took a deep breath to relax overworked nerves.

With mock confidence, Ty nodded to the authority. "Officer, what's going on?" Building adrenalin that needed to escape somehow kept Ty talking. "Where's Brooke? Did something happen?"

The officer ignored the babble of questions because he announced, "Ty Bellin, you're under arrest for conspiracy for fraud, obtaining fraudulent money, and for attempted murder in the first degree of Brooke Bellin."

The false smile on Ty's lips sank as another officer led him from the stand, whipped him around, and matched his wrists to fit the handcuffs.

* * * *

"You're back early," Chloe exclaimed as her business doorbells jingled and she watched Brooke enter. Looking back to the design for a stained glass door she was creating, Chloe lightly proffered, "Did you come back for a lunch break? I'll be done with this in a minute."

Not offering an immediate reply, Brooke walked to the design table and leaned her elbows on top followed by sinking her chin into her cupped hands. "I'm back for a break this whole afternoon. You won't have to keep me company at the courthouse today."

Chloe stopped arranging the glass pieces, and looked quizzically to Brooke. "What do you mean? Is it over?"

Answering honestly, Brooke told her. "I don't know what I mean. The judge dismissed the court for the day."

"Ah," Chloe responded, as if she knew why.

Brooke again took her time with the summary. "When I left, the judge, attorneys, officers, and the two detectives were in his office. It didn't sound like a peaceful assembly as there was shouting."

"For whose side?" Chloe prompted.

"I'm not sure, but Ty was the last to testify and it appeared that Attorney Childs talked about a whole different case by the way he questioned. It didn't sound good for Ty."

The obvious question, "What does that have to do with Scott's trial? Does it mean he's in the court's favor?"

"They did drop the restraining order, but I don't know about the other charge. No one informed me of what was going on, and I couldn't even ask Attorney Childs or the detectives because they never came back to the room before I left. Security still took Scott away, so he hasn't be exonerated yet."

"Yet."

"What?"

"It sounds like you'll be in for a pleasant surprise soon," Chloe said with a lilt to her voice.

"How do you know? I didn't tell you all that happened today." Brooke was tired of all the twisting of facts, leaving her to doubt her analysis supplied by the incomplete scenarios at court and of her personal life.

"I can't explain it. I just know." Chloe left her statement unexplained. "Since I was going to take the afternoon off, why don't we have a late lunch or early dinner? Let's go to the café down the street."

With a weak smile, Brooke agreed.

An hour later at the neighboring café, Brooke responded to the waitress. "No, no thank you. Just another cup of coffee." Brooke pushed her dinner plate to the side as she passed on dessert.

As Chloe repeated the denial of dessert, Brooke's cell phone sounded. Chloe remained quiet as she answered the call and listened intently to the caller.

Brooke sat stunned as she finished the call. Replacing the phone next to the placemat, she managed a weary, yet sincere smile.

"Who was that to make you gain a tad of color in your cheeks, Brooke?"

"If I wasn't so tired, I'd be doing cartwheels," Brooke exclaimed. Gathering the necessary serious attitude, Brooke continued, "That was Defense Attorney Childs. I told you about him, right?"

"I didn't remember his name, but you did tell me about him."

"He just told me that Ty has been arrested. Arrested for good this time. Attorney Childs was brief on the explanation, but he did tell me that Ty supplied his own evidence that…" Brooke faltered at what she was going to say next.

"He…he said Ty was the one who shot me." The tears washed away her initial smile.

Chapter 59

"Let's get back to the house. I'll get the bill. Why don't you go to the ladies' room to catch your breath? I'll wait for you at the counter," Chloe kindly suggested.

Brooke nodded as she used her napkin to wipe the wet stains from her cheeks.

"I didn't tell you the part I initially smiled for," Brooke began. "Chloe, the charges against Scott were dismissed and I already knew that the restraining order had been dropped."

"Brooke, that's fabulous." Chloe threw her arms around her dear friend as they sat together on the living room couch. "I was going to suggest that I stoke up a fire, but I think you should be sharing a warm fire with someone else tonight."

"Do you think so?"

"Of course, I do. Call him. What're you waiting for?"

"I don't know. I guess I'm nervous." Brooke admitted. "Scott and I haven't been together for so long. I almost wonder if he feels the same after all he's been through because of me."

"Well, you won't know until you talk to him."

Brooke hesitated, and then pulled her phone from the side pocket of the jacket she still wore. She thought for a minute to recall the number she hadn't used for so long. Her fingertips knew better, and the number clicked on the phone pad.

Brooke expected to hear the gravelly, sensuous voice she fondly craved. An answering message took its place without the same intensity she waited for. Before the sound to leave a voicemail occurred, she stopped the call. "I can't leave a message. I need to talk to him."

Brooke curled her feet underneath her and tightened her shoulders, vainly wishing Scott would call her. "I may as well tell you the rest of the clipped story Detective Gaynor told me. He talked to me after Attorney Childs." She told Chloe about Ty's video of the shooting and Scott's release. She wasn't able to supply many details until she heard more, which was promised for tomorrow.

* * * *

Scott wrapped a towel around his firm waist. The bathroom held a fog from the twenty-some minute shower he used to soak away the mental pain of the trial.

He blamed the steam of the bathroom for clouding his thoughts because he should rejoice at his rightly deserved release. Only he was alone because he had lost his Brooke. That was more devastating than all the humiliation and inconvenience of what the legal system had forced him to endure.

With this thought crossing his mind repeatedly, he reluctantly left the warmth of the steamed room and moved to the kitchen. He hadn't shopped for an undetermined amount of time, but he did locate a stray can of soup to heat.

Walking past the laundry room, Scott sorted a button-down denim shirt and pair of jeans from a basket of rumpled, yet clean clothes. He stumbled over his feet as he attempted to dress and walk to the living room. Reaching his destination, he gave thanks for the wood already in the fireplace and ready for ignition.

As he approached the lighter that rested on the nearby end table, Scott noticed his cell phone on the same table. He absently grabbed it and checked messages, assuming his former habits. The phone displayed work messages, friends wishing him good luck, and one missed call without a greeting. Brooke's number glowed on the screen.

Everything cleared from Scott's mind except Brooke. God, he wanted her again, but that was unlikely. She'd moved on and he had to. Difficult as it was to imagine that Brooke believed he shot her, what else could he think when he saw her with another man who already had the right to put his arm around her?

Chapter 60

The sun rose the next morning bringing temperatures above freezing. Scott was already in his office to catch up on his workload.

"I left notes on the pending jobs. If you have any questions or need any help to get back in the groove, let me know," Jeff, Scott's foreman, said after going over the recent activity.

"Hey man, thanks for all your help. Uh, I need to get some of the stained glass from Brooke." It hurt to say her name strictly with a business overtone. "Could you get that for me?"

Jeff jerked his head back in amazement. "Sure, but wouldn't you rather get it yourself?"

"No, I have too much to catch up on. Just go in by way of Chloe's business, and she'll direct you to where it's located." This was the easiest way to avoid Brooke.

* * * *

"Well, I did it."

"You got the rest of the information on what happened to end the trial?"

"Yes, but even better," Brooke felt a certain excitement fill her to soothe the pain of Ty wanting her dead. "I…I went to the real estate agent. He said Ty signed the papers. He'll have them picked up at the jail today, and then a 'for sale' sign will go up in front of…of the house." This is what she needed to do before she told Scott her deepest feelings.

"Brooke, I can see you're on the way to a new and happy life," Chloe exclaimed.

"Yeah, all the questions are answered. Granted, there'll be another trial, but the evidence is clear this time."

"I think you do have one more errand to make today."

"What's that?"

"Jeff picked up the other glasses we finished," Chloe hesitantly informed.

"Jeff, not Scott?" Brooke's face puckered by the reminder that Scott was free, hadn't called, and sent his worker over instead of hurrying over himself. She pushed aside the detailed explanation she wanted to pass on to her diligent friend about what went on behind the scene at court.

"Now Brooke, don't get too upset right away. Scott has a lot of things to catch up on. Maybe you should give him a break and go see him," Chloe suggested.

"But I tried to call, and it seems like he's avoiding me. I don't know what I did to change his mind."

"It's been a really rough couple of months for both of you. I don't want to intrude, but I'll tell you one thing. Try one more time. One more time will do it."

Clenching her teeth, Brooke quickly made her decision. She gave Chloe a furtive smile, turned, and exited the house.

Before she changed her mind to alter her course, Brooke headed her car straight to Scott's office. She couldn't turn her mind off during the ride. Questioning the situation aloud, she hoped an answer would pop out of the radio or better yet, her cell phone would ring.

"I know how he feels, or felt, about me. I love him, but never said it. Now, does he still love me after all he went through because of me? Do I have the right to expect him to? I'll tell him right away that I'm in love with him, and then fill in the details of the last few months.

"Good idea. Besides, he still has to deal with me for a few more pieces of stained glass for his job." As Brooke pulled into Scott's parking area, she gained a small amount of confidence.

She knocked and opened the door to his office as she heard him shout, "Come on in." Taking two steps in, she stopped. Any gained strength of mind evaporated as the door shut.

Scott stared straight at her. No expression. No feelings.

"Uh Scott, I thought I would stop over to…to see you." Unoriginal as it was, that's what escaped Brooke's nervous mouth.

"Hello, Brooke." Scott graced her with this plain and unemotional statement.

"Hi." She fumbled with her purse as she grasped its edges in front of her half zipped jacket. He didn't offer another extension to a poorly started greeting. Silence. Transferring her nerves into speech, Brooke said, "Scott, I didn't have a real reason to come over, but I only wanted to see if you're okay."

"I'm fine. I have a lot of work to catch up on."

"Yes, I imagine you do. You've always been real busy." The air grew stale and breathing became desperate. Brooke faltered for another piece of trivial conversation.

"Can I help you with anything, Brooke?" She could see the pain in his brilliant eyes.

Forgetting her original plan, Brooke fought to stumble onto the correct statement. "No, I just wanted to see you. It's been so long."

"I'm sure your friends kept you company," Scott stated in monotone.

"They were good to me, but…" Brooke was ready to cut the small talk when Scott interrupted.

"I'm a little busy here. Do you need anything?" He was always thoughtful, but this was more of a courtesy offer.

Trying to find a safe ground and not waste his time as he insinuated, Brooke mentioned, "I'll have the rest of the stained glass finished for you soon. I heard Jeff picked some up this morning when I was gone."

"Yeah, it was easier for me to send him. If this project is in your way, I can rearrange the stained glass that's finished, and you won't have to work on it anymore."

Brooke's head jerked back in utter confusion at the suggestion. "No, Scott I want to finish it. I enjoy working with you." Her mind tumbled over a dozen questions that popped up.

Scott stopped the scribbling of illegible notes and for the first time, looked into Brooke's eyes. "I know we weren't together much the last few months, but you've moved on and I need to do the same."

She shrunk in her skin and felt like an unwanted ant crawling across the floor. Brooke sensed a weight burden her sensitivity. "I…I don't know what you mean, Scott."

"Maybe he was just a fill-in, but the fact that you wanted him while I wasn't allowed to be in your life makes it hard for me to take us seriously."

She had to get her control back. Without knowing what Scott referred to, she needed to tell him. “Scott, I’m not following what you’re saying. I’m not back with Ty. Matter of fact, I don’t have the paper with me yet, but he signed to have the house sold.” She looked at him expectantly.

Scott set his pen down and pushed the metal chair back from the matching desk. “What about him?”

“Him? Ty? He’s in jail. I assumed you knew that.”

“I do. I’m not talking about your ex-husband. The man you have coffee with.”

Brooke shook her head and tried to make sense of Scott’s incomplete reference. “The man I have coffee with? I don’t know who you’re talking about. I’ve only had coffee with Chloe for the past weeks.” She hadn’t moved any further into the room and all she wanted was to be in Scott’s powerful arms.

With doubt glazing his eyes, Scott responded, “I saw you and a man leave the café, across from the hardware store. He had his arm around you and you appeared happy about it.”

Her mouth fell open. Brooke didn’t have an explanation because she didn’t remember any such incident.

“Take care of yourself, Brooke,” Scott offered to excuse her presence.

Her eyes instantly filled with pain and heartache, mixed with salted water to season them. Brooke lost the train of thought she fought to control and backed to the door. Scott swiveled his chair to a dusty window. It mortified Brooke that he didn’t want to look at her.

The business phone rang. As Scott answered it, she looked around his office, wanting to find a solution before he finished the call. She wasn’t leaving until she had this resolved.

Brooke absently listened to Scott’s gruff voice as he gave orders to an employee. She scoured her mind for a clue about the supposed coffee she shared with another man. Scott couldn’t have been in jail yet. She needed to remember what was going on before that time.

She flinched when Scott dropped the phone on his desk and returned to scribbling notes and searching his desk for information.

“I can’t stand this anymore.” Brooke surprised herself with her outburst. “Do you know how relieved I was when I found out the charges against you were dropped? The only thing I could think of was to run to you and tell you what I've wanted to say for so long." Scott stopped writing and shifted his gaze to her feet.

"I admit I had doubts about dating someone in jail. Who wouldn't? But I kept hoping…hoping that the truth would come out. That we could be more than friends." Brooke sucked in the tremors starting in her voice.

"Brooke…"

"No, stop. I get it. This was too big a test for you." She didn't know whether to start crying or become angry. "I wasn't testing you, and I'm sorry you got mixed up in it.

"You know what? Forget it. Just forget it." A softer expression crossed Scott's handsome face. She had one more point to make. "Oh yeah, I was ecstatic to be able to tell you that there's irrefutable proof against Ty. And the other thing is that he signed the papers for the house to be sold. I'm rid of him. He's out of my life." She took a deep breath before saying, "And I guess I can live without you, too."

Whirling around, she ran to the door. Yanking on the handle, her knit glove slipped forcing her to halt. Scott hurried to catch her.

"Brooke, wait." Her hand remained on the doorknob. "I have no right not to at least listen to what you have to say."

"I've said it all," Brooke stated.

"Then it's my turn." He eased her hand from the knob and turned her to face him. "It's not a habit of mine, but I think I'm acting with a little bit of jealousy and that's not fair to you." She looked up at him, barely able to focus through the tears.

"What's there to be jealous about? There isn't any other man." She wanted to say more, but it was his turn to confess.

"Even if you had an interest in someone else, you came to me."

Anger resurfaced. "You're right. I do have the right to be interested in anyone I choose. Until you realize that I'm not like that, I can't be with you. I suppose you think it's one of the officers or detectives. Better yet, maybe it was the sheriff who served you." Her breathing came rapidly.

Scott dropped his head briefly, then returned his attention to her face. An incredible sadness crept into his eyes. "Brooke, you're right about everything. I was really hurt when I saw a business-type of man put his arm around you. You got in his car and drove off."

Brooke didn't comment.

With a raspy voice, Scott stared up at the ceiling and said, "I was at the hardware store when I saw you."

Brooke slowly began to smile. "I don't think you'd look right wearing a black, wool overcoat."

"What?"

"I prefer men in denim shirts and work jackets versus those who sell real estate."

The grim expression he wore throughout the exchange relaxed. "So you prefer a ruggedly, handsome man? One without a schedule? Someone who didn't entirely keep his cool when a masked man came too near his favorite woman?"

Brooke took a step forward, reaching a hand to touch Scott's shirt.

"So, I was depressed for two weeks or however long for nothing?" The tension crept out of his body as he replaced it with the confident and sexy stature Brooke craved.

"Well, I think the depression may have taught you something valuable." Brooke watched her finger trace a line down the row of buttons on his attire.

They both stood, not sure what move to make next. She remembered the other thing she wanted to tell him. "Scott, I have one more thing to say."

His eyebrows piqued, as if he wasn't ready for another surprise of any kind right now. It was all or nothing, so Brooke finished what she wanted to say. "I've felt it for so long. I swear since the day I met you, although I never actually said it" She reached for his hand. "I'd like the chance to love you, if you can love me back."

Scott didn't pull his hand back. For a moment, he remained silent. "Say it again, Brooke."

She stepped forward and reached for his other hand. "Scott, I want to love you."

It was enough. Scott pulled Brooke to his chest. "Brooke, I already love you. I always have and always will." He released a hand and raised her chin. He softy kissed her mouth and wiped away the salt deposited by the many misunderstandings and time wasted since her shooting.

All of a sudden, to be in Scott's arms and pressed against his body was the only thing that mattered. Brooke's tongue reached up for his as he began to search the sacred spots of her mouth. Scott gripped her neck and pulled her mouth into his, as if he couldn't get close enough. Straddling her legs with his thighs, he walked her back against the wall where he pressed his strength into her. She readily formed her curves into the gaps Scott left.

Brooke felt his hardness rise against her hip just as he pulled back. She looked up quizzically, as he suggested, "We should go elsewhere."

Still hugged closely, Brooke murmured, "You have work to do." She kissed his neck, loving the heat that burned her lips.

"It can wait another day," Scott urged as his hands stroked her back.

"I'll be patient."

"You've been patient. So have I. It's time," he decided as Brooke felt his body pulse against her again. Scott gently disentangled their anxious bodies and suggested, "Let's go to my house. I want you so much, right now, but I want to do this right."

Brooke easily followed his lead to his truck as he held her at his side. Getting in, Scott lifted the center console and pulled her close once again.

* * * *

He rounded up a collection of candles from the cupboard and fumbled with the wrappers.

"What are you doing, baby?" Brooke giggled as she reached in to help.

"I want this to be perfect and I know you like these candle things." Caught in a non-manly task, Scott averted his eyes to hide his embarrassment.

"You're so thoughtful, Scott."

With the candles lit in his room, Scott began to unbutton his shirt.

"No, let me do it. I want to be responsible for you being naked with me."

With a heavy breath, Scott murmured, "You are responsible, My Brooke."

Her fingers nimbly ran down his shirt, precariously tossing it to the floor. Brooke caressed the line of firm flesh above his belt before she loosened the buckle.

Scott dropped his head back and plunged his hands down the back of her sweater, spreading them to massage the tightness away. "Mmm…Scott, your clothes, all of it, comes off first."

"Whatever makes you feel good," Scott responded.

Lowering his Levi's with one hand, Brooke grasped his briefs with the other. As they slipped below his hips, she leaned in with a wet mouth to capture his rise. She couldn't keep her hands still as they roved to her dressings and unbuttoned, unhooked, and maneuvered them to random piles on the floor.

"You're beautiful, Brooke. Let me in you. In your body, in you…" Scott didn't finish as she rose up and gently bit his nipple. Her lips traveled up his neck and along his jaw until she found his mouth. Sinking her tongue deep into his wetness, she found a home.

He groaned with satisfaction and pulled Brooke's hips against his erection. The touch of her skin catalyzed his slow and grinding plunge to her sweet cavern.

"Scott, pull me closer. Pull me closer," Brooke whispered against his damp neck.

Slowing his motion, he ran his hand through her tangled hair. Scott answered her request with a throaty admission, "We still have one thing to discuss."

"Hmmm…How close we can get?" Brooke offered as she hugged her breasts up to his chest.

Planting his position in her, Scott kissed Brooke's ear and revealed their next discussion, "What month would you like to get married, Brooke?"

Epilogue

The rising sun glinted off a clear solitaire on the hand holding *The Sounder.* Branches of a flowering crabapple edged the east window of the kitchen.

"Scott, when you're done feeding Satchel and Colbee, come here. I want you to hear this." Brooke listened to the tumble of kibbles from the back pantry.

"I'll be right in. I'm just giving the dogs something to do, so we can have a few minutes of peace this morning." She heard Scott chuckle along with a click of the treat door.

Scott strolled to the coffee maker, grabbed the carafe, and came up behind Brooke. As he bent down to refill her cup, he placed a kiss on her cheek. "What's up?"

"I was reading the newspaper and found out that we don't have anything to worry about anymore. Finally." She tilted her head back and returned the affection.

"Oh, I know. You found another friend to adopt to keep the other two company."

"Hmm…That's a tempting idea." Brooke rolled her eyes. Getting serious, she said, "Actually, the results of the trials and pleas are in black and white. The journalist put together an article to sum up everyone and all the crimes involved. The crimes started before I was injured." It was still difficult for Brooke to verbalize the attempt on her life.

"Hey, baby, are you sure you want to relive last fall?"

"I'm fine. Really. I was nervous at first. After I read about what happened with Ty, Marla, and the authorities involved, I think it's better that I did."

Scott covered the ring she wore as he caressed her left hand. "They all got what they deserved, right?"

"Sounds like it." She turned back to the first page, scanning the relevant article. "This piece is in the documentary section. First, it gives background information for the main people involved. Then it tells about the crimes they committed and where they are now."

Colbee and Satchel trotted into the kitchen while licking crumbs from each other's muzzles. Brooke glanced at the two boxers and smiled at their innocence.

"I'll give you a summary, since we already know portions of the story. Let's see. Ty is in prison for up to ten ears. He was found guilty for the shooting, bribery, and solicitation." She paused for a moment, feeling the warmth of Scott's touch still on her hand. "Can't believe I was with him at one time."

Scott rubbed his unshaven face against Brooke's cheek. "I'm here now."

"I know, darling. I know.

"Here's the rest real fast. District Attorney Sabin plea bargained to extortion, solicitation, and falsifying evidence. Marla is in for a shorter time for conspiracy and, this is good, Officer Kaehne was placed in a different police station. Looks like he ultimately helped convict the DA."

Scott moved his hand to the paper, folding it closed. "We can put this behind us now."

"I definitely want to do that," Brooke said as she turned in her seat to face her husband. "Oh, one more thing." Scott raised his eyebrows. "This is good. The journalist put in a plug for your business."

"What'd he do that for?"

"I don't know, but it left a nice ending for a sad story. Anyway, the article read that you're a wonderful person for putting up with all the troubles the whole thing caused you. It mentioned that you finished the landscaping at Maple Haven Bed and Breakfast, and that it's one of the best land renovations in the area."

Scott scoffed. "I doubt it said that I'm a wonderful person."

"I was just summarizing the story. And it's true, you *are* a wonderful person."

Brooke curled her hand around his neck and pulled him to her lips for a tender kiss. Releasing his lips, she told her theory. "We're safe for about ten years now."

"No, you'll always be safe. You're with me, and I'll never let anything happen to your pretty self."

Brooke easily wrapped both arms around Scott's neck and resumed the interrupted kiss.

THE END

www.dawnkunda.com

ABOUT THE AUTHOR

As a former private investigator with a BS in political science and attendance at Thomas M. Cooley Law School, Dawn Kunda has reopened her legal books to create suspense in her writing. She is a member of Romance Writers of America and Wisconsin Regional Writers' Association. When she's not writing, Dawn also enjoys tending her acre plus walking garden of perennials and a self-made waterfall and pond, along with biking, running, and cross-country skiing in the lengthy northern winters. She lives in Wisconsin with her husband and three dogs, of which two are adopted. Dawn would love her readers to contact her with questions or comments at dawnkunda@dawnkunda.com.

Breinigsville, PA USA
08 March 2011

257253BV00004B/48/P

9 781606 019368